THE INFINITE NOISE

THE BRIGHT SESSIONS

THE INFINITE NOISE

Lauren Shippen

TOR TEEN

A TOM DOHERTY ASSOCIATES BOOK

NEW YORK

THE INFINITE NOISE

Copyright © 2019 by Lauren Shippen

Designed by Mary A. Wirth

A Tor Teen Book
Published by Tom Doherty Associates
120 Broadway
New York, NY 10271

www.tor-forge.com

Tor® is a registered trademark of Macmillan Publishing Group, LLC.

The Library of Congress Cataloging-in-Publication Data
is available upon request.

ISBN 978-1-250-29751-8 (hardcover)
ISBN 978-1-250-29752-5 (ebook)

Our books may be purchased in bulk for promotional, educational, or business use. Please contact your local bookseller or the Macmillan Corporate and Premium Sales Department at 1-800-221-7945, extension 5442, or by email at MacmillanSpecialMarkets@macmillan.com.

First Edition: September 2019

Printed in the United States of America

0 9 8 7 6 5 4 3 2 1

This book belongs to two people.

To Betsy, who taught me how to read and therefore gave me my life.

And to Briggon, who gave Caleb life and, in doing so, taught me so much.

THE INFINITE NOISE

1

CALEB

Oh god, it's happening again.

I squeeze my eyes shut to make the dizziness stop. It doesn't work. I open them again and focus my eyes on my usual seat, like looking at the horizon when you get motion sick on a boat. I steady my feet the best I can and walk into class, navigating the rows of desks like they're choppy waves. People take their seats around me and I'm caught in a whirlpool, getting dizzier and dizzier, my seat looking farther and farther away and I can't believe I'm about to pass out in the middle of math.

And here I was thinking math couldn't get any worse.

"Settle down, everyone, settle down," Ms. Ramirez yells from the front of the class. "I know you're all anxious to get your exams back and you will, but we've got to get through class first, so take a seat."

Anxious. Yeah. No kidding, Ms. Ramirez. I'd forgotten we were getting our midterms back until Ramirez dropped a stack of papers on her desk and the entire room tilted as we all remembered what day it is. How does this *never* get easier?

I make it through the whole period, somehow. I absorb, like, zero percent of the lesson—my stomach is sloshing and my feet are unsteady on the ground. I know I'm going to fall over the moment I stand up.

Maybe it's not that bad. Maybe the test went better than I remember. I tear my eyes away from the spot on the wall and take a quick glance around the room as Ms. Ramirez gathers the stack of paper and starts moving around the room. Yep, pretty much seasick faces as far as the eye can see. Not a great sign.

". . . and remember that your workbooks are due on my desk at the *start* of class on Friday, not the end. I know some of you try to sneak in some work during class . . ." Ms. Ramirez is talking like half of her class isn't frozen in fear, but I can barely hear her over the buzzing of dread in my ears. I really am going to pass out.

I watch my hand grab the paper Ms. Ramirez is passing to me as she walks by my desk and feel my sweaty palms dampen the pages. The buzzing is joined by my heartbeat pounding loudly in my head as I turn over the paper.

57.

I got a 57.

The sinking, swirling feeling isn't relieved by knowing. It squeezes around me. Heaviness fills my body and I lose all feeling in my limbs.

Don't pass out, Caleb. Whatever you do, don't pass out.

This is the worst it's ever been. This horrible, overwhelming feeling is crushing me and has been for weeks and weeks. It might actually finish the job this time and leave me totally squashed.

Before it can, the buzzing starts to die down and the swaying of the room slows. I look up to see if someone opened a window—suddenly there's fresh air and sunlight in here—and see Moses across the aisle grinning big at his exam. There's a big 98 circled on his paper. My stomach should drop in jealousy but I find myself feeling weirdly happy for him. Looking at him grinning like a maniac at his test is steadying me for some reason.

"Aw, look, Mr. Popular got a *fifty-seven*," someone says behind me, and it's like the window being slammed shut. "Guess it's true what they say about Football Brain."

Tyler snickers and it cuts into me like splinters. I find my spot on the wall again and stare at it like I'm Superman and could laser-eye a hole in the wall and escape. *Don't turn around, Caleb, it'll just make it worse. You know the moment you look at his smug face, you'll want to choke him with his hoodie.*

The bell rings and I instantly spring into action. I shrug my jacket back on, stuff my test in my backpack, and stand up, my eyes never leaving the spot on the wall. I've moved through this class-room for the past two and a half years, I know exactly where the door is, so I start walking in that direction, don't collect two hundred dollars as you pass Go. Simple. I can do this. I can use my stupid, strong Football Legs to walk the rest of my Football Body toward a doorway.

Goddamn. A 57. Maybe I really do have Football Brain.

"Tell me, Michaels, did your GPA go down each time you got tackled this season, or were you born dumb?" Tyler is right on my heels, which *are* moving *thankyouverymuch*, and I feel my whole body grow hot with anger. It itches at my skin but I just keep walk-ing toward the door.

"Shut up, Tyler," I grind out.

"I'm honestly kinda amazed they even let you play," he crows—loud enough to draw attention, like he wants—as he follows me into the hallway. "I mean, can you even read the numbers on the field?"

There's a fire in my chest, choking out all the oxygen in my lungs, and something else—something weighty and dark, making me taste metal. I do everything I can to focus on moving forward.

"And, aw, look," Tyler says, "little Moses got a ninety-eight!"

I look around to see Tyler snatch Moses's test from his hands and wave it around. Like always, Tyler is dressed like grunge never went out of style and has got that toothy sneer plastered over his face. It always makes me want to hit something.

I should just keep walking, I know I should, but my whole body seizes up and I stop in my tracks without meaning to. Moses's face is covered in flop sweat as he tries to get his test back from Tyler and my heart starts beating like it's been injected with Red Bull.

"C'mon, Tyler, give it back," Moses pipes up, his soft voice barely getting to my ears. I can't breathe. Why can't I breathe? Am I having an asthma attack? Do I have asthma?

"What do you think, guys," Tyler grandstands to absolutely no one. "Is it just impossible to be smart *and* athletic?"

My heart is in my throat now and I feel like my head is in a vise. I want to walk away, get far away from Tyler, but there's this heavy, dark-feeling pit in my stomach that's weighing me down where I stand. My field of vision narrows until all that's left is Tyler's dumb crooked smile.

"I mean, on the one hand we've got running back Michaels over here with a failing grade . . ."

God, I want to wipe that smile off his face.

". . . and on the other hand we've got *fatso* Moses with—"

"Mr. Michaels, that's enough!"

The voice cuts through the ringing in my ears and I come back to my body. There are strong hands gripping my arms, pulling me backward. My face feels hot, air ripping harshly down my throat. I'm breathing heavily, too much oxygen getting into my lungs, making me dizzy.

My hand hurts. I look down at it to find it curled into a tight fist. There's blood on it.

"My office, *now*. Both of you." The voice speaks again, coming from behind me. Principal Stevens lets go of my arms and I fold forward like a marionette whose strings have been cut, panting as I push my hands into my knees to keep myself upright. I squeeze my eyes shut, try to slow my breathing.

"Now, gentlemen!" Stevens yells, starting down the hall. Expecting us to follow. Us. *Tyler.*

I open my eyes and take in the scene around me, the last few minutes hazily coming back to me. Tyler is still on the floor, sitting back on his hands. Our eyes lock and he jumps up, wiping his bloody nose on his shirtsleeve.

Oh. The blood on my fist is his.

Fuck. What did I do?

2

ADAM

I can't believe it's happening again.

"Out of the way, loser!" Bryce yells from behind me and I clench my jaw, willing myself not to respond. Talking back won't win me anything.

Neither will passivity, I guess, because seconds later my shoulder is slamming into the lockers as Bryce pushes past me, *hard*. I try not to flinch when he growls "freak" as he glares over his shoulder at me.

This is a tactic animals use, right? Staying completely still so you don't trigger a predator's kill instinct? Fight, flight, or freeze. As Bryce turns his face the other way to talk to Justin, his scowl transforms into a laugh. Maybe he's laughing at something Justin said, maybe he's laughing at my expense. At this point, I don't really care—he's walking away and that's all that matters. Freeze has its advantages.

But so does flight. Which is exactly what I do next.

More than halfway through the semester and I'd thought maybe, just maybe, we weren't going to do this this year. After all, junior year is when everyone else is finally supposed to start taking this whole education thing seriously, right? Focus on acing the SATs, get good grades, build that resume for college apps? Where do these guys find the time to be bullies?

My feet have taken me automatically to the library—my own special defense mechanism. I don't have the luxury of not caring about my future, so I go inside to get some work done, finding my way to a back corner table that's almost completely surrounded by bookshelves.

"Are you hiding?"

I look up to see Moses Miller standing in the narrow space between two of the perpendicular bookcases that protect me from the world, shifting his weight from foot to foot—a habit he's had since elementary school. It makes me feel like I'm on a boat.

"No," I lie, and he narrows his eyes.

"Because if you're not using this nook to hide, then I'd really like to," he says in that small voice of his, made even smaller by the library-appropriate whisper. I'm probably the only person that Moses is ever this assertive with. A loser can make demands of another loser, I guess.

"We can share," I say, stretching my leg to kick out the chair opposite me. "This nook is prime real estate."

"I know." Moses nods enthusiastically as he sits. "One narrow entrance in the stacks, natural light from the window, view through the shelves of the main study area, and three chairs that aren't broken. It's a miracle nook."

I smile for the first time that day.

"So who are you hiding from?" Moses asks.

My smile disappears.

"Just, you know . . ." I shrug like it's no big deal. ". . . Bryce and his merry band of cronies. You'd think the allure of making dumb jabs at someone's social status would have worn off by now."

"Man, I'm sorry, that sucks." Moses winces sympathetically. "Bryce is the worst."

"Like you'd know," I bite. "Those guys never bug you."

"Yeah, because Justin's my cousin. He'd get in massive trouble with his mom if he and his friends picked on me at school. But

I'm the one that has to spend every holiday with the guy, so who's really losing here?"

"I think we're both losing, Moses," I deadpan.

He nods like this is a known fact of the universe. God, what a depressing thought.

"You're in here a lot, huh?" Moses asks.

"Why do you say that?" I don't like the idea of someone noticing my comings and goings. Two and a half years and I've got my system figured out—I know where and when to be out of the way to avoid Bryce and Justin and the rest of the football team. I don't need Moses or anyone else mucking up my system.

"We have similar routines." He shrugs. "Go to class, avoid the jerks. You know, the Nerd Way of Life."

"Ha, right," I snort.

"Not that I'm *your* level of nerd," he continues, the tip of his nose getting sweaty and red. "I mean, I'm not in any AP classes like you, but I do okay. I got a ninety-eight on my math test." He looks up at me expectantly like I'm supposed to throw him a parade or something.

"That's awesome, Moses," I intone.

"Yeah, it is," he says, nodding. "It *is* awesome, and stupid *Tyler*—"

Moses looks down at his hands, hiding his shiny face, and a few things start to click together.

"So . . . who are *you* hiding from?" I ask reluctantly, wishing desperately that this nook had a door I could lock. It's not that I don't like Moses—it's that Moses reminds me too much of myself, and that's a real bummer to be around sometimes.

"Principal Stevens."

"Wait, what?"

Moses lifts his head and leans forward.

"I don't think *I'm* going to get in trouble for it," he whispers, "but Tyler was making fun of me and then he and Caleb got into this *huge* fight—"

"Caleb Michaels?" I interrupt, my breath caught in my throat.

"Yeah," he breathes. "Tyler was being Tyler and Caleb just decked him. And, I mean, Stevens broke it up pretty quickly, but there was blood all over the floor. It was *nuts*."

"Oh my god," I murmur, trying to imagine quiet, beautiful Caleb hitting someone. I guess that's what football teaches you.

"I know." Moses nods. "That's the first time there's been a fight that bad in years. I don't even wanna think about what their punishment is gonna be."

3

CALEB

Sitting next to a bleeding, pissed-off Tyler outside of Principal Stevens's office was bad enough, but sitting in this unfamiliar waiting room alone, waiting for the ax to fall, is *torture*. Things could have been way worse at school—all we got was a one-day suspension and we have to clean all the science labs for the rest of the semester (though not together, thank god)—but somehow, this entire messed-up situation has led to me sitting here, in a therapist's waiting room. It's eerily quiet, the muted walls and low light making me forget what time of day it is. I begged off when my dad asked me if I wanted him to come in with me, but now I'm wishing he was here. I need something to focus on other than the dread of what this is going to be like and how stiff this couch is.

The office door groans open and a petite, perfectly dressed woman steps out. She looks a bit like the waiting room—simple and subdued.

"Caleb Michaels?" she calls, her voice soft but strong.

"Uh, yeah." I stand up, wiping my sweaty palms on my jeans. "That's me."

"Come on in, Caleb." She steps to the side, ushering me into the room.

"Please, take a seat," she says, gesturing to the couch, which thankfully has more pillows than the waiting room. It's lighter in here—daylight streaming in from the window—and I move cautiously toward the couch, sitting awkwardly. Am I supposed to lie down? Is that something that people still do?

"My name is Dr. Bright," she says as she sits in the chair opposite me. "I'm very glad you've come to see me."

"Yeah." I shrug. "I mean, I didn't exactly choose to be here."

"Do you know why your parents wanted you to come?" Ugh, she sounds so earnest. Why does she have to sound like that? My skin itches and I can't figure out why.

"Because I hurt someone," I mutter when it's obvious she's just gonna stare at me until I say something.

"What happened?"

"This guy in my grade was being a jerk, so I hit him." I shrug, not looking at her. There's something in her face that puts me on edge—like she pities me. I hate that.

"What was he doing that made you want to hit him?"

I'm thrown off by the question. No one else asked that. Not the principal or the school counselor or my parents. No one asked anything. They just assumed we got into a fight because that's what teenage boys do. No one brought what *I* wanted into it.

What I want has not factored into this situation at all. Last time I checked, getting into a fight at school didn't mean you had to go to fucking therapy, but here I am, sitting across from some woman called "Dr. Bright" like she's a Sesame Street character, pretending I don't want to crawl out of my skin.

"I don't know. I don't know that I *did* want to hit him, I just . . ." I trail off, shrugging again.

"Did you feel like you *had* to hit him?"

I nod.

"Why is that?"

"Like I said, he was being really uncool."

"How so?"

"He—well, he sits next to me in math class. And he's a total dirtbag—he's always texting and interrupting the teacher, and I'm pretty sure he cheats off the kid in front of him. And we got our tests back and I did . . . well, I did really fucking badly to be honest— oh, shit, sorry—can I swear in here?"

She seems totally unfazed by the back-to-back cursing, but says:

"People often use profanity to distance themselves from their feelings, so I think it's important for you to find new ways to express yourself." She talks like she's reading from a textbook until a small smile comes onto her face. "But you're not going to get in trouble for it. You can say anything you like in here."

I believe her. I don't know why, but I'm actually starting to feel a little comfortable with her. I guess that's what therapists are supposed to do—make you feel safe—but it's like someone's thrown a heavy blanket over me and I'm getting a little *too* warm.

I must be, like, staring into space as I sort through this because she clears her throat and prompts me to continue.

"You were saying you didn't do well on your exam?"

"I don't—" I stammer. "I'm not good at tests."

"Why do you say that?"

"It's always too quiet, you know? Like, too quiet *and* too loud."

"How do you mean?" Her face scrunches up a little, like she's trying to read something far away.

"I just get, like, stressed out. I have a hard time concentrating." Dr. Bright's face crinkles in sympathy and it gives me the courage to say more. "I don't know, maybe I have ADD or something. I feel like I get distracted by the other people in my class."

"What about them distracts you?"

"I dunno." I shrug one shoulder. "They just . . . everyone's always focusing so hard and they're nervous about passing and it just—it gets under my skin."

"Do you feel nervous when taking tests?"

"I guess. I didn't used to. But now . . . I don't know, other people make me nervous sometimes."

"Is that what caused the fight? This other student was making you nervous?"

"No, he was pissing me off!"

I don't mean to shout, but it happens anyway. Guess I'm not totally over it yet.

"Why were you angry at him?"

"He—I guess he saw my test, and when we were leaving class he started railing on me about it. And I told him to shut up but he just kept going—calling me stupid and stuff. It really ticked me off."

"That's understandable, Caleb." She nods. "It can be very difficult to deal with bullies."

"Yeah, exactly, he *is* a bully!" I say, relieved that she seems to be on my side. "He's always picking on people for stuff they can't help. Like this kid who's pretty good at math—Tyler started picking on *him* too. But like, making fun of him for getting a *good* grade and being chubby. And I just got so mad."

"Is that when you hit Tyler?" she asks, and there's nothing judgmental about it. It's refreshing.

"I guess. I don't know, the whole thing is kinda blurry." I swallow as I think about the white-hot anger that pounced on me like a wild animal. "Tyler was trying to get a rise out of me, I think, and I was just getting really upset, I guess, and, I don't know, it was like—like I couldn't control it. And then he started teasing Moses and I just . . . I went into, like, complete Hulk mode. And I hit him."

"What happened after you hit him?"

"I don't really know." I shake my head. "Like I said, it's all a bit of a blur. I guess he hit me back though, and we, you know . . ."

"Got into a tussle?"

"A tussle?"

Based on the look on her face, she doesn't have people questioning her a whole lot. I think I caught her off guard, and it feels like a little victory.

"Is that not an apt description?"

God, "apt." Where the fuck am I?

"'Tussle' makes it sound like we're kids on the playground. It was a fight. You know, between men and stuff." Even as I say it, I'm not convinced.

"Of course," she agrees. Her mouth stays completely still, but her eyes light up with a small smile. She's not buying my bullshit. It's nice.

"I mean, I did give him a black eye. And his nose was bleeding pretty bad," I add, like that somehow makes it better. The smile in her eyes goes away and her mouth gets tight.

"How do you feel about doing that?" she asks quietly.

"Not good," I admit after a second. It's not like I've never gotten into it with someone before. I mean, football is already a really physical sport, and then you add trash-talking into the mix and things can get kinda rough.

This was different though. Instead of running to tackle someone on the field—pumping my legs, bracing my body for the impact— it was like someone else got behind the wheel and threw my fist for me.

"Caleb, are you all right?"

"Huh?" I snap out of my daydreaming to see her watching me with concern. I realize my whole body has tensed up and I'm clenching my fists by my legs, driving them into the couch. I stretch out my hands, feeling the stiffness in my knuckles. "Uh, yeah, I'm fine."

"What do you mean by 'complete Hulk mode'?" she asks, tilting her head.

"I went total rage monster on the guy," I say, thinking that oughta cover it.

"Does that happen to you a lot? You turning into a 'rage monster'?"

The way she says it makes me want to laugh. But the laugh dies in my throat.

"Uh, yeah, sometimes. Lately. But it's like—" I stop myself, trying to find the words while also wondering how much I should tell this lady. I'd already put on a big show about how it was just a fight, no big deal, but there's something *not* normal happening to me. I can feel it. And even though grown-ups are always telling us that hormones make us crazy, this feels . . . worse than that. More dangerous.

I look at her again, weighing my options. She's been pretty chill so far—way chiller than every other adult who's tried to talk to me about this. Maybe she won't even try to lock me up in some kind of loony bin.

"It's like I've got split personality or something," I say.

Jesus, Caleb, why did you lead with the craziest way of explaining this? Keep it together, dude.

"I mean, no, not split personality," I rush to say. "I'm not crazy." Her eyebrow raises the tiniest bit. Oh god, now I've said the one thing that all actually crazy people say. Nice going. Well, if she already thinks I've lost it, I might as well tell try to actually explain things, I guess. "It's that—well, I dunno, I feel like it's coming from somewhere else, you know?"

"What do you mean, somewhere else?" she asks calmly, like I'm making any sense at all.

I feel prickly all of a sudden, like there are little tiny ants underneath my skin. It makes me want to jump up and down, but I really *would* look crazy if I did that, so I just clench and unclench my fists a few times before continuing

"It used to be that, when I would get mad, I knew what it was about. But now . . . now it's like there's all this *stuff* that just, like, jumps into my body and makes me go nuts. And it's too much so I get mad and then when I get on the other side of it, it's like I wasn't even there." I trail off, pulling my fists into my lap and looking at them so that I don't have to look at her.

"When did this first start happening?" she asks, her voice totally neutral. She's not mocking me or calling the men in the white coats yet, so . . . so far so good, I guess.

"I don't know, a couple of months ago." I shrug. "I only really noticed it at the start of this semester."

"Do you get angry a lot?"

"What counts as a lot?" I snap, unable to keep the sarcasm out of my voice. It feels like she's digging into me and I'm afraid of what might come pouring out.

"Do you feel that your anger gets in the way of your day-to-day life? Or overpowers other emotions?" she asks calmly, not rising to whatever challenge I'm throwing down at her. I deflate and decide to cooperate a little while longer.

"I guess. I mean, I guess it overpowers the other stuff. When I'm mad, that's all I can think about. But it's not like I'm walking around super angry all the time, it's—" I stop myself again, unsure about how much I want to say.

"It's what?" she prods. Guess I'm not getting out of this. I close my eyes for a second, exhaling loudly, and decide to just let everything come out. Maybe if I do, she'll stop digging and my skin will stop feeling like Pop Rocks.

"It's *everything*. Like, yeah, I get angry, and when I do it's like I'm possessed or something, but that's not the only thing. I get really sad sometimes and I don't know why or I get stressed during tests but it's, like, *out-of-control* stress, like my whole body is buzzing and I'm just gonna vibrate into oblivion, you know?"

"That sounds overwhelming."

"Yeah, it *is* overwhelming!" I nod enthusiastically, unable to stop talking now that I've started. "It's really overwhelming and I can't rein it in, I can't do anything about it—things just build and build and then they explode and it's like I don't have a choice in it, like my body just reacts without me making a decision!"

By the end I'm practically shouting. I'm out of breath, like I just ran suicides. She barely reacts, pinning me with a completely unreadable expression on her face. It makes me feel calmer for some reason—the itchy feeling under my skin has gone away and I feel something slot into place.

Now that all that's been released, I'm feeling dumb, like I got carried away. I try to brush it off.

"But, like, I'm sixteen, so that's probably normal, right?" I say, faux-casual. "I mean, getting into a fight with someone isn't that big of a deal. Although apparently my parents disagree, because they sent me here instead of grounding me like normal people."

"Do you think you shouldn't be here?" She doesn't seem insulted, which is strangely a relief.

"I don't know. I mean, I know I shouldn't have hit him," I admit.

"It sounds like it's not just about that," she says.

"What do you mean?" I'm feeling unsettled all of a sudden. Nervous. Like some sort of bomb is about to be dropped.

"When your parents spoke to me about you"—the pitying look is back and I hate it—"they mentioned that you've been behaving differently over the past few months. That you've been having mood swings."

"They told you that?" I ask.

"Yes. And based on what you just described, it sounds like they hit close to the mark."

"Uh yeah, I guess. I didn't realize that they'd, you know, picked up on that," I say, rubbing the back of my neck and looking away. "But I mean, everyone has mood swings sometimes, right?"

"True. But your parents seemed to think it was out of character for you. They're worried that it might be an indication of something more serious."

"What do you mean 'more serious'?" I ask. Oh god, I've done it. I've given her reason to think that I'm totally insane and now she's going to send me to some kind of special school for boys who can't control their tempers.

"What, do you think I'm cracked in the head or something?" I joke, trying to play it cool.

"No, Caleb," she says, the pitying look replaced with something softer. "I think you might just be a little different from your average teenager."

"Great," I mumble.

"Caleb, are you familiar with the term 'empathy'?"

"Uh, yeah, I think so," I say after a second. She keeps making hard turns in our conversation and I'm struggling to keep up. "It's, like, being able to relate to what people are feeling, right?"

"Yes, exactly: being able to understand someone's emotional state. Empathy is something most of us experience, but everyone experiences it differently. Some people have a complete lack of empathy—"

"What, like, psychopaths and stuff?" I ask, my heart starting to race.

"Yes, often the people that we think of as 'psychopaths'—people who hurt others—experience less empathy, which can lead to violent behavior. But that's not always true for people who lack empathy."

"Just because I hit a guy doesn't mean I don't care about people," I say, crossing my arms in front of my chest. I don't like what this lady is suggesting. I know I sometimes fly off the handle, but I like to think I'm a fundamentally good dude.

"That's not at all what I'm suggesting, Caleb," she says earnestly. "I think you might be in the opposite position, in fact."

"Huh?"

"I'm curious—these mood swings that you've been experiencing, when do they happen?"

"What do you mean?" I'm thrown again, not following her train of thought. It's frustrating.

"When you're alone, how do you feel?"

I have to think about it for a second. I try to remember the last time I was alone. Last night, in my room, reading before bed. My dad has this archaic rule where Alice and I aren't allowed to have screens on for half an hour before we go to sleep. So I read. The memory floats into my brain and a blanket settles over me again. Except this time it isn't too stuffy. It's light and soft—like this old knit throw that my grandmother made for me when I was a kid. It's made of this really light yarn—cotton or something—and it's cozy but not too warm. I loved sitting out on the rocking chair on our porch on summer nights, all curled up in it. Especially when there would be thunderstorms. I'm transported there instantly in my head—I can smell the mix of the rain and the flowery smell of the yarn and it's like the invisible pressure around me now tightens momentarily, but in a good way.

"Being alone is nice."

I don't even mean to say it, not really. I'm not sure I even realize what I've said until after it's out of my mouth. But I open my eyes (when did I close them?) to see Dr. Bright smiling softly at me, like she understands something. It's both comforting and sorta unnerving.

"You feel calm when you're alone?"

"Yeah," I half whisper, realizing that's what it is. That blanket; that soft, light, barely there warmth . . . it's calm. The awareness of it yanks it away, and I suddenly become fully conscious of where I am.

"Would you say your mood swings happen only around other people?"

"Yeah. Yeah, I guess they do," I say slowly. "That's when I get overwhelmed."

"By other people?" she clarifies.

"Yeah." I take a beat, think back on the past few minutes, try to follow the path of her thoughts and start to put some pieces together. "What did you mean by me being in the opposite position?"

"I don't think you have a lack of empathy, Caleb." She closes her notebook and folds her hands. "I think you have an excess of it."

"What . . . what do you mean?"

Dr. Bright shifts in her seat and for the first time, she looks uncertain.

"There are . . ." she starts, her hesitancy making me itchy again, "people in the world who are different. People who are able to do things that the average human cannot."

"What do you mean?" I repeat, my heart beating faster and faster. I suddenly feel like I'm in a haunted house. Walking through hallways where at any moment something terrifying could come bursting out.

"These people are called Atypicals," she says, and I can hear the weight behind that word.

"Atypicals," I echo.

"Yes." Dr. Bright nods. "And I believe you might be one of them."

"So, are you, like, gonna be a total weirdo forever?"

I look up from my bio textbook to see Alice standing in my doorway. I just got back from my third therapy session and I guess

Mom and Dad had "The Talk" with her. There's a prickly kind of
nervousness skittering up my arms but it doesn't make me want to
tear my own skin off. It's familiar. I guess it must be Alice's? God,
figuring this out is going to be a real pain.

"I guess." I shrug. "I mean, Dr. Bright seems to think it's a pretty
permanent thing."

"Whoa," she says, climbing up on my bed, uninvited.

"Hey, c'mon, don't mess up my pillows," I groan.

"God, you are such a neat freak." Alice rolls her eyes. "Is that
part of your whole thing?"

"Not wanting your sister's dirty feet on your pillows is a totally
normal thing." I emphasize the point by hitting her with one of
the pillows in question.

"Yeah, but you're not normal anymore, huh?" she asks, and my
breath catches in my throat. She's teasing me but it doesn't *feel* teasing. It feels like a genuine question.

"I don't know that I'm really all that different." I shrug. "I just,
you know . . ."

"Can feel other people's feelings," she finishes.

"Yeah," I breathe.

"So what am I feeling right now?" she goads, whatever weighty
thing she was feeling replaced by the desire to irritate me.

"Um . . ." I close my eyes and try to focus on the different sen-
sations, like Dr. Bright has been teaching me the past few weeks.
"You're . . . curious . . ."

"Well, *duh.*"

". . . and you're scared too." I open my eyes to her surprised face.
Saying it out loud makes the fear worse, her feelings making my
stomach a bottomless pit.

"But I don't know what you're scared about," I admit. "I just feel
the feelings, I don't know the why. But I mean, I can guess."

"I'm not scared of *you,* you dummy." She rolls her eyes, expertly
answering my unasked question while sidestepping any actual talk
of our emotions, and the floor comes back to my stomach.

"Wow," I say dryly, "are you an empath too?"

"'An empath' . . ." she echoes. "Sounds so official."

"Well, yeah, I guess it is official. Dr. Bright even said that I'm one of the most powerful empaths she's ever known," I add, my cheeks warming.

"So, what . . . are you, like, a superhero or something?" she asks skeptically, but there's a little zing in my chest. She's . . . excited?

"Yeah, because feeling people's emotions is *so* useful," I scoff. "'The Great Amazing Feelings Boy.' That's not a comic I'd read."

Alice laughs so hard she falls off my bed, and I feel normal for the first time in weeks.

4

ADAM

I poke my head out of my nook and hear nothing but the silence of a school out of session. Nothing new there—it's a library after all, and one that not many people use—but hopefully the halls will be similarly empty by now. Four o'clock, on the dot, the last day before winter break. I'm probably the last person left in the building.

Just like that, another semester is finished. And one with a minimum of unpleasant interactions. Also a minimum of *any* kind of human interaction, but having no friends seems a pretty fair trade for days with no surprises, no fights, no class periods spent crying in the bathroom. Not that I ever did that. Figure of speech.

I step out from behind the stacks and immediately jump out of my skin.

"*Jeez*," I breathe, just barely stopping myself from clutching at my chest like an old woman. Caleb Michaels is standing on the other side of the shelf, looking far too calm for someone who was just surprised by another person in a completely silent library.

"Oh, uh, hey, Adam," he stammers. Caleb knows my name? I try to prevent my face from looking *too* obviously thrilled about that. "Sorry, I didn't mean to scare you." A blush blooms over his cheeks. *Now* he looks caught off guard.

"No, it's fine," I lie, heart still hammering in my chest. "I just—I didn't think anyone else was in here. It's winter break."

"I needed a book," he says simply, waving the copy of the collected works of Shakespeare he's holding like it's a novella, not the largest book in the library. I silently curse the long sleeves that are covering up his arms. "Want to get a head start on the reading for next semester."

"Oh, right." I'm surprised and charmed by his diligence. He smiles sheepishly and the surprise gets edged out.

"You know," I start, emboldened by his smile and the quiet cocoon of the library, "you could just check out *Macbeth*. You don't have to lug around every word Shakespeare ever wrote." I nod toward the massive tome he's holding, making even his large hands look small.

"I know." He laughs softly and my stomach swoops. His eyes dart toward me and he blushes even deeper before continuing. "But I figured, I've got some free time over the break, might as well see what the big fuss is about this guy. I've heard *Hamlet* is pretty good," he finishes, eyes sparkling.

"Yeah," I laugh. "Yeah, that's a good one." I want to tell him that it's my favorite, but Caleb's eyes are fully meeting mine now and he's smiling and I'm smiling back and time feels frozen and full of possibility. Caleb, impossibly, gets cuter the longer I look at him. The broadness of his shoulders feels softer, the clench of his jaw relaxes into a beautiful edge, and I can see flecks of blue in the green of his eyes.

"What are you doing here?" he blurts, looking away and breaking the moment. "Don't you have a free period at the end of the day? I thought you'd have been long gone by now."

"Oh, um, I—" I stutter, my brain still stuck on the moment that's been shattered. Wait, how does Caleb know my schedule? I didn't even realize he knew my *name* until two minutes ago.

"No, sorry, it's none of my business," he says, his eyes getting big. "God, sorry, I didn't mean . . . dammit." He's muttering to himself now and the blush has taken up his entire face. I have a

sudden and urgent need to comfort him, to bring back the ease of
just a few moments ago, which is the only reason I say:

"I hide out here."

"What?"

"Um," I start, desperately wanting to backtrack, "no, not hide.
I just . . . you know. Like to wait until the coast is clear." Caleb's
breathing slows and something close to understanding crosses his
face. He's starting to smile again, softer this time, and it makes me
bold.

"You never know what uniformed sociopath is lurking just
around the corner," I say lightly. I'm expecting him to laugh or
shrug or *something* at the dumb joke, but he just looks down, bringing his gaze, and mine, to the jacket he's wearing. His *letterman*
jacket.

Oops.

I'm about to say something more—take back the comment—
but Caleb just shakes his head slightly before looking back up at
me, hurt on his face.

"I'm not—" he stutters, "I didn't mean to—I, uh, I should get
going."

He picks his backpack up from the floor, puts the book under
his arm, and turns away.

"No, wait—" I start weakly.

"Have a good break!" he calls, barely turning his head to look
back at me.

Caleb rushes out, leaving the library empty once again.

The house is as empty as the library when I get there, which is the
case about ninety percent of the time. That's what you get when
you have two neuroscientists for parents. They're good people—and
smart—but most of the time, I think they had me by accident. They
love me, I know, but they love cutting into people more. How's that
for a family hobby?

I kick off my sneakers into the front hall closet and make my way into the kitchen, not bothering to turn on the lights in the hallway. The house is wrapped in darkness and hush—the December sun having set thirty minutes ago—and I decide that the weather and the end of school both call for some hot chocolate. The encounter with Caleb still fresh in my mind, I grab our copy of *Macbeth* off the shelf in the library, thumbing my way through it as I put the milk on to heat. The book is well worn, a feat considering I'm the only one in the house who's cracked the spine.

It's been a bit of an odd upbringing. Once I was beyond the danger age for swallowing small objects, I was given models of the human body as toys. For my tenth birthday, they handed me an anatomy textbook. A lot of people like their jobs, but my parents love medicine like you wouldn't believe. They are endlessly fascinated by human beings and all the ways that we can be broken and fixed. Medical journals pile up in every room of our house because new information is being discovered all the time, and my parents have to learn every piece of biological knowledge that is out there.

Thankfully, I did inherit my parents' passion for knowledge. I just didn't get the medicine bug. I love books, art, philosophy—all the "soft" fields, as my mother would say. My anatomy books gathered dust as I scoured through the family's bookshelves for the rare volume on the humanities. They've got philosophers in spades, which is nice (something about having a "full appreciation for the human brain") but the fiction selection basically boils down to the collected works of Shakespeare and some old science fiction, all untouched until I got my hands on them. I read *Frankenstein* for the first time when I was eleven and my entire world expanded outward. Probably why I have a bit of a fixation on the macabre.

Or maybe it was just having parents who stick knives into people for a living that gave me my love for the grim and gory. Maybe that's why I loved *Frankenstein*. Maybe that's why I—

No, stop it, Adam. Don't go down that road.

I take the milk off the burner and dig the cocoa powder out of the cabinet. I sit up on the counter with my hot cocoa, swinging my legs as I pull out my phone to post a picture of the perfect cup

I just made. Not for the first time, I wonder what it would be like to have someone over—to make hot chocolate or bake *with* someone. To have someone light up the dark house.

I roll my eyes at myself and that particular thought and hop off the counter to turn on the kitchen lights. Just because I get emo sometimes doesn't mean I have to sit alone, in the literal dark, on the first day of holiday break. That's a little too macabre, even for me.

They don't like that I'm macabre, my parents. For two people that are elbow deep in brains half the day, they have some funny ideas about how sunny-side-up their son should be. They think I should smile more, have more friends, hurt myself less. And I do. I *do* hurt myself less. That should be enough. I shouldn't have to be legitimately happy on top of it. I'm in high school. No one's supposed to be happy. If kids aren't hurting themselves, they're usually hurting someone else.

I think of Caleb's blush and furrowed brow when I said "sociopath" and feel worse than I have in a long time. Please, please, *please* let next semester be better.

5

CALEB

"School starts tomorrow, correct?" Dr. Bright asks after a few moments of silence.

"Yep," I say.

More silence. I'm getting used to these standoffs. I just wish I was better at winning them. But Dr. Bright pins me with a stare and I eventually give in, every time.

"I don't wanna go back," I mumble, face heating.

"Why not?" she asks, like the answer isn't obvious.

"Because being in high school when you can feel everyone's feelings is a complete nightmare?" I answer dryly.

"You've made some good strides since November, Caleb," she soothes. I sense it more in her emotions than her voice, and it grates. I don't want to be soothed right now.

"Yeah, whatever," I bite.

"Caleb"—there's that stare again and the soothing hardens—"what have we talked about?"

"Don't deflect emotion with being an asshole," I recite, and there's a small, quick glow within the perfectly even Therapist Mode that Dr. Bright's emotions operate in.

"I don't remember putting it quite that way," she smirks, "but yes. When you're overwhelmed or refusing the input from your ability, you respond with anger. And we don't want a repeat of what happened with Tyler."

"Yeah, I know," I sigh. "It's just easier, you know?"

"What's easier?"

"Feeling annoyed or mad at stuff," I say.

"It might be an easy way to push away the other feelings," she tells me, "but it won't help you *process* them."

We sit in silence again but this time Dr. Bright is the one to break it.

"How was it being with your family the past few weeks?" she asks.

"Um, it was good, I guess," I say. "I mean, I feel like I've gotten used to their feelings, you know? So, like, I'm able to balance them a bit. But it's not like that in school."

"What helps you balance your family's emotions?"

"Well, there's only three of them, so that helps. And even when their feelings are annoying or whatever, I can kinda tell who they belong to. They're familiar."

"Has the color system proved useful?" she asks.

"Yeah, I guess so," I say, thinking about how Dr. Bright feels warm and yellow right now. "Like, it doesn't always make things easier, but it's definitely something."

"Do you think that could help at school?"

"I don't know," I admit. "There's just *so* much. There's too much, you know . . ."

"Input?" she suggests.

"Yeah, exactly. And so I can't process, like, any of it, and that's when I get overwhelmed."

She purses her lips and I feel the itchiness that I've come to know as Dr. Bright working through stuff in her head. It feels like I'm trying to solve a math problem I don't understand.

"The familiarity of your family's emotions makes it easier for you to balance your ability," she repeats. "Is there anyone at school who could do the same thing?"

"What?"

"Is there someone—a teammate or friend—who you feel comfortable around? Someone whose emotions you could focus on when you get overwhelmed?" The itchiness settles as she says this, like this is really a solution to my Problem.

"Um, no, not really," I admit. "I have friends and stuff but no one . . ."

I find myself thinking of the last day of school, going into the library and knowing, just knowing, that Adam Hayes was there. And then he was so startled and his feelings were all over the place, but there was something—

"No one . . . ?" Dr. Bright prompts.

"No one whose feelings fit," I finish. "I don't know that focusing on anybody at school is actually going to help."

"Well," she says, "something to think about?"

"Yeah." I nod. "Something to think about."

But I don't have time to think about it, because the first few days of school are lost in a haze of other people's bullshit. I got to English early today so that I'd have time to settle in before the onslaught of emotions, and it's not exactly working. I have to close my eyes as the other students start coming into the room. I try to sift through the feelings; focus on the colors and try to figure out what I'm going to be up against for the next hour.

Red. Anger. That one's pretty obvious. And it's an emotion that I'm *super* familiar with.

Black sludge. I think that one is disappointment. But this is worse—this is dripping sludge. Hot and cold all at once. *Ugh*, I hate this one. I feel it all the time but I can't figure out what's different about it. And it makes me want to jump off a bridge.

Soft blue. It settles behind my eyes and makes my head heavy. Exhaustion. Dr. Bright tells me that being tired isn't a real emotion, but I don't buy it. There's a certain kind of tired—a bone-deep weariness—that definitely qualifies as an emotion.

Off-white. Soft. Suffocating. Sadness.

Red again.

Black sludge.

Black sludge.

Black sludge.

God, it's literally the first week of the semester, can't people just chill?

Pins and needles under my skin. My breathing picks up. Traffic-cone orange. Stress.

Oof, *a lot* of stress.

And then.

Quiet. Blue-green. Not sharp like red and orange, but deep. Endless. It fills me up, empties me out. Clears out the sludge, the pins and needles, but makes me tense. Restless.

I open my eyes. Find his.

Adam.

6

ADAM

Caleb.

Why is it that, for the past week, every time I walk into a room, he's staring at me? It's like he has some sort of radar—he catches my eye wherever I go. If I didn't know any better, I'd assume that some dark, omniscient power was out to make my life miserable. Not that I am particularly bereft in the misery department. But this just seems especially cruel.

His eyes. His *fucking* eyes. Sad and curious and *beautiful* and angry; like he's angry that I'm there. Like he resents my existence. Part of me wonders if he's still upset about the stupid library encounter last semester—the staring started just after that—but Caleb doesn't seem like the type to hold a grudge. And yet here we are, a new semester, and his eyes are always on me.

So who's going to turn away first? Every time I want it to be him—I want to stare him down until he gets scared and has to look away. There's something about him that makes me want to *fight*. But every time his eyes find mine, they look straight into me and make mincemeat of my insides. So I don't fight; I cave. I'm always the one to look away first.

Even if I wanted to fight, I couldn't hold my own against Caleb

Michaels. Not many people could. Tyler has been significantly subdued since the fight, and that's *Tyler*—I thought the guy was fearless. I take one more quick glance at Caleb and try, for the thousandth time, to imagine him breaking a guy's nose. I know it happened, but there's something about it that just doesn't compute. I don't feel threatened when I catch him looking at me. I feel . . .

Never mind. Not a productive train of thought.

I walk toward the back of the room to my desk—conveniently and purposefully located behind Caleb so I don't have to look at his face. The back of his neck is still visible and provides its own unique brand of torture, but it's an easy battle compared to his eyes.

Enough about him. What are we doing today? I squint at the board. We're still on *Macbeth*. Good. No romance in that, not really. Just murder and politics, the best distractions.

"I can't believe he said yes! That's *amazing*."

"Gee, thanks for the vote of confidence, Caitlin."

Perfect. Jessica and Caitlin have settled into the desks behind me and seem particularly excited about the day's gossip. Yay, hooray.

"Sorry, you know what I mean," Caitlin says, trying to soothe her. "It's just that taking the quarterback to Sadie Hawkins is kind of a big deal."

"I know!" I can hear the smile on Jessica's face. I guess she asked Ryan to the dance, then. Even I have to admit that they'll make a nice-looking couple—with their shiny hair, tan skin, and perfect Colgate smiles. It's exhausting.

"Now it's *your* turn," Jessica says. "You need to grow a pair and ask him!"

"Ugh, I know," Caitlin says, "and I will. I promise. Just . . . let me get through this week. I need to nail this *Macbeth* project and then I'll ask him. Seriously."

"Okay, okay," Jessica concedes, "but you need to stop stressing about this paper. You already have an A."

"And I'd like to keep it that way, thank you very much." I can't see her, but I just know Caitlin is preening while she says this. I find her early-morning chatter irritating beyond belief, but the girl is *smart*. And she never lets you forget it.

"Fair enough. Just don't wait too long." Jessica's voice drops to a whisper. "Caleb's one of the cutest guys in our class. Someone is gonna snatch. Him. Up."

I freeze. Mr. Collins has turned to us and started speaking, but all I hear is blood rushing in my ears. I should have expected this—I know I should have—but it still catches me by surprise.

Caleb *is* the cutest guy in our class, even if I would be the last person to admit it (though the first one to think it). But he's never dated anyone. I've never seen him so much as check out a cheerleader. For a while, I thought maybe I'd gotten crazy lucky, maybe Caleb didn't want to chase girls like the rest of the football team, but now I'm not sure. He doesn't check out *anyone*. Since the beginning of the school year, he's gotten quiet and kept to himself and *goddammit* if that doesn't make him even more appealing.

7

CALEB

God, I feel sick to my stomach. What is going on? Ever since he sat down, Adam's emotions have been a total roller coaster. Surprised, sad, angry, annoyed, and now disappointed again, but a little different. The sludge fills my veins and then freezes over. Hardens. What is he *thinking* about?

Adam had never even been on my radar before this year. If you'd asked me what classes we'd shared last year, or the year before, I couldn't tell you. But now my whole day revolves around our shared spaces. It was vague at first—just a general awareness when he was nearby—and I'd hoped I'd come back from break and things would have normalized. But of course they haven't. If anything, his feelings are even more noticeable. They wash over me—different from the molasses I swim through with the rest of my classmates—and stretch to every corner. Blue, filling up my entire field of vision; my whole brain.

His emotions are always a shade of blue. But not blue like the sky; blue like the ocean. And they're warm and soft a lot of the time. Even when he's sad, it's warm and soft. Like sinking into a bath. And sometimes that's nice and sometimes I get pulled under and nearly drown.

Today, things are not soft and warm. The black sludge and the red anger are taking over a bit. Those are always the same, in every person. I don't know why. Black and red can be other emotions, depending on the person, but disappointment and anger always feel the same at their core.

Jeez, save it for therapy, Caleb. Focus on class. Focus. *Focus.*

I step into the car after practice and get an earful.

"Good God, Caleb, you could at least put your pads in the trunk. You *reek.*"

"Sorry, Mom. Hold on." I hop out and stuff my gear in the back. I'm not sure it improves the smell though, because she still rolls down all the windows when I get back in.

"Is there a reason you can't use the school's showers? Does your father put up with this every day?" She sounds incredulous. She hasn't picked me up at school for a while—Dad's writing has been keeping him at home for the past few months so he's taken over chauffeur duties.

"Ha, yeah, he does," I say, "and I can't use the showers, it's way too weird."

"Why?" I feel her familiar orange concern wrap around me in a suffocating hug. "You're not . . . ashamed of your body, are you?"

"God, Mom, *no,*" I scoff. She's always doing this—inventing more and more reasons to be worried about me. As if me having a pathetic super*whatever* isn't a big enough problem to occupy her brain. "*No,* no, it's just . . ." I can feel my face reddening as I trail off.

"Just what?" she jabs, her concern like hot, yellow pokers sticking out of her.

"Guys think about a lot of . . . stuff in the showers," I mumble, powering through the humiliation, focusing on minimizing her concern. "And it's weird to be around that. Even if *I'm* not thinking about that . . . that *stuff,* I can still feel it from the other guys. And those kinds of emotions are *not* something I need to know about my teammates."

I feel the yellow pokers turn into understanding.

"Oh . . . right, of course." She *sounds* a little embarrassed, but I don't feel it from her. Only sympathy. My mother is sympathetic to a fault. "I can understand that."

She shudders a bit at the thought and looks over at me, a smile beginning to form. There's a bubbly rush of air that tickles my lungs and we both burst out laughing.

My smile is threatening to break my face apart and I turn toward the open window, feeling the wind and the sun on my face. It's in moments like these that I don't mind my Problem all that much.

I thought I knew what happiness felt like. That free, high-soaring feeling when you're laughing with someone, doubled over, abs aching. It would make my body feel light and strong and untouchable—like I've floated so high, no one could ever pull me down.

That feeling doesn't compare to what it's like now. If I was in the clouds before, now I'm in space, soaring in a bubble among the brightest stars.

Whenever that happens, I feel like maybe my Problem is worth it. Worth all the sadness and anger. But then the sadness and anger come around again and I forget what the joy felt like in the first place.

But right now I'm still smiling and closing my eyes against the sun. I can feel my mom watching me out of the sides of her eyes.

"What, Mom?" I sigh.

"Nothing, sweetie. I just like seeing you happy," she says with a smile. I can feel a bit of sadness drop into her happiness and it ripples outward, extending toward me. I open my eyes and look at her. She still has a smile on her face, but it feels a little strained.

And just like that, it's over. The bubble of joy has burst and I come careening back down to Earth. My mom's not overly sad, just a little bittersweet, so I level out before crashing into the surface. That's what's nice about my parents—I usually don't yo-yo as much around them as I do at school. They're level-headed grown-ups, so it's easier to deal with.

"I've made you sad now, haven't I?" she asks knowingly, seeing the look on my face.

"Only a little. I'm fine," I reply truthfully. "I know you're worried about me."

"Oh, Caleb, I'm never worried about you. It's other people that make me worry."

I don't really know what she means by that, and I don't ask. Just because I can feel her emotions doesn't mean I understand them. Adults are so freakin' weird. Their emotions might be easier to read but then they're always saying cryptic shit like that.

We spend the rest of the car ride in a comfortable silence. As we pull up to the house, I can feel my dad and my sister reaching out to me. Not in the sense that they know I'm there. It's not like their emotions are looking for me. They just . . . find me. I've gotten so used to the way my parents and my sister feel that their emotions are easier to identify.

My dad is in heavy concentration mode and it makes me itch to sit down and get my homework done. My sister is somewhere in the house daydreaming. There's a hazy pink fog around all of her emotions and she's sleepy/happy. It mixes with my dad's focus and leaves me feeling a little off-balance. Like when you stand up too fast and your vision goes fuzzy for a second.

"David! Alice! We're home," my mom shouts as we step inside. "Caleb's with me!"

That's the new warning cry of the Michaels family: "Caleb is here." Code for: "make sure you've got your emotions in check because the super-weird family member is going to make you feel awkward for having them in the first place."

"Thanks for the warning, Mom." I roll my eyes. "Wouldn't want anyone to be caught off guard by the family weirdo." I don't say it with much heat, but I still feel a twinge of annoyance from my mom.

"Come on, Caleb," she says, "you know it's not like that."

"Nah, I know," I agree. "I get it. You guys have to protect yourselves."

"Not from you, sweetie." She turns to me and rubs my arm. "Never from you."

The warmth of her hand on my arm spreads through me as the

exasperation gives way to those familiar yellow pokers, this time with a softer edge.

"You don't feel like you have to hide from us, do you?" she asks, her worry wrapping around me like a blanket.

"No. No way," I assure her. "I love being around you guys. It's . . . easier."

She smiles and the blanket loosens without leaving completely, her ever-constant concern for me creating a warm haven.

8

ADAM

"How's your AP prep coming along?"

My parents and I are having the rare weeknight dinner together, and it's been nonstop questions about school. Eating together is usually reserved for Shabbat, which I've never fully understood, as my dad isn't all that religious and my mom isn't even Jewish. But that's how my dad grew up and I guess it's a good excuse to have a family meal. On Fridays, my parents are capable of shifting out of work mode and having an actual, human conversation. But when they *do* catch me in the middle of the week, it's like being interviewed by a college admissions board.

"It's fine," I tell my mom as I shuffle the nondescript pasta dish around my plate. My folks are geniuses but *my god*, are they bad at cooking.

"Do you need any help? You know that your father and I would be more than happy to—"

"Yeah, I know, Mom, thanks. I've got it covered."

"How's debate club going?" my dad asks. I know that they don't really care about debate club—they don't understand why I'm in it in the first place—but it's nice of him to ask, I guess.

"Understand"—that's such an imperfect word. I love imperfect words. My parents do not. And yet they embody the conflict of that one so well. My parents "understand" why I'm in debate, why I like Shakespeare and Shelley, why I hole myself up in my room and listen to Bon Iver; they perceive the meaning. They grasp the concept. But they don't really *understand*. Not in the greater, metaphysical sense. They keep putting their big brains together to puzzle out the equation of their son, and—even though they get the math, they know how to do the long division, the addition, the subtraction—they can't quite comprehend the answer they end up with.

"It's good," I say, knowing I need to at least try to give him something more than that. "Me and Caitlin are going to be on the same team for our first competition."

"Caitlin and I," my father reminds me gently.

"Right, Caitlin and I," I mumble, annoyed at myself for being so lazy in my speech. Mom and Dad definitely aren't going to be happy about me majoring in English in college if I can't even get basic grammar right.

"She's at the top of your class with you, right, sweetie?" my mom asks, a little pride sneaking into her voice at the fact that I'm still doing so well in school despite, well, despite being *me*.

"Yeah, she's really smart. We're not usually on the same team because it's—it's a little unfair to the other kids, I guess," I say sheepishly, not wanting to come off as arrogant. "But our teacher thought it'd be good to mix things up this semester, so . . . yeah, it should be pretty interesting."

I want to sink into the floor. I hear what I'm saying and how I'm saying it and even *I'm* bored by it. I'm sluggish and dull and I know they can tell and I want to break out of it—be animated, engaged; the vivacious, charming son they want me to be—but I just can't.

Talking to my parents is impossible. Talking to *anyone* is impossible. It's exhausting. Everything always sounds better in my head—my brain runs a mile a minute, I'm *clever* in my head—and then I open my mouth and *nothing* comes out.

There's something not right with me, I know that. I don't feel my feelings in the right way—this is not a new fact about Adam Hayes. Either I feel everything too much or I feel nothing at all, and I honestly couldn't tell you which is worse. Right now, I'm inclined to say the latter, because that's where I'm at in this current moment. I'm like a balloon with all the air let out, and I don't know how to inflate again.

I thought I was doing better this year, or at least, I'm *appearing* better from the outside. My parents look at me with less concern in their eyes, they don't make me leave the door open all the time, I don't want to hurt myself anymore. As much. Well, I *don't* hurt myself as much anymore. It doesn't matter what I want. I'm good with not doing/getting/having what I want.

I'm good at a lot of things. I'm good at biology, at English, at debate, at piano. I'm even good at talking, if it's in front of a class or an auditorium and not the terrifying one-on-one conversations where you're expected to have a normal emotional response and give normal social and emotional cues. *That* I'm not good at. I do not excel at having feelings. Or, really, I don't excel at having the *right* feelings. And I wish I had the energy to hate that I'm this way.

My parents' voices drift in and out of my head and it sounds like I'm listening from underwater. I'm sinking further and further and can't be bothered to swim up.

By the time the water clears from my ears and my brain resurfaces, I'm standing at the sink doing dishes. The repetitive motion is calming me, bringing me back to my body in a way that I'd been missing during dinner. As I come out of my daze, I notice the faint sounds of my parents in the dining room. It sounds like they're arguing, which is . . . unusual. My heart rate picks up a bit as I turn off the faucet and move to the closed swinging door between the kitchen and dining room.

". . . Sanchez wants to publish," I hear my mom say.

"What? Why now?" my dad asks.

"He thinks the project was mishandled."

"Then he shouldn't have abandoned it," my dad says sharply.

So they're arguing, but not *with* each other. That's a bit of a relief, I guess.

"You know he was never really on board as the rest," my mom sighs.

"Are there even any subjects left to back him up?" my dad asks wearily.

"Just the one."

"That doesn't mean that he—"

"It still works." My mom sounds a bit awed when she says this, and I can imagine the expression that's on her face. It's how she sounds when she explains a concept to me that she finds particularly interesting. It's her geek-out voice.

What the hell are they talking about?

"You mean—the subject can still—?"

"Yes." I can practically hear my mother nodding excitedly. "Well, not exactly—not as strongly or cohesively as before. But there are residual effects. Heightened perception—"

Her voice gets quieter and I lean toward the door.

"But not the same that we see in atypical—"

I lean a little too much in my eagerness, and the door jumps a bit, swinging slightly on its hinges. My parents stop speaking and I rush back to the sink, turning the faucet back on and loudly continuing the dishes.

Atypical what? The cloud that's been hovering over me today is lifted as my curiosity burns inside of me and dries up all the dampness in my bones. My parents' work has always been a bit of a mystery—they work for a hospital and sometimes consult for outside projects that are usually pretty confidential—but this . . . this is something else.

The door swings open and I try not to tense up as I hear someone walking up to me. I turn my head slightly as my dad puts some more dishes in the sink.

"I can do the rest of these, *boychik*," he says a little too cheerfully. "You go upstairs and finish your schoolwork."

"I already did all my homework," I say.

"Of course you did." He's smiling at me like I'm the best son in the world, and for a moment I forget about the weird argument and bask in it. "Then go read or something. You do enough around here."

"Okay, Dad." I give in, trying not to be too suspicious. "Is everything okay?"

"Yes, everything's fine, Adam," he assures me as he picks up the sponge and starts scrubbing away at the pasta pot.

"I thought I heard you and Mom arguing about something." I shrug, trying to act casual.

"It's nothing. Just a little work drama." He smiles, his eyes going big like, *Aren't adults silly.* Normally I'd agree, but there's a tightness around his eyes that makes me question the levity.

"Dad," I say flatly, showing him that I'm not buying it. He sighs.

"Scientific innovation is hard, Adam." Oh god, am I gonna get some sort of inspirational science talk? I did not sign up for that. "It's hard and imperfect and there's not always a right answer. There's so much left to discover about the way the brain works, and there's no perfect way to go about it."

"Okay . . ." I can't tell where this is going. He sighs again, puts down the sponge, and leans against the kitchen counter. I guess we're really getting into this, then.

"Your mom and I worked on a project a few years ago that was pretty out there but ended up yielding some great results," he explains. "We were able to gather a lot of really important new data."

"What kind of project?" I breathe, more awake than I've been all day.

"You know I can't tell you that," he says with a sad smile. And yeah, I do know. This is something that never quite made sense to me—how could my parents expect me to want to follow in their footsteps if they can barely tell me about what they do?

"Did something go wrong?" I ask, still not understanding why they both seemed so freaked out only a few minutes ago.

"No, no, not at all. Not with the project itself, anyway." He takes off his glasses and rubs at his eyes.

"Yeah, that's not cryptic at all, Dad."

He huffs a laugh. "Sorry, sorry. I wish I could explain the whole thing, but the long and short of it is that there was someone else on the project who didn't think what we were trying to do was possible. They wanted us to stop trying."

"But you didn't."

"No, we didn't. That person left, we kept going, and it worked. Now they're wanting to talk about the project, try and debunk our discoveries—"

"But I thought it was totally confidential."

"It is," he says, matter-of-fact. "They probably won't end up publishing, but it's just adding a little stress to things."

"Why?" I ask.

"It could jeopardize funding for future projects if people think we're exaggerating our findings," he explains.

"But you're not," I say, not even a question. There's no way my parents would ever give anything but the facts.

"No, we're not. But sometimes people have a hard time believing things that are . . ." He trails off, and I see his brain working to come up with a way to explain this to me without actually *telling* me anything. "Well, some of our work deals with the more unusual aspects of the brain. It can be a stretch for some people to understand."

"Like what?" My curiosity is raging now. Seriously, if they had wanted me to take a bigger interest in science growing up, they should have started with "unusual aspects of the brain."

"Ah, I can't tell you that." My dad grimaces a bit, before deflecting. "At least not yet. Someday we'll have a *long* conversation about the wonders of the human brain."

He waves his hands above his head and spins around goofily. I can't help but smile.

"Oh joy," I laugh, rolling my eyes. "Just what I wanted."

My dad does one more twirl, his eyes twinkling, and I'm reminded of all the ways that he and my mom used to make learning fun when I was a kid. I feel my smile get bigger and a knot in me loosens.

"It's good to see you laugh, Adam," he says, smiling warmly at me.

I know he doesn't mean it as a jab—I know he's just happy that I'm happy—but I'm suddenly self-conscious of my own joy. Oh, right, this is what this feels like. Why is this usually so hard for me to get to?

My smile cracks just a little and I feel the water start to wash over me again, pressing me down. I watch the small collapse reflected in my dad's eyes.

9

CALEB

I hate this I hate this I hate this I hate this I hate this I hate this I hate this—

"Mr. Michaels?"

Mr. Collins's voice snaps me out of my hamster-wheel brain and I look over to his desk to see him giving me a pleading look, like his eyes are telling me, *Just say something, kid, you're making an ass of yourself.* Because right now I'm standing up at the front of the class, silent, my sweaty palms making the ink smudge on the papers in my hands.

Oral presentations are not a strength of mine. I'm nervous already—I don't like public speaking of any kind—but *everyone* is giving their presentations today so *everyone* is nervous. And now I have Mr. Collins feeling nervous *for* me, which is a whole weird different thing than just feeling someone else's emotions. Feeling when someone else is anxious is one thing, but when they feel that way on my behalf, it's like I get stuck in this weird feedback loop where I'm nervous and then I'm nervous that I'm nervous and then I get self-conscious about being nervous and that makes me *more* nervous and . . . well.

I hate this I hate this I hate this I hate this I hate this I hate this I hate this I hate this—

"Shakespeare's *Macbeth* is a grim contemplation of fate versus free will—"

I'm reading on autopilot and my voice is shaky. It makes me feel so small and stupid. My hands are trembling and my mouth is so dry and I hope the sound that's coming out is coherent because I'm pretty sure I'm blacking out from the stress.

My body feels like it's filled with bees. Bees that are moving through the molasses in my veins and using the sludge to build a hive in my stomach. At any moment, I'm going to move my mouth to form the word "Banquo" and a whole swarm is going to come pouring out instead, attacking the class and earning me an F.

At least then I wouldn't have to finish this goddamn presentation.

10

ADAM

"—so, yeah, um, on the fate side, we have the actions of the—the Three Witches . . ."

Oh god, I *hate* this. He looks so uncomfortable and I can hear the nerves in his voice and it makes me want to both run away and hide and also go up there to give him a hug. Caleb isn't the type of guy who swaggers through the school like the hotshot that he easily could be, but he's confident. He has every reason to be: rising football star, reasonably good student (or at least, he used to be), nice guy, solid family, crazy good-looking. How could he not be beloved?

Seeing him like this—anxious and unsure of himself—is like seeing a bird with its feathers plucked clean. There's something naked and vulnerable and *wrong* about it. I don't get why he's so scared. English is the easiest AP by far, and we all know that oral presentations don't count as much toward your grade as the essay assignment. I know a lot of students hate giving presentations, but he seems freaked beyond reason.

Caleb keeps clenching his hands, making his already crumpled notes wrinkle even further. He's barely looking at the pages, his eyes darting around the room like he's expecting someone to leap out from the shadows and attack him at any moment.

"As for Lady Macbeth, we can see, that, uh . . . we can see . . ."

His eyes widen and he looks frantically back at his paper—oh god, he's lost his place. This is like watching a slow-motion car crash, except the person behind the wheel is the cutest guy in your class, who can raise the temperature of the room a few degrees by lifting the corner of his mouth in a smile, and watching him crash and burn is maybe the worst thing anyone could witness.

He's tripping over his words as he looks up in terror at the class. And for some godforsaken reason, he's now staring right at me. Again. I'm holding on to my notebook for dear life, feeling the edgings of it cut into my palms, hoping that either I'll pass out or he'll pass out or the whole class will just drop dead, but he looks so scared that all I can do is stare back and try to silently communicate, *You can do this. I believe in you.* And it's true. I do. My entire body is full of the wish that he gets through this, that he doesn't give anyone reason to make fun of him like they make fun of me, that he doesn't have to feel like crap when he leaves this classroom. Every atom I contain wants to see him succeed, and with that anxiety comes just the slightest bit of relief—like air is filling me up for the first time in days.

When I walked into school today, I'd been numb to the frantic stress around me. Now, I'm boiling over with nervous energy and the strange relief that comes with feeling *something* for the first time in days. Watching Caleb struggle is painful but also a much-needed jolt of adrenaline.

I'm completely frozen in place, worried I'll be trapped in the amber of this stress-filled moment forever, when his shoulders relax slightly and he looks back at his notes and continues. The whole thing takes maybe seven seconds, but it feels like a hundred lifetimes. As he gets back into a groove (or as much of a groove as Caleb can get into when giving a presentation, I guess), I'm a giant exhale personified. I feel wrung out, like I just absorbed all his stress simply by watching him go through that moment of panic. And *god*, I still have to give my own presentation.

I hate this. And I smile, just a bit, because that's *something*.

11

CALEB

Wow, Adam is really good at this. I mean, I knew he was a bit of a brainiac, but he just got up there and opened his mouth and all this super-smart stuff started coming out in this easy, confident way that I've never seen him pull off around, you know . . . other humans.

I guess we've never been in a class where we've had to give presentations before. We shared a math class for a few years, but then he got onto the advanced track and now I think he's in AP calc, which I am for sure *not*. The only other subject we have together this year is Latin and you can't really speak Latin, so it's not a class big on oral presentations, thank god.

It's weird, we've been in school together for five years now, at least, and I don't know that much about him. His parents are big-deal doctors or something and I guess he wants to do medicine too because he's taking all the AP science classes with Caitlin. She gave her *Macbeth* presentation first, to the surprise of no one, and completely nailed it. I like Caitlin—she hangs out with the team sometimes and she's smart and intense in a way that's sort of comforting. I don't have to try so hard with her because she always seems to know what she feels. Sometimes the emotions get really big and make me feel out of sorts, but mostly she's chill.

Adam's feelings are big too. They rush into me whenever we're in the same room, like they're demanding attention. His emotions are massive and unwieldy in a way that's frustrating but also . . . I don't know. They make me feel things. Like, feelings of my own.

Jesus, that's dumb. The Great Amazing Feelings Boy strikes again.

But I think that's why I've been so much more aware of him this year than in the past. At the beginning of the year, I thought I was completely losing it. Because I was feeling all this stuff and didn't know why, and on top of it, sometimes I felt like there were these arms or tentacles or something that would reach out and wrap around me and make everything confusing. I was on a roller coaster—I didn't know what was up and what was down, and it wasn't necessarily bad, sometimes it was thrilling, but I also felt like I was going to throw up half the time.

Right now, Adam seems to actually be enjoying himself for once. Normally he's so sad. Like, *really* sad in a way that I can't begin to understand. Sad in a way that sometimes stays with me all day, even when I leave school and everyone else's feelings wear off. But as he's talking about *Macbeth*, there's a confidence to him that I've never felt. And a joy. He's not just good at this—he *loves* this. After I take a second to wrap my head around that incredibly foreign concept, I realize I like the feeling. It's a bit like how I get when I'm playing football or talking about *Harry Potter* with Alice—like there are these bubbles moving through my veins and sugar on my tongue, cotton candy on my fingertips. It's light and full all at once and always moving forward. Energetic.

That's how Adam feels right now—like a bird has spread its wings inside of his chest and is ready to take flight. It's strong and fragile all at once. He knows what he's doing and it's almost like I can feel the rhythm of his heartbeat—steady but fast and excited in a way that I could tap my foot to. His enthusiasm is electrifying, even if it's for something as annoying as Shakespeare. I find myself admiring him a little for it—he doesn't just want the good grades, he genuinely cares. I don't know why that's a relief, but it is.

He finishes with a flourish, landing his point (whatever the fuck his point was—it all went over my head, and I got a bit hypnotized by the way the rhythm of his heart matched up with the movement of his lips), and he rocks forward a bit on the balls of his feet as he lowers his notes. The smallest smile crosses his face and he gives a not-subtle sideways look at Mr. Collins.

"Very well done, Mr. Hayes," Mr. Collins says with a nod of his head, giving Adam a genuine grin.

The curve of Adam's smile widens and I can feel the warmth of pleasure rush into him at Mr. Collins's comment. It feels like winning a football game or solving a hard math problem on my own.

Adam relaxes, leaning back on his heels for a second before walking back toward his desk. The smile has shrunk in size but not feeling—it's now just a private smile for himself. Well, and me. But he doesn't know that.

As Adam walks down the aisle between the desks, resident blockhead Bryce pulls the old "cough and say an insult" trick, coughing out, "Suck-up," just as Adam walks past him. It's so dumb and childish, and a lazy insult on top of it, so I expect Adam to brush it off. That's what I would do. But instead I feel him cave in, like someone has put their fist around the bird inside his chest and squeezed until it breaks. The familiar wave of deep blue sadness descends on him once again, this time streaked with angry red lines. He resents Bryce and he resents that he cares what Bryce thinks. But he does—he *does* care. He cares so much that his smile disappears with no sign of returning.

Bryce's smirk follows Adam as he slumps down into his seat and then Bryce turns back around to laugh with Justin. They're both idiots. I know that they're my teammates and all, but they bug the hell out of me sometimes. I can feel Bryce's stupid, shiny victory and I have to push against the impulse to laugh with him. His self-satisfaction pokes out the corners of my gut—it doesn't fit and I know it's because I'm not letting it fit. I don't want to be a part of this, but his dumb feelings are making themselves known to me whether I like it or not.

The rest of the class passes in a haze as the black sludge creeps in on me once more, but with an extra stomach-dropping edge to it. Usually it's dark and heavy and oppressive and all of that *sucks*, but this is worse somehow. It's not dark, it's . . . the absence of light. Like some sort of void. It doesn't weigh down on me, suffocate me. It's empty—just total nothingness. But it's sucking me in and I feel like if I go inside of it I'll stop existing entirely, and that scares me, but at the same time it would be a relief.

The bell rings.

"All right, everybody, nicely done today," Mr. Collins says with a clap of his hands as he stands up to open the door. "Have a good weekend. Mine will be spent reading your *Macbeth* papers, so, for my sake, I hope you made them interesting."

"Shakespeare is *always* interesting, Mr. Collins," Caitlin quips as she breezes past him, Jessica rolling her eyes as she leads the way out of the classroom.

"See, that's the kind of quality brown-nosing you all should aspire to," Mr. Collins says enthusiastically. "Nicely done, Ms. Park."

"I do what I can," she responds, not even looking back as she walks through the door.

I'm stuck in my seat, concentrating on not getting sucked into Adam's black hole. I'm facing the front of the class but I can feel him angrily shoving his books into his backpack behind me. I try to focus on my own annoyance instead of Adam's feelings. This keeps happening—he feels sad or angry or whatever and somehow I end up carrying all of that and it's so fucking unfair. Why can't he just push everything down like everybody else?

Adam gets up and rushes out of the classroom, expertly avoiding the leg that Bryce had stuck out to trip him. I mentally cross my fingers that Adam will take the void with him, but I know it's a hollow wish. I'm caught in his orbit and it's going to take me the rest of the day to shake this off.

I pack up my things and move into the hall, not paying atten-

tion to my surroundings, but then there's a sharp, red spike of anger that comes shooting out of the swirling vortex of despair. My
head snaps up to find the source.

"What, do you think you're better than me or something?"

Bryce is growling, looming over Adam by the lockers. They're
clearly in the middle of some sort of argument, and Adam, the
idiot, is staring right back, his body ready for a fight. Adam isn't
necessarily small—I mean, I've got a bunch of inches on him since
I hit my growth spurt this summer—but Bryce is an offensive tackle.
He's *huge*. And there's Adam, clenching his jaw and staring Bryce
down like they're evenly matched. I'd be impressed, if I didn't think
I was about to watch Adam get pummeled into the ground.

"I didn't say that, Bryce," Adam spits back, moving just the
slightest bit forward. Ooh, that was stupid. The drumbeat of
Adam's fear is pounding in my head—he's all false confidence
and bitterness and this will not end well.

Bryce draws himself to his full height, puffing out his chest and
looking down at Adam like he's ready to step on him.

"You think because you stand up in front of the class and say a
bunch of smart-ass nonsense that you're better than me?" There's
that hot-cold black sludge again and I think it's Bryce's. *Oh*. He's
insecure. Bryce is worried that he's dumb.

The next spike of anger is so strong, so piercing, that I'm starting to get worried that Adam is gonna snap and attack the guy. The
angry heat is starting to sink into my pores and I feel myself filling
with lava—I've gotta get ahead of this.

"Hey, c'mon, Bryce, just leave the guy alone," I say weakly, taking
a step toward them.

Adam's anger is momentarily taken over by the yellow-orange
of surprise. There's something else there too. Something softer and
a little . . . squirmy. I don't have time to think about what it might
be before:

"What, don't tell me you liked this nerd's presentation?" Bryce
scoffs, but I can feel the heat of nervousness from him.

"Who cares, Bryce, just go to third period." Based on Adam's
building lava and the tangled, anxious frustration coming from

Bryce, I don't think my stepping in is doing much in the way of calming things down.

"Chill, Michaels, I've got a free period next. I could do this all day," he singsongs, getting into Adam's face as Justin chortles behind him.

"Well, as delightful as this is, I *don't* have a free period, so I'll just be on my way to calc now." Adam rolls his eyes, a pretty ballsy move in my opinion, and starts to move out of Bryce's shadow.

"What would you do with a free period anyway? It's not like you have anyone to hang out with," Bryce taunts, fist-bumping Justin. The King of Weak Insults strikes again and I'd be moaning at the cliché of it all except I can feel the comment lance right through Adam's anger and hit him in the blue place. The wind gets knocked out of me for a moment and the sting of the insult feels close to actual physical pain. It's like I'm watching Adam bleed out in front of me and I can't do anything to stop it.

"Shut up," Adam growls, rounding on Bryce. His anger is still there but it's erratic, pieces of it flying all over the place before getting sucked into the quicksand of hurt.

"What are you gonna do about it, Hayes?" Bryce goads. "The way I see it, it's two against one, and I don't think you could phone a friend, even if you wanted to. No one's gonna come running to save a freak like you."

I take another step toward them, ready to intervene, but moving closer means being hit with a wave of *angerfrustrationsadnessdoubt* that turns me inside out. Before I know what's happening, words are coming out of me.

"Just leave him alone, Bryce, can't you see he's sad enough?"

The hallway goes a bit silent. I hadn't even noticed there were other people there, but students are still milling in between classes and it seems we've drawn a bit of an audience, because people are starting to whisper and a few of them are openly staring. Guess I was a bit louder than I meant to be.

But none of that matters when I feel like I've been punched in the stomach. I want to throw up and also maybe start crying, and that's so stupid because it looks like Bryce has stopped his bullheaded quest to get into Adam's face. He's staring at me weirdly, like I'm some sort of alien. Or maybe he's staring at me that way because I look like I might throw up and/or cry. He nudges Justin's shoulder, says, "C'mon," under his breath, and they walk away. I'm left facing Adam and then I realize why I feel the way I feel. Adam's eyes shutter as he looks at me, the life drained from his face. My stomach is in knots and I don't know if it's mine or if it's his but it makes me want to collapse on the floor right then and there.

I make an aborted step toward him, opening my mouth to say something, who knows what, but he picks up his bag and flees. That's the only way I can describe it. He just full-on runs away.

Another villain vanquished by the Great Amazing Feelings Boy. Hooray.

12

ADAM

Oh my god.

Oh my god.

I need to go to calc but my legs aren't working properly—it feels like I'm walking on two Twizzlers. I detour to the boys' bathroom, rushing into a stall and leaning up against the door. Breathe in deep. And out.

I can't believe that just happened. An honest-to-god knight-in-shining-armor moment from the object of my stupid, illogical, uncontrollable teenage affection and *that's* what happens? He defends me by calling out the fact that apparently I am noticeably some sort of depressed emo loser? What kind of messed-up twist of fate is that?

Stupid Bryce. Just because he's a complete cretin doesn't mean I should be punished for it. But he always does that. It's like he woke up one day and decided, "Hey, that Adam kid is smart and therefore the reason I'm not. I'm going to harass him until I can leech all his intelligence for myself or he punches me in the face and I get to beat him up. Whichever comes first."

It doesn't matter about Bryce. Bryce is a dunce. Bryce I can deal with (even if being called a freak hurt more than I'd like to admit).

It's Caleb that's the surprise element in all of this. Why did he—
how did he—

My heart and my brain are running circles around each other
as I replay the moment in my head. It felt like he saw right through
me. How did he do that? Is he really that perceptive? Or am I just
that obvious?

If someone who barely knows I exist is noticing that I'm low,
then I'm being sloppy. I need to get this under control. Because if
my classmates are picking up on it, then my parents will start to
pick up on it and they'll start hovering again and I'll be back with
the doctors and the open doors and I just . . . cannot have that.

I stand in the stall for ten more minutes, waiting for the coast
to clear. Waiting to not be this way anymore. Waiting to leave this
place, and these feelings, forever.

13

CALEB

Every part of my body aches and the euphoria of winning the game is beginning to float away as Coach Buckner lectures us on all the things we could have done better tonight. Can't the guy ever just enjoy the moment? I can feel that he's proud of us—we played a hell of a game—but it's buried under his anxiety about the season. I get that it's his job and all, but the dude is way too invested in high school football.

"Jesus, do you think Old Buck could ever just give us a break?" Ryan moans after Coach leaves, sinking down on the bench to untie his cleats.

"Oh who gives a flying fuck what that prick thinks," Bryce practically shouts, "that last touchdown was *legend!*" He slaps Ryan on the back and I can feel Ryan brighten a little bit at the chorus of compliments from the team that follows Bryce's swaggering.

Ryan smiles, high-fiving and fist-bumping the guys in between getting out of his various pieces of gear. Despite what happened earlier, I'm reluctantly grateful for Bryce in this moment. As the quarterback, Ryan has a lot of pressure on him, and I know he wants to do everything perfectly. His self-doubt about how he played was really starting to bum me out—like the weight of the world was coming down on my shoulders. Apparently all he needed was some hyping up from the team idiot.

"Hey—Mr. QB. I hear Jessica Hernandez asked you to that Sadie Hawkins thing," teases Henry, the team sleaze. The guys all ooh and wolf-whistle, shoving at Ryan playfully. My stomach swoops and my heart rate picks up.

"Yeah, she did. Not that it's any of *your* business," Ryan shoots back, swatting his towel in Henry's direction. A blush is creeping up Ryan's neck and I feel warm all over. My face scrunches in confusion as I pull my jersey over my head—is Ryan nervous? Why would he be nervous? He's always talking about girls. I don't understand why this is any different.

"Dude, she is *hot*," Justin says, and there's a murmur of agreement through the locker room.

"*Super* hot," agrees Henry. "I certainly wouldn't mind taking a bite of that sexy burrito." Henry does a little dance, spinning his jersey above his head like a lasso, and the instant spike of white-hot rage from Ryan almost makes me fall over.

"*Dude*, shut the fuck up. That is offensive on literally so many levels," Ryan says, chucking an elbow pad right at Henry's face.

"What, don't tell me you haven't thought about tapping that? And now she's asked you to the dance . . ." Henry trails off, wiggling his eyebrows suggestively. I feel like I'm biting into Styrofoam—my teeth squeaking and sliding unpleasantly at Henry's words.

"You know, Henry, not all of us are creeps just looking for a lay," Ryan counters. "It's not like that. She's a really nice girl."

"Oh yeah, she is. *Real* nice," Henry says. I *really* hate the way that Henry feels. It's cold and sharp and thin-edged—I never notice it cutting into me until it's already gone too deep. I try to hold on to Ryan's feelings instead, but that might be an even worse idea.

"I think you should probably shut up now, Henry," Ryan warns, and Henry's ice turns hot.

The white-hot anger from Ryan isn't jabbing out quite as much anymore, but has turned into molten lava that's mixing with toxic acid coming off of Henry in waves now. I'm trying to breathe deeply through my nose and not pay the increasing tension any mind. But Ryan is pissed that Henry is running his mouth and Henry is pissed that . . . what? Ryan isn't joking around with him? Whatever is going on, there's a lot of anger swirling around and that is *not* a good environment for me to be in.

"Aw, c'mon, Ryan—"

"How 'bout you, Caleb? You going to that dance?"

My head snaps up at Ricky's voice, which has successfully cut off whatever dumbass thing Henry was about to say. The lava still bubbles, but more quietly than before, and I gratefully play along with the change of subject.

"Uh, I don't know," I say. I haven't thought about it at all— school functions haven't really been my thing this year, for obvious reasons.

"Of course he's going! I mean, look at this face, someone's gonna ask this cutie out." Ryan's got his arm around my shoulder and his other hand smooshing my face. The lava is frothing but cooling and I allow myself a little smile at Ryan's friendly ribbing. He's burying his anger under the teasing and I relax a tiny bit.

The locker room breaks out into playful conversation about girls and the weekend and I take a few more deep breaths, letting the tension seep out of my chest and into my sore muscles. I beg off the guys' invitations to go out for a victory burger—claiming some bullshit family obligation—and finally get on my way home.

I know that's not what I'm supposed to do. I'm supposed to want to hang out with the guys, celebrate our win, hit on cheerleaders . . . whatever. But it's all too exhausting. It only ever leads to a stomachache from everyone else's feelings and my teammates looking at me weird when I get distant and quiet. I don't know what people think about me—about the fact that I don't really have any friends—but I try to get away from them before I can find out.

But when I get home, it isn't exactly the relief it usually is. My dad is on deadline, my mom has been dealing with a major crisis at work, and Alice . . . well, I actually have no idea what Alice is doing. She's in some sort of mood and for once, I can't tell what kind, so I'm just all out of sorts. My parents apologize for missing the game and congratulate me on the win, but no one's heart is in it. By 9 P.M., I'm lying on my bed, scrolling through my phone and trying to block out everything else. I guess I could turn on my Xbox, but even that feels like too much work. I'm completely wrung out.

After a little while, the strings that connect me and my family start to dissolve into the air—they're falling asleep. My insides uncoil and I feel alone for the first time all week. I get a moment of enjoying the silence before something inside of me tries to make itself known.

Oh. Right. I have my *own* feelings. I sort of forgot about those. Honestly, I'd like to keep forgetting about them.

I put my phone away (watching clips of the guys' post-game celebration is definitely not adding to the calm feeling) and pick up *The Aeneid*—might as well get a head start on our next unit. But as much as I try to lose myself in the Greek tragedy of it all, I can't stop thinking about Adam.

Despite my fist's history with other people's faces, I don't actually like hurting people. And I think I hurt Adam today. Actually, I'm pretty damn sure I hurt Adam today. That's sort of the benefit (well . . . *curse*) of my Problem. It's not fair that when I hurt somebody, I have to feel hurt too. And then I feel guilty on top of that and . . . well . . . it all really sucks.

I lie *The Aeneid* on my chest and stare up at the stupid stick-on glow stars Alice made me put on my ceiling. I've hurt Alice before, I know I have. She's my sister, I'm bound to get into fights with her. But it didn't feel like this. Hurting Adam hurts *more* and I don't know why. Maybe because when I piss off Alice we're still stuck living together and I get to be around her feelings enough to know how to make it right. Or at least, I know when she's mostly over it and it's safe to approach again. With Adam, I don't know if he's over it. Based on how he felt earlier today, I would be surprised if he'd already forgotten about it. But maybe he has. Maybe he's out with his friends (does he have any?) and the whole dustup he had with me and Bryce is a distant annoyance in his brain. Maybe he's fine and I'm just overreacting because the moment I'm given space to have my own feelings, they all rush in and overload my brain until it goes completely on the fritz.

It's only 10 P.M. and I know it's a weekend and my life should probably be more exciting than this, but I turn off the light and try to go to sleep.

14

ADAM

Looks like they won the game. I try to rustle up some school pride or happiness at this, but come up empty.

I really shouldn't be Instagram-stalking Caleb but I can't help myself. I know this is probably a betrayal to my generation but: social media is such a curse. Back in the Stone Age when my parents were dating, all they could do was wonder what the other was doing when they weren't together. They didn't have to be exposed to every second of every day, every person the other was hanging out with, every experience they were missing out on. They could just let their imaginations run wild.

I don't have to wonder if Caleb has spent the entire evening thinking about our terrible encounter earlier today like I have—I *know*. I know he hasn't, because he's been thinking about football and winning and the girl he's inevitably sharing a milkshake with at the local burger joint the football team frequents because apparently we live in a fucking CW show.

And why should he be thinking about it? He tried to do a nice thing for someone he barely knows and I reacted like a complete weirdo. Nothing to write home about. A blip in his day and a loud, screaming, neon warning sign in mine.

"Whatcha looking at, honey?" my mom asks from the doorway, snapping me out of my reverie.

"Nothing," I say, shoving my phone in my pocket and turning the sink back on. Jeez, what used to be the semi-relaxing cool-down time of washing dishes has apparently become "corner Adam and ask him about his life" time.

"Oh really?" She grins. She places the rest of the dishes on the kitchen counter and I shrug as I hand her a plate.

"Are you going out with friends tonight?" she asks, unable to keep the hopeful note out of her voice.

"What do you think?" I scoff, not looking her in the eye.

"What about that Caitlin girl?" she suggests. "It sounds like you two have a lot in common."

"We have a lot of *classes* in common," I correct her. "She's really popular," I add after a moment, as if that explains everything.

"What's wrong with that?" God, my mom cannot let anything lie.

"Nothing's wrong with that, Mom," I say, exasperated. "But I'm, you know, *not* popular, so we don't really run in the same social circles."

"What about the other kids from debate?" she presses. "You never hang out with any of them outside of school?"

"Not unless we need to practice."

"I'm just worried about you, sweets," she says, putting down the plate and brushing my curls down.

"I know you are, but you don't need to be," I assure her, even though we both know that's not exactly true. "I like being alone. I'll make friends in college."

"You know, you don't have to save up—you can have friends now *and* in college," she teases gently, giving me that big-eyed "worried about my little boy" mom look. It's a killer look.

"Yeah, thanks, I know that," I say, rolling my eyes. "But not a lot of high schoolers want to hang out with the depressed gay kid. I'm not exactly first on people's lists for keggers."

"Well, first of all, you're not to drink if you get invited to any 'keggers.'" She raises her eyebrows and takes another plate from me. "And secondly, I think people might surprise you. I know you sometimes feel worlds away from everyone else—"

"Mom, please—"

"But that doesn't mean people can't relate. I'm sure there are other kids at your school who struggle with mental health or their sexual identity—"

"I'm not struggling with my 'sexual identity,' Mom—"

"You know that's not what I mean," she says sternly, pinning me with a look. Uh-oh, somehow we've wandered into Serious Talk territory. "I just mean that, while you are a very special young man for many reasons, you are not the only—as you put it—'depressed gay kid' in the world. But if you never give anyone a chance, you'll never know."

I turn off the sink and start to put the dry dishes away.

"Look, I know that, but that doesn't help me. I don't want to hang out with someone like me. And that's sort of the point, isn't it? *I* don't even like me, why the hell would anyone else?"

"Adam."

Fuck. Why did I say that? Now she's got her Very Concerned voice on. She puts her hands on my shoulders and turns me around to face her.

"*I* like you."

"You're my mother, you have to like me—"

"I like you and your father likes you"—she talks over me—"and anyone who gets to know you will like you. Sometimes that's enough. We don't always have to love ourselves in order to receive love from others. Sometimes that's how we learn to love ourselves."

"Okay, Mom, I get it." I shrug her hands off my shoulders and turn back to the sink, where I pick up a sponge before remembering that I've done all the dishes already. I toss the sponge back and start wiping my hands on the dish towel, pointedly not looking at her. I know this conversation is probably far from over but I really, really don't want to be having it.

"Adam, I just don't want you to—" she starts, and, yep, this is *exactly* the last thing in the world I want to be discussing.

"I know, Mom. But I'm fine." I turn around to face her as I say this, knowing I need to sell it. I can see the growing panic in her face. If I'm not careful, she'll go DEFCON 1 on me—call in the therapists, start checking my bathroom for sharp objects, keep tabs on where I am at all times . . . that's a hard pass from me.

"Really, I'm good," I reiterate, looking her unblinkingly in the eye. She looks skeptical and I reach for the emergency lever on Mom-Calming. "I actually sort of made a friend today."

Um, what?

I remember reading something once about enhanced interrogation techniques (a nice term for "torture") and how if anyone is interrogated for long enough, they'll eventually say something, even if it isn't true. That's what getting a stare-down from Rebecca Hayes is like. I always crack. Even if it means creating more problems for myself, I'll tell her what she wants to hear. I would bug my mom a lot more about her work—especially after that conversation with my dad—if I thought I'd ever get anywhere.

"Really?" Her whole face lights up and my stomach plummets in guilt. Why, oh why, did I say that?

"Um, yeah, sort of," I mutter, throwing the dish towel on the counter and moving around the kitchen trying to find something else—*anything* else—to do.

"Well? Tell me about them!" she demands after a moment. Why haven't I made up some imaginary homework by this point and escaped upstairs? How is *this* how I'm starting my weekend?

"I don't know, it's not a big deal, Mom. I was just in an argument with this guy in my English class and this other guy intervened and it was kind of nice. So I guess you're right—people can be nice and I should give them a chance. Cool, good talk, Mom, I'm gonna go upstairs now," I say all in a rush, moving toward the doorway with my head down.

"Wait just a minute, young man. What kind of argument?" she asks, crossing her arms and getting back into stare-down mode.

"It was nothing." I plaster a fake smile over my face. "Just about our class presentations."

"Adam, darling, are you being bullied at school?"

"Jeez, Mom," I groan, "are you trying to hit on every single after-school special tonight?"

"I'm just—"

"Worried about me, yeah, I get it," I snap, and my mom's face crumples up just a little. That's not fair. You're not supposed to feel bad for your interrogator.

"I'm just tired, okay? It's been a long week," I say by way of explanation and pseudo-apology.

"Okay," she murmurs, her face softening as she pushes my curls off my face again. "Go and relax. But I want to hear more about this new friend later!"

She calls the last bit out to me because the moment I heard "go," I bolted. I know not to turn down a clear opportunity for escape.

I rush up the stairs and into my room, flopping down on my bed and burying my face in my pillow. Why did I tell her about Bryce and Caleb? Now she's going to mention it to Dad and I'm going to get the two-pronged questioning tomorrow.

Caleb isn't my friend just because he got in between me and Bryce. His intervention wasn't even all that nice. Why did I tell her that it was? Is my wishful thinking just running that wild? Am I really so pathetic as to pretend that I made a connection with someone who I've had exactly two terribly awkward encounters with?

I grab my battered headphones off my nightstand, turn on Jónsi, and burrow into my blankets. Maybe if I stay in bed long enough, I'll just cease to exist.

15

CALEB

The fact that therapy has been the most exciting part of my weekend so far makes me feel *really* pathetic. Most of the time I just tell Dr. Bright about my week, do some "mindfulness" exercises, and then she gives me some stuff to think about for next time. That's it. Pretty standard stuff for a pretty nonstandard Problem. But when she asks me how I'm doing today, I find myself cracking and finally telling her about Adam.

"He just sort of . . . drowns everything else out." I shrug, knowing that that barely encapsulates the way his feelings get into every corner of my brain.

"Isn't that preferable to feeling what everyone in the class feels?" Dr. Bright asks. "You don't sound very happy about it."

"No, of course I'm not happy about it, that's literally the point," I snap. "I can't be happy, because he's so miserable."

"Do you know why he's sad?" she asks calmly, and instead of being grateful for her steady emotions today, I'm just annoyed.

"No, how the fuck would I know that, I'm not a mind reader! Look, I just—I just know that he's sad."

I wince at the tiny drop of pity I feel from her. I don't know if

it's for me or for Adam, but it makes me grind my teeth. I'm jabbing at her for no reason and I hate myself for it.

"Does Adam's sadness have a special color to it?" she asks. "Is
he sad over his grades? His family?"

"Like I said, I'm not a mind reader. But I mean, I don't know,
it's pretty general. He's lonely, I guess," I admit. I think about all
the times I've noticed Adam over the past few months and how few
of those times involved him talking to another person. "Yeah, he
feels alone. He doesn't have a lot of friends, so I guess that makes
sense. Actually I don't think he has, like, any friends . . . so."

"Perhaps that's why you only feel him when he's around,"
Dr. Bright suggests. "His loneliness isolates you from feeling anything else."

"Yeah, maybe. I mean—look, people are sad and lonely all the
time, it's high school. He's just—he's just different for some reason,"
I finish, really hoping we can move on from this topic. Thinking
about it is like poking at a bruise.

"Earlier you said you made something worse this week," she reminds me. "Did that have to do with Adam?"

"Yeah, it did," I admit softly. The bruise feels like it's being
punched now.

"What happened?" she asks.

I tell her about the class presentations and Bryce being a dick
and then *me* being a dick, and through it all she just nods and nods
and I just feel worse and worse.

"Sometimes, people don't want others to see their sadness,"
Dr. Bright says finally. "Adam probably thought he was hiding it
well and the fact that you noticed frightened him. It brought into
focus just how unhappy he is."

She's right and sitting there all calm and static and it's making
my blood boil. Instead of keeping me calm, her concern feels cloying and too warm and I worry I'm going to suffocate under it if I
don't fight my way out.

"I knew how he was feeling and instead of fixing it, I made him
more unhappy. You're always talking about this like it's some sort

of stupid gift, that I can help people. But I always just fuck things up," I bite, wanting to blame something, anything, for the way I feel.

"That's because you haven't learned how to control it yet," she tells me evenly. "You're so young and you're dealing with so many of your own emotions that handling others' is going to be over-whelming. Being a teenager is hard, you know that." The sickly-sweet pity is mixing with the fire in my gut as she continues, "I've said before that I think this ability gets easier as you grow older—"

"Yeah, I know, I know," I interrupt. "Being a teenager is rough, there are hormones and all that stuff, blah, blah, blah. That doesn't change the fact that I suck. It's not an excuse. Someone was sad and then I opened my mouth and now they're sadder. And I don't know what he's going to do or how he's gonna react, or if he spent the whole weekend thinking about it—and would you stop that!"

All of a sudden, I'm yelling and I can't stop.

"I can feel your fucking pity bleeding out of you and I don't need it! I'm not some pathetic emotional loser, okay? I'm not like him!"

I'm tightly coiled on the couch, feeling like I'm going to ex-plode and start breaking things, but Dr. Bright remains cool and expressionless. I let myself sink into her feelings and find the pity gone, light warm concern in its place.

"Caleb, it's all right," she soothes. "I don't pity you. I'm empa-thetic to what you are feeling. Surely you of all people can under-stand that, right?"

"Yeah." I exhale, my muscles loosening, fists unclenching. "Yeah. Right. Sure."

I take a couple more deep breaths, letting my feelings level out before the heat of embarrassment takes over.

"Look, I'm sorry," I mumble. "I just—your feelings are normally pretty quiet, so it just surprised me, that's all."

"I see." Her brow crinkles and there's a flash of something I don't recognize before she continues. "I think you are being too hard on yourself. You are not responsible for what other people feel. But, as I was saying earlier, you can choose how to respond to it.

You need to get these outbursts under control. Think before you speak. And that will only be possible if you learn to filter the incoming emotions. I think it's possible you're not in control of your own feelings because they are being overpowered by others—that's why you need to learn to balance them."

"Yeah, I know," I sigh. "I just—I don't want anyone to get hurt. That's all."

Something warm flares, but it's not pity. There's sun on my face for a moment before the sharp edge of Dr. Bright's now familiar curiosity pokes into me.

"I have an idea," she says brightly. "I think you've been given a unique opportunity."

"Awesome, more unique opportunities," I mumble.

"If you couldn't do what you can do, do you think you would have noticed that Adam felt worse after you intervened?"

"No, I guess not," I answer. "But, I wouldn't have gotten involved in the first place if I couldn't do what I do."

"I just mean that you know now that he's feeling worse. And maybe you can help make that better," she explains, a spark in her eye. "I think you should talk to him on Monday. Try and become friends."

"Why the hell would I do that?" I ask, confused. I've literally just told her about how guilty I feel over making Adam feel worse and now she wants me to spend *more* time with the guy?

"You said yourself that he's lonely," she explains. "He could probably use someone who understands what's going on with him. And it might help whatever misplaced feeling of guilt you have if you befriend him."

"Using my ability to make someone feel a certain way is exactly what I'm trying to avoid," I argue. "Isn't that an abuse of power or something?"

But Dr. Bright won't be talked out of the idea. She seems to think that the fact I'm feeling Adam's emotions so strongly is important. That maybe he's someone I could use in school to focus on and learn how to better balance stuff.

We do some meditation exercises to practice—I try to feel her feelings and then make them fit alongside mine or tune them out. I'm definitely not good at the second part, but I do okay on identifying her feelings. And I'm pretty pleased with how impressed she feels, until her face turns serious and concern creeps in.

"Caleb," she says gently, "you're making excellent progress—you're picking up on nuances and layers that you haven't been able to reach until now—but, given what happened with Adam this week, you need to be careful about blurting things out."

"Why?"

"It's important that you keep your ability to yourself," she says, before launching into a new mindfulness exercise that she wanted me to try for that week. I want to keep asking about it but something in my gut tells me she won't say more.

So here I am, Monday morning, standing in the doorway to English class, bracing for battle. My hands tighten on the backpack strap slung over my shoulder as I take a beat. I've got a few minutes before class starts. I can do this.

I give myself a moment to adjust to the feelings swirling around the classroom. There are only a few people here, with more filing past me as I stand next to the door, so I'm able to cut through all the noise pretty quickly to find what I'm looking for.

Adam is sitting at his desk, earbuds in, writing in his notebook. The vast, empty vortex isn't there today, thank god—in its place is a calm, blue pool. It's not tranquil and nice, like the kind of placid peace I find when I meditate in therapy. It's an ocean that's deep and mysterious in that way that's scary but also sort of comforting. I'm letting it wash over me and I feel settled in my body one second and like I'm too big for my skin in the next.

After a moment adjusting to the back-and-forth tide of his feelings, I decide it's safe to approach.

He either senses my movement or feels me staring (which I guess I have been doing for, like, a minute) because Adam looks up and my feet falter for a second. But the Michaels don't back down, so I keep walking toward him and the deep blue clears away as something warm and pulsing rises up. It gets caught somewhere in my rib cage and the nerves hit me all at once. I'm scared to talk to him now but I can't look away and my feet keep carrying me toward him. I'm about to blurt something out when suddenly Caitlin appears in my field of vision.

"Hey, Caleb." She smiles, flipping her hair casually over her shoulder.

"Oh, uh, hi, Caitlin," I stammer, totally wrong-footed. God, she just popped out of nowhere, how did she do that? The warm pulse in my rib cage stutters out like a dying star and splatters across my insides, leaving a dripping ooze in its place.

"Do you have a second?" she asks in that way that she does, where she already knows the answer or at least expects you to give her the answer she wants.

"Uh, sure," I say, feeling sluggish.

"So there's that Sadie Hawkins dance coming up," she says, a slight shake entering her voice. My eyes finally zero in on her face, and as she comes into focus, I'm pulled into her feelings. I feel hot all at once, like I've gotten a sunburn over my whole body, and the bees of stress take up residence again in my stomach. Except, wait, no, it's not bees. It's something else. Something writhing and light and not totally unpleasant.

I'm adjusting to the feeling when I notice that she hasn't said anything for a few seconds and is looking at me expectantly. Am I supposed to say something?

"Yeah?" I say vaguely, just to be safe.

"I was wondering if you wanted to go with me," she says, a pretty blush appearing on her cheeks. She *is* pretty, I think, but I'm too distracted by the squirming and the heat and the dripping ooze on my ribs to appreciate it. So distracted that I've completely lost track of what she's talking about.

"What?" I ask.

"I was wondering if you wanted to go to the Sadie Hawkins dance with me," Caitlin repeats slowly, like I'm being a bit stupid.

Which I guess I am. I can tell from the look on her face that she's sort of already regretting asking me. And then I realize I haven't given her my answer yet.

"Oh, uh, yeah, sure, Caitlin," I say, even though going to a school dance is absolutely the last thing I ever want to do.

"Great," she says with a smile. I smile back automatically, infected by her happiness. It swoops in and clears out the ooze, but leaves the squirming heat behind. "Do you want to—"

"All right, everyone, take a seat," Mr. Collins calls from the front of the room, interrupting whatever terrifying question Caitlin was about to ask.

"We'll talk later," Caitlin whispers, like we share a secret, and I smile back, filled with a momentary warmth. Caitlin's easy familiarity with me is like putting on an old, comfy sweatshirt that I'd forgotten I have.

As I sit down, I think about how Caitlin and I used to be pretty good friends. Maybe even best friends. She lived down the block from us and we'd play kickball in the street and hide-and-go-seek on rainy days. Her mom would make us grilled cheeses and Caitlin would lend me her favorite Boxcar Children books. It was easy and nice.

And then that thing happened where boys and girls get awkward and weird around each other and we stopped hanging out for a few years. I joined football and she went into every advanced class and we just didn't see each other. In sophomore year, our groups started converging and there was a time when I thought maybe we could be best friends again. But then my Problem started up and there was something about Caitlin's feelings that scared me. Even now that I'm more comfortable with the whole empath thing, there's a sureness and subtlety to her emotions that I just do *not* get.

You'd think that knowing what people feel all the time would make you closer to them. But it doesn't work like that. Instead, sometimes I feel this canyon between me and everyone else and I worry that, no matter what I do, I'll never be able to reach across it.

As Mr. Collins drones on about *The Aeneid*, the tether of Caitlin's feelings slowly dissolves and I have a moment to myself. I'm already regretting saying yes to the Sadie Hawkins thing. I've avoided all optional school events like the plague since the beginning of the year and I'm pretty sure that a dance will be a minefield of emotion. People being excited, disappointed, nervous, crushing on one another, *drunk*. There's always that one group that shows up drunk, and I'm dreading it. I went to a football party a few weeks ago and a couple of the guys were drinking. It makes my Problem so much worse.

My personal time to wallow about this is apparently over, because I'm reassaulted by the dripping ooze between my ribs. It's slimy and hot-cold and is simultaneously giving me nausea and heartburn. It reminds me of the sludge, but it's not just disappointment—there's an edge to it that I'm not used to. Though I've never felt this from him before—whatever "this" is—I know it belongs to Adam. Like always, it slots right into place alongside my own feelings, but this time, it weighs me down. I'm suddenly glad I didn't try to talk to him.

Adam is definitely one of the quieter kids in our year. He keeps to himself, doesn't participate in a lot of school stuff. Yeah, he can be a bit of a smartass sometimes, but he's not loud. Unless he's arguing with someone in class or giving a presentation, he doesn't make himself known.

So why do his feelings keep making themselves known to me? There's no canyon between us—I don't have to reach. His feelings swell up like a wave, crashing onto my shore, pushing me deeper into the sand.

Before I know it, the bell is ringing and another class has gone by without me writing a single thing down. Crap. Hopefully I can borrow Caitlin's notes. That might be a good perk of going out with her. Is that what we're doing now? Does saying yes to a dance mean we're dating? I have no idea how this works and there's no way I'm talking to the team about it, so I guess I'll just have to wing it. The thought makes me want to run away and hide somewhere.

"Mr. Michaels." Mr. Collins's voice calls me over as I walk toward the door.

"Yeah?"

"Aren't you forgetting something?" he asks, his eyebrows raised expectantly.

"Um." I rack my brain for what the hell he could be talking about. "Have a good day?" I try.

"Your *Macbeth* essay," he offers, understanding that I'm not trying to be fresh, I genuinely don't know what he's talking about. "I gave you the weekend, but you need to turn it in."

"Oh, right." I exhale, reaching into my bag. "I totally blanked. Here you go."

I hand him the essay, self-conscious that it's a few pages thinner than it should be, despite the fact that he gave me an extension. He takes it from me, but the eyebrows don't lower. Uh-oh, orange pulse of concern is back.

"Is everything all right, Mr. Michaels?" he asks. Jeez, he sounds so sincere. This guy cares way too much. It's nice but it's also a *lot*.

"Yeah, I'm fine." I shrug.

"It's just that you seemed a little distracted in class today." He frowns, leaning back against his desk and folding his arms across his chest. The pulse grows stronger and reaches out to me like a hug. But like a hug from your distant, maybe not-even-really-related elderly aunt who hugs you too long and too tight and asks you too many, too personal questions.

"Did I?" I ask unconvincingly.

"Well, can you tell me the main themes we'll be looking for in *The Aeneid*?" he asks, raising his eyebrows even further as he gives me a skeptical look. Those things are going to disappear fully into his hair any second now.

"Um . . ." I stall, rubbing the back of my neck and looking toward the door, hoping I'll spot a fire in the hallway or something. ". . . the hero's journey?"

"Nice guess," he allows, the concern momentarily distracted by amusement, "but that's not what we were talking about and we both know it. What's going on, Caleb?"

Oh boy, there's the first name again. That's not a good sign.

"Nothing," I tell him, shaking my head a little too vigorously.

The eyebrows crease toward each other. "I'm just—I'm a little distracted."

"I saw Caitlin talking to you before class. Did she do something to upset you?"

"What? No. No, Caitlin's great," I rush to say. No need to have other people dragged into this weird mess.

Mr. Collins is ready to pounce and ask another question and I feel the orange concern squeeze me just a little bit tighter.

"She was asking me to the Sadie Hawkins dance," I blurt out, panicking slightly. "So I guess I was just thinking about that."

The worry loosens its hold on me and I feel like I can breathe again. Mr. Collins straightens from his lean and his face breaks into a smile.

"Ah, I see." He smirks. "Well, I understand that it can be fun to daydream, Mr. Michaels, but please at least try to pull your mind from Ms. Park and focus on the lesson next time."

I open my mouth to correct him, a bit embarrassed by what he's suggesting, but he's emitting this pat-on-the-back understanding that's overtaken the concern completely, so I decide to cut my losses and roll with it.

"Right. I'll do that, Mr. Collins." I nod.

"I was a teenager once, you know. I get it. Just don't let it happen again." He mock wags his finger and moves around to behind his desk, effectively dismissing me. I bolt.

16

ADAM

"Okay, so the topic is same-sex schools."

"And we have to build arguments both for and against, right?" I ask, as Caitlin effortlessly twists her hair into some sort of updo. I'm sort of mesmerized by the movement. Sometimes I think girls have a completely different understanding of physics. Or maybe it's something that anyone with long hair can do. I'd be tempted to try it for myself if my hair didn't grow straight out, defying all laws of gravity.

"Yep," she confirms, "although no pro arguments are immediately leaping to my mind." She shudders at the horror of it all.

"What, you wouldn't want to go to an all-girls' school?" I ask.

"God, no," she scoffs. "My older sister went to one—a *Catholic* one at that—and the stories she would tell . . ." She lowers her voice and looks around as if there's anyone else in the library (there's not, of course). "Drugs, sex, rock and roll—the whole thing. Except, you know, not rocking and rolling. Terrible hazing and mean pranks and stuff. It sounded like a nightmare."

"Yikes," I say truthfully, "that does sound rough."

"Yeah, she was pretty happy to graduate." Caitlin's eyes go wide as she digs in her bag for a pen. There are two ballpoints sitting on top of my notebook, but I can't bring myself to offer her one. I'm still grinding my teeth over having to watch that awful court-ship ritual between her and Caleb. Before she started talking to him, I could have sworn . . .

Never mind. I refuse to be small and petty and jealous about this. Caitlin is smart and not unkind and nice-looking if you're into that sort of thing and she actually *did* something about her crush on Caleb. I need to suck it up and be a good debate partner, even if it feels like my insides are rotting away every time I look at her perfect ponytail.

Caitlin pulls a pen from her backpack with a victorious "Aha!" and I crack open my notebook in response.

"But, I mean, all high school kind of sucks, right? Whether you're with all girls or all guys, there's always going to be some de-gree of conflict," I say, pushing aside my green monster to think about how we could structure our arguments.

"True, but I do think there's something to be said for the differ-ent social contracts that people follow in either single-sex or mixed settings." I watch as Caitlin transitions seamlessly from gossip mode to A-student mode. "An argument could be made for the fact that men and women behave more civilly in mixed groups in order to appeal to the opposite sex. If the factor of potential partners is taken away, a same-sex group has the capacity to slip into all of their worst inclinations. I mean, look at the whole 'locker-room talk' stuff or 'boys will be boys'—that's a direct result of the hypermasculinity that's perpetuated in some all-male environments."

"Okay, that's a good point." I nod, my brain kicking into high gear as I work through the different pieces of her reasoning. "But couldn't it *also* be argued that same-sex environments provide safe spaces in which people can be themselves because there *isn't* the pressure to appeal to potential mates?"

Caitlin smiles broadly at me.

"I think we have the basics of each side of our argument," she says brightly, and we both start scribbling in our notebooks. I sud-denly feel energized—arguing with Caitlin is like taking a shot of espresso, in the best way.

"Though . . ." Caitlin starts, sounding a little hesitant, "it should also probably be mentioned that neither of those arguments works for every individual." She trails off and I look up from the Pro-Con table I'm drawing in my notebook to see her giving me a significant look.

"How's that?" I ask, a sense of dread sneaking up on me.

"Well," she begins awkwardly, "that logic wouldn't necessarily apply to people who feel same-sex attraction. For instance," she finishes, her eyes darting away from me. I do my best to hold in a massive sigh.

"Right, yeah, that's true," I agree, also avoiding eye contact. "But only like, what, five percent of the US population is gay, so I don't know how much we need to make that a part of our case."

"That's fair." She nods in a way that makes me think she probably would have agreed with whatever I had said. "But I just think it's always good to look at every angle of an argument."

"Yeah, totally," I say, looking back down at my notebook.

For a few moments, our quiet corner of the library is filled only with the sounds of putting pen to paper. But there's a weird tension in the air.

"Tense" actually doesn't seem to cover it. What's the word for when you're sitting at a table with someone you don't know all that well and they maybe just implied that you're gay and you *are* gay and you think they were trying to be inclusive or something but you kind of shut them down because they asked out your crush earlier and you really don't want to be having this conversation and now there's all this weird, unsaid stuff in the air that's making it hard to focus on your debate prep?

Is there a word for that?

Before I can finish going through my mental thesaurus, Caitlin starts talking again.

"So . . . do you have any plans for the Sadie Hawkins dance?" she asks, faux-casual. Why is she asking? Does she want me to ask about *her* plans? Oh god, I do *not* want to hear about whatever sock hop fantasies she has about Caleb.

"Um, no," I answer, not looking up, "dances aren't really my thing." Hopefully she'll leave it at that.

"Gotcha," she says, but I don't think she does. "A little too cool for school, are we?"

"What?" I look up at her in surprise, but when I catch her smiling I realize she's probably mostly kidding.

"To your earlier point," I deflect, trying to steer us back to debate, "isn't Sadie Hawkins pretty . . . heteronormative? I wouldn't think you'd be into the whole mandatory 'girls ask the guys' thing."

"Eh"—she shrugs one shoulder—"it's pretty archaic, I'll give you that. But, I don't know, it can be a nice excuse to actually jump in and ask somebody out. Some guys still aren't super comfortable with a girl making the first move, no matter what *I* feel about heteronormativity."

"No offense, but I don't think you want to go out with any guys like that," I find myself saying.

"Ha, you're probably right." She tosses me that big, confident smile again and my mouth curves up involuntarily in response.

Are Caitlin and I . . . bonding?

"Hey, no offense—" I start.

"That's the second time you've said that in, like, thirty seconds. I'm beginning to think you *do* mean offense—"

"What are you doing?" I blurt.

"What?" I've rarely seen Caitlin Park confused, so the look on her face is just a tiny bit satisfying.

"Why are we talking about boys instead of doing debate prep?"

"Do you have something against talking about boys?"

"You know I don't," I say pointedly, almost giving voice to the thing that she's been talking around.

"Then what's the problem?" She asks it like I'm being ridiculous. There's a very real chance that I am.

"I don't know, we've just never talked like this before. I'm not just all of a sudden gonna be your gay bestie." I wince the moment I say it.

"No one's asking you to be, Adam," she says defensively. "I'm just trying to be nice. You know, get to know each other a little."

"But *why*?" I feel like we're speaking two completely different languages.

"Because this is the first time we've spent any time together in three years and you've been in every single one of my classes and we're constantly competing for the top spot in those classes so it seems like maybe we might have some stuff in common?" she says in one breath, exasperated. She isn't looking at me and her face is red

"Oh."

"What, have you never talked to any of your other debate partners about non-debate stuff?" she asks, sneaking a look at me.

"Um, no." I think back on other debate study sessions and realize there haven't been many. "Mostly I just do all the work and then tell everybody what part of the debate they're taking."

Caitlin slumps.

"Yeah. Me too," she says, moping. "I thought I'd try something different."

"Sorry I was such a weird asshole about it," I say.

"It's okay," she says with a laugh. Dimples appear on her cheeks and my stomach turns over at the mental image of her and Caleb both laughing prettily at a dance.

"And hey, you were right," I concede, shaking the jealousy as best I can. "We do have something in common. We're always the ones doing all the work for group projects."

"Very true." She nods. "I think this'll be different." She smiles at me again like we understand each other. What a novel thought.

"Yeah," I agree halfheartedly. I don't have any illusions that I'm suddenly going to become best friends with Caitlin, though thinking about it does spark a little hopefulness in me. I can't think of the last time I made a real friend. But I have no idea how to do this.

Apparently, Caitlin does, and is not done with the heart-to-heart portion of this program.

"I really wasn't trying to, you know . . . *girl talk* with you or any-thing." Caitlin rolls her eyes at her own choice of words. "I just don't see the point in spending any amount of time with someone and not learning anything about who they are."

I see the earnestness in her eyes and give her a small smile.

"I think that's where you and I differ," I suggest, mentally kick-ing myself at shutting her down at every turn. Adam Hayes—king of self-sabotage.

"Good to know. Then that's the last we shall speak of frivolous things," she says loftily. "See? I did learn something about you. I learned that you don't like people learning about you."

She's smirking, leaning her chair on its back legs as she folds her hands in her lap.

"Wow, you really always have to have the last word in an argu-ment, don't you?" I say, smirking back.

She shrugs smugly.

"Aren't you glad to have me as a debate partner?" she asks in that way that's not really a question, rocking back and forth on the chair legs. Her self-satisfied smile is taking up her whole face and it's infectious, dissolving the cloud that so often hangs over my head. This kind of verbal sparring is my *raison d'être* and I'm about to counter when—

"Hey, Caitlin?"

Caitlin nearly loses her balance, her chair tipping dangerously far back before she catches it, slamming forward, her palms smack-ing the tabletop.

"Caleb!" She jumps up, her voice like a shout in the quiet li-brary. Caleb has appeared out of nowhere, like he has the ability to just materialize silently in the library whenever he wants. I haven't spoken to him since the Incident on Friday and I have absolutely no idea what I would say to him now. I do my best to dissolve into the bookshelves behind me.

"Sorry, didn't mean to sneak up on you," he backpedals awk-wardly. His hand is clenching around his backpack strap and it feels like he's looming over the table.

"Oh," he says, his eyes landing on me. "Hey."

I just nod, my voice stuck somewhere between my heart and my throat.

"What's up?" Caitlin chirps, and I try not to notice the hearts in her eyes as she looks at Caleb. I especially try not to think about how my eyes probably look the exact same way. This whole thing is mortifying.

"I was just wondering if I could borrow your notes from English yesterday? About *The Aeneid*?" he asks sheepishly, glancing down at his feet. I take the opportunity to stare at him a bit, and his whole body is rigid. Except there's also a squirrellyness to him, like he's ready to bolt at any second. This could not be more different from our last library encounter. He must not be thrilled to have found me when looking for a private moment with his date.

"Oh, yeah, sure," Caitlin says, her posture relaxing somewhat. "I don't have them with me but I can e-mail them to you when I get home?"

"That'd be great." Caleb nods eagerly.

"I didn't take that many. It was pretty basic—just an overview of the themes we should be looking for as we read, that kind of stuff."

"Cool, yeah, I just totally spaced out, I don't know what happened." He rubs the back of his neck, looking down again.

"You'll catch up in no time, I'm sure," Caitlin offers, swaying slightly.

"All right, well, I'll let you get back to it," Caleb says, gesturing at the table, where I'm still sitting in complete silence like some weird forgotten puppet. "Sorry to interrupt."

"It's fine," Caitlin assures him. "We just got started."

"Yeah, but I know you've been stressed about the competition coming up—" Caleb cuts himself off midsentence and there's a flash of panic on his face.

"Uh, yeah, I guess I have been." Caitlin's face scrunches up and that's now twice in one day I've seen her confused. What in the world is even happening? "God, I must be talking about it all the time."

But she hasn't been. She always seems insanely confident in debate club. I've never overheard her and Jessica talk about it either, and I feel like I get the full rundown every day sitting in front of them in English. I had no idea she was nervous about our competition. I wonder if that's why she was going on and on about the dance just now—was she trying to distract herself?

"Yeah, well, anyway," Caleb says, edging away from the table, "I'm sure you guys will do great."

"Yeah." Caitlin nods, some confidence reentering her voice. "Yeah, I mean, we've got the dream team right here." She throws a grin at me and I give a single nod in concurrence, my ability to speak apparently still out of reach.

"Right, yeah, for sure." Caleb stumbles briefly, having backed into another table. "Well, good luck with all the . . . debating. I'll see you guys later."

He brings his hand up in a strange little wave before turning around and rushing out of the library. Caitlin looks after him for a moment before slowly retaking her seat.

"Yeah, I see what you mean," I say as brightly as I can. "If you waited for a guy like that to ask *you* out, you might have been waiting forever."

The comment leaves a funny taste in my mouth—joking about Caleb this way feels weird and wrong—but Caitlin's shoulders relax slightly and it's almost worth it.

"Yeah, we'll see," she says, rolling her eyes. "I don't know, part of me thinks he only said yes because he was too flustered to say anything else."

She shrugs it off.

"Well, never mind about all that," she says, full bravado back. "We have a moratorium on talking about personal things and we're sticking to it."

We smile at each other as we both refocus on the study materials in front of us.

"Exactly," I say, trying to match her renewed energy and falling completely short.

But as Caitlin talks on about the history of same-sex institutions,

I can't get Caleb's panicked face out of my head. Has he been . . . spying on Caitlin or something? That seems like a stretch, but she was definitely caught off guard by his stress comment.

Clearly I'm not the only one who Caleb can see through.

17

CALEB

All right, take two. I can do this.

Yesterday caught me a little off guard. I knew Adam was in the library—could feel his feelings like a homing beacon—but I didn't realize that he and Caitlin were debate partners now. Based on his feelings, he was equally thrown by the whole thing. He felt surprised and panicked and . . . embarrassed. And then I let slip that I knew Caitlin was stressed, like an *idiot*, after promising Dr. Bright that I would lie low, and I just really don't want to be thinking about that conversation at all anymore.

But after seeing how Caitlin and Adam seemed to be getting along, I'm even more determined to talk to him. Maybe he won't be totally against me trying to apologize. But I think the key is to approach Adam on his own, which is what I'm doing now. Well, he's not entirely on his own—there's a bunch of other kids in the hallway, but at least Caitlin and Bryce aren't going to come popping out of nowhere at any second. Hopefully.

Adam is crouched at his locker, trying to get a book that's jammed at the bottom, and I'm hit with the waves of frustration coming off him. It's all tangled and irritated, like when you pull your earbuds out of your bag to find a mess of wires that hardly resembles headphones.

I take a deep breath and walk toward him.

"Hey, Adam."

His head snaps up at me, and *oof*, instant flood of panic. It feels like I've missed a step going down the stairs; my stomach drops and my heart starts pounding; rivers form in the lines on my palms. Adam's eyes are wide and that light, fluttery feeling swoops into my gut once more. At least this time it feels less invasive—probably because there's so much other stuff to distract from it.

Adam is just staring at me with those big eyes, frozen in place. I always thought the expression "deer in the headlights" was a bit of an exaggeration—I mean, who actually looks like that? But taking in Adam now, it feels like running into some strange, unexpected creature in the woods that doesn't know if you're going to hunt it or help it. I feel guilty for a second before I remember the "uniformed sociopath" comment and a righteous indignation settles in. Just because I'm on the football team doesn't mean I'm like Bryce and Justin. Adam assuming that I am is totally unfair. I've never done anything to make him suspicious of me—I *helped* him the other day.

Okay, well, "help" might be a stretch. He actually seemed to have Bryce handled pretty decently, and I think I probably just drew more unnecessary attention to the whole confrontation.

I suddenly realize I've said his name and nothing else and I am essentially towering over the guy in what's probably a pretty intimidating way. He's still got his hands on the book stuck in his locker and I decide to set aside my bruised ego for a moment and help out. I crouch down next to him and he jolts back a bit. The fluttering in my gut intensifies.

Adam yanks his hands away as I move mine toward the book. I pull at it—a biology textbook that's seen better days—until it finally comes free. As I hand it over to Adam, we both stand suddenly, staring blankly at one another.

"Uh, thanks," Adam says in a low voice, looking down at the

book that we're both holding from either side. I let go of the book like it's scalding hot and shove my hands into my pockets.

"Yeah, no problem," I say, trying to remember why I came over here in the first place. He won't meet my eyes, so I'm left looking at his eyelashes. The way they flutter as he blinks draws attention to the unsteadiness in my stomach.

"I liked your presentation on *Macbeth*," I say a little too loudly, trying to overcome the not-unpleasant twisting in my gut. "It was really smart. I'm not sure I understood all of it but, yeah, good job and everything."

Now I'm the one looking away, too afraid to watch him while I fumble through this, but I sneak a glance at him and see an odd expression on his face. He's staring at me like *I'm* the strange creature he's stumbled upon in the wilderness.

"Uh, thanks," he says again, and there's the tiniest wince on his face, like he knows he's repeating himself.

"Do you want to grab lunch later?" I blurt, causing a sharp pinprick of anxiety-fear from Adam.

"What?" he asks flatly.

"Uh, we have the same lunch period, right?"

"Yeah . . ." he says, a not-quite question.

"Well, do you want to eat together?" I ask again, feeling more stupid with each second that passes. I want to sink into the floor.

"Why?" He narrows his eyes at me and something gets jerked back from my torso—like there's a fishing line between us and he's just reeled it in. "Are you looking for an English tutor or something?"

"No," I respond, a little insulted. I'm not doing *that* badly. This is not going very well. "I was just thinking it might be cool to eat together. It's Pizza Wednesday," I finish weakly, like that will explain this extremely weird, out-of-the-blue conversation.

"Oh," he says, and there's so much in that one little syllable, even if I can't read every piece of it. The tenuous connection between us grows a little stronger, like maybe he's thinking about casting his line back into the water, and a small bubble of hope starts to grow in my chest. Does it belong to him? Or am I really that desperate to hang out with someone who doesn't make me hate my own empathy?

"So . . . ?" I prompt, after a few seconds have passed with him just looking at me like he's trying to solve a particularly difficult math problem.

"Yeah. Okay. Sure," he says, sounding a little more confident with each word.

"Cool. Cool." I nod, faux-casual. "Want to grab food and meet me outside? The bench behind the gym?" That's my favorite spot to eat lunch because it's pretty isolated and I can eat in peace.

"Sure." He draws out the word, narrowing his eyes at me again, and I feel a storm starting to swirl in my stomach, like the pressure you feel right before it downpours. Again, I find myself a little insulted by whatever's running through his head. Does he think I don't want to be seen with him or something?

"No, no, I'm not—" I start, automatically responding to his feelings. He narrows his eyes at me and I course correct fast. "I just find the cafeteria really overwhelming. Where you choose to sit is always such a thing and it's so stuffy and crowded so, yeah, I just like to eat outside."

The clouds of his feelings clear a bit and something dawns on his face.

"Oh," he says, a revelation, "that's why you're never in the caf." He's saying it mostly to himself, nodding, and I take a page from Mr. Collins's book, quirking an eyebrow at him.

"What?" I ask. Has he noticed my lunch habits? That's . . . I don't know what that is.

Adam's face instantly gets red and I feel the heat of his embarrassment inside and out. Seems like he *has* been noticing my lunch habits. Huh.

"So, the bench behind the gym?" he deflects. "I'll see you there." He puts the biology textbook in his bag and slams his locker.

"Okay, yeah, see you there," I say, feeling off-balance by the whole exchange, but not hating it.

He rushes away and as I'm watching him walk down the hall,

he turns his head slightly over his shoulder, like he's checking to see that I'm really here. He sees that I'm staring and the smallest smile crosses his mostly confused face. Something in my stomach flutters awake and I don't know if it's his feeling or mine but, for once, I don't really care.

18

ADAM

Did I enter some kind of alternate universe when I walked into school this semester? There's no way that Caleb Michaels—*Caleb Michaels*—just asked me to eat lunch with him. That's something that happens to Daydream Adam. Daydream Adam is the person I think about when I'm walking home or Mr. Collins is lecturing about something I've already read five times. Daydream Adam never gets bothered by Bryce, he doesn't stress about schoolwork, he doesn't get depressed, he doesn't hurt himself. Daydream Adam is cool and confident and beat Caitlin to the punch in asking Caleb out. Daydream Adam has his life together.

Real Adam is hyperventilating in a bathroom stall for the second time in as many weeks. I'm going to be late for class—*again*—but I can't really be fussed to care. In less than an hour I will be having lunch with Caleb. Caleb who helped me get my textbook out of my locker's clutches like some sort of teen-movie heartthrob. Caleb who was awkward and infuriatingly adorable as he talked about Pizza Wednesday.

Maybe he won't show up. Maybe this is all some cruel joke. That seems like the most likely explanation, despite the fact that Caleb doesn't seem cruel.

But maybe . . .

Maybe he meant it. Maybe Caleb really does want to get to know me.

I honestly don't know which outcome scares me more.

19

CALEB

"Uh, is right here okay?" I ask, gesturing to the picnic bench table with my cafeteria tray. I don't know why I'm asking, I told him to meet me out here, but then we ran into each other on our way outside and I'm just trying to fill the silence.

God, why did I do this? I don't have lunch with people. I eat with the team on Fridays but the rest of the time I come out here and listen to music. It's the break in my day that makes the rest of school even slightly tolerable, and here I am awkwardly forcing social interaction instead. The day is unseasonably warm and I can't tell if it's that or standing next to Adam that's making me sweat under my jacket.

This was a bad idea. I'm never listening to Dr. Bright again.

"Yeah, this is good," he mutters, setting his tray down and swinging his skinny legs over the bench. The nerves coming off him are like painful sound waves off of a loud speaker—it makes my teeth chatter and my rib cage shake and I really am never listening to Dr. Bright ever again.

"This is a nice spot," he says when we've settled across from each other. He's taking in his surroundings (avoiding looking at me, I think) and squinting into the sun in a way that makes me think he doesn't spend a lot of time outside. Now that I'm looking at him in the daylight instead of the heinous fluorescent lights inside the school, I notice how pale he seems. It's not the actual hue—his skin is darker than mine—but there's something that tells me he is seriously lacking vitamin D.

"Yeah," I respond automatically, staring at the dark circles under his eyes. "Yeah, I like it out here. It's quiet."

The waves of anxiety pull back a bit and a tingling itchiness reaches under my skin. Curiosity. It doesn't make me twitch in the way it usually does, but I squirm a bit, wondering what it is that he's curious about.

I don't have to wonder, because his eyes open from their squint and look directly at me (making the squirmy feeling worse) as he says, "I'm surprised you don't eat with the football team. They definitely seem to have a good time during lunch."

The last part comes out a little bitter and I don't even need to feel the poker of anger from him to know that he's resentful.

"They're not all bad, you know," I say, trying not to break eye contact even though there's something about looking directly at him that feels like standing at the edge of a cliff. "Nobody even really likes Bryce all that much. And Justin is an idiot who'll follow anybody around," I add for good measure, and because it's true.

"If they're so great, then why aren't you eating with them?" he asks, a challenge in his voice. He's baiting me and I don't get why so I try to push through the curiosity and nerves and find what he's feeling underneath all of that.

I hit a wall. Like, a real, physical wall. That's what it feels like, at least. Behind the nerves is hard, thin steel. Adam's trying not to feel something but it's not working all that well.

"I like being alone," I blurt out when I realize I haven't picked up the gauntlet he threw. It's the wrong thing to say not only because it's fucking dumb but also because something shutters even further in him, the steel growing thicker.

"Oh," he says, a complete sentence. "I can leave if you want . . ."

As he trails off, I realize he's disappointed and then I know what the wall's about—he doesn't trust me. He probably thinks I've asked him to lunch just to be mean or pull a prank or have something to use against him. But then why did he say yes in the first place?

"No, that's not what I meant," I rush to explain, remembering how he felt when he went all "frightened woodland animal" before and not wanting to give him a reason to run away. "I just meant . . ."

Now it's my turn to trail off. I don't know what I mean to say—I can't tell him that I don't eat with the team because being in crowds is hard because of my Problem. That carrying on a conversation with more than one or two people is nearly impossible, especially when everyone is feeling something completely different.

"I get it"—he nods, unscrewing the cap on his iced tea—"You can be alone with one person."

He says it so matter-of-factly but it sends me reeling. That's exactly it. With one person, my Problem can be nice—sometimes it's easier to connect, to get ahead of the conversation, to understand someone. In a group, it becomes noise.

"Yeah," I say, unable to keep the surprise out of my voice. "Yeah, um, how did you know that?"

"You get this look on your face sometimes when you're in a big group," he says, staring into his yogurt as he idly swirls it around with a spoon. "Like you're powering down or something. People will be goofing off around you and you're just off in your own little world."

"What?" I ask blankly, unsure how to take . . . well, *any* of that, really. That's the second time today he's made it sound like he watches me and, based on the blush that's creeping up his neck, he definitely has been.

"Um, no, I didn't mean—" he starts, wide eyes snapping up from his Yoplait to look at me. The moment our eyes connect, I'm slammed with the hot, face-melting embarrassment that's running wild through his body.

"I just—not that I—" he continues, and I don't know if I should jump in or what. "I'm just observant." He stops abruptly, like that's enough of an explanation.

"Okay," I say, giving him a pass. He knows I'm not buying it—I can still feel the terror and caught-out feeling from him—but I can't exactly throw stones about being observant. Maybe if I let him get away with this, he won't notice my more observant moments.

"It's just—well, I keep an eye on your friends sometimes," he says eventually, and I can't help my eyebrows raising at that. "No, not like, in a weird way. I just keep a lookout, you know? If I can see them coming, I can usually avoid them. And so I've . . . noticed stuff. You're not like them. Or, at least—I mean, I don't know you, so—I just mean that you don't ever seem as into that crowd as everyone else."

He's babbling and fiddling with his watch—a massive, leather-banded thing wrapped around his bony wrist—as he talks. I can feel the impulse in him to get up and bolt, so I decide it's probably time I let him off the hook.

"They're not my friends," I say. Why did I say that? Why do I keep opening my mouth to say something to this guy only to have something completely different come out?

"Bryce and Justin, I mean." I keep going, because why the fuck not, I guess. "Yeah, I hang out with them and everything but you're right, I guess. It's not really my scene."

Mouth, meet brain. Brain, meet mouth. You guys should get to know each other a little better.

Adam smiles a tiny bit as he picks his yogurt back up and I feel something uncoil inside of him. He likes being right. Though I could have guessed that from everything about him, it still gives me a warm feeling in my gut. And that's when the random thought pops into my head of I *want to make him smile again.*

I'd been thinking of this lunch as sort of a charity case—therapy homework that would relieve some of my guilt about fucking things up last week. But as I'm sitting here, I realize that I want to impress Adam. That's why I'm running my mouth about Bryce and why seeing his lips curl around a spoon feels like a victory. I'm not exactly sure where that impulse is coming from, but I want to chase it until Adam starts smiling more than he frowns.

"Do they bother you a lot?" I ask, because I guess we're really getting to know each other now.

"Define 'a lot,'" he snorts. Adam's smirking now, in a way that I think could be described as "wry," and it gives me that edge-of-cliff feeling again.

"You don't seem that bothered by it."

"I'm not, I guess." He shrugs, taking a swig from his iced tea. "At least, not most of the time. They're idiots—no offense—"

"None taken. Like I said, I'm not exactly best buds with those two."

"Right." He narrows his eyes at me, like he still doesn't quite buy that. "So anyway, most of the time I'm able to shrug it off. It's not like some huge deal or anything."

Bzzzzzt.

When I bother to pay attention, my Problem works like a flawless lie detector. There's a little spike of anti-calm that pops up in people, and nine times out of ten it's because they're full of shit.

Adam is so full of shit.

"You're full of shit," I say.

Mouth, brain—what did we *just* talk about?

"What?" He jolts, every emotion in his body spiking again, and I want to slam my head into the table. The Great Amazing Feelings Boy totally face-plants. Again.

20

ADAM

"What?"

Did the golden boy just tell me I was full of shit? Yet more evidence that I've fallen into some weird Twilight Zone version of my life.

"It *is* a big deal," Caleb says, his face set with determination. Determination to do what, I don't know, and that sends a rush up and down my spine. "It sucks that they bother you. You shouldn't have to deal with that."

"What?" I ask again, mouth hanging open slightly. This lunch has been going surprisingly well so far—just the fact that it's even going in the first place is a real shock to the system—but I keep feeling like I'm four steps behind in the conversation. That is *not* a feeling I'm accustomed to and it frustrates me, but also sort of thrills me, if I'm honest.

"Just—what did you ever do to them, you know? Justin and Bryce, I mean. Have you ever given them a reason to be mean to you?" He says it in a way that's nonjudgmental, like he actually wants to understand the situation from my perspective. That's new.

I finally close my mouth as he says this, put down my yogurt, and start in on my pizza. My stomach is too tied in knots for me to want to eat anything, but I need to focus on something that isn't his stupid perfect face.

"I don't know," I mumble into my pepperoni. "I don't think so. I'm just an easy target, I guess."

This is mostly true. But Caleb is looking at me like he knows that isn't the whole story. He's got that stupidly enticing open expression on his face that says he knows I want to say more; that makes it feel like it might be okay if I said more.

"I called Bryce stupid once in seventh grade," I say, risking a look at Caleb. His eyebrows shoot up in surprise and I feel the need to defend myself.

"We were arguing about something in class," I explain, "and he was getting on my nerves so I called him stupid. I know that's not okay, but, in my defense, I didn't think he'd hold a grudge about it for five years."

"That's not much of a defense," he says, squinting at me skeptically as he shovels pizza into his mouth. Why the hell do I find that endearing?

"Yeah, I know. Thanks," I bite back. "Two wrongs don't make a right. I get it."

"Hey, I can't judge you. I'm, like, the king of putting two wrongs together." A little frown crinkles his face and I have a million more questions now.

"I have a hard time believing that," I scoff, and his face crumples a bit more. Okay, maybe I should dial down the snark a bit—it seems like he might actually want to talk to me, which is . . . well, this whole thing is just incredibly surreal.

"I just mean, you seem like a stand-up guy," I continue. A *stand-up guy?* Oh god, I'm turning into my mother.

"A stand-up guy?" he echoes, the frown turning into a small, self-conscious smile that makes him look vulnerable and cocky all at once and *man*, I am so screwed.

"Oh shut up," I mumble into my pizza. So much for reeling

the snark in. "I just mean that I can't imagine you calling anyone stupid."

"I think *you're* a little stupid," he says, and I snap my eyes back up, ready to fight. But he's still gently smirking and—is he *teasing* me?

"Excuse me?" I ask, mock-scandalized, trying to play along.

"I mean, first you call Bryce stupid to his face—" he starts, counting on his fingers.

"Yeah, five years ago," I say in my own defense.

"And then you try to go toe-to-toe with the guy, which is just completely idiotic." Caleb is fully smiling now and I swear, sunlight is literally bouncing off his teeth and blinding me. "Bryce is huge, there's no way you ever could have taken him, especially with Justin standing right there."

"I'm not gonna run scared from some dumb bully like Bryce," I growl, crushing the lighthearted atmosphere that Caleb had been building. "I'm not a coward."

"I never said you were," Caleb says earnestly, "but you have to know when to walk away. You're not gonna win a fight against Bryce—"

"I wasn't trying to fight him—"

"Are you sure?" he asks, like he already knows the answer. He's staring me down and, once again, it's like he's looking right through me.

"Listen, I get it. But trust me: fighting is not always the best solution." He deflates and it looks like I've ruined something good by opening my damn mouth. Again.

"Wow, look at you, oh wise one," I say dryly, trying to pull the conversation back up to where it was before I got all defensive and weird. "Did you read that on a fortune cookie?"

He looks back up at me, his mouth quirking on one side.

"Even better—personal experience," he says sarcastically. The smile doesn't reach his eyes and I know I haven't quite fully repaired whatever it is I broke.

"Oh, right." I nod, trying to pretend like I haven't been thinking about what would drive Caleb to punch someone for months. "Is that what you meant by being 'the king of two wrongs'?"

"Yeah, a little." He shrugs. "I mean, that fight *definitely* wasn't worth all the crap that it led to."

New questions crowd out the dozens that are already filling my head. Did Caleb really get in trouble for that? I think he had to do some school service or something, but maybe his parents were really strict? There's definitely more to that story and I'm itching to ask. But I think we're maybe back on some sort of normal footing in this conversation and I don't want to throw that off

"But mostly I meant . . ." He trails off, bending his head down to his food and glancing up at me nervously. At least, I think he's nervous—he's got the same frightened-animal look that he had in the library.

"I meant, with you. Last week," he mutters, not looking at me.

"What, with Bryce?"

"Yeah."

"What do you mean? Like you said, he'd probably have beaten my face in. You stopped him," I say, my heart beating fast as my brain relives that moment for the thousandth time since it happened.

"Yeah, but I was kind of a dick about it," he says, finally making eye contact with me again. "And I'm sorry about that."

Huh. I didn't see that coming.

"Don't be," I say. Now it's my turn to avoid eye contact. If he feels bad about last week then that must mean he could tell I was freaked out, and that's *really* not a conversation I want to get into.

"No, I am," he insists, and I feel his eyes boring a hole in the top of my head. "I'm sorry I said all that stuff. It isn't any of my business."

"Why *did* you say it?" I blurt out. Okay, I guess this *is* a conversation I want to have.

"I don't know," he mumbles, and I'm not sure I believe him. I don't think Caleb is a very good liar. But he *is* hiding something.

My curiosity is burning under my skin, each question a little spark running through my veins. I want to ask him how he always seems two steps ahead in every conversation. I want to ask him how he knows I'm sad. I want to ask if he's been feeling bad about this all weekend like I have. I want to ask why he invited me to lunch today. I want to ask if we're going to do it again.

"Do you want the rest of my pizza?" I ask instead.

21

CALEB

God, talking about this stuff is fucking frustrating. I'm catching Dr. Bright up on the week, but feelings are messy and annoying and trying to describe them is even worse.

"Usually, it's that the feelings are all just jumbled up," I try to explain, "like in most of my classes, when there are a bunch of different people feeling a bunch of different things. But then sometimes, it just takes over and kind of finds . . . like a, like a home in my chest. Like with Adam."

"What do you mean it finds a home?" she asks.

"Well . . . I don't know." I shrug. "It's like . . . when I'm around him, whatever he's feeling just sort of settles into me and sits there. Next to my own feelings. Like, his sadness, or whatever, becomes my sadness."

"Does that happen with anyone else when you're one-on-one with them?"

"Yeah, I guess." I think about the only other people I'm comfortable around. "Like, when my mom is worried, I feel worried. And I know it's hers but I also feel like it's mine a bit. It's got a different color to it from my own, but sometimes the edges blur together and it creates a new kind of color. Does that make sense?"

"It does," she says, and I believe her. "So, for example, if your emotions are yellow and Adam's are blue, you get green."

"Right, yeah." I nod, relieved that she understands. "Yeah, and with him, it's like everything becomes green. With other people, it's a lot of yellow and a lot of blue and then a little bit of green between them. God, this is a fucking stupid way of talking about things."

"No it isn't. In all my years as a psychologist, I have yet to discover a perfect way to talk about emotions. Visualizing them can be very helpful." She smiles and I feel infinitely less dumb. "So with Adam it completely blurs together? You can't tell the difference between his emotions and yours?"

"Not exactly. I mean, sometimes he's blue, and he stays blue," I say, thinking about how strong the blue can be sometimes. "But yeah, sometimes, his feelings make green and I know that they're his feelings but they feel real to me. Like more real than other people's."

I feel stupid as I say it but Dr. Bright just nods like it makes perfect sense to her. She asks a few more questions about Adam and before I know it, I've recounted the entire lunch to her. As I'm talking, something solid and satisfied settles into me.

"So his feelings didn't overwhelm you?" she asks, and I feel bad about having to deflate her pride.

"Well, they did, sort of. I mean, I could feel them really strongly—he was nervous and confused and excited—but I was kind of all of those things too and it was just . . . it didn't rub me up the wrong way like Caitlin's emotions did." I think about the strange squirmy, hot feeling from Caitlin and how the same kind of thing from Adam didn't feel nearly as bad and realize they must have been completely separate feelings after all.

"I mean, it was a totally different set of emotions, I guess," I say mostly to myself, "but they seemed to fit. Like, I could feel his emotions fine, but I could also feel mine pretty well. And I apologized for shouting at him last week and that made him less nervous and then it was just . . . I don't know, it was easy."

"I'm very pleased to hear that, Caleb." She smiles, and my face warms. "Were you able to control how much of his emotions you were feeling? Balance them out a bit?"

"Um, I'm not sure. I didn't really try." I honestly didn't feel like I had to, but admitting that feels like a trap for some reason. "Sometimes it did it on its own—like, it would be softer at times and bigger at other times and . . . ugh, I don't know how to describe it."

"Try a visual comparison again," she suggests. "See if that helps."

"Yeah, but I don't think the color thing applies."

"Then try to think of something that does. What else have you encountered in your life that was similar to this experience?"

"Um . . ." I think. The colors of Adam's emotions don't change but the levels do. There's a rise and fall to them, except it's not consistent, it's unpredictable.

". . . it's kind of like—" I start. ". . . it's kind of like the ocean."

"The ocean?"

"Yeah," I breathe. "You know when you're standing at the edge of the water and the waves come up the sand to your feet and sometimes there's, like, a strong wave and your whole leg gets wet? It was sort of like that. The more we were talking, it was like his feelings were the water. I could feel them all the time, but sometimes there would be a big wave and the feeling would sort of cover everything up for a moment and then go back again. But I was always myself, you know? It wasn't like I ever became the ocean too. I didn't get washed away."

"Well." Dr. Bright blinks but it's not surprise, it's that warm feeling again. "That is quite the analogy. I'm very pleased to hear that further exposure to Adam has made it easier to balance your own emotions with others'." The warm solid feeling is so comforting I don't want to tell her it's still hard to balance with most people.

"I'm curious," she continues, "the ocean as you describe it is often thought of as a very calm place. Does Adam make you calmer?"

"I guess so. But, I mean, sometimes waves get really big and scary too. Like, when we really started to talk about the guys who were making fun of him, there was definitely a really big wave of anger that sort of took me under for a second. I got really, really angry too and had to take some deep breaths like you taught me to calm myself down."

"And where was your anger directed? I know in the past you've had a hard time with other people's anger. It's made you want to lash out at the source. Did you get angry at Adam?"

"Uh, no. No, I didn't. It was—I was angry at those guys. But I was sort of angry with them to begin with. Well, not sort of. Like actually, really fucking angry."

"Do you think you would have done something if those boys had come by in that moment?"

"I don't know. I mean, the breathing helped, but, yeah, I mean, I was still pretty mad. But I won't hit anyone again, I mean, I promise."

"I know you're trying, Caleb, but remember why you're here. You haven't been handling your anger—or the anger of others— particularly well," she says gently. "I'm happy to hear that the breathing is helping you, but we still have a long way to go on that front."

"I know. But that was ages ago. I didn't even know what was going on at that point, that I was feeling other people's feelings. I'm not dangerous, I promise."

"I know you're not dangerous, Caleb." She smiles. "You're a very kind boy. You would never hurt someone intentionally, I know that."

"Right." I nod. "Yeah, thanks."

"I'm proud of you, Caleb," Dr. Bright says. "It can be scary to put yourself out there like that, but it sounds like the lunch went very well."

"Yeah." I nod. "It did."

Dr. Bright smiles softly and I can feel the warmth shifting to something else—she's about to give me new homework for this week, I just know it—and I keep talking before she can change topics.

"I think I want to do it again," I blurt. "Get lunch with him, I mean. I liked hanging out with him and, I don't know, I feel like he probably could use a friend."

The warmth swells in time with Dr. Bright's smile.

"I think that's a lovely idea, Caleb," she says. "It sounds like you two have a real connection."

The way she says it makes me shift nervously in my seat but I can't claim that she's wrong. I felt more at peace watching Adam fiddle with his watch and avoid my eyes than I do anywhere else in school.

"Yeah, we do, I guess," I admit. "It's not weird, though, right? For me to be his friend when I can feel that he's lonely? That's not, like, breaking some kind of rule or anything?"

"There aren't really hard-and-fast rules with this," Dr. Bright tells me. "As long as the ability itself stays a secret, many Atypicals use them to improve their lives or the lives of others."

"So, like, there are really other people like me?" I ask.

"I can't talk about my other patients, Caleb," she deflects, dis tracting me with a new mindfulness exercise before I can ask the questions that are sprouting in my head.

Between the pleased and proud feeling that Dr. Bright sent me off with and my phone telling me I have a text from Adam, I'm riding pretty high. It's a nice day—crisp and sunny—so I walk right past the bus stop near Dr. Bright's office to take a different route home.

I open the text to a link to a Hozier song. Adam is one of those guys who's always got his headphones on, and he has *a lot* of opin ions about music. I didn't know a ton of the stuff he mentioned at lunch on Wednesday, but we did agree that music is good for block ing out everyone in school sometimes. He told me about this Hozier song that didn't make it onto his first album but that Adam says is really great. It makes him feel less afraid to walk down the hallways.

Okay, so he didn't say that last part. I sort of figured it out by the strong feeling he got when talking about it. Like he was taller and less vulnerable to attack. I could use a little of that feeling myself.

Sometimes being out and about in the city can be way too overwhelming. All those people feeling all those different things, weaving in and out of my body like hot and cold breezes. But today, I put on my headphones and click on the link to listen. "Arsonist's Lullaby" starts to play and I tune out the world around me, focusing on typing back a thanks to Adam. Texting him back brings up all the feelings I had during our lunch, and that warm, solid feeling moves into my chest again. Even just thinking about Adam makes me feel a little less like a sponge that doesn't get a say in what it soaks up.

As the song winds down, I start to feel jittery, the protective shield around me beginning to crack. I can feel my heartbeat kicking up as buzzing enters my head, making me slow and dizzy. Whatever peace I'd had just a second ago is being destroyed by someone's emotions.

The feelings are grating at me—making me clench my jaw and shove my fists into my coat pocket. Something isn't right. This isn't just the noise of a busy street's feelings. This is coming from one place.

I look around me for a person in crisis. A rush of anger and sadness has pushed into me, making it hard to breathe. Someone who feels this way has to be noticeably upset, right? You can't just carry this with you all the time.

But looking around me, I don't see anything out of the ordinary. People rushing to work, talking on their cell phones, a college student trying to get signatures on some petition, a homeless man sitting against a building—normal city stuff.

No, the only thing out of the ordinary is me.

22

ADAM

I don't know how it happens, but after that first awkward, amazing, painful, incredible lunch, Caleb and I keep going. Exactly a week later, I find myself taking my Pizza Wednesday pizza out to the bench behind the gym and sitting down like I belong there. And that's when things get really bizarre—Caleb comes out, sees me, and sits down *like I belong there*. We sit in the cold and stare at each other for a few seconds before Caleb does this little blinking thing like he's resetting. Then he launches into a story about how he thought it might be worth it to read *The Aeneid* in the original Latin and get some extra credit for both classes and I'm so charmed that I momentarily forget how to breathe.

And then it just . . . becomes a routine. Every day, we both find our way to this isolated bench and eat lunch together. And then we start texting every day. And then the texting leads to playing Xbox Live together (I never thought I would have a reason to dust off my Xbox, but here we are), and sending each other music and actually really *talking* at lunch. First about school and then eventually about football and debate and slowly, tentatively, about our actual, real stuff.

"What's wrong?" he asks exactly three weeks after our first

lunch (not that I'm keeping track), popping a pepperoni into his mouth.

"What do you mean?"

"You're—" He catches himself. Caleb does that a lot. He'll start a sentence and then abruptly stop talking, like he's afraid a monster is going to leap out of his mouth and terrorize the locals.

"I'm . . . ?" I prompt, acting like this behavior is totally normal to me now, even though it makes the skin on the back of my neck prickle.

"You just seem a little bummed out, that's all." He shrugs, averting his eyes.

"What're you, a human mood ring?" I quip, but my heart is picking up speed at his observation.

"You're just really obvious, dude," he counters.

I sigh, playing up the drama of it, trying to act like I'm not a ball of self-doubt and exhaustion. I'm mostly comfortable around Caleb now; I don't feel like he's going to bolt or say one day, "Gotcha! Joke's on you, I never actually wanted to be your friend." But I still feel like I'm splashing around in the shallow end. Even when we talk about serious things like our futures or parents, there's a lightness to it, forced mostly by me and my stomach-clenching fear of Caleb finding out that some days I can't get out of bed because my brain doesn't work right.

Caleb rolls his eyes (fondly, I think. I hope) at my overdone sighing and gives me The Look. The Look that I saw that first lunch: the "you're full of crap and you better start talking now because I don't have the patience" look.

"My parents are on me about college apps," I say, finally giving in.

"What? Already? Jeez, I knew they were intense, but . . ."

"Your parents haven't started giving you grief about it?" I ask, disbelieving.

"I mean, we've been touring campuses and stuff," he says with a shrug, "and they get on me about studying for the SATs, but they haven't been crazy hyped about it or anything."

"Wow," I deadpan, "I can't imagine that."

"Dude, are you okay?" His eyes are doing that puppy-dog thing they do that makes my stomach flip over and dissolve. I get a flash of Caleb and my mom teaming up to do a Good Cop/Bad Cop routine and quickly determine that the world (least of all my sanity) would never survive.

"I've got a little less than a year to get my apps ready," I deflect. "I'm really not that worried about getting them done."

"You know that's not what I mean," he says, staring me down. And no, I don't know that, because I *never* know what Caleb means. What does he mean by these lunches? What does he mean when he looks over his shoulder at me in class? What does he mean when he reads me—*me*, who tries so hard to move through school completely unnoticed—like an open book?

"No, I don't, Caleb," I say honestly. "I'm fine."

"No, you're not." He's adamant, getting worked up. "You've been sad and jittery for days and it feels like the kind of sad you get when your parents are putting pressure on you, but I'm not sure so I wish you'd just talk to me about it!"

He's practically glaring at me, like he's mad that I'm having feelings. I sit there in a stunned silence and watch the frustration on his face melt into panic. His eyes widen and I can see his brain catching up with his mouth.

"I'm—" he starts. "I didn't mean—I don't know what I'm saying." He shakes his head and stares down at the table.

"How—" My lips release sound I didn't plan on making and I can feel my heartbeat in my fingertips. "Why do you say I've been sad and jittery for days?" I ask, even though there's so many more things I want to ask.

"Because you have been," he mumbles.

"No, I haven't," I lie. I've barely seen Caleb this week, where is he getting this from?

"Yes, you have, I can *feel* it." Caleb spits it out and looks up at me.

"What?"

"I just mean—I—" His eyes dart around and his face is turning red, out of frustration or embarrassment I have no idea. "I can just tell, okay? You're not that good at hiding it."

"Ouch," I say, trying to sound casual as my heart starts racing in panic.

"No, c'mon, I didn't mean to hurt your feelings—I mean—*fuck*." Caleb brings his hands up to his head, running his fingers frantically through his hair. My brain takes a quick detour from keeping up with this incredibly odd conversation to thinking about how much I wish I could replace his hands with mine.

"Caleb, are *you* okay?" I ask earnestly, partly to get the focus off of me but partly because he is looking increasingly not okay.

"Yeah, no—I'm fine." His hands come around to cradle the back of his neck as he looks up at the sky, inhaling deeply. "Sorry, I don't mean to be so weird all the time."

"I don't think you're weird," I say, mostly truthfully.

He scoffs.

"Trust me, you would," he says grimly.

"What?"

"Do you want to come over on Friday?" He tilts his head down from staring at the sky and I'm taken aback by the question and the sudden eye contact.

"What?"

I say "what" approximately three hundred percent more in conversations with Caleb than with anyone else. It is deeply confusing.

"We've got that stupid Sadie Hawkins thing on Saturday and I still have no idea what suit to wear so do you want to maybe come over and help me pick one out?" There are those goddamn puppy eyes again.

"Why on earth do you think I'd be good at that?" I ask, gesturing down at my oh-so-fashionable jean jacket/black T-shirt/black jeans combo.

"I don't know, because you're—" He stops himself again, and this time his face gets even redder. Oh. So the elephant in the room has finally been acknowledged. Sort of. And apparently this elephant comes with stereotypes.

"I don't know, dude." He breezes past the awkward moment with a roll of his eyes before I have a chance to reply. "I just need a second opinion from someone who's not over the age of forty and not my kid sister. Doesn't really matter if you know anything about clothes or not. Then, I don't know, we could watch a movie or play Xbox or something."

"Yeah, okay." My mouth is continuing to say words before my brain has a chance to think. I don't know if Caleb is asking to distract from the earlier weirdness or because he genuinely wants to hang out, but I'm not going to pass up an opportunity to see if his family are all as freakishly perceptive as he is. Plus, I can't remember the last time I went over to a friend's house.

Friends. I guess that's what we are now. The warm feeling I get in my stomach from that thought almost distracts me from the genuine smile that takes over Caleb's face as he nods and says, "Cool. Cool, cool." For the first time all week, I don't feel sad and jittery, and there's something in Caleb's eyes that tells me that, somehow, he knows.

23

CALEB

My palms are sweating as I make my way down the stairs. I don't know why I'm nervous about talking to my parents about Adam but I am. The whole thing—this weird month of hanging out and becoming friends—has been between the two of us and no one else. I've talked to Dr. Bright about it but, I don't know, it still feels special and protected and I'm afraid to disrupt that.

As I walk into the kitchen, feelings wash over me, momentarily drowning out the sound of my family's voices. Mom is stressed but happy, Dad has got that weird little buzz that I think is, like, a writer's high, and Alice is feeling . . . like there's warm sunlight on her face. I pause for a second in the doorway, trying to figure it out. It's not too bright or hot—it's almost like the sunlight is coming *from* Alice instead of shining down on her.

"Hey, loser." My sister's voice cuts through the wave. "What are you doing?"

"Alice, don't be rude to your brother," my dad chastises as he puts some sort of casserole on the table.

"What's up with you?" I ask, snapping out of it and moving to sit down.

"What do you mean?" she asks.

"You're all . . . warm," I say dumbly.

"Alice got an A on her math final from last semester," my mom fills in, and I feel the warm sun from her too. There's something familiar about it and not just in the sense that my family's feelings are familiar. I think I felt this recently from someone else. Suddenly, it snaps into place.

"*Oh*, you're proud," I say, the feeling coming into focus.

"And what's wrong with that?" Alice asks defensively.

"No, nothing," I say. "I just didn't know what you were feeling." I think back to this emotion coming from Dr. Bright and feel an extra layer of warmth from the idea that she's proud of me.

"Sheesh, you couldn't recognize pride? This family might have a self-esteem problem if you haven't felt that before," my dad jokes.

"Caleb?" I feel a spike of worry from my mom.

"No, no, I have," I rush to explain. "I just don't think I've really paid attention to what it was before. But, you know, it's getting easier to sort through everything, especially with you guys."

We're all sitting at this point, comfortable in our dinner routine, but my comment brings the flow of emotions to a weird stuttering stop. My family is mostly used to my Problem by now but I think it still freaks them out when I talk about it. Probably a good time to change the subject.

"So, hey, um," I start a little too loudly, "would it be cool if my friend Adam came over on Friday?"

For once, I don't really get a read on what everyone feels about the question, because my heart is in my throat and my palms have become the Atlantic Ocean again. I don't see any reason why they would say no but it feels like the question has a lot riding on it. I've got this idea in my head that if I don't make an effort to "solidify the friendship"—as Dr. Bright puts it—then Adam will just get bored and stop having lunch with me.

And here's the thing—I really like having lunch with Adam. I mean, lunch was already my favorite part of the school day because a) food and b) I get to be alone with my own feelings for once.

But it's even better with Adam because then I'm not just stewing in whatever moods I've collected throughout the morning and because, well, his feelings are kind of great. I mean, the kid is stressed to the max all the time and there's the deep blue water that is so strong sometimes I don't understand how he even breathes, but he's funny and smart and his feelings don't make me want to crawl out of my own body. That seems like something worth solidifying.

"Who's Adam?" my dad asks.

"Uh, he's just this guy at school," I say.

"He's in English with you, right?" my mom asks.

"Yeah. Latin too."

"Are you guys going to study on a Friday night?" my dad asks, disbelieving.

"No. No, we were just gonna hang out." I shovel casserole into my mouth to distract from the rising tide of staticky confusion coming from my parents.

"Oh," my mom says, a silent conversation passing between her and my dad that not even my Problem can figure out the content of. "Well, of course he can. You know you're allowed to have any friends over."

"Exactly," my dad agrees. "We look forward to meeting him."

They're talking to me but looking at each other, their eyes having that separate conversation. There's a swirl of feeling coming from them—confusion, concern . . . maybe a little hopefulness or something—and their emotions are in sync in a way that's totally unique to them.

I guess if you've been married for that long, your feelings start to feel the same. It'd be cool if it wasn't so fucking strange. Even Alice, who had been texting covertly under the table until now, is picking up on the weird vibe, her face a question mark as her eyes dart between them.

"Okay, what?" I drop my knife and fork and they clatter on my plate as my parents' eyes snap to me. "Whatever it is, just say it. I'm not *actually* a mind reader, you know."

"Sorry, sweetie." My mom's face crumples in sympathy. "We just didn't realize you were making new friends! It's been a while since you've had anyone over and we're happy that you're getting back out there."

"Don't make him sound like he's some sort of sad spinster," Alice says indignantly. A little ball of warmth swells in my chest. Alice shares my hatred of being pitied and it's nice to know that we'll always back each other up when it happens.

"We're just happy you're socializing, son." My dad awkwardly pats my hand. Alice rolls her eyes.

"It sounds like you're having an easier time with things," my mom suggests, and I feel that light, tentative spark of hopefulness reach out for me.

"Yeah, I guess." I shrug. "I don't know, it's a little easier to deal with it around him."

"His emotions don't overwhelm you?" my mom asks. She's met with Dr. Bright a couple times to talk about how to raise someone like me—an "Atypical" kid, I guess—and it leads to dumbass therapy questions at the dinner table.

"I mean, sometimes, yeah, but I mostly have it under wraps."

"Mostly?" my dad asks.

Fuck. Can't give parents an inch, can you?

"He hasn't picked up on anything weird, I don't think," and *god*, why did I just say that? My nervousness had pretty much gone away but it's back now and it's not entirely mine—my parents are worried about something.

"You haven't told him anything, right, Caleb?" My mom's voice is gentle but I feel the anxious edge to it.

"No, of course not!" I say. "But would it really be so bad if I did? I mean, it's not like I can move stuff with my mind or anything, I don't get why it has to be this big secret!"

"It doesn't have to be a big secret," my dad says, and there's something about this whole conversation that feels like my parents have rehearsed it. "But remember what Dr. Bright said, you have to be careful about who you tell."

"Yeah, whatever." I stare down at my half-eaten dinner. "It's not like I was planning on blurting it out, I barely know the guy. But I just—I hate being the freak with the secret, that's all."

"You're not a freak, honey." Now it's my mom's turn to pat me, this time on my shoulder. "But we just need to make sure you stay safe."

"What? Safe?"

My parents glance toward each other, something significant passing between them, and I feel a tight coil of stress squeeze their hearts. They're—they're *actually* concerned about something. Scared.

"Guys, what's going on?" I lean forward, my eyes darting back and forth between them. Out of my peripheral, I see Alice leaning forward as well, phone long forgotten in her lap.

"Caleb, we just want you to be careful about how much you use your power," my dad says solemnly.

"'Use my power'?" I echo disbelievingly. "I don't use it, it just happens to me."

"Exactly." My mom nods. "And while that's still the case, it's important that you keep it as quiet as possible. We are thrilled that you're making new friends"—my dad nods vigorously in agreement— "but we just want to make sure that you're not being . . ." She fishes around for a word.

"Careless," my dad fills in. "It wouldn't be good for anyone to find out about what you can do unless you're sure that you can trust them."

"Why?" Alice asks before I can.

"Because it's not something you want to broadcast," my dad answers.

"But why?" I push.

"Because there are people out there who . . ." My mom trails off, looking at my dad, and he gives her the slightest nod. "Who might not appreciate what you can do."

"Why the fuck would I care about them?" I snap.

"Language, Caleb," my dad chides.

Whoops, I didn't mean to swear in front of them, but the staticky feeling is swelling through my body and making me squirm.

I feel like an exposed wire jerking through the air, ready to land in a pool of water. My parents are legit stressed and I don't get why.

"Sorry, I just . . ." My brain is buzzing and I can feel my parents' orange, warm concern pushing through the static, and that's a toxic combination for my ability to think. I'm squeezing my eyes shut, trying to keep it together, but the stress-concern-fear loop keeps going round and round and I'm trying to catch the end of it to pull it back but it's moving too fast for me to grab on to. The thought crosses through my mind that I wish Adam were here so I could hold on to his feelings.

"Caleb," someone says, their voice a hot, smothering steam.

"Mom, don't—"

"He's—"

"Sh, just let him—"

"Alice, we can't—"

"Okay, but let me—" A cool hand covers mine where it's gripping the edge of the table.

"Caleb?" My sister's voice travels with the cool breeze of calm that's coming through her hand. "You need to breathe, dude."

I inhale and open my eyes. My family is still sitting at the table, their eyes wide but their bodies uncharred. I didn't explode in a fit of electric rage. I grab on to the buoy of calm my sister has thrown to me and try to use it to clear the humming in my head.

"You guys can't just throw stuff at him without explaining it, you know that," my sister lectures my parents like *she's* the adult. Twelve and the only one in the family who's learned how to keep her head in a crisis.

"We're sorry, son." My dad looks shamefaced and my mom looks close to tears. God, everyone had been in such a good mood when we started dinner (all of ten minutes ago, I realize, even though it feels like hours), why did I have to ruin it?

"What the hell is going on?" I choke out, my throat still tight from the poisonous combination of feelings that's been running through it. "What are you guys so stressed about?"

My mom blinks away her unshed tears and takes a deep breath.

"When we first took you to Dr. Bright, she explained that there are—" She pauses and I feel like I'm about to be told that I have three months to live. I unthinkingly turn my hand over and squeeze Alice's. "There are people who like to keep tabs on people like you—people who can do special things."

"These people aren't dangerous"—my dad takes over, giving me an earnest look that I don't believe—"but she thought it was best that they didn't know about you. We don't want anyone trying to meddle in your life or telling you how to live it."

"We just want the world to be open to you, Caleb." My mom smiles at me.

"And it wouldn't be if these people knew? I mean, who the hell are they?" My parents let the curse slide as they share another inscrutable look.

"Well, to be frank . . . we don't know." My dad exhales, and I know he's telling the truth.

"Are you saying there are superspies after Caleb?" Alice scoffs, voicing the insane thought that was running through my own head.

"Of course not, sweetie," my mom says. "No one knows anything about what Caleb can do, and we're going to keep it that way."

"That's why it's important to trust the people you tell," my dad explains. "We're not saying never tell anyone, but just be careful about who you trust."

"Yeah." I find myself agreeing. "Okay."

My parents smile at that and I venture out of Alice's cocoon of calm to check in with their feelings. The stress and concern are down from eleven to one and the pastel pink exhale of relief is filling them up.

I pull my hand away from Alice's and with it try to pull back into my own feelings. All that I find is a swirl of confusion twisting around a weight of fear in my gut.

24

CALEB

"Okay, I know I said I don't know anything about clothes, but you absolutely cannot wear that."

Adam is giving me the most incredulous look he has (which is pretty incredulous) as I step out of my bathroom in my dad's old prom suit.

"Nope, no, no way." He punctuates each word with a shake of his head. He's sitting on the floor, leaning against my bed and absently spinning a hat between his hands. The sight makes something squirm in my stomach, but in a good way. I'm a little surprised at how comfortable he seems—how well he fits into my space—but I think . . . I think I like it.

Things started out awkwardly—we didn't know how to behave around each other outside of our lunch bench, my parents were too eager and too polite—but once we got into the bad-movie montage of me trying on different outfits and Adam realized I don't mind when he laughs at me, it started to gel. It got *easy*. I'm actually actively enjoying spending time with another human outside of my family, and I know in my bones that Adam is having a good time too.

"What, you don't think powder blue is making a comeback?" I

spin around to show the suit off and Adam chuckles. Something warm blooms in my chest and fans outward, like it does every time I make him laugh. Might be his, might be mine, might be both of ours.

"No offense to your dad, but I don't think powder blue was *ever* cool." He laughs.

"Well, that's the last of it," I sigh as I flop down on the floor next to him, undoing the top button of the ancient tuxedo shirt. "We've officially gone through all my remotely nice clothes. So unless I can show up in my football uniform . . ."

"Hey, with how you look in it, she might not mind." Adam snorts and I blush, uncertain. He goes still—hot, embarrassed anxiety filling the space between us. The hat, which had been spinning in midair like a pizza, drops to his lap. He looks at me sideways before snapping his eyes forward and stammering out, "I just mean—I see the way the cheerleaders look at all you guys when you're in uniform. Guess it's a cliché for a reason. Personally, I don't get it. With the red and white, you all just look like massive candy canes."

The panic he was feeling starts to cool, but something else sharp takes its place. Adam picks up the hat again and continues spinning it, but his hands are shaking slightly. I find myself absently wondering where the hat came from—I must have tossed it out of my closet at some point. I'm mesmerized for a moment, watching it move around and around in his fingers. It reminds me about how Adam told me he plays piano. I'd really like to see him play sometime. I'm staring at his hands, that sharp thing grating at me when I realize: he's lying. I don't know if he's lying about the cheerleaders or thinking we all look like candy canes, but he's lying.

"Huh, yeah," I say dumbly, realizing I need to say *something* but not knowing what that is. There's a right move here, I know there is. But knowing someone's feelings doesn't give me a guidebook on how to respond to them. That I have to make up as I go along.

"You should go with the second outfit," Adam continues, a little too loudly, like he's trying to distract me from my own thoughts. "The one with the skinny tie and the vest."

"You don't think it's too hipster?" I ask, letting the weird moment pass. No point in lingering when I have no fucking clue what to do about it.

"Hipster isn't always a bad thing." He finally looks at me again, a slight smile lifting the corner of his mouth.

"Just didn't think I was the type of guy who could pull it off," I mumble.

"You should have more confidence in yourself, Caleb," he says seriously, like my self-esteem is what we've been talking about this whole time. My heart lurches at his words—how does he see the things no one else does—and I give a knee-jerk response.

"Yeah, well, I'm not the only one," I say, snatching the hat out of midair and donning it dramatically.

"Ooh, them's fighting words," he laughs, his eyes smiling more than his mouth as he reaches for the hat that's now on top of my head. I bat his hands away, which just makes him laugh more, and soon we're caught in a weird not-quite-slap-fight where we're just sitting on the floor shoving each other.

I'm breathless with laughter as Adam's pure joy zips into my body and combines with my own. I've never felt this from him before. He gets amused, yeah, but this kind of carefree happiness is new. I'm completely intoxicated by it and I shove him harder, as if it will release more of the bright light of joy like hitting an old cushion releases dust. I clearly shove too hard because Adam starts to fall backward and he automatically grabs the lapels of the hideous blue tux jacket, nearly pulling me down with him. My arms windmill for a fraction of a second before landing on either side of him, holding us both up.

What happens next is . . . weird. The light of joy doesn't go out but it kind of stutters and bursts. He's still happy but there's an added layer of fluttering anxiety that begins to cut through. The pulse of his nerves is out of sync with my heart, which right now feels like it's going to spring from my chest. The battling rhythms make my skin tingle and my forehead break out in a sweat. All of a sudden, I'm a boy made of nerve endings alone.

Dr. Bright tells me that, when I get overwhelmed by someone's emotions, I should try and focus on what I see—on the concrete things in front of me. I do this now, drinking in Adam's wide-eyed expression like it's going to soothe the fire building in my veins. It doesn't work. His mouth opens slightly like he's going to say something and my heart lurches at the possibility. But no sound comes. Instead his eyes start moving around my face, like he's doing the same thing—trying to cling to reality so he doesn't get dragged under by the wave of emotion that's moving through the air.

My heartbeat has slowed, or it's sped up and his has slowed. Or his has sped up and mine has stayed the same—I'm losing track of what's what and who's who but all I know is that we're in sync again and those butterflies have invaded my stomach once more. They're both welcome and unwelcome—a nice, warm feeling that makes me want to hide. I suddenly become aware of the warmth coming from Adam's body. My arms aren't touching him, but I can feel his rib cage expanding as he breathes, like the air between his sides and my forearms is being sucked out with each inhale.

His fingers flex slightly on my lapels and I don't know if it's been seconds or hours since he first grabbed them. I should say something. I know I should say something. But, as with so many things, Adam beats me to it.

"Yeah, the vest and skinny tie for sure," he mumbles, releasing his grip and folding in on himself slightly as he turns away from me. The fluttering feeling turns sour; the physical withdrawal tearing the feelings away with it. I pull my arms back and wonder at how hollow they feel. Like I just put my fingers into an electrical socket, making my whole body bright, and now I'm living in a primitive world lit only by daylight.

What the *fuck.*

25

CALEB

"You look really nice." Caitlin smiles at me as she closes the car door behind her.

"Thanks," I say gruffly. "Adam helped me pick it out."

I have no rational explanation for why I say this other than it seemed important that she know. Credit where credit's due and all that.

But that's not totally it, is it? I bring up Adam because he should be here. I like Caitlin, and I notice she smells good as she walks toward me, but if there's anyone I want to stand next to in a poorly lit gym, making fun of the DJ and avoiding our classmates, it's Adam. I'm not really sure what to do with this information.

Caitlin is saying good-bye to her parents and I think her dad says something cringingly dad-ish to me as he waves. I respond on autopilot, but now that I'm thinking about Adam, my brain is pre-occupied replaying that weird moment from last night. My body is remembering that butterfly feeling (mine or his?) as Caitlin takes my arm to lead me into the gym and new butterflies swarm into my stomach. The feelings clash like nails on a chalkboard and I try to smile and nod through the grimace I'm feeling as Caitlin smiles up at me and says something.

God, this was a bad idea. I knew this was a bad idea. I shouldn't have said yes when she asked. Dr. Bright said that we could just go to the dance as friends but I know in my gut that Caitlin wants something more.

"Caleb, are you okay?"

"Huh?" My eyes refocus on Caitlin and I realize that she's been talking for the last thirty seconds and I have no idea what she's been saying.

"You just look . . . I don't know." Her face crinkles prettily as she hears herself admit that she doesn't know something. Kind of a new feeling for her, I'm guessing. My mind instantly leaps to the fact that Adam is the same way and, goddammit, this was definitely a mistake.

"Yeah." I nod enthusiastically to make up for the weird panic moving through my brain. "Yeah, I'm fine. Just, uh—I've got a headache, that's all. It's not that bad, though," I add, feeling her concern warming my insides. It's nice. I definitely prefer it over her butterflies.

"Oh good." She looks relieved. "Because, I don't know about you, but I plan on dancing."

She lets go of me and shimmies goofily as she pulls open the door to the school. Crap, was I supposed to do that? Get the door? She doesn't seem bothered by my lack of chivalry; she's smiling at me, the concern melting into soft, lukewarm liquid, and I try to put Adam out of my mind. Caitlin's great. She's witty and smart and clearly gets that I'm out of my element. This is going to be fun.

This is not fun.

I'm trying to be a good date—dance and talk with Caitlin, smile at her friends—but there are just too many people feeling too many things and I lose focus every other minute. I'm about to escape to the bathroom to sit in silence for a few minutes when someone calls out my name.

"Michaels! How the hell are you, my man?"

I turn to see Henry swaggering toward me. He reaches out a

hand, pulling me into a completely unnecessary handshake like we're old school chums who are running into each other at a ten-year reunion. God, this guy is such a tool.

"Hey, Henry." I grimace as he claps me on the shoulder with his free hand. I take a moment to look him over as I adjust to his feelings. He's wearing a well-fitted suit, his blond hair perfectly slicked back, an insufferably smarmy expression on his face. Everything about him is slimy. His feelings slither into my body and make me restless.

"So, you gonna get with that or what?" he whispers, jerking his head toward Caitlin, who's dancing and laughing with Jessica as I get punch for us. My eyebrows reach toward the top of my forehead as I give Henry my best blank stare. I don't want to play this game with him. The moment I start to go along with it, it will become harder to keep his feelings at bay.

"We're just friends," I reply, hoping that will end this conversation. But Henry smirks and tilts his head at me as if to say, *Oh really?* There are phantom bugs crawling over my skin that I recognize as Henry trying to get something. It's the same sensation I feel whenever he's making excuses for skipping practice or getting an extension on a project—the bugs start crawling and a second later he's smirking at our coach or our teacher and they're apologizing to him.

For a while, I sort of thought maybe Henry was special like me. He seems to always get what he wants by just flashing his pearl-white teeth or talking smooth. It's like being hypnotized by a snake. But once I was able to separate his feelings from everyone else's, I realized he wasn't like me. He doesn't have any kind of supernatural ability to get what he wants. He's just . . . determined.

"So you won't mind if I take a crack at her?"

"What?" I'd assumed our conversation was over, but Henry's question snaps me out of my daydreaming and back into my body. There's a little spark of cold fire in his feelings now, right in my stomach, and it's making me hungry in a way that's not going to be satisfied with the too-sweet cookies sitting next to the not-sweet-enough punch.

"If you and Cait are just buds, then you won't care if I try to get in there." He smiles, the flame of determination growing up my torso and frosting over my lungs.

"She hates being called Cait," I say for lack of a response, and because it's true.

"Thanks for the tip, pal." Henry winks, slapping me on the shoulder again, before sauntering away toward Caitlin. He takes the cold fire and the skin-crawlers with him and I'm left holding two glasses of lukewarm punch and wondering if I just gave him permission for something I have no right to give permission for.

Henry reaches Caitlin and Jessica and starts dancing goofily at them. I've seen this move before—he's trying to break the ice, and the girls laugh, mostly out of politeness. The static pinpricks of their annoyance jump out at me and I involuntarily flinch as I step a bit closer to the dance floor. I'm cautiously edging into the radius of their emotions, knowing that whatever the combination is going to be, I might not handle it all that well. I count to ten as I try to gently probe into the swirl of feelings and find out what I'm dealing with.

Before I'm able to gauge the situation, Henry reaches an arm toward Caitlin, grabbing her by the waist and pulling her close to him, swaying awkwardly. She gives that polite laugh again, but this time there's a razor edge to her smile that makes the jabs of annoyance sharper against my skin. My whole body is tense, my shoulders starting to reach toward my ears.

Caitlin tries to spin away from Henry but he pulls her in tighter, forcing her to dance with him. Caitlin's annoyance grows hot with anger and I need to defuse this before it gets out of hand.

"Hey, Caitlin, here you go," I shout over the music as I hand her the punch. She smiles at me, moving away from Henry again, and I feel the hot static of anger-annoyance relax slightly. She opens her mouth to say something but Henry grabs her again, spilling the punch over her hand.

"Hey!" She swats at Henry with her free hand, smile now completely gone. The irritation spikes—wait, no, it's not irritation, this is pure anger. I haven't felt this from Caitlin before and for a second, I'm completely overwhelmed. When most people get mad, there's a build—a burning that grows hotter and bigger until it explodes. This isn't like that at all. It's as if there's been a volcano of molten-hot lava inside of Caitlin this whole time, lying dormant underneath layers of kindness and ambition. Now, all of a sudden, the volcano might erupt.

"What?" Henry laughs, a different kind of heat building inside of him. A kind of heat that, from him, makes me feel radioactive. "Come on, don't you want to dance?"

Both his arms are around her now as Caitlin does her best to angle her body away from him. Jessica and I are standing on either side, wondering what we should be doing.

"Back off, Henry," Caitlin bites, pushing him away, spilling punch all down the front of his perfectly cut suit jacket.

"Jesus," he shouts, looking down at the pink liquid seeping into his clothes. "God, you don't have to be such a bitch!"

"It's not my fault you can't take a hint!" Caitlin yells back, and they're starting to draw the attention of our classmates.

Henry recovers from the spill quickly, puffing out his chest and taking a menacing step toward Caitlin. Toxic rage is pouring out of him. The air is thick and I can almost see the heat waves rising off of Henry. Caitlin's volcano stalls for a moment and all at once, it's like I've had seven shots of espresso—my hair is standing on end and I'm having a hard time breathing. Caitlin is scared.

"Henry, go clean up," I say, stepping between them, my back to Caitlin.

"Don't tell me what to do," he spits. "Your girl here owes me an apology."

"Oh my god, you're deluded." Caitlin leans around me to snarl into Henry's face. The fear abates for a moment as the red-hot anger takes over. How Caitlin hasn't completely combusted at this point is a total mystery to me.

"You're the one who owes *me* an apology," she snaps.

"I was just trying to have fun—"

"What about forcing a girl to dance with you is fun?"

They're shouting over each other now, completely ignoring the fact that I'm towering between them. Henry is mad and Caitlin is mad *and* scared and I can't fix it. Knowing what they feel doesn't help because I can't do anything about it. I'm too buried in the emotions. I shouldn't have come over here. I should always just stay out of it, but *I'm* angry about what Henry was doing and that just piles onto the garbage dump of other people's feelings that's building around me. I can't even hear what Henry and Caitlin are saying now because the fear is stuffing cotton balls in my ears and the anger is making my vision go white. Adrenaline and panic are fighting each other for space in my body and I can't catch my breath. I'm drowning, choking on lava, burning in the heat.

The next thing I know, Henry is off-balance, stumbling backward, away from my outstretched arms. When did I put my arms out? What happened to the drink I was holding? My shoes are wet—I guess that's what happened to my drink.

"What the fuck, Michaels?" Henry barks, regaining his footing and angling his anger at me. Oh god, that is so much worse. I'm now getting a direct feed on his rage and I feel like an ant under a magnifying glass in the sun. Henry takes a step forward and I push him again.

"Go away, Henry," I say through clenched teeth. I'm a ticking time bomb and I want to tell Henry, want to warn him against making this worse, but he's being an idiot, so blinded by his own anger that he can't see I'm blinded too.

"This has nothing to do with you," he hisses.

"Leave her alone." I'm getting into his space now, hoping he's not so stupid that he'll think he can match me in a fight.

"What are you going to do? Hit me?"

I guess he is that stupid.

Molten rage moves through my body, taking control of my arm and charging it up for a punch. I'm about to smack Henry's dumb, smug face when—

"Mr. Michaels!"

"So . . . that was definitely a first for me." Caitlin breaks the silence finally, the tentative curl of her feelings reaching out to me.

"Huh?" I'm still too numb and overwhelmed to form actual words. I feel like a sponge that soaked up way too much water and has now been violently wrung out.

"Getting kicked out of a dance," she continues. "Can't say that's happened before."

I look over at her to see her smile slightly—she's trying to tease, but I know she's nervous. I nearly lost it in there, and I know how scary that can be. And now she's walking around the dark football field with me after a guy practically attacked her in the dance and, god, I'm such a dick.

"I'm so sorry, Caitlin," I breathe, my shoulders collapsing around me. "I never meant to—I just got so—But I wouldn't've. I wouldn't've." I finish nonsensically, but something in her relaxes.

"I know, Caleb," she says, "and you have nothing to apologize for. I actually—well, I appreciate it. You, standing up for me."

"Oh, yeah," I say. "It's, uh, it's no problem."

"I was about ready to punch him myself," she says. "God, he's *such* a douchebag."

"Yeah, he really is." I huff a laugh.

"He's just got one of those punchable faces, you know?" She smirks.

"Yeah, he *really* does." I smile back at her, and there are the butterflies again.

"I'm still sorry, though." Maybe if I keep talking, I can banish the butterflies. "I didn't mean to ruin your whole night. You could have stayed, you know."

"I know. But it was kind of lame anyway." She shrugs. "This is more my speed."

Caitlin is smiling sweetly at me and the butterflies are fluttering from my stomach up into my throat and I need to be honest with her, stop this feeling before she acts on it.

"Hey, Caitlin." I stop walking and turn to her. I really don't want to look at her perfectly symmetrical face but I'm not going to be a coward about this.

"Yeah?" she asks, blinking prettily up at me.

"Um, so, like," I start, "you're great. I really—I mean, you're smart and funny and cool and I really like being friends with you."

"Okay . . ." Her eyes narrow.

"But, um." The butterflies are starting to wilt but it might just be my own anxiety drowning them out. "I don't know what you expected. Like, I don't know if this was supposed to be a date or not but, um . . ."

I'm waiting for her to cut me off—hopeful that she'll rush to correct me, tell me that she never thought of this as a date—but based on the blush rising on her cheeks, I don't think that's going to happen.

"I'm not, um," I stutter, "I just mean that . . . I like you like a friend. I'd like for us to be friends. Just friends."

I exhale and stare at the ground as the butterflies whirl around in a frenzy before flying out of my body, hopefully for good.

"Oh," she says. "Oh, right. Well . . . thanks . . . for telling me, I guess." She nods, looking away from me, and there's something weighty and bitter settling into the place the butterflies used to be. I have the sudden urge to wrap Caitlin up in a hug but I have a feeling that won't be well received in this particular moment.

"I'm—I'm sor—"

"It's fine, Caleb, really." She looks up and meets my eyes, a sad smile on her face. "I like being friends with you too."

Even with the sludge of disappointment weighing me down, I know she means it.

26

ADAM

The bench we're sitting on is so cold, I'm already turning numb even though we've been here for five minutes. I thought Caleb's insistence on sitting outside during lunch was just because he wanted to avoid the cafeteria, but apparently it applies to all sorts of settings. I wanted to stay in the coffee shop, where it was warm and cozy and Fleet Foxes–soundtracked, but Caleb just marched out the door the moment the barista handed him his hot chocolate.

I try to *not* find it adorable that six-foot-something, football-playing, letterman-jacket-wearing Caleb drinks hot chocolate (with whipped cream) but I'm failing.

"Hey, you okay?" I ask, holding my latte up to my face so my nose doesn't freeze off. "You've been weirdly quiet for the past five minutes."

My heart is pounding a tattoo of *please say you're okay please say you're okay.* From the moment Caleb walked into the coffee shop, I knew something was off. He's been surly and distant and meeting today was *his* idea—I'd never be so bold as to suggest two hangouts in one weekend—but now I'm worried that he's going to friend-break-up with me, which is completely ridiculous because,

first off, that's not a thing, and second, are we even good enough
friends now to *stop* being friends?

This entire situation is ridiculous. Just the very idea that the
golden boy would want to hang with the weird nerd is absurd. I've
been lulled into a false sense of security and now Caleb is going
to tell me that it was all part of some bet and my life really will be
a bad teen movie. Or—even worse—he's going to tell me that, sure,
hanging out has been fun, but Friday night got a little too homo-
erotic for his tastes. My brain has been working overtime the last
thirty-six hours trying to purge the memory—Caleb's arms on
either side of me, his face close to mine, his eyes big and wandering, looking at me like he was going to, I don't know, *do* something
that would almost certainly kill me instantly with surprise and
joy—and now it's the only image it seems able to produce.

"Yeah, I'm okay, I'm just—" Caleb pauses, which gives me a second to push away the thought of Friday and refocus on him. He
looks twitchy and sad and the latte curdles in my stomach in anticipation of what he's going to say next.

"The dance went really bad last night." He exhales, not looking at me.

Oh. This is about the dance. Not about me. That makes sense.

All right, so I may have been spiraling there for a second. Time
to get back on track, Adam. You want Caleb as a friend? *Be* a friend.

"What happened?" I ask gently, giving my best "I'm listening
very attentively" face, though I'm not entirely sure I want to hear
the answer. If this is about Caitlin, I might genuinely throw up
my latte. But even that thought crossing my mind churns my
stomach—I don't want to be the weird, jealous guy who's pining
after his friend and blaming Caitlin for simply existing. I'm psych-
ing myself up in my head, convincing myself that, no matter what,
I'm going to be there for Caleb because I care about him regardless of any other feelings I might have, and I've gotten completely
sidetracked in my own social anxiety maze so that I practically get
whiplash when Caleb speaks.

"I tried to punch Henry in the face." The words come out in a
rush and Caleb winces as he says it. I choke on my drink—narrowly

avoiding a full-on spit take—and before I can think about what I should say, I blurt—

"What? What the fuck, *why?*"

Caleb smiles, which is the last reaction I expected.

"What?" I'm suspicious, thinking he's pranking me and is just so bad at hiding it, but then he turns to look at me.

"I've never heard you swear before," he says, grinning. "It just caught me off guard, that's all."

"Oh." I deflate. "Well, yeah, you've been a bad influence on me. Clearly." I let myself make eye contact with him and my stomach swoops. His eyes are soft and fond and I want to crawl under this bench and freeze to death. My face doesn't get the memo, though, and I'm starting to smile in return so I hide it behind my cup as I ask him again what happened.

"He was being a dick," Caleb declares, like that's enough. It is for me, but probably not for Principal Stevens.

"Henry's always a dick," I agree.

"Yeah, but he was being particularly dickish last night," Caleb grumbles.

"How so?"

"He . . ." Caleb clenches his jaw and I'm taken aback by the anger on his face. For a moment, my brain sputters like an engine as it tries to reconcile the image of Caleb, who drinks hot chocolate and laughs at my dark sense of humor, and Caleb, who got suspended for attacking another student and who looks like he could rip someone in two right now.

"He was being really creepy to Caitlin," he grits out, his eyes laser focused at some faraway point in front of him. "He was trying to dance with her and she didn't want to and he kept trying and she kept pushing him away and then they started yelling at each other and I just kind of lost it."

"Right," I say quietly. So this *is* about Caitlin. Well then. Fuck.

"I didn't hit him, though. It didn't get that far. And I wouldn't have—I mean, I wanted to, but I wouldn't have hurt him." Caleb turns to me and the ball of rage that I was sitting next to mere sec-

onds ago is gone. His eyes are pleading with me, asking me to
believe him.

"That's good," I say, for lack of anything else to say. "That is
good, right? I mean, you don't want to get suspended again."

"Yeah." He nods. "Yeah, it's good. I mean, Principal Stevens was
not happy"—as I suspected—"but I don't think I'm gonna get into
too much trouble. I mean, we did get thrown out of the dance, but
so did Henry, so, all in all, it turned out okay."

"God, that sucks."

"Eh, it was whatever. I was kind of over the whole thing after
that anyway." He shrugs, the earnestness gone as he reverts back
to Standard Caleb Mode.

"Yeah, I can imagine." I try to mirror his sudden casualness,
leaning back against the cold wood. "Another guy hitting on your
date definitely puts a damper on things."

"She wasn't my date."

He says it so flatly—is he disappointed by that fact? Relieved?
I sneak a look at him out of the corner of my eye and get no
answers.

"Why'd you get so mad at Henry, then? You weren't jealous?"

Why do I always need to poke at the bruise?

"Fuck no," Caleb scoffs. "I was *pissed*. Caitlin's a really good
person, she doesn't need that kind of shit from anyone."

"True," I agree, "but she can definitely stand up for herself."

"So? Doesn't mean I don't want to stand up for her too." He's
starting to look mad again and I'm not sure what I've stepped into
here. "She was really annoyed and angry and scared and I think
that was all making it hard for her to get rid of him and I could tell
that Henry wasn't going to stop—he was feeling so . . . charged up
or something, and so I needed to do something. I don't think
there's anything wrong with that."

He sinks into himself as he finishes his rant and I have no idea
where the hell any of that came from or what I should do next.
Something about what Caleb just said is bugging me—demanding
that I pay it closer attention—but I can't quite place it. I push it

aside for the time being and try to do what I've been trying all along: be the Friend.

"Listen, Caleb," I start, not really sure where I'm going with this, "I'm sure Caitlin's grateful and everything, but you don't have to fight everyone's battles for them. Just because you got into a fight a while ago doesn't mean you're, like, the designated knight for the whole school."

Caleb shoots me a look.

"I know you don't really follow school sports or anything, but you know our mascot is the Knights, right? So I am, actually, literally a school Knight."

I want to laugh at this but instead the sour look on Caleb's face taps into my acidic side.

"Just because I don't come cheer you on at every game doesn't mean I'm blind, Caleb," I spit out. "I know our mascot is a knight, but that's a silly school symbol, not a fucking code you have to live by."

"Why are you so annoyed by this?"

"I'm not annoyed," I lie, "I'm just frustrated."

"What the fuck is the difference?" he shouts, and I guess we're doing this. We're having a stupid squabble about absolutely nothing in an empty park in the middle of February.

"Is this about breaking up the thing with you and Bryce way back?" he asks, saying "way back" like it wasn't a little over a month ago and we've been friends for ages. For some reason, that annoys me more.

"No, it's not about that," I say. I'm not sure *what* exactly this is about, but I'm not about to admit that to him. "I just don't get why you feel like you always have to step in the middle of these things. Don't you want to avoid getting into trouble again?"

"Yeah, of course I do." He's gripping his cup so tightly I'm worried hot chocolate will start flowing out of the top and burn his hand. "But I can't just stand by and let other people get harassed."

"I'm not saying you should, but that doesn't mean that it's your job to handle it. You should have just gotten a chaperone or something."

"I know it's not my job," he bites, "but I couldn't help it."

"What do you mean?" I demand. I know I'm being obnoxious—like a dog with a bone—but something about this conversation is rubbing me the wrong way and I need to get to the bottom of it. Caleb's free hand is clenching and unclenching on top of his thigh and that's when I realize why I'm so worked up. He's lying. Or, at the very least, he's hiding something. Whatever it is, he's not telling me the whole truth, and that stings.

"What do you mean you can't help it?" I ask again when he stays stony-faced. "You're sixteen years old, Caleb, I'm sure you can resist punching a classmate in the face."

"It just—it hurt too much and I lost track of what I was doing," he spits out. His face suddenly goes pale, like he only just realized what he said, and before I can even ask what the *hell* that means, he jumps in again, defensive.

"Never mind, you wouldn't get it," he grinds out, looking straight ahead and across the park toward nothing. Apparently, no one else thought it would be a good idea to sit outside in below-freezing weather in a park where all the plants died months ago. The bitterness of the air is making me impatient and irritable and I either need Caleb to start being honest with me or I need to leave.

Instead, I just poke more.

"I'm never going to understand if you don't tell me," I say, trying to keep my voice as even as possible. "I don't get why you're freaking out about this. What do you mean it 'hurt'?"

"I'm not freaking out, I'm—" And then he does that infuriating thing where he stops himself from speaking, snapping his mouth shut like he's trying to trap his own words.

"You're, what, Caleb? You're what?" I bark, turning to sit sideways on the bench so I can face him head on. I can see him better now, but the slats of the bench dig into my thigh like individual icicles. Heat is radiating off of Caleb's body and I want to burrow into it, wrap my arms around him, place my numb nose into the crook of his jaw. The impulse surprises me because it isn't the usual kind of "wrap my arms around Caleb" kind of impulse. He's in pain and I want to hold him, comfort him, tell him it's all right, but I can't. I don't know why he's hurting and so I can't make it better. I feel totally powerless.

It is the worst feeling I have ever felt. For a brief moment, I understand what my parents must go through on a daily basis with me and suddenly I'm unable to breathe.

"Nothing. Just forget about it, okay?" And with that, Caleb stands abruptly.

"No, come on, you know you can tell me stuff. What's bothering you?" I follow him, standing but not moving away from the bench. It feels like I'm holding something precious and fragile that a soft breeze could blow away, taking it from me forever.

"Nothing, okay? I'm sorry for—you don't need to worry about it." Caleb finally turns to look at me and there's something helpless in his eyes. "I don't want you worrying about it."

"I'm not worrying about it," I insist, even though I am. "I just want to know what's going on with you."

"There's nothing going on with me!"

"Yes, there is, Caleb!" I'm gripping so hard on the precious thing in my hands so that it doesn't float away that I just might break it instead. "And you never talk to me about it and I get that maybe you're not comfortable, but I'm not going to judge you or anything. You can tell me. I want to know."

"God, Adam," he exclaims, "just because you're a know-it-all doesn't mean you deserve to know absolutely everything."

That stings more than I'd like to admit, and I see my flinch reflected on Caleb's face. That bugs me even more—why should he look hurt over something *he* said?

"And just because you're the jock," I counter, "doesn't mean you *have* to be so emotionally stunted!"

The flinch is bigger this time and the bottom of my stomach drops out.

"You don't know what the fuck you're talking about," he bites.

"Look"—my voice drops—"I'm sorry, okay? I'm just confused."

Caleb closes his eyes and breathes deep.

"I know, I'm sorry, I—" He swallows his next words again and it makes me want to shake him until they fall out. "I'll—I'll see you at school tomorrow, yeah?"

"What—"

"I've gotta go meet my mom. Thanks, uh, thanks for the hot chocolate—" He's backing away now, color high on his cheeks, eyes darting around the way they do when he's nervous. He's about to bolt—the soft breeze has come and the fragile thing is being blown out of my hands.

"Caleb—" I start, not knowing what magical words could make him stay.

"I'll see you tomorrow, Adam," Caleb calls out as he walks backward away from me, before turning more nimbly than I would have thought possible. I'm left watching his hunched letterman-ed shoulders rushing away down the brick path.

Only when he reaches the edge of the park do I remember that he paid for our drinks and yet he was the one to say thank you.

I might be shit at this whole "being a friend" deal.

27

CALEB

"And that's when Principal Stevens broke us up and threw us out."

I deflate further into the couch as I finish telling Dr. Bright my story. Her hands are folding in her lap, the crease between her eyebrows as pinched as when I started. The traffic-cone orange of her worry has softened a bit, turning into that glowing pulse that always reminds me of my mom. It's cut through with the treacly syrup of pity. I want to snap at her, tell her I'm not some sad little boy who lost his temper, but instead I bite the inside of my cheek and wait for her to say something.

"You said you don't remember pushing Henry the first time— what happened, exactly?" Her head tilts and the pity gives way to bubbly curiosity. I relax at this return to normalcy—Dr. Bright trying to figure me out is way more comfortable territory than Dr. Bright worrying about me.

"I don't know, I just—I got so wrapped up in the anger, I guess. I pushed him before I even had a chance to think about it."

"Was it similar to when you got into the fight?" The orange glow pulses stronger, pushing the curiosity to the edges. Dammit. Why does she have to *care*?

"No" is my knee-jerk response, but then I think about it for a second. "Yeah, I guess, maybe a little. It's just hard when it's coming from all sides, you know? Henry was angry and Caitlin was angry and so was *I* and that just made it impossible to push away. I know you've told me to try and separate my feelings from everyone else's but it's really hard to do that when I'm feeling the exact same thing."

"Did Henry's and Caitlin's feelings feel like your own?"

I shrug again. "Not really. I don't know, it—it sort of hurt?"

"The feelings hurt?" A surge of traffic-cone orange.

"I mean, not *hurt* hurt." I squirm a bit on the couch, the heat lamp of her worry making me sweat. "Just, like, it didn't feel right in my body."

"You've experienced that before, correct?"

"Yeah, I guess, but this was just—it was just way more intense." I avoid looking at Dr. Bright because I can tell she's doing that thing where she just stares at me in silence until I start talking more. But I can't keep talking. I don't know what to say.

I don't know how to describe what it was like. I don't know how to explain the feeling of being squeezed into a space that's too small while at the same time being pushed apart by everything that's being poured into your body. I don't know how to tell anyone what it's like to be in the middle of trying to figure out your own feelings when all of a sudden, something you don't recognize invades every corner of you and starts tossing your stuff out to make room for their own.

It's having a stranger take you over except it's not a stranger, because you recognize pieces of it, you've felt this all before, except this isn't like that because it's not yours, it's theirs, and now you're stuck with a funhouse-mirror version of yourself living inside of you.

How the fuck am I supposed to explain that?

So I don't. I explain something else instead.

"Okay, maybe it wasn't more intense this time, maybe it's just that . . . I guess I thought I was doing better." I had meant to deflect but now there's something else bubbling up. "I thought I was, you know, regulating shit better, and I guess I'm not because this totally dragged me under and there was nothing I could do. I hate that, I hate feeling powerless and like I'm gonna fuck up and not even know it—not even have a say in what I'm doing. And I hadn't felt like that in a little while and, yeah, I knew that going to the dance might be risky but I like Caitlin, even when I don't totally like her feelings, but I just wish—"

I snap my mouth shut, only just realizing what I was about to say. Dr. Bright's curiosity is dancing toward me again, but it's shoved aside while I deal with my own surprise and confusion.

"You wish what, Caleb?" she probes.

"I wish Adam had been there." I breathe out, still taken aback by the truth of that statement. I didn't know that. I didn't realize that's what had been missing. That I'd been vulnerable to Henry's gross emotions because Adam wasn't there. "It's—it's easier when he's around or whatever."

"It's easier to regulate other people's feelings?" she asks, and my skin itches at the question.

"Yeah." I nod. "Yeah, it is. Is that—is that weird? That I like his feelings that much?"

Goddammit, another thing I didn't plan on saying. That wasn't what I meant at all. I meant to ask if it was weird that he made things easier but another truth came out instead, masquerading as a question.

"Do you think it's weird?" Dr. Bright tilts her head.

"I think this whole fucking thing is weird," I scoff.

"Caleb."

"I don't know, okay? I don't know anything!" My hands flop uselessly in my lap in my exasperation. "I don't know why Adam makes things easier or why I like being around him or if that's weird or if I should think it's weird or if other people think it's weird. I just know that it's been better this past month. Everything's been better."

The silent stare is aimed at me again—she knows I have more to say.

"And I guess I know that it's always sort of been there." I try to stay nonchalant. "Like, even before I got to know him, there was *something.* I didn't—it wasn't comfortable yet, you know? I didn't know how his feelings fit inside of me but there was something about them. Well, ever since this whole thing started up at least. I don't know that I ever really noticed him that much before. But then it was like . . . once my ability started up, it was like there was this buzzing feeling I could never turn off. It only got quieter when we were in the same room."

"Was it a good buzzing or a bad buzzing?"

"It wasn't good or bad. It was more that I just knew he was there. And then when I could tell his feelings apart from other people's, I was . . . I was curious, I guess. There was something about it that made me want to know more. And that's not usually how it is— normally, I just want to get away, be by myself. But, even when I don't get what he's feeling or he's feeling crappy, it's like his feelings make my own feelings make sense to me."

I'm grimacing at my own rambling but I don't know how else to put it. Something about Adam makes me feel whole in a world where other people's emotions make me into a human jigsaw puzzle where all the pieces are from different boxes.

"Like how we were talking about the colors a little while ago," I try to explain. "If he's blue and I'm yellow, being around him makes everything green instead of just a mess of a bunch of different colors smashed together and I guess . . . I guess I just really like being in that green place. It's just really . . . things are clearer when they're green. They're easier to understand. Like getting to the green helps understand the yellow even better, you know? God, that sounds really dumb, doesn't it?"

"It doesn't sound dumb to me," says Dr. Bright, and I don't feel the lie-detector buzzer go off. "It sounds like the two of you have a very meaningful connection."

"Yeah, whatever." I roll my eyes. "I'm probably just gonna fuck it up anyway."

"Why do you think that?"

"I'm pretty sure I already have. We hung out earlier today and I was *so* weird, I know I was, and I don't know what to do about it."

Silent stare. The rest comes out in a rush. Damn, why does that always work on me?

"I told him what happened at the dance and I was kind of sloppy about it and mentioned that I couldn't help getting mad at Henry and Adam didn't understand that—I could feel his confusion but also his, like, I don't know, his curiosity about it? Except it wasn't like the curiosity I get from you, it was sharper and rougher, like . . . scared, I guess."

"Suspicion?" she asks, her face perfectly calm. But underneath: bright traffic cone spike—no, a flare—a flare and a siren. I rush to put them out.

"No, no, I don't know if he's suspicious—I mean, that'd be a weird thing to be suspicious about, right? There's no way he could figure out what I am. But I think he thinks I'm hiding something. Which I am, but I don't know how to tell him it's not something bad without telling him what it is."

"Do you want to tell him?" she asks, and the flare glows steadily.

"I don't know," I say honestly. "I don't want to stop hanging out with him, I know that. But I feel like I'm just gonna keep being weird and he's gonna realize he doesn't actually want to be friends with me."

Dr. Bright puts her notebook down, folds her hands in her lap, and stays silent. But it isn't the kind of silence that's trying to get me to talk. There's anxiety coming from her but she's not nervous or scared. It's a quiet anxiety, like she's uncertain about something. Hesitant. I twist my own hands, cracking my knuckles and trying not to feel like I'm waiting for an ax to fall.

"Caleb," she says, not looking at me, which totally freaks me out. "You're very special."

"Oh boy, here we go," I mutter, having heard some version of this talk from her before.

"I just want you to be careful." She looks at me now, the orange concern replacing the hesitation. The flares and sirens are gone—this is warm, soft, caring concern, *just* close enough to condescension to make me itch.

"So that the people who are interested in people like me don't find me?" I snap, feeling that little zing of victory when Dr. Bright looks surprised. My triumph is snuffed out quickly by the towering black-red-orange burst of worry that catches in my throat.

"My parents talked to me a bit," I rush to explain, wanting to bring Dr. Bright down from whatever freakout she was about to have. Her shoulders rise as she takes a deep breath and the burst is gone as quickly as it appeared.

"It's not to say you can never tell anyone, Caleb," she says softly. "I just want you to be careful."

"Yeah, that's what my parents said," I grumble. Her sympathy sticks in my teeth like toffee. "But I don't understand—what's the worst that could happen?"

"You're not in danger, Caleb," she says, sidestepping the question completely. "But people like you are sometimes mistreated, and I want to avoid that ever happening to you."

Her words should freak me out but any fear is dampened by her cloying concern. I start to open my gummy mouth to ask more questions, but she quickly changes the subject before I can.

"Why don't we do some meditation?" I look up to see her smiling kindly at me, and it makes the toffee easier to swallow.

28

ADAM

I'm shooting lasers through the back of Caleb's neck in Latin but he has yet to turn around and look at me. Too scared to text him after the park yesterday, I walked into school determined to make things right between us. Instead I slunk to the back of the class-room and looked down when he rushed in late. I don't know how to fix things—I'm not even sure things need to be fixed. I've re-played yesterday over and over in my head and I can't put the pieces together. He got so worked up so quickly and I said something wrong without meaning to and now he won't look at me.

The class flies by without me conjugating a single verb, and be-fore I can shove my books back into my bag, Caleb is out of the classroom. I hurry to follow him, seeing his back move swiftly down the hallway, when I hear someone call my name.

"You okay?" I turn to look at Caitlin, confused as to why she's talking to me until I remember that we'd planned to do more de-bate prep during lunch today. Looks like I'm spending lunch in the library instead of at the table outside that I'd started to think of as *our* table. At least I'll be warm.

"Yeah, I'm fine." I shrug my bag onto my shoulders. "Just a little braindead from declensions."

"I always thought you were crazy for keeping up with Latin."
She shakes her head as she starts to lead the path down the hallway to the library. It's loud—lockers slamming left and right, sneakers squeaking on the scuffed-up linoleum, people making lunch
plans—but Caitlin doesn't seem bothered by the mass of bodies
and noise swirling around her.

What is that like? To move so confidently through the world
that you don't even flinch when a football goes soaring over your
head?

And then I remember Caleb's balled-up fists when he was de-
scribing how Henry was harassing Caitlin at the dance and realize I'm being narrow-minded and petty and just because Caitlin
swishes her hair over her shoulders effortlessly as she glides through
school doesn't mean she never has reason to flinch.

She's talking about how Spanish is so much more valuable than
a dead language like she's trying to sell me a Rosetta Stone and I
resist the urge to roll my eyes.

"You're not wrong," I agree, "but I've got those pesky doctor parents who have lofty medical school dreams for me, so Latin was
pretty much *the* option."

"Ah." She nods sagely and looks sideways at me. "Aren't parents
fun?"

I half smile as we step into the library. It's like entering a weird
parallel dimension where everything is muffled and musty. The
noise from the hall fades away as we move through the shelves to
the back table that we've been studying at for the past few weeks.
We sit down, pulling out our lunches and settling into our usual
debate prep rhythm, placing index cards strategically around the
table and cracking open our notebooks. Technically, eating isn't
allowed in the library but, as always, no one is here. Not even the
librarian.

"How was your weekend?" Caitlin asks around a bite of her
sandwich.

"Eh"—I shrug, also chewing—"it was all right. Nothing eventful."

She hums like she knows I'm being coy and I realize the next step in this conversational waltz is for me to ask her about her weekend. But I already know. And I feel weird about that. Should I tell her I know? Or just wait for her to tell me? Caitlin and I aren't friends, per se, but working on debate these past few weeks, we've become friend*ly*. If I'm really doing the whole friendship thing with Caleb, who's to say I can't have more than one?

"I heard the dance was pretty eventful." I swallow, peanut butter sticking in my throat, colliding with the anxiety that's already balled up there.

"You did?" She looks up from the notecards and I give a sort of sympathetic grimace to let her know I'm on her side. "Oh, Caleb told you?"

"Yeah." I nod, swallowing again, trying to get the peanut butter down. "He felt pretty bad about the whole thing."

I shouldn't be spilling Caleb's feelings to her but I need to talk about it with someone, *anyone*. I'm lost and confused and worried that everything Caleb and I were building is ruined, and I need a little perspective.

"He shouldn't," she snaps, before sighing, her shoulder slumping. "Henry was the one being the jerk. Caleb did what he thought was right. He probably didn't need to take it quite as far as he did but . . ."

"At least it didn't lead to an actual fight," I finish.

"Right." She nods. "Though it was pretty close. If Caleb wasn't going to hit him, I honestly might have. It's good the chaperones intervened when they did." She looks uncharacteristically downtrodden and I feel that powerless feeling again.

"I don't think anyone would blame you for laying into Henry," I offer. "In fact, a good portion of the student body might throw you a parade."

She smiles a bit at that, pushing aside her sandwich to work the ponytail magic on her hair. I'm about to steer the conversation to the work we need to get done, but Caitlin's frowning down at her notes, her mouth twitching like she wants to say something.

"You and Caleb are friends, right?" she asks, looking up at me.

"Um, yeah." I nod, playing it cool, even though my stomach is swooping at the thought that other people see Caleb and me as friends. It's not all just made up in my head. Caitlin has noticed. "Yeah, we hang out sometimes."

"Do you ever—" She stops herself but it's not like when Caleb does it. She's not swallowing around something that wants to burst free, she's being tactical. Years of fierce competition for the top spot in the class have made me very familiar with Caitlin's tactical face.

"Do I ever what?" I press, completely unable to guess where this could be going.

"Do you ever get, like, a *weird* vibe from him?" I must look offended because she rushes to elaborate. "Not bad weird, just . . . I don't know, he's just . . ."

The back of my neck is prickling. I think I know what she's trying to say. But there aren't even really words for it. The fact that Caitlin is having a hard time explaining the uncanniness of Caleb comforts me a bit, but it also freaks me out. If she's picked up on something too, then it's not just me being overly dramatic.

"Really perceptive?" I offer when it's clear she's not going to finish her sentence.

"Yes!" she shouts, eyes wide. The sound echoes in the abandoned library and we both flinch at the loudness.

"Sorry," she whispers, "sorry, I just—yes, that's exactly it. He's *perceptive*. Weirdly perceptive."

"Does that bother you?" I ask.

"No, not really, it just kind of catches me off guard sometimes, you know?" Caitlin's shoulders relax as she leans back in her chair. "I've just never met anyone who knows what's going through my head like that. After the fight, we walked around the field so he could blow off some steam and he was—he just knew exactly what I was feeling. It was unreal. And also, like, a little embarrassing."

"What do you mean?" I ask, suddenly very curious. Caitlin's face is getting red and she's picking at the corner of her notebook, a nervous habit that seems out of place with her easy confidence.

"Just . . ." Her face reddens even more. "Like, we were having an okay time, you know? Just walking around the field and talking. And he'd been so nice the whole night, standing up for me and everything, and I sort of thought . . ."

"Oh," I say, as I realize where she's going. "Right."

I would very much like to evaporate now, please.

"And he knew," she continues. "He knew I was thinking about, I don't know, kissing him or something, and before I had a chance to say anything or *do* anything, he turned me down."

"Oh," I say again. Caleb turned Caitlin down? *Caitlin Park?* Oh god, stupid hope, what are you doing here? Go away go away go away—

"And, I mean, I guess it's nice to save me the embarrassment," Caitlin says, the heat starting to leave her face, "but it's not like I was being obvious about it. At least, I don't think I was. But he just blurted out that he wanted to just be friends, and the way he said it . . . I don't know, it felt like he'd read my mind."

"Yeah, he does that." I shrug, feeling increasingly weird in this conversation. I suddenly want to hear more about what he said—if he gave an explanation for just wanting to be friends—but it's starting to feel like talking about him behind his back.

"He does it with you too?" Caitlin asks, looking at me finally, and the awkwardness in the air intensifies.

"Yeah, a bit. Sometimes." I pull my notebook closer to me and click my pen. "We should probably get to work, we only have, like, twenty minutes left."

"Right, yeah, of course." She nods and transitions into school mode and a breath of relief collapses out of me.

I drop my bags on the kitchen counter and go digging into the cabinets for coffee. It's now been two days without talking to Caleb and I'm starting to lose it a little. I hadn't realized how dependent I'd become on Caleb—on our lunches, our texting, me sending him music and him not understanding half of it. He didn't make things better, necessarily—he didn't chase away the clouds when they loomed heavy and dark over me—but he did make it easier to ignore the impending storm. Caleb makes me feel clever. He makes me feel interesting.

I spent hours tossing and turning in bed last night, picking up my phone to text him before putting it back down. I did that over and over again. I still haven't texted but neither has he, so I'm not sure what to do.

I do know that caffeine is desperately needed if I'm going to get all my schoolwork done but, just as I reach up for the nice espresso beans my parents keep for after-dinner coffee when they have friends over, I hear my mom's voice.

"Adam, what are you doing?" She sounds amused, probably smiling at the fact that I've got my knee on the counter, my other leg dangling in midair as I reach up for the bag like a little kid going for the cookie jar.

"Nothing." I hop off the counter and put on my best innocent face.

"I thought we agreed you'd cut down on the coffee," she says sternly. "Half a cup in the morning is fine but that's it."

"I just didn't sleep all that well last night and I have a lot of work to do," I explain, like that will actually convince her. She reaches around me to shut the cabinet before opening another and pulling out a box of tea.

"How about a nice cup of Darjeeling," she says, not asks, already pulling the kettle from the stove and moving to the sink to fill it with water. I sag against the counter and nod.

"Did you have a good day at school, sweetheart?" she asks, her back to me as she turns on the burner.

"Eh, it was all right." I pick an apple up from the counter and start absently passing it back and forth between my hands. "How was yours?"

She doesn't answer right away, which causes me to look toward the stove. Her shoulders are tense and there are a few curls poking out from her usually perfectly coiffed updo. When she turns around to grab mugs from the shelf, I notice the bags under her eyes like bruises on her dark skin.

"Mom?" I'm instantly alert. "Are you okay?"

"I'm fine, darling." She shakes her head like it will cast off whatever's haunting her. "Just a—a tough day at work."

"What happened?" I try not to sound too curious but I'm sure I fail—though I don't take as much interest in the sciences as my parents would like, that hushed conversation in the dining room still looms large in my mind. Not to mention, I haven't seen my mom look this burnt out in a while.

"We just received some bad news about one of our projects, that's all." She smiles weakly at me.

"Does this have to do with the guy you worked with that was going to try and debunk your research?" I ask, desperate to get more of that story.

My mom looks surprised at the question, like she didn't expect me to have that information.

"Did your father tell you about that?" she asks. Whoops, guess Dad never filled her in on our conversation. She doesn't look angry or upset though. Just intrigued.

"Yeah," I admit, looking back down at the apple still in my hands, "a little. He didn't tell me all that much, just that you guys were frustrated with this person."

"Yes." She nods. "We certainly were. That's all resolved, thankfully."

"So then what's the bad news?" I press. Her mouth is a thin line as she puts the tea bags in the mugs.

"Adam," she starts, voice in Serious Talk mode, "what your father and I do, it's very complicated."

"Okay . . ." I draw out the word, hoping she'll give me more than that.

"And it's also very secret—"

"Yeah, I know." I roll my eyes, really tired of this speech. "You guys sometimes do research outside of the hospital for, like, the government and stuff. But, come on, you're brain surgeons, not spies. I don't get why everything has to be so top secret."

"Brains can be top secret depending on whose brain it is," she says, matter-of-fact.

"Well, *that's* a fucking creepy thing to say," I blurt.

"Adam," she gasps, "language!"

"Mom," I say, laughing humorlessly, "you're talking about top-secret brains, I think I can swear."

"It was a joke," she deadpans.

"Sure," I say skeptically. A slow snake of steam hisses out of the kettle, bolstering the tense silence that's descended over the kitchen.

She turns off the burner and slouches onto the counter next to me in a gesture so casual that I'm reminded my mom is actually a human being and not just the lady who runs my life and takes care of me. When did my parents become *people?*

"Someday," she sighs, "I'd love to tell you everything about our research. I know you never like coming to the hospital and that you don't have a love for science like we do—"

"Despite your best efforts," I mutter under my breath.

"But"—she ignores me and moves to take the kettle off the heat—"I think you'd find some of our research interesting. And some of it is important for you to know."

"What do you mean?"

"There's things about the world that you don't know," she says.

I turn to look at her, to find a completely blank expression—her professional mask pulled down. God, I hate that face. I'm used to seeing it directed at patients at the hospital or other doctors, but never at me. Seeing it now makes me feel small.

"Then just tell me," I plead, wanting her face to soften and for her to be my mom again. The professional mask hardens into a faraway look that makes her seem ten years older before she tilts her head to look at me. All the smoothness fades as her expression crinkles, eyes warming. There she is.

"Not yet. I'm going to protect you as long as I can." She gives me a small, sad smile as she pushes a cup of tea into my hands.

"Mom, you're kind of scaring me," I admit, trying to keep my voice steady. I take the scalding mug from her, hoping the warmth will make me feel less unsteady in this conversation.

"I'm sorry, love." She brings her hand to my face, patting my cheek. "I didn't mean to." Her hand travels to my shoulder, which she squeezes, looking at me with the intensity of love that I'm pretty sure only parents possess.

"Today . . ." she begins, before taking a deep breath and starting again. "I've been helping out on something in an unofficial capacity. An—someone I know who's worked on some of our projects has a patient who's in a coma."

"Haven't you worked with lots of coma patients?"

"Yes," she says, "but this is a little different. It's a very unique case and I was consulting to try and find a way to wake this person up. I thought I'd cracked it but today—we tried something that I thought would work and it didn't."

"Oh," I say like I understand. "That was the bad news?"

"Yes."

"But you'll just try something else, right?" I suggest hopefully, hating the defeated tone of my mom's voice. "I mean, there's gotta be something that'll work."

"We've been trying for two years and . . . nothing." She shrugs like "that's just the way life works sometimes" and I want to shake her. That's *my* job. To get knocked down and refuse to get back up. Rebecca Hayes is supposed to *fix* things.

"I'm going to keep trying," she insists, seeing the way I deflate, "but I'm getting very frustrated. And he's—it's a young man. Not as young as you, but in his twenties. Too young to be trapped in his own body."

"God," I breathe, "that must be awful."

"Yes, I imagine it is," she agrees grimly.

We stand there, our backs leaned against the counter, drinking our Darjeeling in a bleak silence. I want to ask more questions—*know* more—but I also want my mom to wrap me in a hug and tell me the world isn't a scary place where the most brilliant minds I know can't help a twenty-something in a coma. I also want to put my arms around her and tell her it's going to be okay, that she doesn't need to worry about me, that I'll take care of her. But I don't do any of that.

I stare straight ahead, pressed shoulder to shoulder with the woman I call Mom, but who is known by most other people as the brilliant Dr. Hayes. There are always things I thought I could count on but, here I am, standing in the kitchen I grew up in with a woman I realize I barely know, and it occurs to me that maybe I don't know anything about the world at all.

29

CALEB

Wednesday dawns frosty and dark. Well, okay, I guess it doesn't dawn at all, then. I hate this time of year—waking up in darkness, coming home in darkness—the whole world made small and cold and claustrophobic. The lack of light makes everyone's feelings press in on me, and most days feel like being trapped in an unlit meat locker with hallucinogenic gas pouring in from the vents instead of air.

It's been a bad week. And, fuck, it's only Wednesday.

I've been trying to lie low after the whole Sadie Hawkins mess, but any time I stop to think about the weekend—the almost-fight, Caitlin's butterflies sitting on top of the acid from the dance, her face when I blurted out that I didn't feel the same way she did, the fight with Adam, the fact that Adam still hasn't texted—I want to sprint out my front door and run and run and run and never look back.

But it's been impossible to run away with the memory of the fear-anger-hurt cocktail from both Henry and Caitlin still fresh on my tongue. It's left a bad aftertaste in my mouth that I haven't been able to shake in four days. Getting that close to losing my temper again has brought everything close to the surface in a way that makes me skittish and worried. School is a nightmare. Well, more of a nightmare than usual.

I pull myself out of bed and go through the motions of breakfast with the fam. My parents are a whirlwind of activity, my mom packing her briefcase up before I've even scarfed down half my Eggo, and my dad on the phone with his editor about his newest pages. Alice and I roll our eyes at each other from across the breakfast table but our hearts aren't in it. There's a manic energy in the house, made more urgent by the soft darkness that's just beginning to lift outside.

"So, weirdo," Alice quips around a mouthful of cereal, "get into any more fights this week?"

"Shut up," I mumble, not in the mood for Alice's jabs.

"Jeez," she says with a groan, "so sensitive this morning."

"It's early," I bite back.

"It's always early," she says sagely. "What's got you all worked up?"

"What do you think?" I gesture to the parent-created chaos around us and Alice winces, I think in solidarity. I'm having a hard time getting a read on what she's feeling—there's too much interference. Mom and Dad are both in high-stress mode—a buzzy caffeine feeling that I'm sure makes them productive but that just puts me on edge.

"So when's that weird goth kid coming back?" Alice asks. I choke a bit on my waffle.

"What?"

"The guy who was here Friday." I can hear the unspoken "duh" in her tone. "He seemed cool. I liked his T-shirt."

"Oh, are you a Twenty One Pilots fan now?" I laugh. "How do you even know that band?"

"I'm twelve, Caleb, I know how to use the internet, *god*." She gives me a particularly pronounced eye roll. "So . . . is he, like, your new best friend or something?"

"Don't be stupid." I give her an eye roll of my own. "I'm too old to have a best friend. And, besides, we kind of got into a fight this weekend, so . . . I don't know."

There's no rational explanation for why I tell her this, other than I'm desperate to talk to anyone about it. I haven't spoken to Adam since the park on Sunday and it's driving me nuts. For the past few days, I've felt him staring daggers into my back and he's still upset but I can't even tell why anymore. I don't know if he's upset from our argument or because we haven't talked since or because he's decided he doesn't want to be friends anymore. Whatever it is, I don't know how to fix it.

I know the solution to this is to get close enough to get a better read on his feelings, but I'm terrified of the answer. I was acting pretty weird and harsh on Sunday and it wouldn't surprise me if he just decided I wasn't worth the trouble.

"Dude, did you spend your whole weekend getting into fights?" Alice snaps me back to reality. A spoonful of cereal is lifted halfway to her disbelieving face.

"It wasn't that kind of fight," I explain. "I'm not even sure it *was* a fight."

"You know," she says dryly, "you're getting a lot better at explaining yourself."

"Shut up," I groan, "I just—I was all worked up from the dance and I told him about it and he didn't get why I was so angry at Henry and I sort of let slip that it hurt and I couldn't help it and then he wanted to know more about that and I snapped at him and left."

"Smooth," Alice deadpans.

"Alice—" I stare at her pleadingly, not having the patience or the energy for her smart-ass antics this morning.

"Have you tried, I don't know, *talking* to him?" she asks, like she knows everything.

"No," I admit. "His feelings have been kind of jagged—like sharp *toward* me—and it hasn't seemed safe to approach."

"You should talk to him," she says sensibly.

I take a sip of orange juice, avoiding eye contact with her. Alice's feelings are starting to edge toward pity, and looking at her will just make it ten times worse. She doesn't usually feel bad for me like this—that sticky, sunset-colored gum that clogs up my joints—so I must look pretty glum.

"Yeah," I assure her. "Yeah, I will."

But I can't. School is a toxic whirlwind of emotion and I can't block it out. There's the prickly static of stress, face-melting embarrassment, dripping hot-cold sludge of shame/disappointment; twisty, twirly butterflies. My body is a mess. I want to burrow further into myself. I want to tear off my own skin.

Ever since the dance, everything's been right on the surface. Feelings swoop in and mix around and I'm too off-balance to regulate it. The thought of having a voluntary conversation with another human makes my stomach roil. The thought of simply *being near* another human makes me want to crawl underground.

The prickly, face-melty, dripping, twisty emotions combine to create a thick, poisonous molasses. Sometimes socializing—sometimes simply being—is like having liquid anise poured into my veins, until my blood runs thick with it and all I taste from my tongue to my toes is black licorice. I hate black licorice.

Somehow, all of that just makes me miss Adam *more*. Yeah, his emotions are overwhelming and sometimes unidentifiable, but they *fit*. It's like a Picasso painting. All the pieces don't fit together—the eyes, the mouth, the nose—they're in the wrong place, the wrong shape, the wrong size. But the whole thing together just makes sense. Looking at a Picasso painting, you get what that guy was going for. It's a whole person. Sometimes Adam's feelings get inside of me and show me my odd, misshapen bits but in the process, it's like being put together. The thought of having lost that makes my stomach churn.

The lunch bell rings, my morning gone in a haze of jumbled body parts that don't quite make a face, and I bolt for the exit, not even stopping at the cafeteria to get something to eat. The cold air hits me like a wall as I burst out of the doors, clearing a bit of the bitter taste from my pores. I inhale deeply, closing my eyes and letting the noise from the hallway fade as the door shuts behind me.

I walk toward my lunch bench absently, shaking my head like I'm trying to get water out of my ears. I'm tired and wrung out but I also feel whole in a way that I haven't felt all week. I'm watching my feet, concentrating on the sound of my shoes on the hard ground, when something comes out to greet me. Soft. Blue-green. Hesitant. Warm. I want to lean into it.

I look up from my shoelaces as the bench comes into view.

Adam.

"Hey," I say, my steps slowing. He's sitting on the bench like he has been for the past month and I'm both relieved and resentful of it. I don't want to deal with any potential emotional minefields right now. I just want to sit in peace for thirty minutes until I have to go back into the swirling vortex of doom that is the student body today.

But the blueness fills me up, rounds my edges, and clears my head. The black licorice gets replaced with glorious green and, no, I was wrong before—*this* is what being whole feels like. Adam's emotions clear out everything; they quiet the infinite noise of the world and let me find the yellow parts of me that hurt. Residual anger here, stress about my math exam there, social anxiety all over. It's all mine and I haven't had a chance to look at it the entire day. It isn't lost—the Picasso painting is actually a face and I'm more content than I've been all week.

"Hey," I hear Adam say, sounding like he's underwater. I shake my head again as he keeps talking.

"I hope it's okay that I'm sitting out here." He comes into focus as the haze clears. "It's Pizza Wednesday."

Before I even consciously make the decision, the green is pulling my smile up. The warm, soft feeling grows in my chest, butterflies swooping in as Adam gives me the slightest smile. One corner of his mouth lifts a bit but his eyes are glowing as I swing my legs over the bench seat. I know I'm giving him a big smile and not saying anything like a complete freak, but the rush of butterflies rising into my lungs keeps me from caring. Minutes ago I was drowning in molasses. Now I'm flying.

The other corner of his mouth twitches like he's trying to keep the butterflies in too and he glances down at his plate, his dark eyelashes casting shadows on his cheeks.

I've never wanted to kiss anyone more.

Oh.

Oh.

"Caleb?" He's far away again as I hear blood rushing in my ears. "Caleb? Are you okay?"

The cold, blue spike of his worry is like dunking my head into a bucket of ice and I snap out of my own thoughts. He's looking at me again, the sparkle gone from his eyes as they fill with concern.

"Yeah," I grunt, my voice sounding not like me at all. "Yeah, I'm fine. Sorry, I—"

I can't tell him that I was thinking about leaping across the table and kissing him but I need to say something to explain why I've been—I'm assuming—staring at him, open-mouthed and blank, for the last few seconds.

"I just realized I didn't actually get any pizza," I say.

"Do you want my other slice?" he offers. That tentative smile is back on his face. He's looking at me fondly—like he *missed* me— and I feel like I need to sit down. I *am* sitting down. Jesus, get it together, Feelings Boy.

"Um, yeah," I say, "thanks."

He pushes the pizza toward me and I reach for it, heart in my throat as I think about what would happen if I brushed my hand against his. But by the time the thought finishes crossing my mind, his hand is picking up his own slice and lifting it to his mouth. His mouth that I'm totally not watching like a creep now.

Oh my god, *what* is happening?

"So." He chews, putting the slice back down and wiping his hands on his jeans. There's a bubbling anxiety rising up my esophagus so I stuff pizza in my mouth to try and shove it down.

"I want to apologize for Sunday," he finishes.

"What?" I nearly choke. "Why? I was the asshole."

"I think we can agree that we were both assholes," he says, and I want to argue but I don't. He's right. If I'm being honest, Adam hurt my feelings too. And that hurt was buried under *his* hurt and sometimes my life is just so unfair. But I can't explain that to Adam so I don't know how to apologize for hurting him.

"But I think it's safe to say that I was the bigger jerk," he continues. "I'm sorry for prying. Your business is your business and I shouldn't have pushed."

"No." I shake my head, wiping the grease from my mouth with the back of my hand. "No, I'm sorry for being so weird. You were just worried about me. I get it, I can be kind of . . . obtuse sometimes?"

"Obtuse?" The butterflies surge and I can't even begin to guess what that's about.

"You're not the only one with a vocabulary," I tease, and he laughs, just a little. It sets me on fire. But not in the lava anger way. This is a green fire lapping at my skin, keeping me warm and making me want to get up and jump around, like I'm stepping on hot coals.

"I'm very impressed." He smiles and it's like sinking into a hot bath. Comforting and all-encompassing. He fiddles with his watch and I'm hypnotized by his fingers pulling on the strap. They're skinny and trembling slightly, like they were in my bedroom when we were picking out an outfit for the dance. I flash back to the moment on my floor, with my arms on either side of his body, and instantly feel like I'm going to throw up. But in a good way. Is that even a thing?

I really like Adam. As in, *like* him like him. A lot. I like the way he barely ever fully smiles and I like how excited he gets about Shakespeare and I like the way his feelings feel.

The butterflies are rising through my body again as Adam takes another bite of his pizza. They're lifting everything up, pushing everything out to make room for the fluttering. My heart isn't even beating anymore—it's been replaced with light, flapping wings that send pure light into my blood vessels.

"Are you okay now?" he asks, mouth pulled down in concern. I know he's worried from the expression on his face, not his feelings. I can't find that worry anywhere in my body. Everything is drowned out by the tingling in my gut. And suddenly I'm seized with the anxiety of who it belongs to. Is it Adam's? Does he get nervous and light-headed when we're together too? I hope he does, but at the same time, if this is his feeling, then maybe it's not mine. Maybe Adam likes me and that's what I've been feeling this whole time and I haven't had a genuine emotion of my own in months except for the fucking anxiety I'm feeling right now and I realize I haven't answered Adam's question but right now I want to throw my pizza down and never stop running.

"Yeah," I lie. "Yeah, I'm good now."

"Wow," he deadpans, "you really are one of the worst liars I've ever met."

"Shut up," I mumble and, just like that, things are normal again.

Adam complains about the epic round of college tours his parents have planned for spring break ("A week in the car with my parents, Caleb, what the hell am I gonna do?") and I tell him about how Caitlin stood up to her dad for me when he was pissed that we got kicked out of the dance. I make it sound ridiculous—like Mr. Park was one step away from pulling out a shotgun—so that I can see Adam laugh again. We spend five minutes straight speculating on what Mr. Collins does with his weekend ("I bet he plays Scrabble against himself," Adam says) and complain about our Latin exam.

I feel full with a happiness that's laced with impatience. My knuckles have turned red from a combination of the cold and my constant hand-rubbing, but I'm reluctant to put them into my pockets. Adam's hands sit on top of the table—constantly moving, picking at the corner of his juice carton, curling into the edge of his watchband—and I like looking at our hands on the graffitied wood slats of the table, inches away. I can't feel the warmth from his hands but just imagining it drives me to distraction. It would be one quick move to put my fingers through his but I'm too paralyzed with fear and the fragile hope that's bloomed inside of Adam (inside of me? I'm beyond being able to tell). He's happy. He's happy that we're talking, that we're here, sharing space and *being*.

And I'm happy. I'm happy for those same reasons or maybe because he's happy but I'm not sure there's a difference.

Far too soon, the bell rings and we start to make our way back inside. There's a string between us, drawing me closer to him as we walk through the doors, and my stomach is churning at the thought of breaking that connection and going to my next class. I don't want to go away from him.

And then Adam asks me if I want to hang out this weekend and he smiles in that way that sits more in his eyes than in his mouth and I can feel the warm rush of joy, pure blue-green ocean water filling me up and clearing the anxiety away, and I realize that I'm not strong enough to break the string, even if I wanted to.

30

ADAM

I wake up with a dull throbbing behind my eyes. I keep them closed, breathing deep, hoping it will go away. It doesn't.

I should check my phone—did my alarm go off? Why am I awake? What time is it? Do I need to be at school? Panic climbs my ribs like a ladder. I should check my phone. I don't.

I could roll over. That would be so easy. Just roll over, open your eyes, reach one hand out to grab your phone. That's nothing. You can do that. You don't even have to leave your warm blanket cocoon.

Turning my body one hundred and eighty degrees is completely impossible. I'm too tired. I didn't get enough sleep. I got too much sleep. I should go back to sleep. If I have school, my parents will come get me. I should get some rest.

I don't.

It's five minutes later, twenty minutes later, two hours later—who knows?—when I remember that it's Saturday. Good. I can just stay here. I don't need to check my phone. I can stay here and sleep.

———

My brain is cataloguing every detail of the pattern on my wallpaper like it's memorizing the information, but the moment it enters my brain, it evaporates. My head is empty. My head is too full. I'm drowning.

A loud crash jerks me awake—when did I fall asleep again? Was I sleeping? I hear my dad yell, "Sorry! Sorry, I'm fine!" from the kitchen, where it sounds like he's making breakfast for twenty people.

Oh shit. My aunt Annabelle is coming over today for brunch. I'm supposed to be up for that. A new wave of anxiety fills me but my body immediately rejects it. I don't have the energy to be anxious. A blessing and a curse.

"Adam?" my mom calls from the hallway. "If you're up, could you go help your father with breakfast?"

To call back or not to call back, that's the question. Well, no, actually the original version stands in this situation—to be or not to be. One of the most famous lines and, in my opinion, kind of the wrong question. It's not "to be or not to be," Hammie—you *are*. Whether or not you like it. The question is *how*?

While I'm lying here contemplating *Hamlet*, my mother knocks on my bedroom door.

"Adam? Sweetie?"

If I don't answer, she'll come in to wake me, and I don't have the wherewithal to face another human right now.

"Yeah," I shout, my voice tense, "I'm awake."

She says something else that gets lost somewhere between my closed door and my ears processing sound and then I hear her move down the hall. I need to get up now. I need to get up and get dressed and help my dad and hang out with my aunt and be the functioning human my parents so desperately need me to be.

How, Hamlet? Help a brother out.

———

The next thing I know, I'm sitting at our dining room table, pushing eggs around my plate, trying to work up the strength to eat them. I don't remember getting eggs. I don't remember sitting down. There's little spots of white and green mixed in with the yellow—my dad has made scrambled eggs with cream cheese and tarragon. My favorite. The thought of eating any of it in this moment makes my stomach roil.

Why the special eggs this morning? Are we celebrating something? Sound makes its way through the cotton in my ears—voices, two women, one man—and I look up blearily from the mess of food I've created in front of me. Oh. That's right. My aunt is here. I knew that.

"Adam," a muffled voice says, "do you not like your eggs?"

A deep inhale through my nose brings the scent of coffee into my brain, shaking my consciousness a bit. My dad is talking to me. I have to respond. If I don't say anything, that will be suspicious and, as much as I don't have the energy to deal with my parents now, I *definitely* don't have the energy to deal with them on high alert.

"Yeah." I flash what I know is a weak smile in the direction of my dad. "Yeah, sorry, I just don't think I got enough sleep last night."

They know it's a lie, but as long as I'm present enough to be lying to them like a teenage son is supposed to do, their worry will be at a minimum. That's the important thing. Just keep them from worrying.

It's not that they don't have reason to worry.

When things got to be too much I would need to let some of it out. By whatever means necessary. All that toxic feeling, the anxiety, the walls closing in; those could all be briefly solved with a sharp edge. Heavy, rib-crushing weight would descend over me and the only way to relieve it was by opening myself up.

But sometimes the problem wasn't that things were too much. Sometimes they weren't enough, and a blade could fix that too.

Because I don't wonder "to be or not to be" and I don't even always wonder "how." There have been times when the question is: "Am I?" Times when I can't feel my own heart beating in my chest, when the color gets sapped from the world, when opening my eyes feels like running a marathon. I never know if I'm going to snap out of it, if I'm ever going to feel anything ever again. I always know I should feel afraid of being trapped in that gray world forever, but I never have enough energy to feel fear.

I don't know what's worse—feeling like the world is going to end or feeling like the world isn't even worth ending. All I know is that cutting into my skin helped. Until it didn't.

I don't do it anymore. Okay, I don't do it anymore *much*. The summer before my sophomore year, I was trying to carve out my loneliness from my torso and my shaking hand pressed too hard. One hospital trip and parent-induced rehab later, it feels like so much more of a risk. I always knew that it was something I shouldn't be doing, of *course* I knew, but that didn't matter. The guilt and shame that came after each time didn't outweigh the relief from doing it in the first place. Until that summer.

The fear on my parents' faces my whole sophomore year, combined with the various coping mechanisms group therapy gave me (I've baked more in the past year than all other years combined), have kept me on the straight and narrow. I may sneak it in here and there when things get particularly bad, but apparently the potential of disappointing my parents is terrifying enough to block out all the other stuff the majority of the time. Causing myself pain means nothing to me. Causing them pain is unacceptable.

"So, Adam, how is your semester going?"

I hear the clinking of Annabelle setting down her fork before my brain processes her question. She's looking at me with the laser focus that she seems unable to ever switch off and it sparks just a bit of life in me. I like when Annabelle looks at me like that. It makes me feel important, puts me on my toes. Talking with my aunt is like debating with Caitlin—frustrating and rewarding in equal measure.

I wish Annabelle weren't here today. Or I wish I wasn't like this right now. My body is completely unable to understand or feel that exhilaration at this moment.

"Um," I stutter, caught off guard by all of a sudden having to interact with the people I'm eating breakfast with. "It's going well." I pat myself on the back for saying "well" not "good"—if I thought I was a freak about language, I'm nothing compared to Annabelle. She uses it like a weapon.

"I hear you're in debate club?" Of course that would interest her. If words are her weapons, debate club is like a gladiator stadium.

"Yeah." I nod, the scrape of my fork over my plate keeping everything in focus. Out of the corner of my eye, I see my mom's hand tighten minutely around her knife. Right. She hates the whine of utensils against dishes. I should stop aimlessly moving my cutlery around. But my mom won't call me out on it. She would never do anything to make Annabelle think that she has a less-than-perfect family.

The competitive spirit between my mom and her sister makes me and Caitlin look like kids on a playground. Annabelle works some high-powered job where she's in charge of a bunch of people—I honestly have no idea what she does—but she lords her upper management position over my mom even though my mom has about two more degrees. They're constantly measuring their careers against each other, one wordlessly trying to one-up the other. I'm pretty sure my mom uses the fact that she has a spouse and kid as a way to get more cosmic life points against Annabelle. But Annabelle also knows that she's my favorite relative and she buys me books I actually want to read, so I might be a bit of a draw as far as pawns go.

Honestly, how did anyone expect me to be adjusted and not filled to the brim with neuroses with role models like these?

"I'd love to come see you compete sometime." Annabelle smiles, all teeth and no spark in her eyes. The tension hasn't left

my mom's hand and the air in the whole room is thick with stress.
Did I miss something? Mom and Annabelle's monthly spat? Did
my dad say something dumb? Or is it me? I'm not doing a good
enough job of pretending to be human and they're starting to
notice and soon the weight of their collective concern is going
to fall from the sky and crush me. I have to get the situation under
control.

"Um, yeah," I say, doing my best to inject enthusiasm into my
response and almost certainly failing. "Yeah, we've got a competition next month sometime."

"Son"—my father's stern voice cuts through the tension before
layering on more—"are you sure you're all right?"

"Yeah," I repeat, "I'm totally fine. Sorry, I'm just a little distracted today."

"Fun plans for your Saturday?" Annabelle asks, her smile finally
warming her eyes. She winks at me and I want to appreciate it—
want to goof off with my aunt in these rare moments when she lets
her hair down—but it just makes me flinch.

"Uh, no, not really." I shrug before my whole body involuntarily
seizes up in panic. I'm supposed to see Caleb tonight. He's coming over. He's coming over to *my house* and I haven't even asked
my parents about it yet because by the end of school on Thursday,
a damp cloud had descended over me and I've spent the last
seventy-two hours wallowing in it.

The conversation at the table has moved on—Mom and Dad
are talking about one of their newest areas of potential research
and Annabelle looks deeply interested in a way that makes me
think she isn't only looking for weak spots in my mother's pride.
There's no further inquiry about my weekend plans because "um,
no, not really" is par for the course when it comes to the life of
Adam Hayes. My parents don't expect me to have friends. They've
tried—getting me to sign up for more extracurriculars, offering to
let me throw small (read: very pathetic) parties at the house—but
they know a lost cause when they see it.

"What about Caleb? What's he doing this weekend?"

How much time has passed? Did they finish talking about work so soon? I look up from my plate again to see three pairs of highly intelligent adult eyes staring at me. I replay the last thirty seconds of my life, trying to remember what was happening around me as I was being pulled further into the dark spots of my body.

Conversation came to an abrupt halt—my mom cut my dad off as he was saying something. But not to interrupt something—to make him stop talking. Because *I'm* here. They must have been discussing some of their top secret stuff and then remembered that I'm also present and put the kibosh on that. Damn, I should have been paying a lot more attention.

Now I see my mom's question for what it is: a desperate attempt to change the subject while there are minors present. I should never have told her about Caleb. Except I've been to his house and we hang out in the coffee shop and the park and my mom knows I almost never go anywhere. If I'm not around here or at school, she can guess where I am.

"Um," I start, knowing I need to say *something*. Guess I should just jump in with both feet. "I actually invited him to come over and hang tonight, if that's okay."

My parents *beam*. It's like a switch gets flipped and light comes on in their faces. My body summons up the energy to be just a *little* insulted by that when it occurs to me that this is the first time I've had a friend over in . . . years. It's been years. So, yeah, okay, they have every reason to look happily surprised.

"But I don't know that we're doing that for sure," I blurt, wanting to dampen their expressions so I don't have to be blinded. "We didn't make any concrete plans or anything."

"Well, text him," my dad laughs. "Make concrete!"

"Who is this person?" Annabelle asks, rolling her eyes at my dad ever so subtly.

"He's a friend of Adam's." My mom grins. "Very nice young man. Football player."

"Mom, what?" Panic seizes me again. "How do you know that? You haven't even met him."

"Your school isn't very large, sweetie," she says, matter-of-fact. "It wasn't hard to look him up. And I assume he's a nice young man because he's friends with you." She doesn't even give me the courtesy of looking ashamed at how embarrassing literally every part of that statement is. I want to crawl under the table.

"Ooh, football player." Annabelle smirks. "Is this *nice young man* a potential paramour?"

Now I *really* want to crawl under the table. My mom and dad exchange one of their Looks, this time with a disturbing twinkle in their eyes. Oh god, am I that obvious? Of course I am. Everyone and their mom (including mine) knows that I have a crush on Caleb. Apparently, the only person who *doesn't* know is the boy himself.

"No," I say, blushing, "it's not like that, we're just friends."

A few more speculations about Caleb's character are made and then some general commentary on how nice it is that I'm bonding with someone from my class. I nod and grimace through it, but the moment I see an opening, I lie about needing a shower and bolt upstairs.

I *do* need a shower, but the thought of it exhausts me. Turning on the water, getting undressed, getting in, washing my hair, drying myself off, getting dressed again. It's so much work. Too much. Instead, I reenter the cocoon of my bed, with no intention of ever coming back out again, even though I know Annabelle will want to catch up more at some point. I spare a second to wonder how long she's staying today before even that takes too much energy.

The brief flashes of panic I felt at the thought of Caleb during breakfast have worn off, leaving an empty shell behind. I'm tired on a primal level. I'm tired in a way that makes me feel like I am carrying the missed sleep, the physical toil, the mental anguish of all of my ancestors. I should text Caleb now and tell him that he can't come over tonight, tell him that I've got homework or family time or I'm too depressed to function.

I can't say that. I know I can't tell him the truth. Because that's not how we work as a society. We don't have the liberty of telling each other, "Hey, I'm having a depressive episode so I'm sorry for being distant or weird or useless or making myself bleed. I wish I could say that this is a one-time thing and will never happen again, but it isn't and it will. I don't want to be around you right now or during those times at all, but I would love if you took care of me and sat silently in the corner of the room for when I need someone to hug me. You will get nothing in return except for maybe my friendship when the cloud lifts and I can be human for two seconds. Hope that's all good with you!"

But we don't say that. We say, "I'm fine." We say, "It's nothing." We make excuses that we know aren't true and that *they* know aren't true but we both pretend anyway like we've all agreed to have this collective hallucination together. And it gets us nowhere.

There's a tiny, weak voice in the back of my head that's saying maybe Caleb would understand. I want to believe it. And it's true, Caleb is a surprisingly . . . sensitive guy, but I don't think we're at the point where I can just dump all this stuff on him.

Then again, will I ever get to that point with anyone? What does that look like? Do my parents tell each other about all their ugly, self-loathing thoughts, the times when even taking a sip of water feels like climbing Mount Everest, the feeling of sharp tension that comes with being around other people? Do they even feel those things?

Maybe they do. Maybe they *did*. Maybe this is normal and every person my age feels like this. Maybe this eventually goes away. Maybe I'll wake up one day and be Daydream Adam, excited to take on the world. I'll roll over in bed with complete ease, smile at my husband, whistle while I make coffee, and go to a job that I love and never want to hurt myself ever again.

That same voice telling me I can trust Caleb is whispering these dreams to me. Like a little spark in my chest, frail and flickering, causing me to hope. But it's no match for the vaporous black cloud that permeates my lungs. The cloud throws the spark into darkness until all that's left is an echoey voice murmuring, "It will always be this way. You don't get to change this. You don't get to leave this behind. You will remain in this oppressive nothing. Always."

31

CALEB

Adam's house looms over me like a storm. I shake it away, chalking it up to the overcast sky affecting my mood, and walk up the front path to the door. A blue mist snakes out of the house, wrapping its way around my head, muffling my ears and threatening to choke me. I swallow around it, closing my eyes as I try to adjust. This is Adam's. I think. It's heavier, more present than ever before, but it feels like him.

I knock on the door. No answer. I knock again before noticing the doorbell button next to the mailbox attached to the front of the house. I push it, hearing the chimes through the closed door. No answer.

This might have been a bad idea. Adam invited me to hang out when we smoothed things over on Wednesday, but I didn't see him the rest of the week and it's dawning on me that just showing up at his house without hearing from him is sort of a strange move.

God, what if he's not even here? The sun is starting to go down, making it feel like it's much later than it actually is, and my hands are stinging in the cold. I shove them into my pockets just as the blue haze gets thicker—it's not a fog anymore, it's a wave. Breathing functions are hard to access for a few seconds and I struggle to maintain my balance, as the feeling is almost a physical force pushing me backward, away from the door.

This was *definitely* a bad idea.

There's a shuffling sound coming through the door and I see a shadow in the window. Either someone is coming to answer my knocking or I've interrupted a serial killer in the middle of a spree and this night is about to take a turn. The wave—roiling, hot-cold, suffocating—has set my teeth on edge and made my eyelids heavy. Despite the chill and decreasing daylight, there's a part of me that wants to lie down right here on Adam's front stoop and go to sleep forever.

The turn of the door handle wakes me up a bit and a familiar dark-haired head pokes around the corner. Adam's curls are more of a mess than usual, and it makes my stomach twinge. I want to soothe his hair, make it look less crazed, but I also want to indulge running my fingers through it. He looks like an odd, black-and-white version of himself—sapped of color, full of contrast; circles under his eyes, his freckles black against the unnatural paleness of his dark skin. He squints at me around the door like he's looking into the sun and it makes me itch, the blue getting into my blood vessels and making me skittish.

My system is rejecting whatever this is instead of slotting it into place like usual. It feels different—bigger and more unruly. I push through it to try and focus on what's in front of me, the reality of the moment. Adam's long fingers curl around the edge of the door as he pulls it open wider and it's like the door was a barrier between us, keeping his emotions at bay. Now it all rushes in, the suffocating blue with the bitter taste of nervousness.

"Caleb," Adam croaks, "what are you doing here?"

"Sorry." I throw up my hands in a placating gesture, like I'm trying to calm a spooked woodland creature. "I thought we were hanging out, but if this is a bad time . . ."

"Shit," he breathes, "I meant to text you. I'm sorry."

His words are apologizing for not texting but the strain in his voice makes it sound like he's sorry for something much bigger. Black sludge seeps out of him, mixing with the blue wave, creating a slow whirlpool that numbs me as it sinks into my skin. As I watch him press his eyes closed, I realize what that uniquely sharp sludge is—he's disappointed in himself. He thinks he's let me down.

"It's okay," I assure him, "we can hang out tomorrow if you want—"

"No." He steps over the threshold as if to stop me from leaving. "No, I mean, you're already here. You might as well come inside."

"Are you sure?" I ask.

"Yeah." He nods sluggishly and turns back into the house. I follow slowly, worried that if I step in the wrong place, I'll drop into the whirlpool and drown. The house is dark and quiet, making the wave that's pressing down on me even stronger. But I'm soothed by the lack of light. These feelings rushing through my body don't want to be seen.

Adam turns to me, hands stuffed in the front pocket of his hoodie, and I feel the familiar butterflies. But they flap wearily, like they have delicate wings that will be torn to pieces by the sludge if they move too quickly. I want to ask Adam what's wrong, why he's feeling this way, but before I can—

"Do you want anything? Water, or . . ." He trails off and then pulls one of his hands out of the hoodie to rub at his face. "Sorry, I'm a little out of it, it's been a long day."

"Everything okay?" I ask, even though I know the answer is "no."

"Yeah, it's fine," he lies, and I don't even need to feel the buzzer of nervousness to know he's not telling the truth. "My aunt was over today for, like, the *whole* day and she can be kind of intense so it was just tiring."

"Is she still here?" I ask, even though I'm getting the impression that *no one* is here. Not even Adam, really.

"Nah." He shakes his head. "She and my parents went to some event for a charity they're all involved in or something. I don't know, I wasn't really paying attention when they told me about it."

"I get that." I snort and Adam's lips twitch like he wants to smile but doesn't have the face muscles to pull it off. I rock back and forth on my heels, not sure what to do. This should be awkward—the

two of us standing silently in his front hall with all the lights off—
but everything's too dampened for me to feel weird. I just feel sort
of . . . numb.

"Um." Adam's voice breaks the silence, too harsh for my ears.
"Wanna go upstairs and watch a movie or something?"

"Yeah," I agree, "that sounds good."

As we walk up the stairs, I think about how I was hoping I could
finally show Adam how to play Madden, but now even the thought
of picking up a video game controller exhausts me. When we enter Adam's room, I don't have the energy to look around. I'm in a
place I've thought a lot about in the past few weeks—wanting to
explore Adam's space, learn more about him, understand him—
and all I want to do is lie down on the floor and stare at the ceiling
until I fall asleep.

I get pretty close to that wish. We sit sideways on his bed with his
laptop between us, watching something on streaming. I think it's
funny but I keep zoning in and out. I'm losing time. I don't know if
I've been here for twenty minutes or two hours. I don't know how
many episodes we've watched or even if what we're watching *has*
episodes.

Adam's body is warm next to mine, our shoulders barely touching as we each lean slightly to get a better angle on the screen. It
should comfort me, being this close to him. It should excite me.
But the warmth is dulled by the steady stream of sadness coming
from him. That's what it is. It's sadness. Not the vague, general sadness that sometimes lurks around him, distinctly his but not especially dangerous. This is enormous. There's a thick, soupy fog
gathered around both of us, so large that I'm not even sure Adam
is there. There's only fog.

It's bigger than him and bigger than me and I'm starting to
worry his parents are going to come home from their fancy dinner
to find our mummified corpses on his bed.

". . . Caleb?" A soft voice is calling to me but my eyelids are too
heavy to open. The voice says my name again and my neck spasms,

caught in an awkward angle. I lift my head and open my eyes to find Adam's face startlingly close to mine. My eyes drink his face in, my whole field of vision filled with the brown warmth of his skin, his hair, his eyelashes, his eyes, and then my brain catches up and I jerk backward.

"Sorry," he says, face crumpling. "I just—I have to go to the bathroom and you were . . ."

He gestures to our relative positions and I realize that I'd fallen asleep and somehow ended up with my head on his shoulder. My face heats as he mumbles, "So . . . be right back," sliding off the bed and leaving the room.

I blink a few times, shaking my head to clear the fog. How long was I asleep? I'm still tired all over, but calmer. Sleep can do that for me—detox other people's emotions and leave me at a baseline of my own feelings. I do a mental and physical check—my body is a bit sore from falling asleep sitting up (I must have dozed for a while), but the fog is a little less thick. It isn't gone, just . . . plateaued.

My thoughts are interrupted by Adam reentering the room.

"How long was I out?" I ask, stretching my arms out in front of me.

"Only, like, half an hour." Adam shrugs, climbing back onto the bed.

"Fuck," I exhale. "Sorry, dude."

Everything about this is *so weird*. I've been here for hours and we've said about a total of twenty words to each other. I'm feeling like a bad friend but also like Adam is being a bit of a bad friend by not telling me what's going on with him. But I don't know if that's what people do. Is sitting in silence and then falling asleep normal friend behavior?

Adam is queueing up something else on his computer, very pointedly not looking at me, and I'm suddenly filled with anger. I know it's irrational, but I'm ticked off that Adam hasn't even made an effort to talk to me. If he didn't want to hang, I gave him an out. He didn't have to invite me in just to ignore me.

"What the hell is going on with you?" I ask before I can stop myself. Shit. This is why Dr. Bright keeps telling you to check in with your own emotions, Caleb. So that when they come rushing back, you don't say stupid-ass things.

"What do you mean?" Buzzing starts under my skin as Adam looks at me out of the corner of his eye. I've made him nervous. Good. Maybe he'll actually start talking to me then.

"You've been weird all night," I argue.

"Well, *sorry* for not keeping you entertained," he drones, but I feel the swirl of anxiety and self-disappointment as he says it. Shit, now I feel bad.

"No," I say, backpedaling, "I didn't mean—I'm just worried, I guess."

"Worried?" he scoffs. "What the hell does that mean?"

"It means that I can fee—" I bite the words back, changing the shape of them in my mouth before I speak again. "I can see that you're drowning and I don't know what to do about it."

Adam looks like he's been slapped. Feels like it too. There's the caffeine jolt of fear, a toxic addition to the sludge sundae we already have going on. I want to take it back, want to apologize, but my own frustration is still strong enough to be drowning everything else out.

"If you don't want to be here, Caleb, you can just leave." He fails to meet my eyes and the fear evens into a steady stream.

"That's not—" I'm getting even more frustrated now. "I don't want to leave, I just want you to talk to me. I'm just—I'm here."

Adam's jaw clenches as his eyes wander the room, looking at anything but me. I want to grab his face, steer it toward mine, rattle it and not let go until the truth starts falling out of his head.

God, if this is how Dr. Bright feels when getting me to talk, I owe her, like, a thousand apologies.

"It's not your problem, Caleb." He shakes his head and my frustration wanes a bit. That's the second time he's said my name, and it makes the fluttering in my stomach rise.

"I'm your friend, aren't I?" I say gently. "You know you can tell me stuff."

"Oh really?" he snorts. "Isn't that exactly what I said to you? And you don't tell me jack."

Okay, he has a point there. I know better than to try and win an argument against Adam, but this is so not the same as me not wanting to tell him that I have a superpower. Not that Adam knows that, but still.

"I tell you lots of stuff," I counter, even though I don't tell him anything about the biggest thing in my life.

"But you're hiding something, I know you are." Adam turns to look at me now, his gaze burrowing into me as the fog makes room for annoyance.

"Well, apparently so are you!"

"I don't want to talk about it," he mumbles.

"Neither do I."

We're sitting side by side, arms crossed, not looking at each other, both filled with irritation and sadness, and I'm just about to get up and leave when Adam says—

"We're being assholes again, aren't we?"

My body releases a breath I didn't realize I was holding, my shoulders coming down from up around my ears. I turn my head slightly to look at Adam. He glances up at me through his eyelashes, face set and stubborn, his mouth a tense line.

"Yeah," I sigh, "I think we are."

"Why is this so hard?" he groans.

"What?"

"Being a person."

I wish I could answer him, but I don't know how to be a person either. Sometimes I feel like I'm not even human, but instead some sort of emotion-meter with legs doomed to be crushed under the weight of other people's problems.

Adam is looking expectantly at me, which flatters me as much as it bothers me. Why should I have the answer? I like that he thinks that I have the answer. But I don't. I want to.

"I don't know," I say honestly.

"Yeah," he sighs. "I know."

He exhales like he's seen all the woes of mankind for centuries—
like he's carrying the entire world on his bony shoulders. I want to
reach out and touch him. Take his hand or smooth down his hair
or hold him close until the bags under his eyes disappear.

"Are you sure you're okay?" I ask, genuinely not knowing for
once. The fog is still there, but it's paled, becoming lifeless and
limp where it was once an aggressive, all-consuming force. Adam
feels withdrawn—distant in a way that makes my insides ache.
Even when I get pulled under by the tide, I miss his feelings when
they aren't there.

"Almost never," he laughs darkly. My heart clenches in pain—
my own pain. I would give anything to make Adam okay.

He glances up at me again, before rolling his eyes at my worried expression. He sighs again, quick and overblown, his cheeks
puffing out in drama.

"I don't know," he says after a moment. "It comes and goes in
waves, you know?"

"I do." I nod vigorously to keep from laughing at Adam's choice
of words. "I really, *really* do."

"There's something strange about you, Caleb." He squints at
me and I feel a small curl of curiosity bend out of him and tickle
my ribs. I should be worried that I've shown my hand—that he's
getting suspicious—but then I feel a bit of that good blue softness
stretch out of him and meet my yellow. Suddenly, we're in that
green space and the tiniest ghost of a smile is trying to come to
life on Adam's face.

I look away, instantly shy at the swell of positive feeling between us. It's fragile and precious and I know if I open my mouth
I'll ruin it.

"I don't think that's a bad thing, by the way," Adam says, and I
can hear the small grin in his voice. I want to see it, so I look at
Adam again and the butterflies reenter my stomach, stronger and
more welcome than ever. The desire to reach out to him grows and
Adam is looking at me like he's thinking the same thing. His face
leans closer to mine just a fraction and time stops. There's a fizzy

feeling in my chest but before I can do anything about it (or let him do something about it), panic takes hold of my body and I flinch back.

"Caleb?" Adam's voice is small and I feel the hot rush of embarrassment wipe out all the butterflies like a meteor.

"I'm fine," I lie on autopilot (it's always a lie). "I just—I remembered that I promised my dad I'd help him with something tonight before bed and it's getting to be that time so I should go."

A fight-or-flight response has kicked into gear without my permission and, before I know it, I'm hopping off the bed and moving toward Adam's bedroom door.

"Oh"—Adam stands too, blushing—"okay, yeah, I'll, uh—I'll walk you out."

He does and it's awkward and we just stare at each other when we say good-bye instead of fist-bumping or waving or, I don't know, *hugging* like normal fucking people who might have kissed five minutes ago if one of them hadn't totally freaked out. Half an hour later I'm lying in my own bed wondering what the hell my own weird-ass behavior was about.

I wanted to kiss Adam. I'm . . . adjusting to that. That thought has come up a few times and it's like, that's cool. *That* I can do. I think. It's been a long time since I've kissed somebody. And I haven't kissed anybody since my ability started up, so that's a whole other wrench to throw in the machine.

I've also never kissed a boy. But that's less of a concern than I thought it would be. Like, it doesn't even fucking register as something to worry about. Adam's face makes me feel a certain way—a way that I didn't feel looking at Caitlin at the dance—and that hasn't happened in a long time and who cares if his face is male-shaped.

No, the problem is that I think Adam wanted to kiss me too. Again, not necessarily a problem. For most people—most *normal* people—that would be a good thing. The person you want to kiss wanting to kiss you should be all high fives all around. But it's got me second-guessing everything. What if Adam's wanted to kiss me for a long time? What if the only reason I want to kiss him is because he wants to kiss me?

God, what if none of my emotions are my own? Even now, in my bedroom alone, I can feel my parents and Alice. It's faint but it's there. I haven't been alone with my own feelings in months. How on earth can I trust them?

32

ADAM

"You don't have to listen but I thought it might be good for when you guys go to away games," I explain, trying to look Caleb in the eye despite the fact that I feel like I might throw up. "I know the team kind of drives you crazy sometimes. Especially on the bus. So this can be, like, you know, like a distraction or whatever. And you've got that scrimmage coming up this weekend so . . ."

I've become more inexact in my language since meeting Caleb. But I can't blame him and his inability to communicate clearly (though I do blame some other things for that). He makes me nervous. I'm *always* two steps behind.

Like this past Saturday night. A night when I'm having a particularly bad time and he's cool about it. Yeah, he asks questions, but he doesn't judge me or run away. He sits with me and doesn't make me talk and I'm so grateful that I almost feel better. And then I *do* feel better, the cloud lifts just a tad, and we have a Moment and he gets all weird and leaves.

I want to chalk it up to gay panic. That Caleb could see my feelings written all over my face and had a hetero-freakout. It's Occam's razor: the simplest solution is usually the correct one. Caleb now fully knows that I have a crush, and was trying to be sympathetic to my feelings by excusing himself (un)gracefully.

But something in my hind brain is sending up the alarm at that straightforward (pun not intended) solution. I wasn't lying when I said there was something strange about Caleb. Something . . . queer. And not in the current version of the word (though I'm still holding out hope on that front too)—in the "odd or unusually different" way. If I had spidey sense, it would be tingling all the time around Caleb.

He's holding the thumb drive I just handed him like it's something precious and unfolding the piece of loose-leaf paper I'd pulled from my notebook in first period and hastily scrawled all over. I should explain more—tell him he doesn't have to read my reasoning for why I picked these songs (*please* don't read this in front of me)—but my brain is stuck on Caleb and tingling so I don't hear what he's saying until he's halfway through his sentence.

"—cool. Thanks." He looks sideways at me as he pulls a textbook from his open locker. His cheeks are getting redder and redder and my stomach clenches in fear. Have I embarrassed him? This was meant to be an olive branch—a way of saying, "Don't worry about Saturday, I promise I'm not like that all the time and I won't try to kiss you ever, let's just be friends"—but what if he thinks playlist-making is some sort of overture? That I'm hitting on him with music?

Oh god, that's *exactly* what I'm doing.

"Hey, listen." Caleb closes his locker and turns to me, face serious. Here we go. Caleb was trying to let me down easy and now comes the flat-out rejection. I should have seen this coming when Caitlin told me about the dance—if he doesn't want her, he's definitely not going to want me. I'm just relieved that this is happening between classes, that soon the bell will ring and this won't be a drawn-out process.

"I'm sorry about Saturday," he says. "I didn't mean to just bolt out like that but I—I just had stuff I had to do."

"Oh," I say, confused.

"Yeah," he continues, "it wasn't anything to do with you, I was having a really good time. I mean, I know I fell asleep and every-thing"—he blushes harder—"but it was fun. Thanks for having me over. Or, you know, for letting me in when I just showed up with-out texting first."

"Yeah, of course," I say, "you're always welcome." I'm speaking on autopilot, turning into the consummate host that my parents have raised me to be. My mind is racing. I'm relieved at Caleb's words, but how did he know exactly what I was worried about? Two steps behind turns into five steps behind and I want to tear my hair out.

"Are you—" he starts, hesitant for once, instead of trying to keep the words in. "Are you okay? Like, after this weekend, are you—"

"Yeah," I rush out, "yeah, I'm fine."

He looks at me skeptically, a muscle in his jaw jumping like he's mad.

"You're lying," he says, matter-of-fact.

"Isn't everyone always lying when they say they're fine?" I quip.

"You have no idea." His eyes roll heavenward, his voice heavy with wisdom that he has no right to have. He brings his gaze back down to my face. "But you don't have to lie to me. I don't want you to."

"Haven't we been over this?" I ask, starting to get irritated by the double standard of information flow between us.

"I just . . . I'm here, okay?" he repeats. "Just—if you ever need anything. If you want to talk or whatever. I'm here."

His green eyes are big and earnest and I was not at all prepared for this level of sincerity this early on a Monday morning. Now *I'm* the one blushing and I look away, feeling vulnerable under the scrutiny of his strange x-ray vision. I mumble something in response—an agreement, a thank-you, a deflection, who knows—and it makes him smile a little. That's good enough for me.

The bell rings and Caleb thanks me for the playlist again, put-ting the flash drive into his pocket. He asks me if I want to get lunch later and I nod automatically before he gives me a little wave and goes down the hallway to his class. I watch the back of his head as he walks away, hoping that if I stare hard enough his skull will open up and all his secrets will come spilling out.

33

CALEB

I have a new nightly ritual. I lie on my bed, stare at the ceiling, and think about Adam.

I'm pathetic.

Dr. Bright is always telling me to meditate, and I don't think I can really claim to be doing that, but it's the same idea. Meditation is just so *boring*. Who wants to sit in silence and think about nothing? *How* do you do that? I guess that's the point—clearing my mind is supposed to help me figure out how to balance emotions so that I can be around other people without blowing my lid—but yikes. What a yawn.

So, no, I'm not meditating, but I *am* trying to clear things out a bit. I have to wait for everyone to be asleep before I can wipe my body of feelings that aren't mine, which means that I've been staying up late and then getting less sleep, which makes me less able to balance, which then makes it harder to clear stuff out. It's not the perfect system, but until I can drive myself to the middle of nowhere, it's all I got.

And, hopefully, I *will* be able to do that soon. Mom and Dad are still insistent that I stick to the learner's permit and only drive when they can be there to help. They're worried about road rage, which, yeah, okay, I get it. Maybe being on the road with a bunch of other people while operating heavy machinery is not the best idea for me. But, god, it's annoying to have to take the bus everywhere.

Anyway, back to the nightly ritual of obsessing over Adam. Maybe obsessing is the wrong word. I'm trying to . . . puzzle it out.

I pull the track list he wrote for the playlist he made me out of my pocket. It's crumpled from me shoving it in and out of my pocket for the past four days. I smile as I play with the frayed edges of the paper, reading it for the hundredth time.

Just something to keep you company on the bus—Adam

1. "Can't Feel My Face"—The Weeknd (I don't know if you even realize you're doing it, but you mouth along with the words every time this song comes on.)
2. "Hard Out Here"—Lily Allen (yeah, yeah, it's a girly song, but Lily speaks true.)
3. "Here"—Alessia Cara (I don't think anyone has ever described so well what it's like to party with our classmates. At least, I assume, I don't know; you're the one who actually gets invited, you tell me.)
4. "Strawberry Swing"—Frank Ocean (I know you love Coldplay, but trust me—once you hear this, you'll never go back to the original.)
5. "Grade 8"—Ed Sheeran (idk, this song just reminds me of you.)
6. "Water Under the Bridge"—Adele (all hail Adele—this is my favorite off her new album.)
7. "You're Not the Only One"—Jamie Cullum (words to live by.)
8. "Super Trouper"—ABBA (I'll always be in the crowd in spirit.)

The whole thing is just the most Adam thing that Adam has ever done. He was nice to listen to me complain about how team bus rides drive me up the wall (without a concrete explanation for *why*) but he didn't need to come up with a solution for it. And he definitely didn't need to write out the songs on the playlist and give his reasoning, but that's just who he is. It's well thought out and explained, sentimental but also snarky—reading it is like feeling his feelings. Like feeling his *best* feelings—the times when he's laughing at me or talking about the book he's reading or . . . or looking at me.

I move from the notebook paper to look at my phone, pulling up the texts we exchanged after I first listened to the mix.

> So . . . do you like the mix?
> *You have the weirdest music taste I s2g*
> What do you mean? Most of it is songs I KNOW you like.
> *ABBA???? Really??? ABBA???*
> . . . okay, yeah, the ABBA was all me.
> But you liked it right?
> Caleb?
> *Yeah of course I fucking liked it. It's abba.*
> *Don't tell the team.*
> Your secret is safe with me.
> . . . super trouper.
> *Ur a dead man.*

Reading over the texts, my heart does that stupid thing again where it spasms and it sort of hurts but it also makes me feel energized and nervous, like the way I feel before a big game. Are we flirting? Is that what's happening? I think I might be. Ever since that moment at our lunch bench after our fight, there's like a neon sign inside of me saying, "You like him!! He makes you feel the butterflies!! You want to kiss him!!"

But what if I don't? What if the only reason that sign is glowing is because Adam's the one powering it? The butterflies feel different from the ones I felt from Caitlin—I don't have the impulse to immediately squash them—but I'm still filled with uncertainty. Dr. Bright would say this is why meditation is important—that I need to clear my head in order to understand what *I'm* feeling. But closing my eyes and imagining a river with leaves floating down it or whatever isn't helpful for me. Instead I lie on my bed and stare at glow-in-the-dark stars on my ceiling.

I feel the last of my family members drift off to sleep—my dad, I think, it's always my dad—and my whole body exhales. I do a mental and physical check of myself. I'm tired (what else is new), a little sore from my run earlier (but not in a bad way), and just a bit hungry (again, what else is new). Basically, your standard.

The emotional check is a little more complicated. I'm stressed about a history quiz I have later this week but, in general, looking forward to school tomorrow. That's new. New-ish. And I know exactly why school doesn't fill me with dread anymore like it did at the beginning of the semester. It's because of Adam.

Which leads me to the heart of the matter: what are my feelings about him?

I want to be around Adam all the time. I think about him constantly, I miss him when he's not there, and when he *is* there I want . . . more. I let myself imagine for a second what that would be like and my breath catches in my throat, the pit of my stomach aching. Out of all the feelings I've felt—and I can safely say that it's been a lot, the whole gamut—I've never felt anything like this.

And he's not here. He's miles away, probably in his own bed staring up at his own ceiling, and every cell in my body wants to be next to him. That's a feeling *I'm* feeling, right now, alone in my room. I don't have the excuse of his emotions influencing mine— there's no one else to blame. There's no one else to thank. This is mine.

This is *mine.*

A strange mix of relief and anticipation swirls in my body. Finally, I have something that's my own and it's *good* and no one can take that away from me. It doesn't matter how much other people invade me every day—fill me with things I'd rather not feel, confuse my head and my heart—because this is mine.

But what do I do about it? That's a totally different, terrifying question. A question I'm not sure I'm even at yet. Because it feels dishonest to try and be with someone when I'm only sharing part of who I really am with them. I mean, everyone keeps secrets. But this feels like a *big* secret.

I want to tell him. I *have* to tell him. If I ever want to be more than just Adam's friend, he deserves to know the truth. On Sunday, I'm going to talk to Dr. Bright about it, and if she thinks it's all right, then I'm going to tell him. And then I can tell him how I feel and everything will be fine. No: *better* than fine. Things will be good because I'm pretty sure he feels the same way. As long as he doesn't freak out about my ability, things will be great.

Thinking about it makes my heart leap into my throat in anxious anticipation. The thought of Adam knowing—of *anyone* outside my family knowing—terrifies me. But I can do this. I can be brave enough. Because the alternative—keeping a huge secret from someone who I think is turning into my best friend—just isn't acceptable. I was able to tell Caitlin I just wanted to be friends. I can tell Adam my biggest secret and that I want to be *more* than friends. I can. I'll be brave.

34

CALEB

I am a total coward. Before I know it, almost a month has gone by since Dr. Bright gave me the go-ahead, saying, "If you trust him, you should tell him," and I've stayed completely quiet. School got busy and spring training got intense and Adam was constantly stressed out about his big debate competition (which he totally nailed like I knew he would) and there just hasn't been a good opening.

But today is Adam's seventeenth birthday and I feel like I might spontaneously combust if I don't tell him soon. And, let's be real, with everything Dr. Bright has accidentally hinted at about her other clients, that might be a possibility. We still don't know that much about this—for all I know, I'm gonna get worked up extra bad one day and just burst into flames. That might honestly be preferable over this constant state of standing in the open doorway of an airplane, wanting to jump but being too paralyzed with fear to take that final step.

But first I have to go through the doorway in front of me. I hear footsteps and the creaking of the heavy door on its hinges, opening to reveal Mr. and Mrs. Hayes's smiling faces.

"Come on in, Caleb." Mr. Hayes pats my shoulder as I step over the threshold. I'm bombarded with questions about how I am, about how my parents are, how's school going, so nice of you to come over, Adam's just in the kitchen he'll be so glad to see you—I lose track of the actual words as their excited voices are drowned out by their feelings. Energized nervousness, hopefulness, and the warmth that comes from people's bodies when they're trying to make you feel comfortable.

I've met Adam's parents exactly once before, when they dropped him off at my house a few weeks ago. They came in for about two seconds to do the whole hand shake so nice to meet you thing with my parents and kind of look me up and down before going off to whatever fancy dinner they had that night. Adam's parents go to a lot of fancy dinners.

Standing in Adam's front hall right now is the complete opposite of that night. The first time, they'd been stiff and formal— all dressed up and awkwardly polite to my drab-by-comparison parents. My parents are smart and accomplished and all, but the Hayeses are that kind of smart that makes you feel nervous the moment you make eye contact. Adam is the same way—there's a fierceness to how smart he is. The conversation in our doorway— because the Hayeses never came in far enough to justify closing the front door—was short and devoid of any actual substance, but it lasted long enough for me to know that Adam's parents were suspicious of me. They had their walls up—easy for me to find because they're built with the same bricks as Adam's defenses— and didn't thaw by the time they waved a polite good-bye.

I didn't tell my parents this, that the Hayeses were wary of us. But I think they could tell. They would never admit it, but my parents were a little intimidated. I definitely was.

But now, here the Hayeses are, warm and grinning at me. There's a swirl of bubbly happiness and a frenetic orange stress radiating from them. The wall is gone—they are inviting me in (literally and figuratively) and I'm thrown by being cast in the role of "person to impress." I know what wanting parental approval feels like, I feel it basically any time a classmate interacts with their folks (and sometimes when they interact with certain teachers). It's a desperate, jittery energy, like drinking a soda that's too sweet. This is like that except the Hayeses *are* the parents and I'm the kid, and the topsy-turvy ride I got on when I entered the house is starting to make me feel nauseated. I need Adam.

Like simply thinking it summoned him, soft blue starts cutting through the gummy air, wrapping around me like a shield. My shoulders relax as Adam appears in the doorway to the kitchen, brow furrowed and holding a wooden spoon covered in what looks like chocolate. Our eyes lock and the lines between his eyebrows soften as he gives me the little half smile I've gotten so used to. The response in my body is instantaneous—the blue-green wave washes over me completely, clearing me out and lifting me up.

"Hey," I croak, my throat clogged from the stuff that's been bogging down the atmosphere in the house.

"Hey." His smile grows a little stronger.

"Uh." I blink, knowing there's a next step to this dance but forgetting what it is. Then it clicks.

"Happy birthday," I blurt out awkwardly, taking a step toward him, the hand holding his present—which I'd forgotten about until right now—hanging stiffly at my side.

"Thanks," he says. The blue-green lightens and expands, changing the colors on the butterflies darting between us.

"What's with the spoon?" I ask.

"Oh." He looks at his hand like he'd forgotten he was holding anything. "I'm making a cake."

"On your birthday?" I ask, confused.

"Yeah, of course." He grins and I feel the warm breeze that comes along whenever Adam wants to tease me. "That's kind of *the* day to do it."

"Usually people don't make their own cakes," I counter, unable to stop myself from grinning back at him. He has a buoyancy that I haven't felt in weeks and it's making me carefree and happy.

"I like baking." He shrugs, pleased with himself.

"Adam wanted to make sure the cake was perfect and he doesn't trust his old man to do it right," Mr. Hayes jokes, reminding both Adam and me that his parents are still standing between us.

"Dad," Adam moans, rolling his eyes.

"Okay, okay"—Mr. Hayes throws up his hands in surrender—"I concede, you are the better baker." A brief beam of pride shines from Adam. "So I'll go and deal with the boring dinner stuff. Are you all done in there?"

"Yeah," Adam says, "just put this back with the frosting?" Mr. Hayes takes the spoon from Adam and walks toward the kitchen, making a show of running his finger through the chocolate and taking a taste, winking at me and smiling big. I laugh politely at the dad humor but Adam is oblivious, which is probably for the best, given the quick, hot jab of embarrassment that shot up when Mr. Hayes spoke.

"Why don't the two of you go into the living room and I'll make sure Elijah doesn't burn the house down." Mrs. Hayes shakes her head at the sky and waves an arm toward what I assume is the living room before turning to follow her husband.

Adam shoves his hands in his pockets and rocks back on his heels. We give each other awkward, no-teeth smiles, unsure how to be around each other with his parents making a racket in the kitchen. Adam shrugs and swivels his head in the direction of the living room, his body trailing after like he's being pulled by a string.

We sit down on the big couch, which is so much less comfortable than it looks. I feel stiff, like we're pretending to be adults who come over to each other's homes for their birthdays and sit on settees and talk about stock options or whatever it is that adults do. There's a weird pressure in the air, like we're supposed to be *doing* something. What are we supposed to be doing?

"So . . ." I start, "how's the birthday been?" I'm hyperaware of my body—do I always sit like this, what should I do with my hands, is it weird that Adam and I are sitting on the same couch? Are we sitting too close? Too far apart? The questions run around, outpacing the green, pulling me away from the tether that's keeping me in reality. Adam's voice, like always, pulls me back.

"It's been good," he says. "Pretty uneventful, but good."

"That's good," I echo stupidly. I'm nodding, unable to control my own body. Adam's nerves are starting to entwine with my own and normally that's okay, but these nerves are spiky and slimy and difficult to fit in.

"Do you wanna go upstairs?" Adam mumbles, and I feel the ball of anxiety in my gut loosen a bit. There's something comforting in knowing that even when we're uncomfortable, Adam and I are still on the same page.

"Yeah." I nod and we bolt from the couch and up the stairs. We get to his room and I pause a moment to really look around. The last and only time I was here, I was too deep underwater to take it in. But now that I'm here with a clear(ish) head—full of soft butterflies and simple, uncomplicated happiness—I'm able to absorb it. I have to keep myself from smiling at just how very *Adam* it is. His things are organized within an inch of their life but there are little nods at rebellion throughout—the dog-eared and, no doubt, written-in paperback copies of classic literature on his nightstand, the band stickers covering his laptop, the USB piano keyboard on the end of his bed. I wonder if he composes. I wonder if he's been composing in bed. My whole body goes warm at the thought.

"Oh, here"—I shove my poorly wrapped gift toward him—"before I forget."

"You didn't need to get me anything." He smiles and a soft buzzer goes off. He's not lying, but it's a half-truth. He wasn't expecting a present from me but he's thrilled that I got him one. His pleased surprise is better than any football win or good grade.

"Whatever." I shrug. "Your current ones look like they've seen better days so I just thought . . . It's no big deal." That, of course, is a lie, and we both know it.

He gingerly tears back the wrapping paper to reveal a pair of black, over-the-ear headphones.

"They're not, like, the greatest quality or whatever," I explain, "but they're wireless and, I don't know, it seemed like you could use a new pair."

A foreign emotion is taking over my body—warm and golden, like the sun. But it's not the sun-on-your-face sense of pride. It's . . . softer. Fresher. Like I'm being held close by warm light.

Adam looks up at me, bright joy in his eyes. His mouth is

twisting in the way that means he's trying to hold back a smile, and my heart tries its best to expand outside of my chest.

"Thank you," he breathes, his fingers curled protectively around the band of the headphones. "This is really, really nice." The reverence lacing his voice clues me in to what the feeling is: gratitude. He's grateful. And . . . hopeful. He hasn't looked away from me, our hearts beating in time, and I swear we're standing closer than we were a second ago. I see actual, literal sparks fly between us and it makes me flinch.

"Yeah, you're welcome." I shrug, trying to pretend like I don't know that we both want to ignore the headphones between us and grab at each other. "What else did you get?"

I'm suddenly shy, wanting to slow this train down. If we start something and then he finds out that I'm a total freak, it will be so much worse when I do tell him.

Adam shows me what his parents got him for his birthday—a "new" old watch from his dad (passed down from his grandpa or something), a suit from his mom ("For college interviews," he says, giving a truly epic eye roll), and a nice, probably really old leatherbound copy of Shakespeare's collected works. Adam holds it like it's fragile and priceless and I'm filled to the brim with joyful light. I ask him about his favorite play and he starts talking about *Hamlet* or *Much Ado About Nothing* or something and I should be paying attention but I'm distracted from the words themselves by the way his body leans against his desk, the minuscule smile on his face, the tentative happiness he feels at sharing this piece of himself.

Now. Now is the time to tell him. Take a deep breath, straighten your shoulders, and tell Adam that you're some kind of weird superhuman. That you're not normal but that that doesn't mean there's anything wrong with you. Tell him that you like him. Then kiss him. Just do it. Jump out of the plane.

". . . so, I don't know, we'll see how I feel once I read the rest of them, I'm only, like, halfway through the histories." Adam is shrugging like his Shakespeare obsession is no big deal but I know better than that. I know he's secretly totally jazzed that he's got a musty old copy of all the plays that he can treat like some sort of challenge. I feel his laser-focused enthusiasm: the bubbling in his veins and the tingly sugar crystals on his tongue. I can taste them so strongly it's almost like *I'm* the one who gives a flying fuck about Shakespeare. But it's not enough—I want to know what he *really* tastes like. If the ways he feels when he's excited translate to sweet cotton candy in his mouth; if the big blue waves leave salt on his skin.

"Caleb, are you okay?" Adam asks, a common question from him these days. Like if he asks enough I'll finally tell him what I'm really feeling.

"Yeah, I'm okay." I shake my head to clear it. "I'm good, actually. Really good."

He gives me that soft half smile again and tilts his head. "Where do you go?"

"What?"

"You get this faraway look on your face sometimes and you don't snap out of it until I say something. It's like you're in a totally different world." The cotton candy turns to Pop Rocks as Adam's curiosity takes over in his body, and it makes me anxious. Here it is, the perfect opening, the moment when I'm supposed to step into open air.

"Actually," I start, bracing myself to take the leap.

"Boys! Dinner!" Mr. Hayes's voice cuts through the strings of anticipation hanging in the air and I feel our twin disappointment fall like weights on both my shoulders. Adam sighs, says, "Come on," and leads the way back downstairs.

Soon we're back to playacting—sitting across from each other at the dining room table with Mr. and Mrs. Hayes on either end asking us questions about school like we're being interviewed. The dinner is fine—the food is good and the Hayeses are nice despite how serious they are. Somehow Adam ended up with a diluted version of his parents' intensity, which is really saying something, because he's the most intense person I've ever met.

"How about you, Caleb?" Mr. Hayes asks, making an effort to include me in a conversation I'd completely tuned out of.

"Huh?"

"What are you thinking about in terms of college?" Mrs. Hayes fills in, emitting a supportive warmth that reminds me a bit of the teachers at school. But coming from her, it feels like there's a right answer.

"Oh." I look to Adam for some kind of hint on what I should say, but he's staring at his mom, irritated embarrassment aimed like a laser beam at her. "I don't know. I mean, it's still a long way away. I think my parents and I are gonna do, like, a big college tour road trip this summer or something."

"Not everyone plans their lives out five years in advance," Adam complains, and I learn where Adam got his head-tilt-half-smile expression from. On Mrs. Hayes's face it reads like *You're being an idiot but I love you anyway* and my brain gives me a quick slideshow recap of all the moments Adam has looked at me like that. Hope pushes my heart into my throat.

"It was just a question," Mrs. Hayes shoots back lovingly.

"You're an athlete, isn't that right?" prompts Mr. Hayes, cutting through whatever battle of the wills was about to start between his wife and son.

"Um, yeah," I answer. "I play football. Running back."

"Oh, very good." Mr. Hayes nods sagely. "That's very impressive. Very good position."

"Dad," Adam deadpans. He and his mom are both looking at Mr. Hayes now, fond amusement dancing around them.

"Elijah, you have no idea what you're talking about," Mrs. Hayes teases, her laugh ringing loud and clear, hinting at looseness that I didn't think was possible in Adam's mom.

"I thought I was pulling it off." Mr. Hayes shrugs good-naturedly, joining his wife in laughter. It brings a burst of yellow-sparked joy into Adam's chest and he holds back a laugh, not wanting to give his parents the satisfaction of thinking they're funny.

That's not something I know because of the empath power. Adam doesn't *feel* withholding from his parents. But I know that's what he's doing. I know because I can see him trying not to smile, wanting to roll his eyes and call his parents dorks, because that's what he does. I know him. All empath stuff aside, I know who Adam is. And that makes me feel like more of a superhero than anything.

"You'll have to excuse my husband," Mrs. Hayes says, smiling at me. "He likes to pretend he knows everything about everything, but we're not exactly a sports family."

"Yeah, I sort of got that," I admit, and Mrs. Hayes laughs again.

"He's not the only one who thinks he knows everything about everything," Adam singsongs, side-eyeing his mom. It might seem like he's annoyed or embarrassed, but he's got a mischievous light-footedness to his feelings. He's having fun. Mrs. Hayes is ready to play along, opening her mouth in mock-offense to say something, but I beat her to it.

"Oh, you mean you?" I quip. I feel a thrill of satisfaction from the surprise that darts through Adam as his eyes snap to me.

"Oh-ho!" Mr. Hayes slaps the table like I've scored a point. "He's got your number, doesn't he, *boychik*? You should keep this one around." He shakes his finger knowingly at Adam before tapping his nose.

"Oh my god, *Dad*," Adam groans, the blush on his cheeks like a glowing sun setting over a desert. He looks at me and laughs and I feel my face grow hot too. But it's not embarrassment—Adam is pleased. Proud that I'm fitting into his family, impressing his parents. And I feel a smaller-scale warmth from them too—they're glad that I know how to joke with them.

The approval makes me self-conscious again. I really want to impress his parents. I want them to like me. I want to know Adam even better than I do. I want him to take his dad's advice and keep me around. Just like that, telling him about what I can do feels unnecessarily risky.

I don't have time to dwell on it, as the conversation moves back to college and schoolwork, Adam and his parents debating the schools they should go see on spring break.

"Adam, you can't just tour Yale over and over," Mr. Hayes says. "It's good to look at other schools. You never know, you might find one you like just as much."

"I doubt it," Adam grumbles.

"Still," Mrs. Hayes says, "you don't want to put all of your eggs in one basket."

"Yale, huh?" I ask, a little hurt. This is the first I'm hearing about it, and it sounds like something Adam's been dreaming about for a little while.

"Yeah," he says. "I know it's a hard school to get into but they have one of the best English programs and, I don't know, it's worth applying." Cold air sweeps into me and I brace for the wave that's about to wash over the table. But it doesn't come. Instead, it's the sludge. Pitch black, oozing, burning cold like dry ice.

He doesn't think he can get in. That's why he's never mentioned it to me.

"You'll get in," I say confidently—maybe too confidently, because three pairs of eyes snap toward me. Mrs. Hayes's eyebrow is lifted in a perfect, curious arch over her carefully blank expression and I feel the need to explain. "I just mean, I know you're worried about that, but you'll get in. Everyone thinks so."

"What do you mean 'everyone thinks so'?" Adam asks. Shit. I shouldn't have said that.

"Um . . ." My forehead is breaking into a sweat under the triple-Hayes gaze. "I mean, you're really smart. And we all believe in you. Like, the people at this table. We all think you can do it." I've lost all control over what I'm saying but it's okay because the sludge is starting to crack, like grass growing through concrete.

"Yes, we do," Mrs. Hayes agrees, giving me an inscrutable look. That's a word that Adam loves: inscrutable. He says I'm inscrutable but I don't think I hold a candle to Mrs. Hayes's face right now.

"Absolutely." Mr. Hayes nods strongly, beaming at his son, the sun ray of pride overlapping onto me. But Mrs. Hayes is still staring at me, head tilted like she's trying to solve a puzzle. I've gotten used to a Hayes trying to figure me out all the time, but it feels sharper coming from her. More dangerous.

"Um, yeah." I rub my hands on my legs, trying to distract myself from the ants under my skin. "So don't be worried or anything."

Because it'll be fine." I'm nodding too much, conscious of my beet-red, sweaty face. Thankfully Adam is feeling too contented to notice.

"Well, okay"—he blushes—"thanks, everyone. I guess."

"Cake!" Mr. Hayes shouts suddenly, rising from his chair. Adam and I both jump a bit in our seats at the outburst but Mrs. Hayes just laughs again, breaking her focus on me to put her grinning face in her hands.

"You have to get that man under control," Adam deadpans to his mom. Mr. Hayes has moved into the kitchen, where he is humming something unrecognizable but almost definitely out of tune.

"I gave up on that a decade or two ago, sweetie pie," Mrs. Hayes chuckles, moving to clear the dishes away. Adam makes a gagging face—I'm assuming at the nickname—and Mrs. Hayes just ruffles his hair as she follows her husband into the kitchen.

"So . . ." I lean forward to look at Adam, drawn in by the balmy blue-green tide of his happiness. "What kind of cake did you make?" This prompts a head tilt, smirk, and bubbly playfulness that tells me he's about to tease me.

"How many minutes a day do you spend thinking about food?" He grins, sparks in his eyes creating electricity between us.

"It's an important subject," I toss back. "It is, you know, *necessary* for survival."

"Oh yes." Adam's eyes go dramatically big. "Of course, the ever-important nutrient that is chocolate cake. How could human beings have evolved this far without it?"

"So you made chocolate, then?" I wiggle my eyebrows and he laughs, biting his bottom lip in an attempt to keep the higher ground. My heart squeezes and I twist my hands together under the table so I don't reach out and touch him.

"Fine," he says loftily, "you win. It's chocolate on chocolate. With raspberries."

"Oh man, I could have guessed that." I lean back in my chair and cross my arms, feeling restless, stuck in this stiff chair, forced to look at Adam's smiling face with an entire table between us.

"Oh really?" He leans back also—a challenge—and the sparks turn into butterflies. I'm standing in the doorway of the plane again.

"When Becca M. brought in those fancy-ass cupcakes for her birthday you got a raspberry chocolate one and you were happier than I'd ever felt from—" Adam's smile deflates slightly and I tense, sucking the rest of my sentence down and rerouting. "I mean, you seemed to really like it. I should have guessed it was your favorite."

Adam's not buying it. I'm being reckless and either Adam is going to figure it out (how could he?) or decide I'm way too weird to keep hanging out with. Maybe I should just do it now—rip off the Band-Aid, tell him right here at the table. I lean forward again to say something—god knows what—just as Adam inhales, eyes narrowing, ready to interrogate me no doubt, when the lights suddenly go out.

"Happy birthday to you . . ." Adam's parents re-enter the dining room singing, Mr. Hayes's hand still on the light switch. Mrs. Hayes is carrying a fire hazard of a cake and making up the on-key half of the singing. I join in, somewhere between Mr. and Mrs. Hayes's abilities, and my heart surges at the way Adam looks at me.

The cake is as delicious as I would have expected from the boy who seems to be perfect at everything he tries. I mumble something along those lines and nearly vaporize in my seat at the pleased warmth that rushes through Adam. Mr. and Mrs. Hayes decide to have another glass of wine each, letting Adam have a few birthday sips, and between that and the sugar, the whole atmosphere loosens. We're joking and laughing and I'm basking in the glow of the Hayes family relaxed and teasing each other when I start to feel . . . weird.

My head feels full of loosely packed cotton and there's a slight buzzing in my ears. I'm weightless and sleepy. The conversation around me moves in and out of my understanding and I'm seeing everything through a slight golden haze.

Oh god, I'm getting drunk.

This has happened a few times before at football parties. When

I'm around people who are drinking, I start to feel drunk too. It doesn't matter if I haven't had a drop of alcohol (I did once and, let me tell you, what a disaster), I can't be around drunk people or things start to get fuzzy. Usually it's a combination of feeling frantic and also relaxed—like I could punch through a wall and not feel anything, or say exactly what I want to. This isn't like that. This is softer, more passive, and that's all I've got because things are getting swirlier and swirlier.

Oh Jesus, I'm getting *adult* drunk.

"Caleb," someone says, "are you all right?"

I blink slowly to see that three-pronged stare again. You can do this, dude. Just make up an excuse and leave.

"Um, yeah." I'm speaking slowly, taking care to not slur. "Just a sugar crash, I think. I should—uh, I should go." I stand carefully, getting an instant head rush. I grip the back of my chair, praying to whoever will listen that I don't fall over.

"Oh," Adam says, his disappointment cutting through the haze and sobering me slightly. "Okay. I'll walk you out."

Good-byes happen and all I can hope is that I don't make a complete and total ass of myself. Somehow I make it outside okay, holding on to Adam's mix of confusion, contentment, and worry like a terrible life raft. The clear air and distance from the Hayeses does wonders for my head, and I breathe deep before checking in on Adam.

He's looking up at me, eyebrows creased, mouth slightly downturned. His emotions are a swirl of blue and warm gold and I'm trying to sort through them when he speaks.

"You okay?"

"I'm fine." I shrug. Adam's mouth tightens and I want to correct it. "I'm good," I pivot. "Really. Tonight was really nice, thanks. I mean, happy birthday." I'm floundering, still sobering up and wincing at the confusion coming in waves from Adam.

"I'm sorry I'm so weird all the time," I finish lamely. Adam shakes his head at me like I'm being an idiot. Which . . . fair.

"You just had dinner with my parents," he says. "I don't think we can judge about being weird."

"Your parents aren't weird," I say honestly, but Adam looks at me skeptically. "They're . . . intense."

"That's one word for it," he scoffs.

"But they love you a lot," I blurt, missing his smile. "They think you're so great. And I'm sorry that I made such a bad impression, I know it was important to you. That I not fuck up in front of them. But they don't hate me or anything, so you don't have to worry. I think your mom is maybe a little . . . I don't know, suspicious of me? I don't know, she's hard to get a read on—"

"Caleb, what are you talking about?" Adam interrupts, his eyes bugging out of his head.

Fuck, I really went on a ramble there. I guess I'm not as sober as I thought.

"Nothing." I shake my head, panicking. "Sorry, I'm just—I'm really tired. I should go."

"Caleb . . ." Adam starts, twisting vines of worry-confusion-curiosity wrapping around me. And something else too. Fear. He's scared of me. I have to get out of here.

"I'll see you tomorrow in school," I call out, already halfway down his front walk. "Happy birthday!" I give an awkward wave, avoiding Adam's crestfallen face, and walk quickly down the sidewalk before realizing that I need to call my mom to pick me up. I dial quickly and tell her to meet me three blocks down from Adam's house. For once, I can't bear to be anywhere near his feelings.

35

ADAM

Well, that was fucking weird.

I watch Caleb speed down the street before I turn to go back into the house. Spending time with Caleb means getting emotional whiplash all the time. One moment things are great, the next, he's skittering away like a scared mouse.

As I shut the front door behind me, I think back on the moment before my parents brought out the cake. Caleb leaning toward me, smirking. It felt like . . . flirting. I have to stop myself from thinking that word too loudly in my own head. It's ridiculous. It's not the first time I've felt that Caleb might be flirting, but that doesn't make it any less ridiculous.

"You all right, sweetie pie?" I look up to see my mom holding chocolate-covered plates in the doorway to the dining room.

"Yeah, I'm fine," I say, forcing a smile. "I'm good."

"Want to come help with dishes?" She jerks her head toward the kitchen.

"Don't I get a break because it's my birthday?" I rebut, with a real smile this time.

"Want another piece of cake?" she offers instead, eyes glittering. A small laugh escapes me and I follow her into the kitchen, where my dad seems to be making more of a mess than should be possible when washing the dishes.

"That Caleb is a real *mensch*," my dad shouts over his shoulder, the sound of the faucet nearly drowning him out. I roll my eyes, even though he can't see me.

"Your father's right." My mom places the dishes in the sink as I cut myself another slice of cake. "He's a very nice boy."

"Yeah," I say, not looking at them, "he's cool."

"Was he okay at the end there?" she asks. "He rushed off pretty quickly." She leans against the counter, taking dishes from my dad and drying them, and it looks like I'm getting the double interrogation tonight.

"Hope we didn't scare him off." My dad winks over his shoulder, pausing to kiss my mom on the cheek before turning back to the sink.

"You might scare *me* off." I gag and my mom lazily swats me with the dish towel. She looks questioningly at me and I sigh before continuing. "I think he was fine. He just does that sometimes."

"He's very . . . perceptive," my mom says carefully, and my dad's shoulders tighten slightly.

"Um, yeah," I say, confused. "I guess."

"And he's always like that?" my mom probes.

"Like what?" I ask.

"Rebecca," my dad warns under his breath, and that freaks me out more than anything.

"I'm just asking a question." She turns to him, shrugging innocently.

"And . . . what question is that, exactly?" I put my cake on the counter and take a step toward her, feeling like I'm missing something.

"I just think he's a very unique boy, that's all," she finishes, like that explains anything. My dad turns back to the sink but the tension doesn't leave his body. I pick my cake back up, chewing on it thoughtfully, wondering what tactic I can take to figure out what she's talking about, when my mom speaks again.

"So, are you two dating?"

I nearly choke on my cake.

"Mom!"

"Rebecca—"

"What?" my mom exclaims. "It's just a question!"

"Leave the poor boy alone." My dad shakes his head, laughing, hands covered in suds. My face is burning and I'm still trying to swallow down thick chocolate cake.

"So?" she prompts, and my dad laughs again.

"No, we're not dating," I mumble into my nearly empty plate. "He's not—we're just friends."

"Well, I think you'd make a very sweet couple," she says casually, like this isn't the most mortifying moment of my life.

"You're incorrigible," my dad chuckles, handing her a plate.

"Don't pretend you don't feel the same." She wags her finger at him with her free hand and he shrugs and nods, making an agreeing "you've got me there" sound, and I'd very much like to slink away into nothingness now.

"Okay, wow, well, this has been fun," I say, putting my plate back on the counter and edging toward the hall. "But I'm gonna go crawl into a hole now."

"Sweetie." My mom laughs, putting the plate down and walking toward me. She grips my shoulders, turning me to face her. "We're just trying to say that we're happy for you. Friend or whatever else, Caleb seems great. And we're really happy that you have someone."

"Whatever," I groan, wanting to squirm away, but my mother has a vise grip.

"Happy birthday, my love." She smiles, loosening her hold on me to touch my hairline softly.

"Thanks, Mom," I say. My dad turns off the sink and joins the love fest, and the more I try to get away from them, the more they hold on until we're in a truly horrifying group hug situation. When I finally get free, I give them both icy stares.

"I am so going to over to Caleb's next weekend," I threaten. "He's never coming here again."

36

CALEB

Something is wrong.

I'm sitting in math, trying as hard as I can to block out Tyler's self-loathing and Moses's self-pitying and focus on the board, but suddenly there's a siren in my head. Something is wrong and it's wrong with Adam.

"Ms. Ramirez?" I put up my hand. "Can I have the bathroom pass?"

Ramirez doesn't even pause in her explanation of tangents, simply waving her hand in a "sure, go ahead" gesture. I run up to grab the clipboard and rush out the door.

I know it's Adam. I could recognize his anger and fear anywhere. Even though our connection is strong, and even stronger now that I'm actively thinking about him every second of every day, there are still parts of the school day when I don't feel him. Math is one of those times—Adam has a free period when I have math, so sometimes he wanders far and sometimes he's just in his little library nook working and his emotions are quiet enough that I lose the connection. But the spike of adrenaline I just felt is definitely his.

Without me actively making the decision, my feet are carrying me through the hallways in the direction of the feeling. The

anger grows stronger and stronger—a powerful, deep blue wave—
and I round a corner to find its source. Adam. Squaring off with
Bryce. Again.

What an idiot.

"God, Bryce, what's your damage?" Adam groans and I can
hear the eye roll even if I'm too far away to see it. He's full to the
brim with false confidence—there's too much jittery fear for the
confidence to be anything *but* false—and I stifle the impulse to
run to him, grab him by the legs, and throw him over my shoulder.

"I'll damage *you*." Bryce takes a step toward Adam in a way that
I do not like *at all*. There's sharp-edged sludge cutting up my insides so bad I can barely move.

"Wow," Adam says dryly. "Not even enough brain capacity for
a *Heathers* reference."

"What the fuck are you talking about, fag?" Bryce spits, and my
whole body is lit on fire.

"What'd you call me?" Adam clenches his jaw, stepping to
Bryce, but he doesn't have time to do anything else because before I know it, I'm between them, staring Bryce down like I can
liquify him with my gaze.

"Yo, Michaels, what gives?" Bryce reels back a bit and the anger is cut from Adam's blue-yellow surprise mixed with Bryce's instant spike of panic. Even with their emotions making war in my
chest, I'm so angry I could beat Bryce into the ground.

"What the fuck did you just say to him, Bryce?" I growl.

"Chill, man, jeez," Bryce says, putting up his hands in a mock-
ery of innocence. I can practically feel his pulse alongside my own,
beating frantically with the fear that comes from stepping into
something you're not sure you can get out of.

"I can handle this, Caleb," I hear Adam say. He's defiant and
fucking furious, and for once, it doesn't do anything to my own
emotions. I'm so mad I can barely see the green.

"Yeah, but now *I'm* handling it," I say to Bryce's face.

"Oh yeah?" Bryce sneers. "How exactly are you handling it, Michaels?"

Don't punch him. It will *not* be worth it. Just . . . talk him down.

"Look, Bryce, I'm sorry you hate yourself, but you don't need to take that out on someone who's minding his own business. Just go to therapy like the rest of us."

Way to go, Caleb. Now everyone knows you're in therapy.

A flash of anger bursts out of Bryce's nervousness and then the whole thing is smothered in self-loathing sludge.

"Whatever," Bryce huffs, stepping back. His feelings are all over the place, jittery and sharp. I reach out for Adam's feelings—for that sense of belonging—and find a boiling sea.

"God, Michaels, you're so dramatic," Bryce forces a laugh. "See you around, losers."

There's no sting to his words—just a deep, permeating despair that makes me almost pity the guy. Bryce swaggers away with a speed I wouldn't have thought possible for a swagger. I take a deep breath and turn around to face Adam.

He looks *pissed.*

Wait, he *looks* pissed. I reach out to find the emotion to match his face and hit that wall I haven't bumped up against since that first lunch. What the fuck?

"What the fuck, Caleb?" he asks, crossing his arms.

"What do you mean?" I bite back. "I just saved you from getting your face beaten in. Again."

"I don't need you to protect me." The wall erodes a little and I feel the flutter of nerves before I feel the wave of anger. But I'm not worried about drowning in it—it's not directed at me.

"I know that," I say evenly. "But that doesn't mean I can just stand by and let him talk to you like that."

"He's been talking to me like that for years." Adam rolls his eyes and the wall goes up again.

"What, really? I thought it was just stuff about you being a nerd, not . . ." I trail off, letting the *F*-word hang between us. Impossibly, the wall grows thicker.

"Well, okay, yeah, that was the first time he's gone that particular direction." Adam shrugs. "But I can handle Bryce."

"You shouldn't have to," I tell him, taking a step closer in the hopes he'll uncross his arms, and with them, bring down the wall.

It works. Something in him softens and he looks in my eyes for the first time.

"How did you do that?" He matches my volume, speaking like we're in one of our rooms, not a school hallway.

"Do what?"

"Know exactly what to say to people. It's like you take off their masks."

His eyes are roaming my face like the answers are somewhere in my frown lines. A rush of nervousness—my own—floods my veins.

"I—" I start, having no idea what to say. "I don't know. People are just . . . easy to read." Even as I say it, I know I'm not convincing him.

"Right." He nods skeptically. "Well . . . thanks, I guess. For intervening. Again."

There's a small smile on his face but sadness in his eyes and I want to kiss him into oblivion.

"Yeah," I breathe. "No problem."

37

ADAM

"I can't believe you haven't heard this album yet," I say, typing rapidly on Caleb's computer as he leans over me. I can smell the spicy scent of his shampoo and it fills my head with distracting vapor. I focus on the task at hand: getting Caleb to listen to the newest Panic! at the Disco album.

It's been a few weeks since the double-whammy birthday incident/Bryce encounter and things have thankfully gotten back to normal. As promised, I've been spending weekends at Caleb's with his non-humiliating family but his inferior music collection.

"I mean, I know a lot of their songs," Caleb says, close to my ear as he watches me pull up the album, "but I don't think I even knew they came out with new stuff."

"Well, prepare to have your mind blown." I hit Play on the album and a shrill chorus comes chanting through Caleb's speakers.

Tonight we are victorious

I turn my head to look at Caleb. He's got one hand on his desk, the other on the back of the chair I'm sitting in. He's surrounding me and it makes me feel safe and warm. A grin is blooming on his face, growing with each rhythmic nod of his head as he gets into the groove of the music. I can't help but smile at him in return. Caleb's joy is always infectious, like an airborne disease with symptoms that appear in its victims right away. I'm pretty sure that's not a thing—a virus that makes you smile as soon as it enters your system—but maybe I should ask my parents.

"I like this." Caleb keeps nodding and smiling and my internal organs might start melting from the warmth in my chest.

We end up listening to the whole album while sitting on his floor, like we always do, leaning against his bed. Our arms are pressed together from shoulder to elbow, our hands lying on our outstretched legs. It would be so easy to reach over and take his hand in mine. I glance sideways at Caleb to see him looking at me and smiling softly. My stomach drops and my heart rises to my throat, creating an empty, echoing chamber in my torso.

"You look happy," he whispers over the thunderous chorus of "House of Memories." I wouldn't have even heard him if we weren't sitting so close. The gaping space inside of me tightens impossibly before being filled with a rush of nervous fluttering.

"I am happy," I whisper back. We've somehow gotten closer to each other and I can feel my heartbeat in my ears.

"That's good," Caleb exhales.

My whole field of vision is filled with his face. There's an electric current between us, so strong I can almost see the sparks in the air. I fear if I move too quickly, I'll get shocked. I'm frozen in place, paralyzed by the voltage, as "House of Memories" ends, highlighting the silent space between us. The opening piano chords of "Impossible Year" drift into my ears, giving definition to the ache of longing inside of me. It feels impossible—being this close to Caleb, him looking at me this way. It's impossible that I think he might be about to kiss me.

I hear myself say his name—a question, an answer, a hope— and regret it instantly, want to grab it and shove it back into my mouth, to keep it from smothering the sparks. Because something in Caleb snaps and shutters and before I'm done breathing out his name, he's leaning back and away from me.

"Caleb?" This time the word is a question and I hate how hurt my own voice sounds to my ears. I find myself in a moment that is the photo negative of the one that came before it. Caleb is now making an effort to avoid eye contact, and the electricity has been replaced with dead air.

"Do you want to take a walk?" he blurts out.

"What?" I have that two-steps-behind feeling again and I really, really hate it.

"I just—I need some air." He stands and pulls his letterman jacket from the back of the chair, shrugging it on. I rush to my feet and silently follow him down the stairs, absently waving at his parents when he tells their confused faces that we're going for a walk, and soon we're outside, walking away from his house to who knows where.

"Caleb," I say again, "what are we doing out here?"

His hands are shoved in his pockets, his jaw clenched as he stares straight ahead. He's stiff and quiet and I want to scream at him and shake him because I'm so disoriented from the last five minutes.

"It's kinda warm tonight," he answers flatly. "I don't know, I thought it'd be nice to get out of the house."

The back of my neck is prickling—Caleb isn't behaving like himself and I'm not sure what to do. I'm reminded of my birthday, that sudden shift in behavior and, not for the first time, I wonder if Caleb might have a serious mental health problem. As in, more serious than mine. The thought scares me like it did the first time I had it, but this time it comes with a sense of hopefulness. That, at least, would be an explanation. Maybe, like me, he's been fighting invisible demons this whole time.

"Caleb," I repeat, like saying his name has been working at all. This time I gently grab his arm, stopping in the middle of the sidewalk and trying to get him to look at me.

"Are you okay?" I ask, craning my neck to try and get him to look at me instead of the ground. He steps back from my grasp, scrubs his hands over his face, and sighs.

"There's something I have to tell you," he groans, face in his hands.

"Okay . . ." I try to keep my face neutral but my heart is beating like I'm a rabbit running away from a wolf.

"So, you know that fight with Tyler I got into last semester?" he asks, sounding overly casual.

"Yeah . . ." I answer, and then, when it seems like maybe he wants me to say more, "I remember being pretty surprised when I heard that you'd beat someone up. You always seemed like a really nice guy."

Caleb tilts his head to toss me a small smile before licking his lips nervously. "Yeah, well, I guess people aren't always what they seem."

"Look, I know that sometimes you maybe have, like, anger issues or something," I offer, thinking of the way he was looking at Bryce in the hall the other week.

"Yeah, it's not just that," he sighs, turning away from me again and stepping off the sidewalk to sit on the curb, his body a painful comma curved in on itself. I take a deep breath and sit down next to him, the concrete cold on my legs despite the hint of spring in the night air.

"Well, whatever it is, you can tell me," I assure him, bracing for the worst. I run through all the things I learned in the program my parents sent me to, in group, and remind myself that, no matter what he has, he's still Caleb. He hangs out with me even though I have depression—whatever this is, I can handle it. My mind is running through every disorder I've ever read about in my parents' books: depression, bipolar, a personality disorder—

"Have you ever heard of mirror-touch synesthesia?" he says into his hands.

Okay, that I did not expect. It's a pretty rare condition so I can't remember all the specifics, but I have heard of it and tell Caleb as much.

"Right, well," he stutters, "my therapist thought that'd be a good jumping-off point for this conversation—"

"What conversation?" I start to get annoyed that Caleb's been planning our conversations without me but my mind sticks on the fact that Caleb sees a therapist. I thought his quip to Bryce about therapy was just a figure of speech and I'm about to ask more when—

"The conversation where I tell you I have a superpower," he says, and I'm too baffled to even laugh at the assertion.

"Well, no," he corrects himself, "it's not a superpower, it's a total pain, but it is, like, *not* a normal-person thing. I'm not a normal person."

"You seem pretty normal to me," I say for lack of anything else to say. I have no idea what we're talking about.

"Well, I'm not." Caleb looks at me now, worry darkening his eyes. "I'm special. I can . . ." He trails off before starting again. "So. Mirror-touch synesthesia—people with that can feel, like, the physical things that happen to other people, right? If they see someone get slapped, they feel like they're getting slapped."

"Right . . ." I prompt, hoping he'll start putting the pieces together for me.

"Okay, so, I can't do that." He takes a deep breath like he's walking into battle. "But I can feel other people's feelings."

"What do you mean?" I ask, and then something clicks and I think I know what he's talking about. "Oh, you mean empathy? You're really empathetic?"

"No." He shakes his head. "Well, I mean, sort of yeah. I'm an empath. It's not like I'm just hypersensitive or anything, I literally feel the feelings of everyone around me all the time. Really specifically. It's like being psychic, except it sucks."

"Caleb, there's no such thing as psychics," I say gently. I'm starting to get worried that this is way beyond my capabilities of understanding—is Caleb delusional? How seriously worried do I need to be? I suddenly feel like a child in a way that I haven't in a really long time.

"Yeah, I think there might be," he mumbles before continuing, "but that's a whole other thing."

"You know, Caleb"—doubt and worry are starting to slither up my spine, a knee-jerk response kicking into gear—"you might be hanging out with jocks too much if you think it's abnormal to notice other people have feelings."

It was the wrong thing to say. Caleb's face flinches and crumples. "Don't be a dick," he says defensively. "I'm not messing with you—"

"I didn't think you were," I say, while simultaneously realizing that, yep, that is exactly why I'm getting defensive.

"I know it's something you worry about." He's looking at me earnestly now. "Being pranked or led on or whatever. Because right now, you have a bit of the same feeling you had the first time we had lunch—like you don't trust me. It's all defensive and prickly but also scared."

"What are you talking about." I don't phrase it as a question because suddenly it's not just the back of my neck prickling—there're goose bumps over my whole body. I know what Caleb's talking about. I know *exactly* what he's talking about. That *is* something I worried about in the beginning, and the moment he brought up messing with me, I felt my walls go up.

"I *know*," he says. "I know how you feel. All the time. I don't always understand it but that's why—why I *know* stuff, all right? About you, about Caitlin or Bryce, about your parents—all of it. It's why I get weird sometimes—like when I got drunk at your birthday—"

"You what?" I interrupt but he ignores me.

"You said I'm strange—well . . . this is why." Caleb exhales like he's run a marathon and I feel like a marathon has run over me.

But things are starting to slot into place. All the oddly tense moments, the weirdly perceptive observations—all those times that Caleb is about to say something before gulping it down like a secret—those things are starting to make sense.

But that's impossible. Because even though this explanation makes the past few months make a lot more sense, the explanation *itself* does not make sense at all.

"That's not possible," I push back. "ESP and all that stuff isn't real."

Caleb looks offended at that.

"Not that I don't believe you," I rush to explain. "But just that . . . just because you're maybe more sensitive than other people doesn't mean you can read minds."

"I didn't say I could read minds," he bites, "just emotions. But I've gotten good at piecing together the feelings to figure out what's going on with someone. It's not perfect, but I'm getting better at it all the time. Dr. Bright has been helping me a lot."

"Dr. Bright?" I ask, dazed.

"Yeah, she's my therapist "

"And she says you're an empath?" That beggars belief, but I try not to sound judgmental. "That you're not a normal human?"

"Yeah." He nods enthusiastically. "After the fight, my parents sent me to her and she helped me figure it all out. It's what she does. Works with people like me. Not just empaths, but other people who are special too. But she has seen lots of people who are like me—who are empaths. And it made so much sense, when she diagnosed me or whatever. I got into that fight with Tyler because I was so overwhelmed by *his* feelings. I thought they were mine—all that anger and bitterness—and I didn't know how to balance it. I'm better now. I mean, obviously, I'm not perfect, but I can usually tell the difference between someone else's feelings and my own now."

Caleb's body starts to relax throughout that little monologue and he's looking at me hopefully, as if now that he's explained his therapist and his diagnosis, I'm totally on board and completely able to grasp everything he's saying.

"So . . ." I process out loud, "you feel the feelings of everyone around you and it's sort of like mind reading but also you think those feelings are yours sometimes?"

"Pretty much." He nods. "I mean, it's a little more complicated than that probably, but that's the gist. It's not mind reading, I promise, but it's . . . I don't know . . . I know *a lot* about people now."

That makes my heart beat faster in fear. If this is true (and I'm really starting to believe this is true), I might be in real trouble here.

"Why are you telling me this?" I ask, getting to the important question. I've spent a lot of time pestering Caleb about whatever perceived secrets I thought he might have, but he's always been reluctant to cave. Why now?

"Because you're my friend," he states, and my breath hitches at the intensity of his gaze, "and I want to tell you things. I *need* to tell you things because it's not fair that I know what you're feeling all the time and wasn't even telling you about it."

"I'm sorry, Caleb." I shake my head. "I'm having a hard time believing this."

"I know," he says, "but it's true. And there's a little part of you that knows that. I know you're nervous and scared right now, but you've also got that tiny little glimmer of confidence. You *trust* me."

"Yeah, I do," I concede, "but this is really next-level weird."

"You don't have to be mean about it." He pouts.

"No, sorry," I blurt, "I'm not trying to be insensitive, I just— This is a lot, Caleb. If you really can feel all of my feelings . . ."

"I can," he asserts. "Like, right now you're nervous and scared and all that, but you trust me. But also there's that little pool of, like, sadness, I guess? I don't really know how to describe it, it's so big sometimes. Like when I came over last month—it was really big then. Like a massive wave that turned into a storm or something. And it's weird that I know that stuff because you haven't told me and I have a feeling it's kind of a big deal, so I felt bad not telling you I knew."

I'm starting to get dizzy despite the fact that I'm sitting down. Caleb is looking at me as he says this and it's like having my chest wrenched open and my soul read. He knows that I have depression. He doesn't seem to know exactly what it is—or he doesn't want to say—but he knows. According to him, he's *felt* it.

"I—" I start.

"You don't have to explain yourself," he interrupts, sounding panicked. "I'm not trying to make you feel bad or anything. I'm just—I'm sorry that you feel that way. I know how hard it is."

"Because you feel that way when I do?" I ask, heart sinking at what I think the answer might be.

"Well, yeah, sort of," he says, "but it's not like you're making me sad or anything, it wears off when I'm not around you. And I still feel my own feelings, you know? Wait . . . why are you . . . relieved?"

Caleb is squinting, his head tilted like he's trying to listen to something far away.

"Um, I—I don't know that I am," I stammer, before actually giving it some thought. "I guess . . . I guess I'm glad there's an explanation for why I always feel like I'm missing something around you. You throw me off sometimes and that *never* happens, with anyone. This fills in that blank a little bit."

"Good." He smiles. "That's good."

"Yeah . . ." I trail off, my mind working at a million miles a minute. This is real. Caleb really can feel my feelings—all of my feelings. And it seems like he knows what they are even before I do. Which means, that earlier . . .

"Oh god." I cringe, thinking about our moment on his bedroom floor just twenty minutes ago. And so many moments before that. He's known this whole time. He's known that I have a massive crush on him and that's why he's always so weird during those times, because he snaps out of it and realizes that he doesn't feel the same and changes the subject and oh my god, I've never felt so humiliated in my entire life. And now he's going to feel *that* and I have to get out of here.

"Adam, why are you feeling . . . embarrassed?" he asks, sounding uncertain. "I'm the one who—"

"I have to go." I stand up quickly, edging away from Caleb like the distance will keep him from feeling my embarrassment. Is that how this works?

"Wait, what?" Caleb stands also, stepping toward me, and I try not to flinch back.

"I just—I need some time to process." I start to turn away so I don't have to look at Caleb's puppy-dog face, but he grabs my arm, so that I face him.

"Are you—are we okay?"

"Yeah." I nod, trying not to show my hurt. At least it seems like he still wants to be my friend. "Yeah, we're fine. It's just a lot. But I'll see you on Monday, yeah?"

"Yeah." He drops my arm, looking like I've just told him Christmas is canceled.

I mumble a good-bye and take off down the street, trying not to break apart at his unspoken rejection.

38

CALEB

My whole body is buzzing with nervous energy as I knock on Dr. Bright's office door.

"Caleb, come in—" I don't even wait for her to finish opening the door before I'm bursting through it, pacing back and forth in her office.

"Sorry, I know I'm early, but I just couldn't sit around my house anymore." There are massive waves of worry coming off of Dr. Bright but I'm too tied up in my own feelings to pay it much attention.

"It's fine," she says, closing the door and gesturing for me to sit down, which I completely ignore in favor of pacing more. "Caleb. Are you all right?"

"No, no, I am not fucking all right," I spit, the pacing making me more agitated, which just makes me want to pace even more.

"Does this have to do with Adam? I got your message that you were planning on telling him this weekend."

My mind rewinds to Friday, when I left that message, and it feels like a hundred years ago. God, I was so optimistic then, so hopeful that Adam would believe me when I told him the truth and then we'd finally fucking stop dancing around this thing that

I know both of us feel, but instead I got halfway there and then it completely blew up in my face.

I don't even try to hide this from Dr. Bright.

"Yeah, yeah, I did that. Last night." I'm nodding furiously as I walk back and forth in her small office and I know I must look like a complete maniac. "And it did *not* go well."

"Caleb, why don't you sit down and tell me what happened." She gestures again at the couch and her outstretched arm sweeps a cool breeze of calm over me.

I sit. And I tell her the whole damn thing.

Out of all the bone-headed things I've done in my life, texting the guy I like while in the middle of a therapy session is probably one of the more idiotic.

Telling Dr. Bright everything actually really did make me feel better. It was good to get everything off my chest, but also, as we've just established, I'm a fucking idiot.

Adam was *embarrassed*. He believed me, but he was embarrassed. How could I have not seen that? He *does* like me and he was freaked out that I was telling him I could feel his feelings. Like Dr. Bright just said, he probably thought I was telling him I knew he liked me and was letting him down easy.

"Caleb, what are you doing?"

Out of the corner of my eye, I see Dr. Bright lean forward, resting her elbows on her knees, her curiosity bubbling out and curling into my nerve endings. I focus in on my phone, trying to come up with the perfect words that will rewrite the last twenty-four hours.

"Communicating," I reply, my thumbs moving quickly over the touchscreen. A drop of black-sludge disappointment drops into the whirlpool of curiosity-concern, rippling outward and making my fingers stutter on the keyboard.

"I meant in person, or a phone call," Dr. Bright sighs. "Not texting."

I want to snap at her that she should have specified when saying I needed to communicate more, but I'm too filled up with my own anxiety about all the ways I could screw this up. All the ways that I could not only lose my shot with Adam, but lose him as a friend.

"Yeah, well"—I look up at Dr. Bright, hoping she'll start to understand—"I can't go to school tomorrow without fixing this, and Sunday is his study day so I know he won't want to come over tonight. This'll just have to do."

I hear how whiny and pathetic I sound, and I do everything in my power not to cringe. Dr. Bright's face crumples and she sits back again, her eyes swiveling up to the ceiling like she's just completely given in.

"Very well."

For some reason, that feels like permission to send the text I've typed out, but I'm still freaked about saying the wrong thing and totally blowing it.

"Okay," I start, hoping that Dr. Bright will tell me I'm doing the right thing and it will all turn out fine. "'I'm saying, 'I'm sorry that I upset you yesterday. But you need to know that I like your feelings. All of them. So you shouldn't feel weird or anything about the fact that I can feel them. Because it doesn't have to be weird.' How's that?"

It is not my normal policy to read my texts to a grown-up, but this feels like a desperate situation, and Dr. Bright's advice is what got me into this whole "feelings" mess in the first place. I wouldn't have ever gotten to know Adam if she hadn't suggested it.

That thought makes a rock of fear drop to the bottom of my stomach. I don't want to think about that. I don't want to imagine what my life would be like without him.

"You're going to send it regardless of what I have to say about better forms of communication, aren't you?" she says wearily, and in a weird way, that gives me the confidence to take the leap. I can't lose this. I can't even risk losing this. And if stuffy Dr. Bright thinks I'm being impulsive and dumb, I'm probably doing exactly what I should be doing.

"Yep."

I send the text.

39

ADAM

*I'm sorry that I upset you yesterday. But you should
know that I like your feelings. All of them. So you
shouldn't feel weird or anything about the fact that I
can feel them. Because it doesn't have to be weird.*

What in the hell am I supposed to do with that?

My heart is in my throat and I can't feel my fingertips. I think
I might actually pass out. Wrapping my head around Caleb's
confession last night was hard enough as it is. It shouldn't be
possible—it shouldn't have been so easy for me to believe. But I
do. I totally do. It makes so many things make sense.

But this doesn't make any sense. What on earth is he trying to
say?

The screen is blurring in front of my eyes and my head is swim-
ming trying to parse out this problem. I feel dizzy and confused
and . . .

Hopeful. I have hope. Hope against hope. Confusing hope. It
can't be. But I have to know. My phone still sits in my trembling
hands and I realize that minutes have passed and I haven't re-
sponded. I need to get it together. I can't lose this chance.

I text back.

> How is it not weird? It's so weird. And humiliating.

Just because I have hope doesn't mean I'm going to make an ass of myself. I've already revealed so much by just spending time with Boy Wonder—I can't expose myself more. I need more information.

My phone buzzes.

> *What do you have to be humiliated about?*

Apparently, all plans I had to keep my dignity are completely hopeless. Looks like we're going to drag everything out in the open. I was trying to protect my soft spots, curl in on myself, but Caleb insists on breaking me open.

> Come on, you must know by now. If you can really feel everything I feel, then you must know. No point beating around the bush about it.

But that's exactly what I'm doing. I don't want to say it so *he'll* have to.

I get up from my desk chair and start pacing my bedroom. I'm being too harsh, too prickly. But Caleb knows me, he knows that this is who I am. He can't expect to vague-text me and not get hostile texts back. Right?

> *To be totally honest, I wasn't sure. Sometimes things get really muddled and it was easy to confuse that with my own feelings.*

Oh, goddammit, there's that hope again. I start to compose another text, saying god only knows what, when my hands—still shaking—stop themselves. We're getting nowhere like this.

Here it is, Adam. Now is the time to be brave. Now is the time to jump in and say what you feel and find out how he feels. This is your moment.

I slump down on my bed, the nervous energy of the past ten minutes dissolved like wind sucked out of my sails. I'm not this person. Caleb is. Caleb is the guy who defends the weird kid in the hallway, his non-date at the school dance; the guy who always puts his apple slices on my lunch tray because he doesn't like them and he knows that I do. Caleb is the guy who is terrified to give an in-class presentation but will never cower in front of a bully. And who am I? I'm nobody.

Something righteous and indignant flares inside of me. That's not right. I'm more than this. I don't have to be the sad kid who sits on his bed, staring at his phone, wishing he could say the things he wanted to say. I don't have to be the guy that aces classes but can't even carry on a conversation with his parents or muster the strength to get out of bed some mornings.

The fingers on my free hand curl into my comforter as my other hand clutches my phone, staring a hole through it like that will give me answers.

. . . it was easy to confuse that with my own feelings . . .

What does that mean?

The righteous fire glows stronger in my chest. I'm smart—top of my class, will probably be in the running for valedictorian next year. I see a difficult problem and I solve it. I figure things out. That's just how I work. But I cannot for the life of me figure Caleb out. That is unacceptable.

Before my brain can communicate with my hands, I'm hitting the little phone icon next to Caleb's name. The ringing stops and he doesn't even have time to say hello before my mouth takes on a mind of its own.

"What the fuck is that supposed to mean?" I shout, far too loudly and completely at odds with the small, hopeful-nervous person I am in my bedroom in this moment.

"What do you mean?" Caleb's voice sounds tinny and tight and it makes my heart clench. I try to stay focused—get answers, Adam. Puzzle it out.

"What feelings would you have to be confused about?" I demand. This is it: the heart of the matter. A clear question will yield a clear answer. That's how it works.

"Well, like," Caleb stumbles, "when I'm feeling something and another person is feeling the same thing, I can't tell what's coming from them and what's coming from me."

Okay, so apparently, that's *not* how it works. I want to be patient, want to understand that Caleb is operating off a totally different system than the rest of humanity. He's bound to have a different way of processing, communicating. I should be sensitive to that.

I'm not.

"Caleb, I swear to god, if you don't start making sense in the next ten seconds—"

I'm pacing the room again, unaware of ever standing up, my hands pulling at my hair as Caleb's voice shouts out of the speaker from where the phone sits on my bed.

"I like you too, okay?" It's loud and stops me in my tracks. "Yeah, I could feel something from you but I was never sure because I was always feeling it too. A lot. So you can stop being an idiot and feeling embarrassed, because if anyone should feel embarrassed it's me, the guy who's been so stupid about you that it broke my fucking superpower!"

My heart surges and I stumble forward, leaning my hands on the bed where I placed the phone, bending over it like getting closer to it will be the same as being able to see Caleb's face in this moment. I want to tell him, "Finally, yes, me too, where are you, I'll come there," but my stupid brain cannot let me have one good thing for even one tiny moment.

"But . . ." I start, not consciously knowing where I'm going with this, "I didn't think you—how the hell did I not know you're gay?"

It's not the right thing to say at all. He just confessed actual feelings for me, I'm pretty sure, and here I am harping on sexuality like some sort of senior citizen, but it also feels like an important question to ask. I'm so terrified. If I fool myself into thinking that this could be something . . .

"Oh." Caleb wasn't expecting that question either. "Um, I don't know that I am."

My heart doesn't even drop; it just up and vanishes. There it is. I expected it, I saw this coming, but it still hurts so much that my breath catches in my lungs. I was wrong. I read this whole situation wrong and I am shattered.

"Oh, right, sorry." I can't let him hear how crushed I am. "Never mind—"

"No, no it's, um . . ." He pauses and my heart returns in full force, fluttering madly, counting each second of silence before he says, "Not that I'm not into—" He pauses again and I'm going to completely lose my mind—

"It's just you," he breathes, "I like you."

My stomach is in knots as I pace back and forth. At least I'm not in my bedroom anymore. Turns out Caleb was texting me from his *therapy session*, so I'm frantically wandering the park near his house, waiting for him.

I'm waiting for a boy. I'm waiting for a boy who texted me in the middle of therapy because he couldn't wait any longer, because he wanted to fix things between us. I'm waiting for a boy who *likes* me and, yes, who likes me like that. I think. I hope.

Despite the warmth of the other night, the final gasps of winter are giving their last hurrah and I suck in a deep breath of cold air as I replay the last seconds of our phone call over and over again in my head. He said he liked me and I said "me too" and asked to talk and he said he would leave therapy early to come find me. We should be inside, in one of our houses—the sun has just dipped below the horizon and there's that sharp-soft feeling in the air that comes just before snowfall. But this doesn't feel like something we can hash out indoors, where there are other people and other feelings and so much that can get in the way.

I'm waiting for a boy who can feel everyone's feelings. I'm waiting for a boy who is something more than human.

I've spent the past twenty hours trying to piece it all together— my parents' weird jobs, my mom calling him "perceptive," everything that Caleb's told me, the fact that he has a special therapist who knows about him—and none of those revelations or questions are as important as "I like you too." There's a part of me that's beating myself up for even thinking that way. I hate being the teenage cliché who cares more about romance than actual, real-life superhumans—but wait, that's not a cliché. This is entirely new territory and I can't believe that I'm the one charting it.

I pause in my pacing as I take another gulp of cold air. The park is completely empty—as bare as the trees that line the pathway through it. It's a surprisingly quiet night, as if the city knows that something important is about to happen here and is trying to be respectful. The hush is like a blanket over the block, making everything still.

Inside me, there's a cacophony of sound. My head and my heart are battling it out. My head says, "No way, this can't be. You've read it wrong. This is all a trick, he doesn't have a superpower, and he definitely doesn't like you. Think about it: it doesn't make any sense."

My head is right. It doesn't make any sense. Me standing in the middle of a frigid city park on a school night when I haven't finished any of my homework for tomorrow (like I was going to get *any* work done with everything Caleb told me last night running around my brain) makes *no sense.* But my heart doesn't care.

My heart is screaming *yes.* It's saying, "This is right, this is how it's supposed to be. You knew. Somewhere, deep down, you knew this was true. He's it. There's no version of this story where this doesn't happen."

To which my head of course says, "Stop being a fucking sap, life isn't a story; even if he does like you, it'll be a mess because you're not someone who can be normal about this—"

And just as my head is about to talk me out of feeling excited, hopeful, all a-whirl with infatuation, I hear rapid footsteps behind me and I spin around so fast I nearly trip over my own Twizzler legs.

Caleb comes to an abrupt halt as I turn. He's out of breath, like he's run here (oh my god, did he *run* here?), red-nosed and completely fucking beautiful.

"Hi," he breathes, sticking his hands into his letterman jacket, eyes searching my face. His expression is unreadable and I want to trace the lines on his forehead with my frozen fingertips.

"Hey," I say, my voice faraway-sounding to my own ears. My head has officially exited the proceedings. My heart is demanding I listen to it, pounding against my rib cage and being lifted up by butterflies fluttering madly under my diaphragm.

We stand like that, ten feet apart, our breath curling like smoke between us, and stare at each other. What's supposed to happen now? What do I say? Am I supposed to *do* something? The problem with my head taking a much-needed vacation is that I'm stuck with a heart that wants so much and no executive functioning left to act for it.

"How was therapy?" I ask, like that's exactly how I've been planning to start this conversation. I'm treating this like any other day in the park—like we're at school on our lunch break. But this is different. I know that and I have no idea how to behave.

All I know is that Caleb is looking at me with those gorgeous green eyes and I'm so in love that I momentarily forget my own name.

"Oh, who the fuck cares?" He laughs, and then he's walking toward me. I see it all in slow motion and I'm moving in slow motion too, unable to react to anything that's happening. Caleb is smiling, a spark lighting up his eyes, which haven't stopped moving around my face as he takes two long strides to me. It's like he's trying to memorize what I look like—trying to capture my face in his mind's eye. Like I'm something important, something worth remembering.

In a millisecond, he's right in front of me, his hands coming out of his jacket pockets and rising to my face. I feel his cold palms on my cheeks and I should flinch at the sudden burst of ice but he's leaning toward me and then—

And then.

The cacophony inside of me transforms into a symphony. There's no warmup, no build; just instant, intricate, immeasurably beautiful music. The icy weather is a distant memory—every part of me is drowned in the most comfortable fire. I'm more aware of my body than I ever have been but also my entire world is narrowed down to Caleb's lips on mine.

His fingers wind into my hair, clutching me closer to him, like I'm not the only one who's wasted hours imagining raking my hands through his hair and down to his neck. I'm holding on to the back of his letterman jacket for dear life. Caleb is still moving with the momentum of walking to me—so quick and decisive— that we nearly tip over. One of his arms leaves my head to wrap around my torso, catching me, and I melt. That's it. If I wasn't a goner before, I sure as hell am now.

Minutes pass. Seconds. Entire centuries. It's impossible to tell. With Caleb's arm around me, I feel weightless, like if he lets go, I'll float away into the starry night. There's a perfect, cloudless sky where my brain should be. I'm dizzy. I'm faint.

Oh. I'm not breathing. Like, at all.

We separate, gasping for air, our breath creating a swirl of fog between our too-close faces. Caleb puts his other arm behind my back and I lean away to get a look at him. His face is red and I can't tell if it's from the cold or if he's blushing but it doesn't matter because his smile is enormous, reaching his eyes and beyond. His perfect hair flutters minutely in the frigid breeze and I give in to months—years—of repressed desire and touch my hand to the edge of his hairline. The gesture makes something in his smile soften and I'm embarrassed at giving in to the impulse.

"Hi," he says again, leaning his cheek slightly into my palm as my hand moves down the side of his face.

"Hi." I'm at a loss for anything profound to say but it doesn't seem like Caleb cares. He's looking at me like he just translated a particularly hard section of Latin and it makes me nervous. Unsure.

Oh, hey brain. Nice of you to rejoin the party, but could you give us a second, please?

"So . . ." I start, my head completely ignoring my heart's plea for it to stay out of this, "you like me, huh?"

Caleb licks his lips and closes them around his teeth like he's trying to hold in a laugh.

"Um, yeah." He grins. "Is that not obvious? Wait—" A cloud passes over his expression. "Why are you nervous? Did I . . . was that not . . . good?"

His hold on me relaxes as he starts to move backward. I notice I've been standing on tiptoes, and I'm thrown off-balance by his retreat. I panic and pull him back to me with the lapels of his jacket.

"No, no—" I assure him, "no, I just—I didn't think you would. I thought it was just me."

"I'm sorry I was so weird about everything—" He's trying to apologize for something that neither of us understands.

"No, you weren't weird, *I* was weird—" I interrupt.

"But you . . ." He swallows, looking away from me for the first time. "You too? I mean, with the feelings and stuff?"

It's not an actual sentence but I get what he means. I want to tell him how endearing it is that the boy who can feel everyone's feelings can't for the life of him talk about it, but then I realize I'm not much better.

"Yeah, I do." I nod. "Have the feelings and stuff."

"That's good." He echoes the end of our phone call.

"It's you that I can't . . ." I shake my head, unable to say it out loud.

"What?" Caleb tilts his head.

"You're *you*," I say, like that explains everything. "Of course I like you. I just can't believe you feel the same way. It doesn't—it just doesn't compute."

"Okay, brainiac." He's smiling again, touching my cheek like he can't help himself, and that's good. "Think you can wrap your head around it long enough to let me walk you home?"

"Yeah," I breathe, "yeah, I think I can manage that."

"Good." He's doing that thing again—looking at me like I hold all the answers. Like I *am* the answer.

That's another thing that doesn't make any sense. How is this even possible? He's telling me it's true and I can see it on his face but this is so much harder to believe than the existence of super-powers.

Caleb is grinning like he has the answer but I'm stuck on the equation that got us there.

But then he kisses me again and I realize it doesn't matter how we got there. Caleb is every answer that I need.

40

CALEB

I didn't realize it could be this good.

Now that Adam and I are officially together, my happiness is doubled, tripled, an endless loop of joy. He's happy, which makes me happy, which makes him happy—he doesn't even need an empath power, he just sees me smile—and we just go round and round until we're grinning at each other like total nutjobs.

As April goes on, the world thaws around us and overnight everything is green, inside and out. I don't have to try and hide who I am anymore and Adam's walls start to dissolve. The big, unpredictable waves between us don't seem so scary now. We're floating.

Adam is way more chill about my ability than I thought he would be. I guess his parents do some pretty weird science kind of stuff, so that part wasn't as hard to believe as the fact that I like him. I tease him about that a lot and he doesn't try to swallow his smile.

"What's Dr. Bright's deal?" he asks me one day, tilting his head upward to look at me from where it was resting on my chest. We're lying on the grass in my backyard, soaking up the spring sunshine, and his face is so close to mine I can count his freckles. I want to bend down and kiss the ones on his nose and then I remember that I can and I give in to the impulse. I instantly feel stupid about it but Adam moves his face to kiss me for real and I forget to feel self-conscious.

"So . . . what's her deal?" he repeats a few minutes later, sitting up on his elbows, arms draped over my torso so he can look at my face right side up. "How did she get into this line of work?"

"I don't know." I shrug, making his arms pop up a bit. "It's not like we spend my therapy sessions talking about her."

"But aren't you curious?" he asks. "I mean, you said she has other patients like you—wouldn't you want to meet another empath?"

"Fuck no." I laugh. "That sounds like a nightmare."

Adam's face scrunches up as he thinks it through. "Okay, yeah, point taken. But still, don't you want to know who her other patients are? What they can do?"

In this moment, my answer is yes. I'm filled to the brim with Adam's burning curiosity, a soft fire that makes me want to get up and run around. There's stuff that I get excited about, but I'll never really understand how Adam feels this way about learning so much of the time.

"I guess," I answer truthfully. "I don't know, it seems complicated. I'm only just now starting to get my own life under control, I'm not sure I want to add a bunch more freaks to it."

"I'm the only freak you need?" Adam smirks, but there's a sliver of self-doubt running through the teasing.

"You're not a freak," I say, before smirking myself. "You *are* a total dork, though."

He swats at my shoulder and I grab his hand, maneuvering it into mine, looping my fingers through his. Satisfaction pours out of Adam.

"Well, you're a total meathead," he says and laughs.

"But such a good-looking meathead," I offer, Adam's affection making me feel confident in a way I never feel without him. He just laughs at that, shaking his head and leaning in to kiss me again. But his hunger for more information itches, distracting me.

"I think it's nice you're curious about it," I say, laying my head back down on the ground. "I can ask Dr. Bright about it if you want."

"Do you think she'd tell you anything?" he asks, running his free hand through my hair. He does that a lot.

"I don't know," I say.

"Hm."

"What?"

The fire is turning cold, pulling inward from my limbs to sit in my stomach, hard and light like titanium. Determination.

"I have an idea."

41

ADAM

I don't actually expect Caleb to go along with my half-baked idea, but he does. He hears me out, fiddling with the watch on my wrist where it rests over his heart, as he nods along with my proposal. I think he starts to tune out my rambling at one point, because his eyes soften and seem to get stuck on my mouth, which makes my stomach do somersaults. But he finally catches up because he says:

"You want to spy on my therapist?"

"Spying is such an ugly word." I smirk. He smirks back and, just like that, we're off to the races.

The next three weeks are a total dream. Not only do I have a boyfriend (Is that what he is? We haven't actually defined anything but that's what I'm calling him in my thoughts because it makes the oft-dormant pleasure centers of my brain light up), but he's kind of a superhero. I guess there's never been a "Mr. Empath" or "Super Emotion Man" but the point is: Caleb isn't fully human. And that is just. So. Cool.

While I am curious about Dr. Bright's other patients—and Dr. Bright herself, though I don't think we're quite at the point where I can just introduce myself to Caleb's therapist—I mostly want a concrete excuse to be around Caleb. It's not like there was ever a concrete excuse before—we would just hang out. But now that we're . . . whatever we are, I want to have an activity. A reason for Caleb to keep spending time with me. Because there is no way that Caleb wanting to kiss me and talk to me and be around me is going to last. It feels too much like a dream in the self-deluding sense.

While we had our awkward moments before, there's a new kind of uncertainty that pops up between us now. Things had been . . . tense for a while and now I know why: the double whammy of reciprocated-but-not-confessed romantic feelings and *hiding a freakin' superpower.* But Caleb is still tentative around me. Even though he doesn't try and stop himself mid-sentence anymore, I think he's worried he's going to spook me if he shares too much. Which is just . . . well, the irony is *not* lost on me.

We're sitting on a bench in the small park across from Dr. Bright's office, conducting our second "stakeout," though really, we're paying more attention to each other than the comings and goings of her patients. And here's one of the ways that Caleb is more hesitant: he blushes a lot more now when he flirts, like being intentional about it is embarrassing. I try to tease him about it but, of course, he has to go all sincere on me.

"I'm still getting used to it, I guess," he says into his lap, cheeks red at my laughter.

"Used to what?" I ask, a little breathless.

"Feeling happy," he says, and my breath hitches. "*You* feeling happy." My breath stops completely as those green eyes look up, earnest and probing.

"How did I feel before?" I ask, not really wanting to know the answer. Now I'm the one looking away, uncertain where this conversation is going to lead but knowing it's probably nowhere good.

Caleb must be able to tell, because he says, "We don't have to talk about this. I know it's weird."

"No, come on, I want to know," I plead, like the masochistic idiot I am.

"I mean . . . you were sad a lot. And lonely." He drapes his arm over the back of the bench, his fingertips brushing my shoulder. The stray thought pops into my head that Caleb would make a good doctor—excellent bedside manner.

"You could feel that?" I ask quietly.

"What, you weren't lonely?" There's hope in his voice. He knows the answer, better than anyone, but he still hopes it isn't true. It makes all of my insides ache.

"No, I was," I admit, "I just didn't realize 'lonely' was an emotion."

"Oh yeah, it totally is." Caleb nods, a little more surefooted. He likes explaining his ability to me. "But there's different kinds. When I get lonely, I get really, really sad and kind of, I don't know, hopeless, I guess? You felt . . . tired with it, if that makes sense."

"Yeah, that makes sense." I choke around a lump in my throat. The observation stings in its accuracy. I *was* tired. Because I assumed it would never change—that I would be lonely forever. That no one would ever understand. That no one ever *could* understand. But here's proof that I was wrong, sitting next to me, all flesh and blood and genuine in a way that I've never before experienced. For some reason, that breaks my heart.

Now that I know about Caleb's ability, I see how much what I feel affects him. I start to smile, and look up to see him already smiling. I get sad and his shoulders get heavy. And, as much as it's been nice to not have to explain certain things, it makes me feel helpless. I can't control my own happiness, how am I supposed to be responsible for someone else's? How on earth is this actually going to work?

I'm trying to get us back to the easy flirtatious mood of a few minutes earlier when I see a vaguely familiar shape out of the corner of my eye.

"Oh hey." I swat at Caleb's shoulder and subtly gesture toward the sidewalk in front of Dr. Bright's office. "Isn't that guy one of Dr. Bright's patients?"

"Where?"

"That one over there." I gesture again, trying not to draw any attention to us. "The kind of shady-looking guy."

I'm not sure I would have even noticed him if he hadn't been wearing the exact same outfit and doing the exact same thing he was doing last time we saw him. He's unbelievably average. Average in an almost weird way—like you look at him and the moment you look away, you've forgotten what his face looks like. But if you keep your eyes focused on him, you start to notice how incredibly out of place he looks. He's dressed all in black—black Vans, black jeans, a black hoodie—and leaning against the brick building smoking a cigarette. It's . . . a look.

"Oh yeah . . ." Caleb breathes. "We've definitely seen him here before."

"What do you think his ability is?" I ask, suddenly excited by all the possibilities.

"It's definitely not invisibility," he scoffs. "God, could he look more conspicuous?"

"Seriously," I laugh, "he's really gunning for the role of 'Shady Park Guy Number Five.'" Caleb laughs loudly and I smirk, satisfied. But the sound seems to catch the attention of Shady Guy.

"Ooh, whoops," I whisper, turning my head to talk into Caleb's shoulder, "I think he caught us staring. Quick, look like you're talking to me."

"I *am* talking to you," Caleb says, amused. "I doubt he's looking at us—"

"No, don't look—" I say, but it's too late. Caleb has already turned his body away from me to look at Shady Guy. I stay angled toward him, hoping that Caleb can pass it off as looking around the park and not us staring at some stranger, but Caleb is not always the most subtle person on the planet.

"Okay, he was definitely looking at us, because now he's coming over here," Caleb whispers frantically, turning back and leaning into my space.

"Shit," I mutter. What did I just get us into?

"Oh god, what if he's like, a crazy homophobe coming over here to try and save us from damnation or something?" Caleb says, complete panic on his face. That thought hadn't occurred to me, but it is far more likely than what I'm imagining. And surprisingly, less terrifying.

"What if he's a *dangerous mutant* coming over here to kill us?" I rasp, and Caleb gives me a dubious look.

"I seriously doubt that," he says, and I'm about to rebut when I hear—

"Hey there."

Caleb and I unfurl from the closed-parentheses position our bodies were making on the bench to see Shady Guy looming over us. He's smiling blankly and we should just get up and leave like you're supposed to when a crazy person approaches you in public, but I'm stuck.

"Um . . . hi?" Caleb's arm moves slightly closer around me as he turns his body toward Shady Guy, and it brings me a modicum of comfort.

"Hi," I say, for absolutely no good reason at all.

"Do I know you?" Shady Guy asks.

"No, I don't think so." Caleb shakes his head.

"Are you sure? I could have sworn I've seen you around before." Shady Guy gives a broad smile and, against my better judgement, I'm a bit charmed by it. "Say, are you one of Dr. B.'s patients? Dr. Bright, that is."

"Um, yes," Caleb answers. "Yeah, I am."

"Caleb," I whisper, "what are you doing?" It's one thing to make small talk with a stranger—it's another thing entirely to tell him about your therapist. And any other information that having said specific therapist might imply.

Shady Guy invites himself to sit, settling down on the other side of Caleb, and I give a weak protest, hoping to end whatever this is before it starts.

"Oops, looks like your friend doesn't want me to join you," Shady Guy says, leering at us.

"Boyfriend," I mumble, wrong-footed, and then I'm instantly

angry and embarrassed that I chose this moment to say that word out loud for the first time, without even consulting Caleb first.

"Good for you," he condescends. "Do you mind if I talk to your *boyfriend* for a moment?"

"I guess not," I say blankly. But I do mind. I know in my heart of hearts that I don't want to be talking to this guy any longer. And I definitely don't want him talking to Caleb. But the words leap from my mouth before I have time to decide on the shape of them.

"What's your name, kid?" Shady Guy asks. It squeezes us uncomfortably, my body pressing into the hard metal armrest at the end. Shady Guy drapes his arm casually over the back of the bench and I watch it happen with detached curiosity. It doesn't bother me. Why doesn't it bother me?

"Caleb."

"Nice to meet you, Caleb. I'm Damien," Shady Guy—Damien—says. "And you are?" He leans around Caleb to look at me.

"Adam," I say, my voice sounding small.

"Are you a patient of Dr. B.'s as well, Adam?"

"No."

"Ah, okay. Shame." He grimaces. "So, Caleb, what do you do?"

"Um . . . go to high school?" Caleb answers, a blank look coming over his face.

"No"—Damien rolls his eyes, exasperated—"I mean, what's your ability? I assume you're an Atypical. Dr. B. doesn't have any normal patients as far as I know."

"I'm an empath," Caleb says, like that's not the biggest secret he has. I want to speak up, grab Caleb's hand and get up and leave, but the more immediate part of me wants to stay, see where this goes. Now that he's sitting with us, Damien doesn't seem so bad.

"Huh." Damien looks thoughtful, his mouth twisting like a scar in the middle of his face. "That means you feel the emotions of other people, right?"

"Basically." Caleb shrugs.

"Ah," Damien sighs. "That's a bit of a disappointment."

"I'm sorry," Caleb says, and sincere and righteous anger flares up inside of me, cutting through the out-of-place contentment I'd been sitting in moments before.

"Wait," I interrupt, "why are you apologizing to him?"

"I want him to like me," Caleb says, like he's in a trance.

"What?" I get that Caleb likes to be Mr. Popular, but this is ridiculous. Caleb is looking at Damien like he's the greatest thing he's seen all week, and suddenly I'm drowning in jealousy. I know I should say something, have a discussion with him about this, but . . . I want Damien to like me too.

What the hell is happening?

"Ooh, *that's* an interesting turn of events." Damien grins, settling into the bench, looking like the king of the world. He's actually not as awkward and odd-looking as he first appeared. There's something attractive about him, something seductive—

"Damien?"

We all turn to look toward the voice, and see a girl a little older than me and Caleb, staring incredulously at us. All at once, I notice how sunny it is in the park, how in public we are. I'd forgotten where I was, drawn in by Damien.

"Oh boy," Damien mutters before raising his voice and turning toward the girl. "Well, isn't this just turning out to be a party?"

"Why are you scaring a couple of teenagers?" she demands, walking toward us, arms folded. I'm uneasy—her chambray shirt is covered in paint stains, hair a mess, wild intensity in her eyes. Is this park full of weirdos all the time?

"What makes you think I'm scaring them?" Damien asks sweetly.

"How do you think?" she snarks, jaw twitching.

"Ah, right"—Damien nods—"that pesky mind reader."

"*Damien*," she hisses, looking around her and stepping closer.

Wait, what did Damien just say?

"Oh, don't worry," he says in a placating tone, "we're in privileged company. Caleb here is a patient of Dr. B.'s. Just ignore the other one."

"Hey!" Caleb shouts as I eke out an offended "Excuse me?" My head is a mess. I can't decide who's a friend and who's a foe and all I want to do is put my hand in Caleb's, bury my head in his shoulder, but he feels so far away from me.

"Don't talk to him like that," Caleb says, snapped out of his reverie, and I start to feel the warmth of his body again.

"I think you should get out of here, Damien," the girl says, more fiercely than her hippie appearance and small stature would suggest was possible.

"Don't you want to catch up?" Damien says flirtatiously. "Shoot the breeze? It's been a minute."

"Seriously," she bites, "or I'll call the police."

"Okay, okay." Damien puts his hands up, rising from the bench. "No need to go nuclear. I'm sure I'll be seeing you soon anyway, Chloe. I daresay the tides are turning for ol' Damien."

"Just go," she sneers.

"Ta-ta, kiddos." Damien waves as he walks away. "Nice chatting with you boys."

As he walks away, my head starts to clear, revealing a swirl of frustration. I don't understand what just happened, but all I know is that my boyfriend was giving priority to some strange, older guy while I was sitting here, clearly uncomfortable. Was I uncomfortable? I can't even remember anymore.

I wait until Damien reaches the edge of the park to speak.

"Well," I start, "*that* was interesting."

"Wait . . ." Caleb seems to be recalibrating. "Why are you angry? And why is it the 'angry at Caleb' kind of angry?"

"You can tell the difference?" I ask, momentarily distracted by the finer points of his power.

"It's a very specific kind of angry," he explains. "Like, disappointed and pissed all at once." Yep, that pretty much nails it.

"'I want him to like me'?" I echo Caleb's own words back at him.

"What?" His face scrunches up as he turns to look at me.

"Was that . . ." I don't even want to ask the question but it needs to be asked. ". . . flirting?"

"Ew, what?" Caleb looks genuinely disgusted, which soothes me a little. "God, he's, like, ten years older than us!"

I can tell we're about to get into a dumb argument when I hear—

"Um, boys?"

Both our heads snap toward the girl, still standing over us. Her hand is raised awkwardly in an effort to gain our attention, and I feel foolish having this fight (if that's what it is) in front of her.

"I'm sorry, who are you?" I ask.

"Oh, I'm Chloe." She sticks out her hand for us to shake it. "Nice to meet you."

A mind reader. A mind reader and a fucking mind controller. Or, no, that's not what Damien is, apparently. He . . . pushes thoughts onto people? Emotions? That's what Chloe—the *mind reader*—said.

I wouldn't have guessed that getting coffee with a mind reader would be one of the least insane parts of my day, but it actually shed light on a lot of things. Chloe is a patient of Dr. Bright's too, and she explained Damien's power. How it wasn't Caleb's fault that he wanted Damien to like him. That's how it works—Damien wants something and you want it too. And because Caleb is an empath, Damien's want was doubled. He took the brunt of it for us and I feel horrifically guilty over my momentary jealousy.

Whatever you want to call what Damien does, it's pretty terrifying, and I'm wondering if the name is a self-appointed moniker or a nice piece of prescient work on the part of his parents. Oh god, it really could be psychic parents, couldn't it? That's the realm of reality in which I now exist.

I need to lie down.

No. What I really need is more information. Knowledge is power. Knowledge is king. Knowledge can help me prepare for whatever crazy thing is going to get thrown at us next. It's what's going to help me be a good boyfriend to this incredible, unusual, strange, wonderful guy I'm dating. I need knowledge.

I hop off the kitchen counter, where I'd been sitting, staring blankly into space, and walk into my parents' office to find my dad standing in front of his filing cabinet, flipping through folders.

"Dad?" I ask, feeling like a little kid, "can we talk?"

"Of course." The filing cabinet drawer clicks shut as he turns to face me. "What's on your mind?"

"You and Mom . . ." I start, twisting my watchband around my wrist. "You guys—what you do—your work, I mean—"

"Adam, are you okay?" He interrupts my nonsensical rambling, taking a step toward me with concern in his eyes.

"Do you want some tea?" I blurt, suddenly intimidated by my parents' office in a way I haven't been since I was small.

"Sure, kid." He smiles, patting me on the shoulder, leading me out of the office and into the kitchen.

I go about my familiar tea-making routine in a heavy silence. Paranoid thoughts run around my head—does he know about Caleb? How could he know? What would he do if he did know? Should I tell him?

No. It's not my secret to tell. And it's not that I don't trust my parents, but there are things I don't know about them. That thought scares me more than any other.

"So," my dad says as he hands me a mug, "what's going on?"

"I've just been . . ." How do I ask him about Atypicals without telling him Atypicals exist? "I guess I've been curious about what you and Mom do."

"Okay . . ." he leads.

"Yeah, so," I flounder, "what exactly do you guys do?"

"What?" He smiles a bit, like a seventeen-year-old asking his parents about what they do for a living is silly and strange, which I guess it is.

"I get that you're neuroscientists, but what do you actually *do*?" I ask again.

"Mostly research, these days."

"You realize how vague that sounds, right?" I scoff, and he sighs heavily.

"Adam, we've been over this: a lot of our work is confidential," he explains.

"But *why*?" I press. "You're scientists, you're not spies. And don't give me any of that crap about brains being secret depending on whose brain it is, I get plenty of that from Mom," I add when it looks like he's going to feed me some company line he and Mom have predetermined.

"Son," he starts, and it instantly puts my guard up, "we still know so little about the brain. We've made more progress in the past twenty years than the previous two thousand, but we've barely scratched the surface."

"What's your point?" I ask.

"Knowledge is important," he says, as if that phrase isn't used so much in this house that it might as well be embroidered on a pillow, "but sometimes more knowledge means more danger."

"What are you talking about?" I ask. "What danger?"

"Some people use knowledge as a weapon," he says calmly. "The more we discover, the more opportunity there is for the wrong people to exploit that information for their own gain."

Everything he's saying makes sense. In his rational, warm voice, it sounds like the end of the discussion. But I've lived with my father for seventeen years. I'm his son. He can be as much of a closed book as anyone—other than my mom—but I can still tell when he's hiding something.

"Is that all it's about?" I push. "Hiding information from bad people?"

"What else would it be about?" he asks, and for a brief moment my dad is gone, replaced by some cold-blooded scientist examining a specimen.

"Well, like you said, there's things we don't know about the human brain," I say, thinking of Caitlin and debate and throwing someone's words back in their face to make a counterargument, "so isn't it possible that there are some dangers in the brain itself?"

"Many would argue that there's nothing more dangerous than the human brain." My dad nods and I just barely resist rolling my eyes.

"Spare me the philosopher platitudes," I groan. "You know what I mean."

"No, I don't," he says innocently. "What do you mean, *boy-chik*?"

Part of me wishes I could get the cold scientist back—I might get more out of him than my constantly concerned dad.

"Just . . ." I start, frustrated. He's better at this than me. He knows how to argue and counterargue and keep me distracted, and all I want to know is if my boyfriend is in danger because his therapist has sketchy clients, and I have no idea how to get that information.

"Is there a chance that there are people out there with brains that . . . well, that are dangerous?" I ask. "And not just in the 'people have the capacity for evil' kind of way," I continue, "but in, like, their brains are actually, physically dangerous."

My dad leans back against the counter and fixes me with an inscrutable look. Oh god, he's onto me. But how could he possibly be onto me?

"Physically dangerous in what way?" he asks lightly.

"Like, okay," I say, hating how imperfect my speech is in this moment, "like, a mind reader would be an extreme example. And obviously that stuff isn't real—"

My dad has tensed just slightly, and both my arms are immediately covered in goose bumps.

"But if we don't know a lot about the human brain," I continue, ignoring all the unspoken things that are hanging between us, "then it's possible that the human brain can do, like, inhuman things, right?"

He stares at me, head tilted, before putting his mug down and crossing his arms.

"It's certainly possible," he says to the ground, his voice still in that casual "this is all hypothetical" register that never struck me as odd before now, "but, while there's been plenty of speculation, nothing has ever been proven."

We're getting somewhere now, and I realize I need to be economical with my questions. I want to ask about Damien and Chloe—find out if my dad knows about mind control and telepathy (holy fuck, I still can't believe those things are *real*)—but the most important thing is Caleb. He's always first priority.

"Okay, so, let's speculate." I try to match his casualness. "If someone *could* do something like read minds, how would you deal with that?"

"As a scientist?"

"As a person."

And here it is. The crux of it all. I don't know how to be a boyfriend to Caleb. I wouldn't know how to be a boyfriend to Caleb even if he was just the incredibly handsome football-playing Golden Boy. I especially don't know how to be a boyfriend to someone with a supernatural ability.

"Why do you ask?" The head tilt is back.

"I'm just . . . speculating," I echo, hoping that will be enough.

"How are things going with Caleb?" He pivots and the question is like a shot of adrenaline to the heart. Is he trying to change the subject or is he connecting the dots?

"Things are fine." I nod nervously. "They're good." I let him lead the conversation away from science and into the equally uncharted territory of talking about my relationship with Caleb with my father, keeping an eye out for land mines all the while.

42

CALEB

Dr. Bright's emotions are a swirl of worry, surprise, and anger, all wrapped up in a black tar of self-loathing. Nothing in her body language or face has changed in the last ten minutes as I've described our encounter with Damien and Chloe, but her emotions are telling me that she wants to bury her face in her hands and tear her hair out. I know how she feels.

"Caleb," she says, an entire sentence on its own. "I am so sorry that this happened. Damien never should have confronted you— it was completely inappropriate and I will most certainly be having a conversation with him about it. Though, as much as I like to keep my patients separate, I am glad that Chloe intervened."

I'm glad too, to be honest. I have no idea what would have happened if Chloe hadn't stepped in. I've never felt like that before— I've spent almost this whole year with other people invading my space, my feelings, my brain, but I've never felt like I've been body-snatched. Being around Damien was like freezing to death. I was getting warm and sleepy and compliant, and if things had kept going I would have eventually lost all of my own brain functioning. It reminded me of Henry at the dance—that cold, slimy determination—except, this time, the feeling slithered its way into me and none of my defenses could keep it out.

"I'm sorry we were spying on you," I say sheepishly, and I feel some of Dr. Bright's anger fizzle out. "We shouldn't have been there in the first place. Adam was just curious about the whole thing. And I guess . . . I guess I was too. I mean, even though it was a little scary, it's kind of nice knowing that there are other people out there like me."

Dr. Bright exhales and the black tar strengthens, squeezing my rib cage so hard that I worry it might crack. How does she live like this?

"I should have been more forthcoming with information about Atypicals." She sighs. "It's natural for you to be curious and I should have been more open to answering your questions. I was just . . ."

She trails off, rubbing her hands nervously, two things she *never* does, and my stomach clenches in fear. Suddenly the possibility of having more information seems like a terrible, terrifying prospect.

"I was trying to protect you," she finishes, and the weight inside of me lightens a fraction.

"Protect me from what?" I demand. "You sound just like my parents. I know you guys had a conversation about all this when I first started seeing you and that they're worried about people out there who might want to hurt me, but what has you all so freaked out? I can feel feelings, how much danger could I really be in?"

I'm working hard to make my voice sound casual, scoffing at the idea of some looming, villainous force, but I'm cold all over, heart pounding rapidly in an attempt to warm my blood. Dr. Bright looks at me, and I feel like I'm standing on the edge of a diving board. Wobbling and jelly-legged, unable to jump and unable to walk back. It fits awkwardly in my body and I know it belongs to Dr. Bright. She's uncertain. She's *never* uncertain.

"There's an organization," she says finally, "called The Atypical Monitors."

It's like having six shots of espresso—fear races through my veins like simply saying the name has caused Dr. Bright to summon demons from hell. She's afraid. She's *terrified*. My body is full of emotions that I've never felt from her before, and I'm starting to shut down.

"Caleb?" she asks from above the mud I'm sinking into, "are you all right?"

"It's—" I'm having a hard time speaking around the molasses. "It's too much, I'm sorry. I can't—can we talk about something else?"

I desperately want to know more about these Monitor guys but I'm overloaded, the hard drive in my brain fritzing from a soda spill of foreign feelings. I can't take any more information in or I'll completely lose it. My world is dark and upside down and that's when I realize I've closed my eyes, bending over to put my head between my legs.

Meltdown complete.

I blink and I'm back in my bedroom, the rest of my therapy and the drive home a blur. My mom is standing in the doorway, talking to me, but she's far away. I find my ears again, tune them into her frequency, finding the static of her worry and holding on to it until the waves turn into sound.

"—nothing to worry about," she says, contradicting her own emotions. "Dr. Bright shouldn't have scared you like that."

"She didn't scare me, Mom," I groan, irritated. Sometimes I think life would be easier if everyone could do what I do. "I just got overwhelmed. You know that happens sometimes."

She nods and I can feel that she wants to step into my room, sit down on my bed, put her arm around me. But she won't because she knows she's already too close. If she touches me, I'll just start drowning in someone else's worry.

"I never wanted life to be this hard for you," she whispers, and my vision comes into focus enough to see that there are tears in her eyes. Something in me unwinds. This is one of the things I love about my mom. She's learned that trying to hide her feelings from me just makes it harder for me to process. So she's honest with me about what she's thinking, even if it makes both of us feel worse.

I appreciate it more than I've ever been able to express to her, but I think she knows in that way that moms know.

"I know, Mom." I sigh and we look at each other helplessly, a half-length of room between us. I scoot over on my bed, highlighting the space that was already there. An invitation. She jerks her head in an awkward nod and walks into my room, sitting heavily next to me. I'm already on her wavelength so the proximity doesn't change anything. Doesn't make it worse.

"You're a very special boy, Caleb." She pats my arm and I roll my eyes.

"Yeah, I know." Just like that, I'm annoyed again. "That's what everyone keeps saying."

"Well, that's because it's true," she says earnestly. "Even before we found out about your ability, you were always so sensitive. So caring."

"God, Mom, you make me sound like such a loser," I deflect, her calm, loving presence unable to cover up my own discomfort at having what is shaping up to be a pretty embarrassing conversation.

"You're not a loser, Caleb," she assures me. "You have a beautiful gift. I wouldn't change anything about you."

"But . . ." I lead, wobbling on the diving board again.

"But, when you're a parent, you hope your child is . . ."

"Normal?" I finish for her, feeling like a failure. The genuine love she has for me is in every cell of my body, but that doesn't stop my own body from producing disappointment like that's the only thing it knows how to make.

"Yes," she agrees sadly. "We love that you're you, that you have this ability. But it might make things harder for you. Just like—" She stops herself mid-sentence and I fully understand how frustrating it must have been for Adam all those months. I badly want to know what she was about to say. And then, thinking of Adam helps me put the pieces together.

"Just like dating a guy might make things harder for me?" I grimace and I feel the cloying toffee of pity drip into my stomach.

We haven't exactly had the Conversation yet, because I'm not sure how to have it. Or if we even need to. My parents haven't asked and I haven't told them, but we all know. Or at least, I think they know. If not, I may have just dropped a bomb on my poor mother. But I don't feel any surprise from her, so I doubt it.

"We love Adam," she says, squeezing my arm, and then that rickety uncertainty crops up again. "That is who you're talking about, right? There's not some other boy that we haven't met that you've been secretly dating?"

I can feel that she's teasing me a little—calling me out for not being up-front with her—but there's also a genuine question in there.

"No, Mom," I say, rolling my eyes, "there's no other secret guy. It's Adam. *Just* Adam."

"Well"—she pats my arm again, extremely awkwardly this time—"that's good. He is a very nice young man."

"He is . . ." I start, trying to edge back to the point despite the fact that, now that I'm here, I really don't want to have this conversation. Better to get it over with, though, I guess.

"He *is* a nice young man," I echo, trying to find my words. "He is very nice. And . . . a man."

I look up from my lap to see my mom's bemused expression. She's trying not to laugh at me and close to completely failing. I'm not worried anymore about this conversation going sideways but I really, *really* want to run from the room.

"A young man," I correct for no good reason and because she hasn't said anything yet. My own mortification is heating my insides up, burning out any other emotions I might feel from her.

"Hon, it's okay." She smiles. "Relax. This doesn't have to be a big conversation if you don't want it to be. But I'm also happy to do the loud and proud coming-out thing if that's what you want—"

"Jeez, Mom, that's not what I'm doing. I'm not—" I stop, realizing that what I was about to say isn't true. "Well, I mean, I guess I know what I'm *not*. I'm not straight. I guess. I mean, I like Adam. And that's good. So. Yeah."

I wince at my rambling, relieved that she doesn't need me to explain and yet trying to explain anyway.

"We don't need to do the loud and proud thing," I rush out, before backpedaling. "Not that I'm not proud. It's not like I'm trying to hide it or anything. It's just that . . ."

"You have bigger things to worry about," she finishes. A weight lifts from my shoulders. If I didn't know better, there are times when I'd think my mom was an empath too.

"Right." I nod. "And Adam is cool with all that stuff, by the way. We're—we're good."

43

CALEB

I want so badly for that to stay true. For Adam and me to stay good. But, because I apparently can't catch a fucking break, telling him about me and becoming his boyfriend did not make everything easy. The honeymoon phase or whatever is over and we're not the perfect couple that I'd been fantasizing we'd be.

I constantly have to remind myself that he knows about my ability. That I don't have to hide. I'm training myself out of holding things back and it feels scary and unnatural at first. Like I jumped out of the plane and just kept falling, falling, falling.

He's been there to catch me. Most of the time. But sometimes . . .

That huge, powerful ocean is still there. I thought I could banish it. I thought that not keeping secrets anymore, that giving in to our butterflies, would wipe the black days away. And it did at first. Those first few weeks—spent in my backyard just as spring had fully sprung—were perfect. I walked through my life in a warm, green haze. Adam was my anchor, keeping me from spinning out, and I was a boat for him on the vast, deep ocean that is his emotions, and things were so good that I started thinking about us in cheesy-ass metaphors, apparently.

I've gotten better at telling what's him and what's me—what's yellow and what's blue—but a lot of the time, things are green. And when things are green, I feel right in my own body in a way I never have before.

But then: the sky darkens and the waves roll in and where I was standing at the shore before, looking at the storm swirling over the water, now I'm dragged under. His tide is too strong and I'm too close to the undertow to do anything about it. Adam has learned how to weather this. He's been living with it his whole life. But I don't know how to swim, not in these waters. I drown instantly and sink to the bottom until we separate and the light starts to stream through, slowly leaching the water from my lungs and bringing color back into my cheeks.

Today is one of those days.

"You should just go home," he mutters from under his sweatshirt. We're lying side by side on his bed—his parents aren't home but, even if they were, they would have no reason to be scandalized. We're above the covers, I still have my shoes on, and we're not even touching. Adam is faced toward the wall, swallowed in a hoodie he stole from me (not that I gave much of a fight; he looks pretty cute in it) and even though there are inches between us, it feels like miles of stormy sea.

"I don't want to leave you like this," I say to his back, desperate to reach out and touch but not knowing if it will make it worse or better.

"Caleb, I'm fine," he insists, though there's not much fire behind it.

"You know that doesn't work on me," I tell him. "I'm the one person you can't lie to about being fine."

He sighs and rolls over to look at me. Shadows from his hoodie play over his brown skin turning him back into the black-and-white-movie version of himself.

"There's no reason for both of us to feel this way," he says. "It would make me feel better if you went home and got somebody else's emotions in you." He grimaces at his own phrasing. "You know what I mean. Or, even better, go somewhere you can just feel yourself."

"You need to find a better way to talk about my ability," I joke weakly, and he gives me a pity smile. I hate those smiles. They're placating and fake and only make me feel more helpless. I try to make him smile for real when he's like this—try to make him laugh—but it always feels impossible. Sometimes, it makes it worse.

"Caleb," he sighs, "please. You don't need to be here when I'm like this. I know I'm not exactly the best company right now."

"You're always the best company," I mumble, shimmying closer to him. One blade of grass bursts through the concrete. A single beam of sunlight starts to stream through the clouds.

In the next moment it's gone.

44

ADAM

I wish I could control this. Caleb has the ability to feel the emotions of any human on the planet, and he's getting better and better at controlling that ability all the time. I can't control even one of my emotions. I want to eradicate this feeling forever. I never want to see how it infects Caleb, how it makes him slow and dull and takes away the light in his eyes. I feel like a parasite, a leech that's sucking all the goodness out of him.

And yet, he stays. He stays and is a life raft for me. And we do our best to float until the dark cloud passes and then I try everything in my power to take advantage of the sunny days.

Today is one of those days. I showed up at Caleb's house after the last—and only—meeting for Latin club this semester. The club is only me and one other student, so it's not exactly a big time commitment.

I pull Caleb out into his backyard the moment he invites me in and grab one of the various footballs that's always lying around. Caleb's face lights up in a surprised smile and we toss the football back and forth until the sun goes down. Caleb does his best to explain some plays to me and I do my best to be interested. Football isn't so boring when it's Caleb explaining it.

It eventually turns into a messy touch football game between the two of us that doesn't have any coherent rules or boundaries but which does involve a good deal of tackling, which I am more than okay with.

At one point, I have possession of the ball, running around in the setting sun with no idea what I'm supposed to be doing. Caleb guns for me, grabbing me around the legs and tossing me over his shoulder. He runs to whatever section of the yard he had determined was the end zone and claims a touchdown, despite the fact that I'm still holding the football.

"Well, I'm holding *you*," he says, victorious, spinning around as I hold on for dear life, still slung over his broad shoulders, "so by the transitive property . . ."

"Ooh, look at . . . you," I wheeze out, getting dizzy, "Mr. . . . Smart . . . Guy."

I should be completely humiliated by this ridiculous display of machismo but I'm, of course, charmed. Caleb gives another full belly laugh at my attempt to tease him and reaches up to grab my torso, bringing me back to my feet like I'm a sack of potatoes.

I've dropped the football at some point and wind my arms around his neck as he wraps his arms tighter around me. My feet are barely on the ground, but I don't care. I let him hold me up and we kiss until it's darkness all around us.

45

CALEB

"Um . . . hello?"

The large, garage-like metal door slides shut behind me, echoing through the musty space. It smells like paint and turpentine and a swirl of frustration-inspiration. Like all the people who have made art here—tried to make art—have left some of their feelings behind, just waiting to be soaked up by someone like me.

"Caleb!"

I whip around at the sudden, sharp sound of Chloe's voice to see her smiling at me from another doorway hidden in the far corner of the room. As always, her overalls are covered in paint, her hair a mess, and her feelings distant and strange.

"Sorry." She winces. "I didn't mean to scare you."

"It's all right," I breathe. "I just didn't feel you come in."

"Really?" she asks as she walks toward me. "I'm the only one here right now."

"Yeah." I rub the back of my neck as my eyes track her movement around the room, picking up paints and cloths and brushes and going through what is clearly a nightly routine. "It's . . . I don't know, your feelings aren't as loud as some other people's, I guess. At least, not always."

"Hm." Her face scrunches up in a way that tells me she's reaching out for my thoughts. There's a bubble of uncertainty within her, shaking with fear.

"No, I don't want you to think—" I rush to explain. "It's not like you don't feel things. You feel, like, *a lot* of things," I tell her truthfully. "But I think sometimes . . ."

"Sometimes I'm too in my head to make the feelings big?" she finishes.

"Yeah." I nod. "Something like that."

We smile tentatively at each other and the bubble stops shaking, settling warm and happy in my chest.

"I'm really glad I met you, Caleb," she says. "It's so nice having someone to talk to about this."

"Yeah, I was just thinking the same thing."

"I know." She smirks.

It *is* nice to talk to Chloe. To know that she understands, at least to a point, what it's like to have your mind and body not be your own. I don't have to censor myself around her—don't have to worry about sounding dumb or saying the wrong thing—because she knows everything I'm thinking anyway.

"So . . ." I start, my face warming at the idea of Chloe listening in on my sappy thoughts—I still have *some* dignity left. "You needed help moving some stuff?"

"Yes!" She claps her hands, and a zing of golden excitement races through my veins. "I want to clear away some of my sculpture stuff to make room for Frank's paintings and, well—"

"You're built like a scarecrow?" I tease. She laughs, big and bright, and my whole body feels bathed in sunlight.

I'm about to ask who Frank is when a cloud comes in, smothering the sunlight. My shoulders tense as something big and foreign climbs on top of them. This isn't like one of Adam's storms. This is a tornado, an electrical storm, a fire, and a flood all at once.

"Frank! Hi!" I hear Chloe say over the slide of the metal door. I turn around and feel a spark of familiarity—both in the face and the feelings. Chloe is smiling warmly at the man—Frank—gesturing him into the studio. He's older—maybe thirty—ratty

clothes hanging off his tall frame, the dark skin of his cheeks
sunken into his face. I've seen him before.

"I didn't mean to interrupt," he says, gentler than I could have
thought possible from someone with feelings as big as his. They're
spinning me around—fear, sadness, anxiety—and I can't find still-
ness long enough to grab on to any one of them. I've not only seen
him before—I've *felt* this before.

"You're the homeless man who sits outside the bank," I blurt.
Chloe visibly winces but I barely notice because there's raw, cold
fear clutching my heart.

"No, shit, sorry—" I apologize frantically. "I didn't mean—I've
just seen you around, that's all."

"Frank is a friend," Chloe says in a way that makes me feel like
a child who just broke a fancy vase. "I'm helping him work on his
paintings."

"Oh, right." I nod. Frank is still standing in the doorway, staring at me with big, frightened eyes.

"Frank, this is Caleb." Chloe's sugary compassion is pushing
me to move my feet in Frank's direction. "Caleb, Frank."

"Nice to meet you, man." I stick out my hand like I didn't just
make an awkward spectacle of myself moments ago. He pauses
before taking his hand off the door and reaching for mine. The
moment our palms touch, the tornado starts again, making me
sway. The fear is enormous—bigger than I've ever felt from anyone before—but it doesn't spur a fight-or-flight response. I'm frozen in place, feeling like maybe I should just give in to the fear.
Maybe I deserve it.

"Hey, Caleb, you okay?" A soft hand touches on my shoulder
and I let go of Frank's hand to look into Chloe's concerned face.

"Yeah, I'm—" I clear my throat. "I'm okay."

"Are you . . . ?" Frank starts quietly. It sounds like his voice has
hardly ever been used. His eyes are still wide, his gut-churning fear
still ruling every cell in my body, but there's a tiny burn of curiosity cutting through it.

"Never mind." He shakes his head like he's clearing the cob-
webs.

"I think I'm gonna sit down for a second," I say, moving away from the blast zone of Frank's feelings. It doesn't help.

"Yeah, of course," Chloe says, and I try to grab on to her worry, with no success. She's not Adam.

"You just sit there and get your breath back," she continues, like nothing is out of the ordinary, "and I'll tell you about what Frank and I are working on!"

She's started to move around the studio again, like a butterfly flitting around flowers, and Frank and I eye each other warily from across the room. His feelings are still a confusing swirl inside of me but I don't feel like I'm in danger. Instead, I feel like I am the danger.

46

ADAM

"You can say no, but—"

"Oh god, is there another football party?" I groan dramatically. We're sitting on Caleb's bedroom floor as always and I'm painting his nails with polish we stole from his sister who, incidentally, completely terrifies me with her no-nonsense intensity. I'd never admit that to Caleb, but of course he already knows.

"No, no party," he laughs. A few weeks ago he dragged me along to a team gathering and, while not as terrible as I feared (thankfully both Bryce-and Henry-less), it was definitely not my first choice for how to spend an evening. One upside to Caleb's ability is that he can't stand group situations either, so we bailed early.

"It's just a stupid scrimmage thing," Caleb says, his breath puffing over my forehead as I lean over to paint his right hand with precision. "JV and varsity playing on teams for spirit week."

"Oh yeah, you guys do that every year, right?" I vaguely remember weeks where every hallway and every athlete were draped in the school colors and full of school pride. Obviously, I've never participated myself.

"Yeah," he says, "once in the fall and once in the spring. I'm always on the Red Team."

I look up to see a big grin on his face and can't help smiling in return.

"Is that the good team?" I tease.

"It is because I'm on it." He smirks and I lean forward to kiss the smug look off his face.

"So . . . will you come?" Caleb asks again a few minutes later.

"Yeah, of course." I smile. "Now I get to openly ogle you in your uniform." I waggle my eyebrows and Caleb blushes up a storm. I still get a nervous thrill every time I flirt with him—like there's always the chance that it's going to go wrong—but watching the red rise up his neck into his cheeks is worth the risk.

"I knew you didn't actually think we looked like giant candy canes." He laughs and it's my turn to blush. I want to shove at him but fear messing up the nail polish, so I just smile and shake my head.

"Oh my god," he says suddenly, a surprised look coming over his face.

". . . what?"

"You were jealous," he breathes, like he's just had an epiphany.

"Um, when?" I ask, knowing there could be lots of times to choose from.

"About Caitlin and the dance," he says. "When she asked me, that's what that was. That dripping, oozing stuff in my chest."

"Ew, what?" I laugh. "Is that what jealousy feels like?" I love hearing Caleb describe emotions. He's gotten more and more comfortable explaining his ability to me, and I could listen to him talk about it for hours.

"That's what it felt like then," he says. "It's different now, when you get jealous. Like with Damien—when you were confused about why I wanted him to like me."

"To be fair, I was confused for a lot of reasons," I say. But I want to hear more. "Why was it different?"

"I think because we're together now?" Caleb tilts his head like he's tuning in to the radio of my emotions. "Like, it's less pointed than it was with Caitlin. God"—he shakes his head and smiles—"there were so many things about you that I just didn't get for the longest time."

"But you get them now?" I ask.

"Yeah, I'm starting to." He smiles.

"You know," I say, "you can always ask me what I'm feeling. I'll tell you." I do my best to really believe this, knowing that there are still things I haven't told him, and that Caleb can feel that desire to hide.

Wanting to mean it must be enough, because Caleb says, "I know," and we grin dopily at each other before I ask him to tell me more about the scrimmage. Caleb grows animated, and I keep having to pull his hand back down as he gestures, causing both of us to laugh. It's been twenty minutes and I've barely painted one hand.

"I think Chloe might come to the scrimmage too," Caleb says.

"Chloe the mind reader?" I ask.

"That's the one."

I put down the bottle of polish and lean back on my hands to look at Caleb. He's giving me the puppy-dog look, like I'm going to have a problem with the fact that he's been hanging out with Chloe. Which I don't. Even if I got a little freaked out by the whole encounter with her and Damien, spying on his therapist's patients was my idea in the first place.

"That'll be cool," I say, careful to keep my voice neutral.

"She's really chill," Caleb says earnestly. "I went to her art studio a few days ago and she's really good."

"What kind of art does she do?" I ask, sensing that Caleb wants to talk more about it.

"She says she's mostly done ceramics until now, but she's starting to do a lot of painting," he starts to explain, before continuing with a hesitance I haven't seen from Caleb in a while. "She met this guy—Frank—who used to be an artist too. He's a Marine and, well, he's been having a hard go of it. Homeless and stuff."

"Man, that's hard," I say.

"Yeah." He nods, looking down at his nails. "And I guess he really loved to paint before he joined up so Chloe's helping him get back into it. She's reading his mind and then painting what he can't. I think he's got an injury in his hands or something."

"Wait, what?" I struggle to keep up. Our little stakeouts in front of Dr. Bright's office had been a fun, silly game. But then it opened Pandora's box and a whole new, complicated, unreal world sprang out of it. "She's reading his mind and painting what she sees?"

"Yeah! So, like, he's thinking about what he wants his paintings to look like," Caleb explains, "and then Chloe reads his mind and does the painting for him. Isn't that cool?"

"Does he know that's what she's doing?" I ask, thinking that yes, it is cool, but also completely freaky.

"Oh, yeah, totally." Caleb nods seriously. "They're working on it together."

"So she just up and told this guy that she's a mind reader?"

"Well, no, not really," he says. "It's not like he's just some guy. They're friends. And . . . well . . ." There's that hesitancy again and it still makes me grind my teeth. "I think he's special too. Not like me and Chloe are—he's not an Atypical. But he . . . it's weird. When I met him, I realized I'd actually felt his feelings before."

"What do you mean?"

I'm doing my best to focus on what Caleb is saying as he explains a huge block of desperate emotions that would hit him sometimes when he takes the bus. Caleb is animated as he talks, and my heart swells that he feels comfortable enough to talk to me about this kind of stuff, even if it has messed me up a bit to have my entire worldview completely shifted.

"And his feelings were really different, you know?" Caleb says. "Like, way more intense and louder than other people's. I couldn't feel anyone else the couple times I passed him around town."

"What, like how it is with me?" I ask, trying not to sound jealous. The first time Caleb told me how much more he liked my feelings over anyone else's, I practically passed out from happiness.

"No, not really." He shakes his head. "It's not comfortable in the same way. His feelings are pretty extreme. And they, like, grate on me in a way that yours definitely don't."

"Why?" I ask.

"I don't know . . . Chloe seems to think that something happened to him when he was in the military."

"Hm." I think through the various psychology books I've read. "That makes sense. I mean, if he has PTSD—which it sounds like he probably does, I mean it's so common in vets and if he actually saw combat . . . well, maybe that makes the emotions more intense?"

"Oh." Caleb blinks. "Yeah, maybe. I didn't even think about that."

"Maybe talk to Dr. Bright about it?" I suggest.

"Yeah. Yeah, that's a good idea." He nods.

"Well, wait, if Chloe wasn't talking about PTSD, what does she think happened to him?" I ask.

"Oh, she thinks . . . she thinks he may have been part of some experiment or something," Caleb says. "Like, I guess some of the stuff she's seen in his thoughts is sort of . . . sketchy."

"What?" I laugh. "That's crazy."

"Is it?" Caleb raises his eyebrows at me and I have to concede. Caleb went to a telepath's art studio this week, I guess anything's possible. I swallow in fear, thinking about my dad looking at the floor as he tried to convince me his work was in hypotheticals alone, before Caleb distracts me.

"Anyway," he continues, "he's a nice guy, even if it is a little hard to be around him. He came by right as I was leaving Chloe's studio, and it was like being thrown on an emotional merry-go-round. Like, he's just got so much fear and sadness."

"Yikes." I grimace sympathetically. "Maybe it's best to stay away, then?"

"Yeah, maybe." He shrugs. "I don't know, it got better when he started focusing on the art. And I really feel for the guy. He's trying to get better, which I totally get. He and Chloe have started going to this art therapy thing and it sounds kinda cool."

"Have you thought about joining them?" Caleb gets a bit cagey anytime I ask him about therapy but I can tell that it's important to him. He's so terrified of repeating the mistakes he made with Tyler and Henry.

"I don't know." He shrugs again.

"Sure you do." I smile. "You've talked about using your ability to help people before. Maybe volunteering in a group thing could be a way to get into that."

"Yeah." He smiles back. "Yeah, that's a good idea."

I want to tell him how group therapy helped me. About how music is one of those things that makes me want to hurt myself less. But then I'd have to tell him about the cutting and the rehab and the open doors and I don't think I'm ready for that.

But guilt hangs heavy in my stomach. Caleb has opened up about everything. He's told me his biggest secret, takes the time to describe it to me; he shares what he's learning about Atypicals, and he's the one who was brave enough to make the first move. I haven't even mustered up the courage to have a real conversation about my depression. Here he is, telling me about mind readers and experiments and I can't tell him I've been diagnosed with a fairly common mental illness. Instead, I try to act like I'm the normal one in this relationship—ask him more questions about Chloe and Frank and using his ability for something good and hope that's enough.

"So I hear you had an interesting talk with your father the other day," my mom says, coming up behind me as I wash the dishes. I really should just avoid the kitchen entirely. Then maybe I wouldn't keep finding myself in these situations.

"Uh, yeah, we did." I aim for casual and fall somewhere along the lines of "No, Mom, I didn't drink at the party, smell my breath" levels of suspicious.

"And how was that?" she leads, crossing her arms and leaning against the counter to face me. I turn off the sink and tilt my head to look at her. She's smiling warmly at me, but there's the steely flint in her eye that I usually only see directed toward her sister.

"It was . . . frustrating," I say honestly, knowing the direct approach can be the most effective. "I just wish you and Dad would talk to me about what you do."

"Why the sudden interest?" she asks. "You never seemed to care before. What's changed?"

All right, Adam. If you're going to do the direct approach, do the direct approach.

"Caleb," I say. "He's . . . different."

"I know, sweetie." She smiles and my face heats. "He seems like a really special boy."

"Yeah," I say, staring into the sink, "he is. And I just—I want to be a good boyfriend to him, you know?"

Oh shit. Did I just tell my mom that Caleb is my boyfriend? We haven't actually had that conversation yet. I sneak a look at her to see her smile taking up her entire face. I haven't seen that expression in years.

"I think that's very sweet, Adam." She smirks and I barely suppress the eye roll. "But what does this have to do with the work your dad and I do?"

The steely flint is back and my heartbeat picks up a couple paces.

"You just . . . you're always talking about how different brains are, and Caleb's brain is, you know, different. Like the way my brain is different," I add, the admission like a blade against my skin.

"Oh, sweetie, I didn't realize—" The steel in my mother softens and dissolves, but for the wrong reasons.

"No, he's not—Caleb isn't *like* me. I mean, as far as I know. It's not the same kind of different," I say nonsensically. "He's got other stuff going on."

"What kind of other stuff?"

Direct approach, Adam. That's the best thing. The direct approach.

47

CALEB

I swear to God, the moment this semester is over, I'm not going to think about math for the entire summer. Trying to do trigonometry while surrounded by people who also really hate math is the worst kind of torture. And with Adam off in super-advanced-special-person math, I'm completely on my own.

Moses has been a good emotional touchstone—he's better at math than most people in the class, so he doesn't get caught up in the tangle of frustration in the same way as everyone else. And when that doesn't work, Tyler, weirdly, has been a refuge. I hate his feelings—hate him, hate what I did to him, his now-slightly-bumpy nose a constant reminder—but he spends so much of the class period bored or completely checked out that hooking onto his feelings is usually a complete wash.

Together, though, they're toxic. And today I'm in a radioactive wasteland the moment I step out of the classroom.

"God, just leave me alone, Tyler," Moses spits, louder than I've ever heard him. And here's the swarm: fear, anger, self-hate . . . the complete cocktail I've come to expect from this particular combination of people. I don't even know what they're fighting about today and I really don't care. I just want to get out.

"What are you gonna do, little Moses?" Tyler mocks. "Michaels isn't gonna come and save you. He's too chickenshit after I beat his ass last semester."

I feel the challenge in Tyler's emotions almost before I hear the words. He's full up on bravado, reckless, wanting to get punched. I can't give him the satisfaction.

"Shut the fuck up, Tyler," I spit before I can stop myself.

"Oh, you really wanna go again, Michaels?" Tyler steps toward me, Moses's feelings fading in the background, giving way to the burst of satisfaction in my chest. Tyler wanted this. Tyler wanted to goad me, get into another fight. I'm done caring about the why— I'm so soaked in anger and frustration and fear. He wants a fight? He'll get a fight.

"No, he doesn't," someone says, grabbing my hand and steering me away from Tyler. The hot rage is being cooled by gentle waves of water.

"This isn't any of your business, Hayes," Tyler snarls, and I feel Adam squeeze my hand. I haven't looked at him yet—I'm scared of him seeing too much of me like that—but knowing that he's there is already bringing my blood pressure down.

"What the fuck business is it of yours anyway, Tyler?" Adam says lightly. "Don't you have better things to do than picking on Moses and trying to get your face bashed in by my boyfriend? Again?"

Adam's full of bravado too—not sure this is going to work—but I'm starting to float on his ocean, the sweep of his thumb over mine like the rocking of a boat.

"Whatever." Tyler rolls his eyes and starts to saunter down the hallway. Moses mumbles something to us—maybe a thank-you— and I want to comfort him somehow but I'm so focused on the rhythm of Adam's emotions I can't form words.

"I'm sorry he's such a dick to you, Moses," I hear Adam say. "You should really tell someone about it."

"Yeah, because ratting out dirtbags has historically worked out so well for the snitches," Moses mutters, and Adam's laugh lights up all the happy spots in my brain.

"Yeah, okay, fair point."

"Well, thanks," Moses's light voice finds its way to my ears. I think I nod at him before he scurries away.

"Hey there," Adam says, thumb still rubbing mine soothingly. I finally turn my eyes to him. His face is carefully blank, like he's trying to control his emotions so I don't get overwhelmed. I want to tell him that getting overwhelmed isn't so bad when it's with him. I want to tell him that sometimes the ocean of his emotions is terrifying in its scope, but other times, like now, I want nothing more than to drown in it. I want to tell him I love him.

"Hey" is what I say instead.

48

ADAM

The sounds of bodies hitting each other and cleats digging into the field mix into the noise of the crowd and it overwhelms me. It's been a long time since I came to a school event. Everyone is dressed in red and white, even me—I pull Caleb's letterman jacket closer around me and try not to look too smug that I'm wearing it.

"Wow, never thought I'd see you at one of these."

I look to my right to see Caitlin shuffling into the bleachers to stand next to me, her arms laden with concessions. She grins around the straw of her soda and I grin back.

"Yeah, well, part of the job description now, I guess." I shrug.

"He's got you wrapped around his finger, does he?" she snorts, and I laugh. It's been a couple weeks since Caitlin and I have said more than two words to each other—after the debate competition (which we won), we stopped having a reason to hang out and I got too caught up in Caleb and Atypicals and everything else to make the effort.

Not that I would have necessarily made the effort anyway. Without the built-in time of debate prep, I would have had no idea how to be Caitlin's friend. I feel like she's Technicolor and I'm black-and-white and that the two can't mix together in the real world.

"Adam!"

A girl's voice is calling to me but Caitlin is stuffing a pretzel into her mouth so I look around until I spot Chloe waving from one of the aisles. She makes her way through the crowd to me, wrapping me in a hug that makes it seem like we've been friends for ages. I tentatively hug her back and fumble through introductions to Caitlin.

As they shake hands, I start to have a total out-of-body experience. I'm standing in the school bleachers watching football, wearing my boyfriend's letterman jacket, with a friend on either side of me. When did this become my life?

"Did Caitlin and Caleb used to date?" Chloe whispers into my ear as Caitlin cheers the Red Team on. The two other times I've been around Chloe were like this too—she just jumps into the middle of a conversation. If I'm two steps behind with Caleb, I'm twenty steps behind Chloe.

"Um, no, not really," I whisper back. "Why?"

"She was just thinking about him and I wasn't sure . . ." She cocks her head like she's *actually* listening to something—like mind reading is just trying to hear a stereo in the next room—before nodding and jumping right back in.

"Ohhhh, gotcha," she replies to no one. "Don't worry, she's not jealous of you. She's happy for you guys."

Chloe pats me on the shoulder like she's comforting me for fears I never expressed and turns to watch the game. Guess we're done with that conversation. Whatever it was.

The rest of the game is like that. Caitlin cheers and eats so many pretzels I start to worry about her sodium levels and Chloe has a number of conversations with me in which I don't say a word out loud. She keeps her voice low the entire time— telling me things about our classmates, about her art, responding to my thoughts—having seven conversations at once, all by herself.

The entire time I'm focused on the field. It's surprisingly relaxing having Chloe chatter into my ear. I don't have to worry about saying the right thing or being interesting, because she hears everything. I don't have to hide because I *can't* hide. The lack of choice is a strange relief.

So when she tells me she doesn't mind that I'm paying more attention to Caleb than to her, I believe it. I've never seen Caleb like this. He's tense and aggressive, speeding across the field, pushing other players out of the way when he needs to. In moments when he takes off his helmet to listen to the coach or get a drink of water, his face is serious and angry.

I know this is normal for him. One of the reasons he likes football is because it lets him get out all the rage in a healthy way. I don't get it and I'm not totally sure I approve, but I'm glad it works for him. Even if seeing him like this makes my skin prickle—like being in love with Jekyll and getting a glimpse at Hyde.

"Have you told him yet?" Chloe whispers, and I think back on my own thoughts to find what she's asking about.

"Told him what?" I ask.

"That you love him." She smiles.

"Oh." My face burns. God, while the lack of pressure in conversation in refreshing, knowing a mind reader is also sort of mortifying. And now I've thought *that* and the last thing I want to do is hurt Chloe's feelings so I just focus on answering the question. "No, no, I haven't."

"You should." She smiles like she knows a secret and I want to ask her what she's heard in Caleb's thoughts. But before I can she grimaces, squeezing her eyes shut before sighing and opening them to give me an apologetic look.

"All right"—she winces—"I think I'm officially tapped out."

"Too many people?" I guess.

"Yep." She nods slowly. "Dr. Bright wants me to ease back into group settings, but this may have been a little too much too fast."

She leans around me to say good-bye to Caitlin and then asks me to make her apologies to Caleb. I tell her I will and I wave as she makes her way down the bleachers. Any time I think I'm living the high school cliché, I'm reminded that so many of the people in my life are not normal. At least they're not normal in a way that's interesting and cool, instead of being not normal in the way that means they lie in bed for days at a time.

As I watch Caleb move around the field with a fierce intensity I've never seen from him, it dawns on me just how differently he operates. He's feeling the emotions of the entire team, the entire stadium, and he carries it all on his shoulders like a pro. Not to mention, dealing with me when I get bad. Every part of my being wants to return the favor—wants to know how to comfort Caleb when he gets overwhelmed, how to talk him down when he gets furious. But I have no idea where to start.

Talking to my mom had been a mixed bag. I didn't tell her about the empath stuff but instead borrowed Caleb's mirror-touch synesthesia example. She knows the processes a brain like that goes through, but she's not a psychologist. She couldn't tell me how to be there for someone like Caleb. And where I would normally turn to research, there's not exactly a handbook on this.

I push any thought of my own problems out of my head and refocus on the game. I'm determined to be here for Caleb. To be "green" as he calls it. To be normal.

49

CALEB

As the school year starts to wind down, I settle into a rhythm for the first time since the beginning of junior year. I start to get back on track with schoolwork—though my grades are never going to recover from first semester—go to art therapy with Chloe and Frank, and spend all my free time with Adam. There are still the days where the tide pulls me under, but we start to learn how to balance those days. Sometimes Adam hides from me—only talking to me over Skype or the phone so I don't have to feel his emotions—and sometimes he tries to squash his feelings down. But, when I ask, he lets me sit on the ocean floor with him. It's not exactly pleasant, but I always leave it feeling like I know Adam even better. And I'm grateful for that.

Even when things are green with Adam, my life becomes increasingly not-normal. Hanging out with Chloe opens up the world of Atypicals to me. I try not to ask Dr. Bright too much about the organization she mentioned, and I definitely don't talk about it with my parents, but little by little, I start to realize there's this whole other world out there that I'm a part of. A world of telepaths and mind manipulators and other empaths and who the hell knows what else.

It's all exciting and new until Chloe calls me one day, frantic and worried, and tells me to come meet her. After one minute hearing her talk, I wish I hadn't agreed.

"What do you mean Adam's parents did something to Frank?" I ask, trying to wrap my head around what she's telling me.

"So," she starts, fiddling with the colorful bangles wrapped around her wrist, "I ran into Adam and his parents this morning—"

"Yeah, so you said," I say, to try to hurry her along. I like Chloe but she's easily distracted. I don't know if it's because she's always listening in on people's thoughts or if it's just the way her personality is.

"Right," she says, "and they were really nice, they seem like good people. But I mentioned Frank and . . . they knew who I was talking about. They've met him."

"Okay . . ." I prompt.

"They experimented on him," she finishes, eyes wide.

"What?"

"What, exactly, did Chloe see?" Dr. Bright asks a few hours later after agreeing to do an emergency session with me. She's got her walls up—her perfect therapist exterior—but there's an electric undercurrent of fear running between us like a train track.

"She wasn't totally sure," I say, jittery, "but I guess mentioning the Marines made the Hayes think about their work—I guess they work with the military? I didn't know that. I just always assumed they worked at a hospital."

"It isn't unusual for the military to hire scientists," she says calmly. Calm, calm, calm—I can practically hear the thought running around her head. It's such a lie.

"No, I know that, but Adam's never mentioned it. I feel like that's a pretty big thing to leave out. Especially since Adam has a lot of opinions about the military."

"Is that what's causing you concern?" she asks. "That Adam's parents work in an area he doesn't approve of?"

"No, it's—" I shake my head. "It's the kind of work they're doing.

Chloe, she only got glimpses so she can't be sure, but she said she saw a lot of not-good stuff. They were thinking about Marines they'd worked with—or no, they worked *on*. They were experimenting with them—on them—ugh, I don't know. But she saw Frank. In the Hayeses' heads. They were doing something to him. She said it was a different Frank too—like, younger, healthier. And the Hayeses and some other scientists were doing something to him and a bunch of other soldiers but the soldiers knew about it. So, I don't fucking know what that means."

I may not be able to read people's heads like Chloe can, but just feeling her sick with worry as she relayed what she saw to me gave my imagination plenty to work with.

"Chloe got all this from their thoughts by mentioning Frank?" Dr. Bright asks, like the exact wording of the conversation is what's important here.

"Well, no. After she saw the first bit of something," I explain, "she started talking about Frank more and asking some questions. She's gotten really good at making people think of certain things."

"I didn't know that." A sliver of sharp disappointment cuts through the practiced calm.

"Yeah, it's actually—it's pretty cool," I say. "And apparently when she started talking about other organizations that she's looked into to help Frank—like the art therapy place and the VA and the vet center and all that—that's when she saw this symbol in the Hayeses' thoughts. The one for that organization you told me about, the—the monitoring one—"

"The AM?" Dr. Bright's eyes widen and it's like being shocked by the third rail. "Chloe saw The AM's logo in the Hayeses' thoughts?"

"I guess." I nod.

"Is she certain?" The electrical current grows and sparks.

"She seemed pretty certain."

"She should have called me." Dr. Bright still *sounds* calm but she's given up on trying to hide her fear from me. It makes my whole body static. "If your boyfriend's parents work for the AM, then—"

"No, no, they don't work for them," I say, my instinct telling me that clarity on this is important. "They just—they work *with* them."

"I'm sorry?"

"Chloe was pretty sure about that," I explain. "They don't work for the AM or whatever it's called but they've been working with them on the soldier experiments that they're doing. And Chloe is worried it might have something to do with us."

"What?" Dr. Bright's worry gets caught up in the tangle of confusion and pressure grows behind my eyes.

"Well, she said that she saw the organization logo thing and then a bunch of stuff about Class A. And she says that's what we are. In the categorization of Atypicals or something, that I'm a Class A, we're Class As."

"Yes." She nods. "Yes, that's true. So Adam's parents are working with the military and the AM to experiment with Class A Atypicals who are also soldiers? I'm sorry, that's a bit of a hard story to swallow. I don't think there are enough known Class A Atypicals to populate the military."

"No, the soldiers aren't special like us," I say, trying to work through the confusion knotting my head—pushing aside the whole "Class A" conversation that clearly needs to happen so that we can get to the bottom of this. "Chloe thinks they were using Atypicals to experiment on the Marines. She thinks they did something to Frank."

"That's a pretty serious accusation." Dr. Bright raises her eyebrows at me and a real, genuine calm starts to loosen the knot.

"I know," I breathe. "But, look, I trust her. She knows that she can't be one hundred percent sure without talking to them more, but Chloe thinks that's why I have such a strong reaction to Frank. Because they, like, did something with his empathy."

"That's what she saw in the Hayeses' thoughts?" she asks. "That they were experimenting on Frank's empathy?"

"Yeah, I guess so." I shrug.

"Have you talked to Adam?" There's another shock but it's not Dr. Bright this time. It's my own fear.

"I texted him earlier," I say. "But he and his parents were on their way to have lunch with his aunt and apparently that's usually a pretty drawn-out thing so I don't—I don't think he's checking his phone."

"What did you text him?" she asks, and I want to roll my eyes at the fact that I spend a lot of time talking about my texts in therapy.

"Just that I'm really freaked out," I mumble. "That I'm worried his parents are dangerous. I don't know, it didn't feel like this before, it—" I swallow, worry clawing its way up my throat. "But now that I know Chloe and I know there are other people out there like me, it feels like a them-and-us situation, you know? Like, what if his parents are against people like me?"

"I don't want you to grow paranoid, Caleb," she soothes, her soft, lukewarm comfort reaching out for me. "I know that Chloe has learned a lot about the AM in these past few weeks—and I'm very much responsible for that—but I don't want her filling your head with fears."

"No, no, she's not," I rush to explain, telling myself to remember to ask Chloe later about what Dr. Bright has told her. "But I'm still, like, totally freaked out. If Adam's parents see people like me as something to be experimented on, then how can I know he won't eventually feel the exact same way?"

Even after we got together and things in our relationship shifted, Adam always treated me the same. The thought of him turning on me—of looking at me differently, *feeling* differently, scares me more than I'm willing to admit. Even to Dr. Bright.

"Have Adam's parents ever treated you differently?"

"No, not really. But I mean, I've barely met them," I add, thinking that the first and only time I've had any signification interaction was Adam's birthday. "They're hardly ever around. And I don't think Adam has told them much about me."

"That's good." She smiles. "I don't want you to fret too much, Caleb, but it might be good to keep the Hayeses ignorant of your ability. At least until we find out more."

"Are you—" I have to swallow again, feeling on the verge of
tears. "Are you gonna look into it?"

"I'll make some inquiries," she says. "Your safety is very important to me."

And I believe her. I trust her. The calm radiating from her is
real now and settles around me like a blanket as we move on to
other topics. Maybe I was too caught up in Chloe's emotions
earlier—maybe she was too caught up in some thoughts she mis-
interpreted. Maybe this was all just a really bad game of telephone
and I have no reason to freak out.

Which, of course, is when Adam shows up, freaking out.

"I walked over here from my aunt's house," he pants, Dr. Bright
still standing with her hand on the doorknob after letting him in.
"What the hell happened with Chloe today? She was acting sort
of strange when we saw her earlier, but I just kind of thought it was
Chloe being Chloe."

"She saw all this stuff in your parents' thoughts," I explain, trying to balance my panic with Adam's panic with Dr. Bright's concern. I have terrible whiplash and now I'm going to crack from
stress.

"Yeah, that they work for the military?" he scoffs. "That's ridiculous."

"Well, where do they work?" I ask.

"They work at a hospital," he says, barely leaving out the "duh."
"Because they're doctors."

"What hospital?" I prod.

"The—the one over on First." His face creases in a frown, and
I feel a drop of uncertainty ripple out from the core of his concern.
"I don't know, does it matter?"

"How do you not know where your parents work?" I push.

"They don't talk about it." He throws up his hands, and in doing
so, pushes more of his nervous energy onto me. "A lot of the research they do is confidential!"

"See what I mean?" I turn away from him, pacing the tiny
room. "Who knows what shady shit they're up to!"

A lance of burning-hot hurt pierces through me and I stay faced away from Adam so I don't have to see the pain I'm feeling etched on his face.

"Hey," he barks, "those are my parents!"

"Gentlemen, let's try to remain civil, please."

Dr. Bright's voice cuts through the tension, some of her Therapist-Mode calm—still real and solid—soothing the burn. I'd forgotten she was there—so caught up in Adam's feelings that hers were a distant memory. I can't process like this, and I'm relieved when Dr. Bright agrees to leave us alone in her office, even though I'm left with the swirling whirlpool of anger-hurt-fear that's standing in front of me in the shape of my boyfriend.

My boyfriend who cares about me. Who knows about my weird ability and likes me anyway. My boyfriend who would never put me in harm's way or tell my secret or betray me. I'm being a dick.

"I'm sorry," I sigh, turning to look at Adam and trying to hold myself together. "I overreacted earlier. Chloe saw a bunch of stuff, but we don't know anything for sure."

Adam's shoulders inch down as he exhales, and I step forward to bridge the chasm between us. His face is relaxing and just looking at it makes my insides untwist.

"And besides," I continue, "it's not like you've told your parents about me, so even if they were experimenting on people—"

His shoulders tense in their descent from around his ears and fear grabs my heart in its fist, pushing it up toward my throat.

"Wait." I stop in my tracks. "Why do you feel scared?"

"I—" The blood has drained from Adam's face and he's staring at me in a way that makes me want to look behind me to see what horrible monster is lurking in the shadows. "I did tell them about you."

"What?" My stomach drops to the ground. The fist tightens.

"Only sort of! After I first found out," he says. "I wanted to make sure I wasn't going completely crazy. So I asked some questions, you know? To see if it was neurologically possible. And my dad talked about all this theoretical stuff that mostly went over my head but it made me realize that you weren't messing with me."

"But you never asked him about it again, right? So there's no reason for him to think it has anything to do with me?" I continue hopefully for him. Adam is always asking weird stuff, maybe he's already forgotten about it. But the fist gripping my heart is starting to dig its fingernails in.

"Adam," I prompt, fear rising up my throat like vomit.

"You haven't given me a lot to go on, okay, Caleb?" he says, his face an apology. "You don't tell me how I can make things easier for you, so I had to do some independent research. I talked to my mom about, you know, brain stuff, and I—I—I was trying to be a good boyfriend!"

"By going behind my back and telling your parents my biggest secret? How could you do that?" I can hear my voice climbing higher and louder and feel the edges of Dr. Bright's bookshelves digging into my hips. I've backed away from Adam, trying to get as much distance as possible, but the iron grip in my chest persists.

"I'm sorry," he pleads, "I didn't think it would be this big of a deal. It's just my parents, it's not like I told the whole world!"

"Yeah, but it's your parents who might just be evil scientists who totally fucked with Frank's head!"

I'm spiraling, I know I am. Dr. Bright must be able to hear us shouting, because her worry is starting to snake under the door and twist like vines around my legs, making it impossible for me to run away. Everything in my body is tight—the vines of her anxiety squeezing the blood out of my legs, pulling me into the ground, the fist pushing my heart up, up, up, leaving a dark, cold hollow of fear at my core.

"—my parents aren't dangerous, they would never hurt you." Adam's been talking and I can barely hear him through the molasses.

"I don't believe you!" I shout. "I can feel you panicking and I can feel Dr. Bright worried sick and I just—I can't do this right now, okay?"

I want to tell him to leave, to run away. I don't know what's going to happen next. Either I'm going to have a heart attack and die in front of him or I'm going to break everything in Dr. Bright's office, and I don't want Adam witness to either of those things.

"What do you mean?" Adam takes a tentative step toward me like I'm a dangerous animal. I break completely.

"It's all too much!" The words are being simultaneously pushed and dragged out of my throat. "I'm barely dealing with my own feelings and then everything that's been going on with you, I just—I can't have all this stuff hanging over my head and fucking me up! What if I totally crack—what if your parents or the AM or Damien do something to me and I end up like Frank, my emotions totally out of control—"

"Caleb, nothing's going to happen to you—" Adam, the idiot, takes another step, ignoring the basic human instinct of not going toward a wild animal when it starts foaming at the mouth. But a part of me is grateful for his movement because it spurs my own.

"No, don't—" I step sideways, walking toward the office door. "I need to be alone for a while—"

"Okay." Adam nods, looking at me like I'm a stranger. "I'll walk you home."

"No!" I blurt, terrified by the idea of taking all of this outside with me. "I need to be *alone*-alone. Just—just let me be for a little while, okay?" He nods again and a new wave of fear washes over me, pushing molasses into my veins, making it hard to breathe.

"And—" I choke out, "and don't tell your parents anything else about me." My voice is hard and I feel the edges of it cut through his fear to the blue place that's always inside of him.

"Caleb, you're acting like I betrayed you." His eyes are shiny and my jaw clenches further, teeth pressing into and sliding against each other like shifting tectonic plates. "I didn't do anything wrong, I lo—"

His mouth snaps closed and my stomach plummets. I can feel him wanting to shove the half-said words back into his mouth. I know that impulse well.

"You mean a lot to me," he finishes. "I don't want you to shut me out."

My hand is on the doorknob, the vines dragging me toward where Dr. Bright stands panicked in the waiting room. I don't want to do this. I don't want to turn away from him but I need to get out of the chokehold I'm in.

"I'm sorry," I whisper, opening the door and walking out.

50

ADAM

"Do you experiment on people?" I shout, the kitchen door swinging angrily on its hinges behind me. My parents turn to look at me in surprise. Saturday dinner is bubbling away on the stove and my dad is mid-pour from a nice bottle of wine. I want to break everything in the kitchen.

"Honey," my mom says, a look of panic on her face, "what?"

"Caleb, he—" No, Adam, don't cry, you don't get to cry yet. You have to stay angry.

"That girl we ran into yesterday," I start again, "Chloe—"

"Oh, yes, she was lovely." My dad smiles and I want to shake him until his teeth fall out.

"She's a mind reader," I blurt and, fuck, I really shouldn't have done that. The glass from my dad's hand drops to the floor, spilling red wine over his shoes like blood. It makes my stomach roil.

"Okay." My mom turns the stove off and wipes her hands on her apron. "Let's all go to the dining room and sit down."

"Rebecca—" My dad protests from the floor, where he's picking up glass shards.

"It's time, Eli," she says, and the gravity in her voice makes me want to rewind this entire thing and go back to a time where I didn't know anything. Why couldn't "ignorance is bliss" have been the lesson my parents instilled in me?

Two minutes later, we're all sitting stiffly at the dining room table, staring at each other like there's a bomb on the table that one of us needs to disarm.

"You didn't seem all that surprised to hear that Chloe was a mind reader," I say finally, hands twisting frantically under the table. I wish we weren't sitting down. I wish we could be doing this somewhere I could pace around and smash things.

"She's not the first mind reader we've met," my mother says calmly, like that's not the biggest fucking revelation of my entire life.

"What the *fuck*," I grit out, furious.

"Adam," my dad chastises, "language."

"No," I say, shaking my head, "I'm sorry, I'm not going to apologize for swearing, you just told me that you've known *mind readers* exist. I now have to recalibrate my entire world view, *again*. I think I'm allowed some fucking expletives."

His jaw clenches and he takes his glasses off to rub at the bridge of his nose.

"Fine," he says. "You're right."

"But you've known about mind readers for a little while." My mom tilts her head, and knowing I have the same physical tic makes me disproportionally pissed. "And empaths."

"Yeah," I say unapologetically, "I have. But I don't experiment on them for fun."

"We don't do it for fun," my dad says, and I nearly black out in rage.

"I'm sorry, but what the *hell* does that mean?" I demand.

"What your father is trying to say is that we're doctors." My mother is a stoic column, and every moment she stays calm makes me angrier and angrier. "We're not some mad scientists who are creating Frankenstein monsters in our labs. We took an oath. We look after people. We make them better."

"How?" I ask. "Chloe's friend is seriously messed up from what you did to him."

"Military funding is extremely unreliable, *boychik*," my dad says, putting his glasses back on and entering what I've always thought of as Professor Mode. "That project was defunded. There was nothing else we could have done. We did our best."

"Your best wasn't good enough!" I croak, tears bubbling up again.

"It often isn't," my mom says sadly, and I can hear the weight of the world in her voice. "But we have to keep trying."

"Why?" I ask, not understanding one jot of this.

My dad smiles softly at me.

"Knowledge."

51

ADAM

Just like that, the dream is over and school is a torturous slog again. Caleb won't return my texts, won't look at me in class—he's pale-faced and grim, keeping his head down as he marches through the halls. I want to reach out, say something—*anything*—but I can't get my feet to move or my mouth to work.

We'd only been together for a few months but he'd already changed the landscape of my days. Now I'm back to hiding in the library, keeping an eye out for danger, working as hard as I can to make myself invisible. Not even my nook feels secure enough, so I've taken to sitting on the floor in the dark, dusty stacks.

"Adam?"

My daily self-pity sesh is interrupted by Caitlin, who has some-how tracked me down in this far corner of the library.

"What do you want?" I sigh, not having enough energy to put up with any small talk.

"Um, the *Gorgias*?" she says, inching toward me like I'm a bomb waiting to go off.

"What?"

"*Gorgias*," she repeats. "It's, um—it's right behind you."

My brain catches up to the fact that I'm leaning against the

philosophy books and Caitlin isn't actually here to check on me—
she just wants to read some Plato.

"Oh," I say, turning around to grab the slim volume from
behind my right ear. "Here you go."

I hand her the book and she smiles awkwardly at me. We haven't
spoken since the football game, a fact I am beginning to deeply
regret. Caitlin has been kind to me—has put up with my prickli-
ness more than anyone else has other than Caleb, and now Caleb—
well. I should probably wait for Caitlin to leave before I careen
back into my wallowing.

"Are you okay?" she asks after a few seconds of tense silence.

"I'm—" I start before realizing that this is my chance to course-
correct from the past few months; from getting so caught up in
my own love life that I ignored the friendship of a girl who maybe
needs it as much as I do.

"I'm not great, to be honest," I say finally, and Caitlin grimaces
sympathetically before gingerly sitting down on the carpet.

"What's going on with you and Caleb?" she asks gently. "Did
you guys break up or something?"

"I don't know," I reply, horrified to find my voice thick and my
eyes stinging. "We got into a pretty big fight and now he's not talking to me and I don't know what to do about it."

"What was the fight about?" she asks. "Not that I'm trying—
I'm not trying to pry or anything, I just maybe could help if I knew
what happened? Ugh, sorry, you don't have to tell me anything."

She's rambling, something Caitlin rarely does, and twisting her
hands in her lap. I want to tell her it's fine, tell her that I'm just
happy she's here, happy she's listening at all, happy that she *cares*,
but that all feels too earnest and too honest for the moment. So
instead I focus on the matter at hand.

"I can't really—I can't tell you," I say. "It's kind of a long, complicated story and a lot of it isn't my story to tell, but . . . I screwed
up. I wasn't honest with him about some stuff and now he's scared
off and I always knew that he was going to get scared off but I
thought it would be about the other thing, there's no way I could
have seen *this* coming—"

Now I'm rambling and I don't know how to stop but thankfully Caitlin interrupts me.

"What other thing?"

"Oh." I turn red, angry at my mouth for communicating without my permission. "You know, just . . . the way that I am."

Caitlin looks at me like she wants to say something, like she's weighing all the different arguments in her head, but she stays silent, her eyes turning soft.

"It was never going to last." I stare into my lap, wishing desperately that I could just *stop talking*. "I'll be fine."

"I'm—" Caitlin is at a loss for words and I feel guilty for always putting her in these unique, un-Caitlin-like situations.

"I'm sorry," she says finally. "But maybe—maybe it isn't totally over yet. I've seen the way Caleb looks at you. I was even—I was a bit jealous, at first, if I'm honest. But I couldn't even stay jealous because you two . . . you just *fit*."

And that, more than anything, is what makes the tears leave my eyes and start rolling down my cheeks. I try to brush them away surreptitiously, murmuring a thank-you before hurriedly asking Caitlin about why she's reading Plato when classes end tomorrow. She sees my need for a change of subject and starts explaining why she loves Socratic dialogue so much. I let her voice wash over me and, just for a moment, everything hurts a little less.

52

CALEB

I'm playing quidditch in the backyard with Alice when she asks me why Adam hasn't come around. The question nearly causes me to trip over my own feet and I want to run in the house and not come out until she's forgotten that she asked it. But instead, I gulp in some air, put down the dodgeball we'd been using as a quaffle, and sit on the grass, utterly defeated.

"We . . ." I start, and Alice comes to sit next to me, bringing her sudden concern with her. "I think maybe we broke up?"

Don't cry don't cry don't cry don't cry—

"What?" she asks, incredulous.

"Yeah, I don't know." I pick at the grass. "We just—we got into this big argument about his parents, because they experiment on people like me—don't tell Mom and Dad"—I point a finger at her as she opens her mouth to say something—"and, I don't know, it was a *bad* fight and I said I needed time but now I'm not sure where we're at because we haven't spoken since the last day of school when I said, 'have a good summer,' and ran away."

"Smooth," Alice deadpans, the spike of her worry cutting at my insides. But it hardly registers because my insides are already torn to bits. It's been one week since I last saw Adam, walking into the library on the last day of school—hours after I went up to him to tell him I was sorry, that I screwed up, that I trusted him more than I'd ever trusted anyone before telling him to have a good summer instead—and each day of that week has been a strange kind of torture. But now too much time has passed to text him and I can't feel his feelings when I'm not around him so I'm just lost, the summer stretching out before me like an endless wasteland.

53

ADAM

A summer in Ohio. There's a song about that. If memory serves, it's about how terrible a summer in Ohio is.

Whoever sang that song was right.

54

CALEB

I'm watching the most recent video Adam posted on loop. Looks like he's visiting his dad's family in Ohio. He must be miserable. I wish he would post a photo of his face.

55

ADAM

Caleb must be posting so many selfies specifically to torture me. Or maybe he's posting the same number of selfies he always posts and I'm just acutely aware of them now that I don't get to look at his face in real life.

Whatever the reason, I hate it.

56

CALEB

Adam DM'ed me a photo today. He went to the Rock and Roll Hall of Fame and sent me a picture of ABBA's name on the wall. An inside joke from before we were even dating. "Super Trouper," the last song on the first mix he made me. A nickname. A secret.

Did he send it in mocking or as an olive branch?

I stay up all night trying to figure out the answer.

I don't send anything back.

57

ADAM

Summer is winding down and my boredom wears off, leaving anxiety in its place. I'm going to see him soon. Whether or not I want to, Caleb and I are going to be in the same building, in the same room, completely undefined. We never really broke up, but it's been crickets from him all summer and the uncertainty is eating away at me. If I thought I dreaded school before knowing Caleb, it doesn't compare to the dread I feel after losing him.

58

CALEB

I should text Adam. I should have texted him weeks ago. I should have been texting him all summer. And now school starts tomorrow and we haven't said anything to each other since June except the occasional photo or song.

My heart is making itself sick trying to decide if it's excited or terrified to see Adam's face tomorrow.

59

ADAM

That could have been so much worse.

Caleb and I still only have two classes together, thankfully on alternating days (even though I never thought in a million years that he'd *want* to take AP Latin. The fact that he signed up for it makes dumb stupid hope flutter in my chest), so I only had to see him once today and it was fine.

Well, no, it felt like my intestines were trying to strangle my heart, but I didn't pass out or anything, so I'm counting it as a victory.

60

CALEB

That could not have gone worse.

I wanted to say something to Adam in Latin—I mean, he's the only reason I even signed up for the AP course in the first place—but then I saw his face and his dumb stupid freckles and I wanted to kiss him so badly I nearly passed out.

I really just need to text him.

61

ADAM

"Shove over, queerbo." Bryce pushes me against the locker and my phone nearly drops out of my hand. Adrenaline pours through my body—I don't know that I can muster caring if my phone breaks, but the idea of the whole hallway getting a glimpse at Caleb's feed pulled up on my phone is mortifying.

"God, Bryce, how are you more of a dick with each passing year?" I say, out loud. Fuck. I just said that out loud. I look over at Bryce to see him red all over. He seems to be stunned into silence, because he just blinks at me for a few moments.

Like Charlie Brown and the football, I'd had the hope that senior year would finally put an end to Bryce's regularly scheduled torture. After all, he left me alone most of last semester, though I'm realizing now that was probably just because I was dating Caleb.

"What'd you just say to me?" Bryce blinks himself back into motion and steps toward me, chest puffing out. I really thought I'd make it through high school without getting punched in the face, but I guess we can't always get what we want.

"Just . . ." I start, having no idea how to deescalate this situation. ". . . leave me alone, Bryce. Aren't you tired of this by now?"

"Listen, freak," he whispers, getting close to my face, "just because you and Michaels were a thing doesn't mean you can talk to me like that."

"Hey!"

Both of our faces whip around so fast at the sharp voice our noses nearly graze each other. Caleb is standing a few feet away, jaw clenching in a familiar way that tells me he's trying to keep his shit together. Uh-oh.

"What?" Bryce barks, and anger flashes in Caleb's eyes.

"Leave him alone, Bryce," he grits out, fists clenched at his side.

"It's okay, Caleb," I say calmly, not wanting to handle this on my own but wanting even less for Caleb to do something stupid and heroic that will land him another suspension. "I've got this."

"Yeah, Michaels, he's got this," Bryce mocks, and Caleb takes a step toward us.

"Besides," Bryce continues, "I thought the two of you were over."

That stings more than anything else, even though Bryce is really just stating a fact, rather than trying to take a jab. Caleb flinches and I wonder if he's feeling my sting or is barbed by it himself.

"Doesn't matter," Caleb says, and I want to drown. "You should still leave him alone."

"Why do you always have to be in everyone's business?" Bryce is getting in Caleb's face now and I could easily scurry away to my next class but I'm stuck to the floor.

"I'm tired of you stepping on everyone, Bryce," Caleb spits. "You pour so much toxic shit into this school every single day and you don't even realize it."

"What the fuck are you—"

"And if you don't get your own bullshit under control," Caleb says, steamrolling over him, large and looming and full of terrifying strength, and a shiver runs up my spine, "I'll crush you into the small, pathetic bug that you really are."

They stare at each other, barely breathing, until Bryce breaks, rolling his eyes and stepping back. He opens his mouth, probably to deflect and say "Whatever" as always, but Caleb beats him to it.

"I mean it, Bryce."

Caleb is unmoving and steely-eyed. Without saying another word, Bryce adjusts his backpack on his shoulder and walks away. He's halfway down the hall before Caleb's shoulders collapse and his fists unclench. I want to reach out for his hands—still white-knuckled and stiff—but he just glances at me from the corner of his eyes, mumbles, "Um, sorry," and takes off in the opposite direction.

I think that's the end of it. The vanquishing of my bully as the last act of affection Caleb will ever show me. I'm grateful, but seeing him fighting what must have been so much emotion makes me miss him like a physical ache.

I think that's the end of it until, later that night, I get a text.

Hey. Can we talk?

"Mom? Dad? Can we talk?"

My parents look up from their reading—medical journals for both, like the consistent dweebs that they are—and squint into the setting sun to meet my eyes. They're ensconced on the patio, trying to soak up the last moments of summer, and I can read the surprise on their faces. We haven't exactly been talking very much this summer.

"Of course, sweetie, what is it?" my mom asks earnestly.

I sit down, leaning my elbows onto my knees, my hands clasped together like I'm delivering terrible news. They both lean forward as well, and the air instantly becomes tense.

"Caleb texted me," I blurt. That wasn't at all how I wanted to begin. I'd been aiming for Serious Adult Conversation here and ended up at Son Freaks Out About Ex-Maybe-Still-Current-Boyfriend Telling Him They Need to Talk After Saving Him from School Bully Like a Goddamn Hero.

"That's . . . good," my dad tries, and my mom nods in solidarity. They like Caleb. They've made a point of telling me so over and over again this summer, which, as you can guess, was actually the opposite of helpful.

"Yeah, maybe. But here's the thing—no matter what he says or what he wants—" I swallow around the hope that's been clogging my throat since the moment I heard my phone buzz "—I need you guys to be . . . cool about it."

"We've always liked Caleb," my mom says earnestly, and I roll my eyes, "and we'll be happy as long as you're happy. You know we don't have any problem with you dating as long as we get to know the boy first."

"Yeah, believe it or not, that isn't actually what I'm talking about," I bite, running my hands over my hair. I can't let my parents steer this conversation away from what I actually want to talk about. I have to be the one to stay in control.

"I'm referring to the fact that you both work for an organization that hurts people like Caleb—"

"Now, son, you know that isn't true—" my dad interrupts, and I want to groan in frustration. Yes, I know that isn't what my parents do, or so they say. They spent the whole summer telling me that they've only done a couple of projects with the AM and that they've always involved volunteers. That the experiment with Frank was a military operation and it went wrong but Frank knew the risks. That my parents want to *help* Atypicals and that sometimes means doing radical things.

I don't know if I've ever experienced anything as jarring as no longer trusting my parents. I believe that they love me, that they want the best for me and the world, but I'm not sure we have the same ideas on how to go about ensuring that. I've played it cool, listening carefully as they talked *at* me all summer, explaining how all their work is legal and safe and totally aboveboard. And I know that they believe that. I'm just not sure if they should.

"I just need to know that you're not going to do anything to him." I raise my voice to talk over their protestations and they both turn silent at the stern look on my face. "I need to know that you're not going to tell anyone about him or do—I don't know, *anything* that could make him feel more different than he is."

"Of course, darling," my mom says, her eyes big and pleading. "We'd never want to hurt Caleb. Ever. How could you think that we would?"

"I know that we've kept you in the dark a long time," my dad says, laying his hand over my mom's in solidarity, "but we won't do that anymore. We promise."

My mom nods fervently in agreement. There's still an open wound that hasn't gone away since I first learned about what my parents do. I still don't trust them completely and, while that injury may never heal, their promises will have to be enough to keep it from bleeding.

62

CALEB

The crisp, warm scent of fall is in the air and I try to focus on the leaves crunching beneath my feet instead of the warring emotions inside of me. I'm nervous, excited, worried, sad, hopeful—the whole damn spectrum. The fact that it's all my own doesn't make it better.

"Hey," I say, trying to contort my face into something resembling a smile. "Thanks for meeting me."

"Yeah." Adam is looking at his shoes, scuffing them against the concrete.

"Do you wanna sit?" I ask, gesturing to the bench. Our bench.

We sit and I stare at the path in front of us. The path where we first kissed. It feels like a million years ago. It *was* a million years ago.

"Sorry that we haven't really been able to talk at school," I begin, heart pounding in my chest like it's going to flop out and die on the path where it first felt full. "I just—it's been kind of a crazy two weeks with football and classes and my mom getting on my ass about college applications—"

"It's fine, Caleb, I get it," Adam interrupts, and I hit a wall over and over again. "I'm actually kind of surprised you wanted to talk to me at all."

"Of course I wanted to talk to you," I say, "I miss you."

"Yeah," he says, "so you texted."

It's like we're back where we started except worse. I can barely feel anything from him, my own nerves drowning everything else out.

"Didn't you . . ." I don't want to ask the question but I have to know or I might die. "Did you miss me?"

I immediately regret it and rush to put the words back into my mouth.

"No, never mind." I wave my hands around like that will literally clear the air between us. "Forget I asked—"

"Yeah, Caleb," he says, and the wall cracks slightly. "Of course I missed you. Can't you—can't you feel that?"

I feel an aching longing, yeah, but I've felt that all summer. I have no way of knowing if it's his or if it's mine. I explain this to him and he repeats himself.

"I have missed you," he says, breathing life back into me. "A lot."

"I'm sorry. I don't know if I've said that yet. I'm *really* sorry." I can feel a rant building but I don't care, I have to get this out. "I freaked out and fucked everything up and I know I've been a shitty boyfriend—" My breath catches in my throat as any tentative hope is crushed under the weight of reality. "Well, I guess I haven't been much of a boyfriend at all and I just . . . I'm sorry, okay?"

Every word I say is like a small hammer chipping away at his walls but I've barely made any progress. He pivots his body away from me and it stings.

"What do you want from me, Caleb?" he asks wearily. "I don't hear from you for months and then you stand up for me with Bryce and now . . . Why did you ask me to meet you?"

Time to just lay it all out there.

"Dr. Bright says I can't make decisions for you. And I think that's what I was trying to do," I say, admitting that I didn't get here on my own, I needed help from my fucking therapist. I take a deep breath before diving into the next part, cracking open my chest for him to do whatever he wants with it. "I care about you *so* much and I didn't want to make your life more complicated or make things harder for you so I guess I just . . . I shut you out."

Another shuddering inhale. God, this is hard. His blue warmth is starting to bleed through the cracks in the wall and I want to cry with relief.

"I was a fucking coward," I finish. And then—just when I was hoping a dam would burst—the wall just dissolves, letting the blue-green wash over me, clearing out the muck in my veins for the first time in months.

"I feel like I should apologize too," Adam starts, and I immediately jump in to stop him.

"No, just let me," he insists. Another deep breath in for both of us. "I've spent a lot of time thinking about this—about us. And I think I was too wrapped up in my own shit before. I was so worried about making you feel sad that I didn't think. I didn't let you in. And I put a lot of pressure on you to be the stable one—the *normal* one—in the relationship, which is pretty fucking ironic. Your power is cool and everything but I don't need you to be my superhero. And I'm sorry if I felt like you had to be. I don't think you're a coward."

Leave it up to Adam to come out with an entire articulate speech while I sit here with random words spilling out of my mouth. I try to take it all in—really process what he's saying—but my brain is stuck on one thing.

"But I *want* to be your superhero," I say, my hand itching to take his but uncertain if we're there yet. "I want to make things better but . . . I'm just not sure I always can."

I'm crippled under my own black sludge but a sliver of affection cuts into it, lifting it off of me.

"You make things better just by being there," he says, really looking at me for the first time since we sat down. He laughs despite himself and my heart soars. "I mean, I never thought I'd even be friends with you, let alone . . ."

We smile carefully at each other as we simultaneously realize that this thing might not be ruined.

"You've made things so much better." His fingers reach out to touch mine, braver than me. "I don't think I told you that enough."

"Oh." I smile down at our nearly joined hands, shy. "Well. That's good."

"So . . . what does that mean?" His fingertips tap a nervous rhythm on my knuckles. "Do you still want to, you know, go out?"

The shimmering light of his hope fills my brain and my whole face is a grin. The Great Amazing Feelings Boy rides again, this time feeling stronger than ever.

63

ADAM

"I'm game if you are." Caleb smiles, his face split open in happiness, and I can't help but laugh.

"You are such a jock." I shake my head, grinning at him, and he squeezes my hand. God, how I missed this.

"Meathead," I mumble.

"Dork," he replies, stepping into our familiar rhythm.

Against all odds, I'm filled with hope again. Things might be okay. He hasn't run away and I haven't found a hole to crawl into. We're sitting on this bench, holding hands, beaming at each other like lovesick fools, and things might be okay.

Things are going to be hard. I have no illusions about that. Caleb still has an Atypical ability and I still have depression. Caleb still gets angry and I still want to hurt myself. My parents are still scientists who've done things I can't imagine, even if they've tried to convince me of their good intentions. There are still Chloes and Franks and Damiens out there that are going to make Caleb's life complicated. There's still an organization that we barely know anything about but that makes Caleb go pale whenever it's mentioned.

Things are going to be hard. But for the first time, I start to wonder if things might be easier together.

But first: communication.

"Okay," I start sternly, "but we have to agree on one thing."

64

CALEB

"Okay, but we have to agree on one thing," Adam says, suddenly serious again, and my heart would clench if it wasn't already buoyed up by so much joy.

"Okay . . ." I play along. "What?" I would be freaked out if I wasn't feeling Adam's giddiness. I don't know what he's about to say, but whatever it is isn't serious enough to drown out his happiness so I can't be fussed to worry about it.

"Neither of us is going to be the normal one," he says practically. "I think it's best we just accept that."

I huff a laugh, a slight breeze of relief bolstering the joy even more. Adam beams at me, the biggest smile I've ever seen, and I bask in the warmth. I can't help but kiss his curved lips, chasing the taste of sunlight, before giving him my answer.

"Sounds good to me." I smile, an entire sun in my head. A whole solar system. "We'll be weird together."

ACKNOWLEDGMENTS

When I started *The Bright Sessions* back in 2015, I could never have anticipated what it would become. It was meant to be an experiment, a way to explore a new-to-me form with some actors I admired, a chance to stretch my legs as a writer. All these years later, and the world of Dr. Bright and her patients has become my entire world, a world that so many people have joined me in, both as collaborators and listeners. It was never my creation alone and there are so many people who need to be thanked for helping me make this story.

To the actors who first filled the world of *The Bright Sessions* with their voices: Julia Morizawa, Anna Lore, Charlie Ian, Ian McQuown, Andrew Nowak, Alex Marshall-Brown, Phillip Jordan, and Alanna Fox—thank you all for coming along on this journey with me. And thanks most of all to Briggon Snow and Alex Gallner, who were the first people to give voice to Caleb and Adam and give them life. Hearing your voices in my head made this book possible. An enormous thanks to Mischa Stanton and Evan Cunningham, who create the auditory landscape of *The Bright Sessions* and who inspire me every day.

To Matthew Elblonk, for seeing something in my writing and

always believing in me. I'm so grateful to have an agent that so deeply understands me, and even more grateful to call you my friend.

To Ali Fisher, who made having an editor the opposite of the scary thing I feared it would be. You've made my writing so much stronger, made me smile with your notes, and related to my Fannibal tendencies. There's no one I'd rather ride with in the Reaper's War.

To all the people who made me love reading in the first place, especially T. A. Barron and Seann Alderking, who put fantasy books in my hands when I was a child and expanded my universe infinitely outward.

To the communities of people that have held me up: my New Year's gang, FTH, my Glow Up Crew, my Time Stories team. Thank you for sending me memes and giving me joy when I got buried in work. And a deep, heartfelt thanks to the audio drama community—especially Jeffrey Cranor, Joseph Fink, and all of Night Vale—for the paths you've paved, the inspiration you've provided, and the kindness you've shown me.

To Brendon Urie, for giving me music for fifteen years. You took me from my own emo phase all the way through writing Adam into existence. Neither of us would be who we are without you.

To my parents. Thank you for always supporting my dreams of telling stories and for filling my life with so many stories from the very beginning. To my sister, Betsy—you could fit in literally every single one of the above categories. You've given your voice and your expertise to *TBS*, you put so many books in my hands and taught me how to read them, you have held me up my entire life.

Last but certainly not least: to all of you. To all of you who pick up this book and see a little (or a lot) of yourself in Caleb or Adam, whether you're in high school or high school is a distant memory. There's nothing I can say to make those painful moments less painful, but I hope knowing you're not alone brings a bit of comfort.

To every person who has been following Caleb and Adam's love story for the past few years and beyond: thank you. You keep me green.

Stay strange.